Metafiction and Metahistory in Contemporary
Women's Writing

Metafiction and Metahistory in Contemporary Women's Writing

Edited by

Ann Heilmann and Mark Llewellyn

palgrave
macmillan

First published 2007 by
PALGRAVE MACMILLAN
Houndmills, Basingstoke, Hampshire RG21 6XS and
175 Fifth Avenue, New York, N.Y. 10010
Companies and representatives throughout the world

PALGRAVE MACMILLAN is the global academic imprint of the Palgrave
Macmillan division of St. Martin's Press, LLC and of Palgrave Macmillan Ltd.
Macmillan® is a registered trademark in the United States, United Kingdom
and other countries. Palgrave is a registered trademark in the European
Union and other countries.

ISBN-13: 978–0–230–00504–4 hardback
ISBN-10: 0–230–00504–7 hardback

This book is printed on paper suitable for recycling and made from fully
managed and sustained forest sources. Logging, pulping and manufacturing
processes are expected to conform to the environmental regulations of the
country of origin.

A catalogue record for this book is available from the British Library.

Library of Congress Cataloging-in-Publication Data
Metafiction and metahistory in contemporary women's writing/edited
   by Ann Heilmann and Mark Llewellyn.
       p.   cm.
   Includes bibliographical references and index.
   ISBN-13: 978–0–230–00504–4 (cloth)
   ISBN-10: 0–230–00504–7 (cloth)
   1. English fiction—20th century—History and criticism—Theory,
   etc.   2. English fiction—Women authors—History and criticism—
   Theory, etc.   3. American fiction—20th century—History and
   criticism—Theory, etc.   4. American fiction—Women authors—History
   and criticism—Theory, etc.   5. Women and literature—Great Britain—
   History—20th century.   6. Women and literature—United States—
   History—20th century.   7. Fiction—Authorship.   I. Heilmann, Ann.
   II. Llewellyn, Mark, 1979–
   PR888. W6M35 2007
   823.9′099287—dc22   2006052783

Printed and bound in Great Britain by
CPI Antony Rowe, Chippenham and Eastbourne

Contents

**Part III: Generic Experimentations with
Gender and Genre**

Acknowledgements

The chapters in this book are, apart from the final one, based on papers that were delivered at the 'Hystorical Fictions: Women, History, Authorship' conference, which the editors co-organized at the University of Wales Swansea in August 2003. We would like to thank, on behalf of both ourselves and the authors in this volume, all those who took part in the event, be it as speakers or as audience members, for their stimulating contributions to what proved to be an invigorating debate. Thanks are also due to our readers for helpful comments, and to Paula Kennedy, Christabel Scaife and Helen Craine at Palgrave Macmillan.

Notes on the Contributors

Sherry Booth is Director of Core Composition at Santa Clara University, Santa Clara, California, and a senior lecturer in English. She teaches courses in writing and literature, and is a member of the faculty in the Program for the Study of Women and Gender. Her research interests and publications include nineteenth-century Scottish rhetoric, ecofeminism and fiction by contemporary women writers who address issues of nature and the environment in their work. Her current project is the literary wolf.

Christine Colón is Assistant Professor of English at Wheaton College in Illinois, where she teaches courses in English literature, Latin American literature and women writers. She is the author of published articles on Jane Austen, Joanna Baillie, Anne Brontë, Adelaide Procter, Wilkie Collins and John Keats. She is currently working on a book on Joanna Baillie.

Sarah Falcus, after completing a PhD on the maternal in the fiction of Michèle Roberts, studied for a postgraduate teaching qualification in Further, Adult and Higher Education. She is now a lecturer in English at Liverpool John Moores University, UK. Her research interests lie within the field of contemporary women's writing, particularly women's revisions of religious tradition and women writing the maternal.

Sarah Gamble is Senior Lecturer at the University of Wales Swansea, UK, where she directs the interdisciplinary Centre for Research into Gender in Culture and Society (GENCAS). She is the author of *Angela Carter: Writing from the Front Line* and the editor of *The Routledge Companion to Feminism and Postfeminism* and *Angela Carter: A Reader's Guide to Essential Criticism*. She has also published articles on a variety of topics, including transgender theory, *Bridget Jones' Diary* and the novels of Carol Shields. Her most recent book is *Angela Carter: A Literary Life*.

Ann Heilmann is Professor of English at the University of Hull, UK. The general editor of Routledge's Major Works 'History of Feminism' series, she is the author of *New Woman Fiction: Women Writing First-Wave Fiction* and *New Woman Strategies: Sarah Grand, Olive Schreiner, Mona Caird*. She has (co)edited two other essay collections, *Feminist Forerunners* and *New Woman Hybridities* (with Margaret Beetham), and four anthology sets, most recently *Anti-Feminism in Edwardian Literature* (with Lucy Delap and a contribution by Sue Thomas). She has co-edited (with Mark Llewellyn) a critical edition of *The Collected Short Stories of George Moore*.

Katharine Hodgkin is Principal Lecturer in the School of Social Science, Media and Cultural Studies, University of East London. She has published a number of articles on early modern culture, and is co-editor (with Susannah Radstone) of two volumes of essays on memory, *Contested Pasts: The Politics of Memory* and *Regimes of Memory*. She is currently working on an edition of an early seventeenth-century autobiographical manuscript (*Women, Madness and Sin in Early Modern England: The Autobiographical Writing of Dionys Fitzherbert*) and a monograph, *Madness in Seventeenth-Century Autobiography*.

Jeannette King is Senior Lecturer in English at Aberdeen University, UK. She is the author of *Tragedy in the Victorian Novel*, *Doris Lessing* and *Women and the Word: Contemporary Women Novelists and the Bible*. She has recently published a monograph on *The Victorian Woman Question in Contemporary Feminist Fiction*.

Georges Letissier is Senior Lecturer in nineteenth- and twentieth-century English Literature at Nantes University, France. He has published articles in French and English on Peter Ackroyd, A. S. Byatt, Dickens, George Eliot, Alasdair Gray and Graham Swift. His main field of research is post-Victorianism in fiction writing. He has written on post-Dickensian narrative fiction in *Refracting the Canon in Contemporary British Literature and Film* (ed. by Susana Onega and Christian Gutleben). He is the author of a book in French on Ford Madox Ford's *The Good Soldier*.

Mark Llewellyn holds a research position in the School of English at the University of Liverpool. He has co-edited special issues of *Women: A Cultural Review* (2004), *Women's Writing* (2005), *Critical Survey* (2007) and *Feminist Review* (2007). His research interests range from understandings of 'authorship' in seventeenth-century poetry (the subject of his doctoral research) to the novelist George Moore (1852–1933), and contemporary women's writing. He has published refereed journal articles and book chapters in each of these fields; he has co-edited (with Ann Heilmann) George Moore's collected short stories in five volumes and is working on an AHRC-funded project on the Victorian Prime Minister William Gladstone's reading.

Rachel Morley, a former journalist, is now a doctoral candidate at Macquarie University, Australia, where she is working on a creative-writing PhD. She has published papers on a diverse range of topics including biography and autobiography, Australian women's boxing, and on the Victorian poets Katharine Bradley and Edith Cooper – an aunt and niece who wrote together under the pseudonym 'Michael Field'.

Michael Sinowitz is Associate Professor of English at DePauw University in Greencastle, Indiana. He completed his doctorate at the University of Miami, after receiving undergraduate degrees in English and History from Boston University. He is currently revising *Waking into History: Forms of the Postmodern Novel*. He has published 'The Western as Post-modern Satiric History: Thomas Berger's *Little Big Man*' in *Clio* and his essay, 'Graham Greene's and Carol Reed's *The Third Man*: When a Cowboy Comes to Vienna', is forthcoming from *Modern Fiction Studies*. He is also working on a book-length project entitled 'Body Politics: History, Genre, and the Body in Patrick O'Brian's Aubrey-Maturin Series'.

Johanna M. Smith is Associate Professor of English at University of Texas-Arlington, where she teaches eighteenth- and nineteenth-century British literature. She has published extensively on *Frankenstein* and on nineteenth-century literature and culture. Her most recent book is an anthology of life-writing by British women of the long eighteenth century, and she is completing a book on women in the public sphere in the period 1750 to 1850.

Julia Tofantšuk is a doctoral candidate at Tallinn University, Estonia, currently working on a thesis exploring gender and identity issues in the writings of contemporary British women authors, particularly Jeanette Winterson and Eva Figes. A special focus is the question of history as presence, space and process that is as provisional and invented *en route* as the (provisional) identities constructed within it. She has published articles in Norway, Germany, Hungary, Poland and Lithuania, most recently contributing to a volume on *Jewish Women's Writing of the 1990s and Beyond in Great Britain and the United States*.

Maria Vara received her undergraduate degree from the School of English, Aristotle University, Thessaloniki, Greece, and her MA in Studies in Fiction from the University of East Anglia, Norwich, UK. She is currently a doctoral candidate at Aristotle University, where she teaches courses in writing and literature. Her research interests include women's fiction and literary theory. She has published articles in Greece, France and the UK on detective fiction, Gothic and the fairy tale, most recently contributing to a volume on *The Reception of British Authors in Europe: Jane Austen* (ed. by Anthony Mandal and Brian Southam).

Diana Wallace is Principal Lecturer in English at the University of Glamorgan, UK. She is the author of *Sisters and Rivals in British Women's Fiction, 1914–39* and has recently published *The Woman's Historical Novel: British Women Writers, 1900–2000*.

Introduction
Ann Heilmann and Mark Llewellyn

In the last decades of the twentieth century and into the new millennium, historical fiction, particularly that written by women authors, has been transformed from an essentially escapist form of literature with a predominant interest in the romantic into a genre at the cutting edge of postmodern conceptualizations of the past and of contemporary worlds. Writers like Margaret Atwood, A. S. Byatt, Angela Carter, Tracy Chevalier, Eva Figes, Daphne Marlatt, Michèle Roberts, Rose Tremain, Sarah Waters, Jeanette Winterson and others have reinvested history's role in literature and literature's place in history with a new importance. This book examines the dynamic experimentation within historical fiction by contemporary women authors from North America, Australia and the UK. Ranging from the popular to the literary, the fictional to the factual, and covering those narratives that defy categorization, the chapters assembled here represent new and varied approaches to the subject of how contemporary women fiction writers use and reconfigure history in their work.

We have designated the texts under discussion in this volume as 'metafictions' and 'metahistories'. Metafiction, for our purposes, is best defined by the following statement by Patricia Waugh:

> Metafictional novels tend to be constructed on the principle of a fundamental and sustained opposition: the construction of a fictional illusion (as in traditional realism) and the laying bare of that illusion ... to create a fiction and to make a statement about the creation of that fiction. The two processes are held together in a formal tension which breaks down the distinctions between 'creation' and 'criticism' and merges them into the concepts of 'interpretation' and 'deconstruction'.[1]

In the case of this book, the 'formal tension' Waugh indicates is provided at an additional level by the other term in our title: the 'metahistorical'. By 'metahistorical' we mean those works of both fiction and nonfiction in which one of the author's primary contentions is the process of historical narrative itself. As Hayden White defines it in *Metahistory: The Historical Imagination in Nineteenth-Century Europe* (1993), metahistory denotes a recognition of the 'historical work as . . . a verbal structure in the form of a narrative prose discourse'.[2] The ways in which history is written after the events it describes and the manner in which narratives more generally are constructed within a historical moment as literature provide the crucial critical undercurrent beneath the chapters that follow. What most unites the chapters gathered here is the fact that the texts they discuss are, in themselves, part of a process of critique; their authors seek through the very act of writing to deconstruct and reinterpret aspects of the historical process which have previously silenced or been closed to their female subjects.

This does not mean that the chapters in this book are to be read as somehow separate from other trends in contemporary literary studies or that they are divorced from a sense of literary tradition; we are not arguing that the authors selected are creating a new genre or that historical fiction by women did not exist before them. Indeed, quite the opposite is true, and the readings presented here are, like the texts they discuss, in sympathy with an aesthetic reading of the historical narrative process, albeit one that is theoretically, critically and politically (feminist) informed. As A. S. Byatt has commented on her own desire to write historical novels,

> It may be argued that we cannot understand the present if we do not understand the past that preceded and produced it . . . But there are other, less solid reasons, amongst them the aesthetic need to write coloured and metaphorical language, to keep past literatures alive and singing, connecting the pleasure of writing to the pleasure of reading.[3]

For women, the pleasures of writing and reading are arguably intensified when dealing with the historical. Pushed to the margins of the literary and historical canon up until the latter third of the twentieth century, it is in part by reclaiming historical events and personages as subjects and participants in contemporary fictional accounts that women writers can begin to assert a sense of historical location. In this sense, it is by interrogating the male-centred past's treatment of women at the same time as seeking to undermine the 'fixed' or 'truthful' nature of the historical narrative itself that women can create their 'own' (counter-)histories; it is in such acts that the metafictional and metahistorical combine. Women writers' impulse to reassess not only their own position in history but also the nature of that history's right to represent the 'truth' has coincided with a wider cultural challenge to what constitutes 'History'. The growth in 'new histories' of women, gender, ethnicity and sexuality since the late 1960s, for example, has prompted a change in educational practice as well as public perception. Recent women writers have engaged with this to the extent that, as Diana Wallace remarks,

> the woman's historical novel of the 1990s looks less like a nostalgic retreat into the past than a complex engagement with the ways in which representations of history change over time... The novels of the 1990s... contest the idea of a single unitary and linear history. They emphasise the subjective, fragmentary nature of historical knowledge through rewritings of canonical texts, through multiple or divided narrators, fragmentary or contradictory narratives, and disruptions of linear chronology.[4]

Thus, women writers in particular have risen to the challenge of a changing, postmodern understanding of the nature of history, the historical process and the (in)validity of any individual account's claims to accuracy or, ultimately, objective truth. This has made the possibilities of resurrecting, altering and (re)imagining women's historical lives greater, and has also provided a seemingly more secure future for the genre itself.

That history has become a more pressing subject in recent literature more generally is indicated by the spate not only of fictional works but of critical theory's engagements with this material. During the last twenty years, significant work has been carried out on the genre of historical fiction, notable examples being the writings of Hayden White,[5] Linda Hutcheon,[6] Steven Connor,[7] Peter Middleton and Tim Woods,[8] and Jürgen Pieters.[9] Of these, Hutcheon's *A Poetics of Postmodernism* (1988) has been the most influential, and the term 'historiographic metafiction' is used frequently in critical discourse as a short-hand for the kinds of theorized approaches to the historical in literature which have become part of mainstream culture since her book was published. Hutcheon's own definition of the term suggests how it

> refutes the natural or common-sense methods of distinguishing between historical fact and fiction. It refuses the view that only

history has a truth claim, both by questioning the ground of that claim in historiography and by asserting that both history and fiction are discourses, human constructs, signifying systems, and both derive their major claim to truth from that identity.[10]

Given that history and fiction are both grounded in narrative, the two remain interdependent on one another. Historical fiction could therefore be viewed as the quintessential mode of postmodernism, in that it continually raises questions and concerns about the very fabric of the past and the present. As Hutcheon writes, '[p]ostmodern fiction suggests that to re-write or to re-present the past in fiction and history is, in both cases, to open it up to the present, to prevent it from being conclusive and teleological.'[11] The distinctive feature of such fictions in Hutcheon's view is to be found in their eagerness to explore how narratives and histories work within and around one another.[12] It was Hayden White, almost thirty years ago, who argued that this relationship be explored for what it could teach both historians and creative artists about the role, status and authority of historical narrative. As White wrote,

> Historians are concerned with events which can be assigned to specific time-space locations, events which are (or were) in principle observable or perceivable, whereas imaginative writers – poets, novelists, playwrights – are concerned with both these kinds of events and imagined, hypothetical, or invented ones ... What should interest us ... is the extent to which the discourse of the historian and that of the imaginative writer overlap, resemble, or correspond with each other.[13]

Underlining as they do the 'imagined' nature of history as a discipline and its similarity to creative writing in terms of narrative drive and 'story', White's comments hint at the possibility of a criticism that is aware of the flexible play between these two spheres of discourse. Yet while historical fiction as a genre has continued to explore the tensions between history and story, criticism has been rather slower in attempting to deal with such material, particularly in the context of women's writing.

As Peter Middleton and Tim Woods indicate at the start of their 2000 book on memory and time in contemporary fiction,

> contemporary historical literature has become an extremely active sphere of argument about history and the rediscovery of its elided

potentialities, as well as an often highly conflicted struggle over what should be remembered and what forgotten.[14]

The 'elided potentialities' here might cover a multitude of absent things, but they undoubtedly should include the potential of so many women and their stories. Some studies of historical fiction or the presence of the past in contemporary culture have made reference to the specificities of women's engagement with the historical, such as David Leon Higdon's *Shadows of the Past in Contemporary British Fiction* (1984),[15] which carries chapters on Jean Rhys and Margaret Drabble, or John Kucich and Dianne F. Sadoff's edited collection *Victorian Afterlife: Postmodern Culture Rewrites the Nineteenth Century* (2000),[16] which engages with women's responses to history and use of historical fiction or film in the work of A. S. Byatt and Jane Campion. But neither of these texts focuses on gender as a fundamental issue in the production of such work. Historical fiction written by women, therefore, remains a relatively neglected area of literary study. Aside from Diana Wallace's wide-ranging but Anglo-centric *The Woman's Historical Novel: British Women Writers, 1900–2000* (2005) and Jeannette King's carefully focused *The Victorian Woman Question in Contemporary Feminist Fiction* (2006),[17] there are no critical works which deal specifically with international contemporary women writers and historical fiction. Yet historical fiction remains a female-author–dominated genre: look for historical narratives in the popular fiction bestseller lists, for example, and it is the names of Philippa Gregory and Sarah Waters which dominate. Part of the reason for this is that women, along with members of minority ethnicities and nonheterosexuals, need a narrative history. As Wallace points out in her book, 'exclusion from recorded history, whether as a subject, reader or writer, is a serious business';[18] the authors whose work is explored here take that challenge seriously.

Our book seeks to fill this important critical lacuna and expand the kinds of authors discussed not only by focusing entirely on women writers, but by broadening the geographical, generic, cultural and canonical scope of the works under consideration. With its emphasis solely on women writers, this book marks out new territory in the field. The distinctive qualities of *Metafiction and Metahistory in Contemporary Women's Writing* are its focus on British, North American and Australian women writers; its exploration of both fictional and factual re-engagements with history by women; its combination of chapters on established and lesser-known authors; and its varied theoretical and literary critical approaches.

The book is divided into three sections. The first, 'Towards a Reconceptualization of History and Identity', probes the fictional manipulations of 'history' as a paradigm for exploring and exploding national, ethnic, linguistic and gendered identities in the British, Canadian and Australian writers Angela Carter, Stevie Davies, Daphne Marlatt, Helen Darville (alias Demidenko), Eva Figes and Jeanette Winterson. It begins with a chapter by a historian: Katharine Hodgkin's discussion of historical novels in the context of seventeenth-century history is a particularly useful beginning for this book. Hodgkin's aim is to question the relationship between 'history' and 'story' and to discuss how a historian responds to the process of reading historical fiction. Hodgkin rightly asserts that contemporary historical fiction frequently underlines the apparent connections between chronologically separate lives and experiences through the use of 'dual temporalities', a device through which the interrelationship of past and present 'is self-consciously and self-reflexively foregrounded through interlocking stories' (p. 16); such stories establish the relationship between periods most often through women. The examples cited range from Rose Tremain's *Restoration* and Jeanette Winterson's *Sexing the Cherry* (both published in 1989) to Stevie Davies's novel *Impassioned Clay* (1999). It is to the last of these that Hodgkin attributes the emergence of her own interest in the fundamental relationship between historical fact and historical fiction, reality and imagination. While critical of aspects of Davies's novel and its apparent gestures towards popular misconceptions of the three types of seventeenth-century woman highlighted in Hodgkin's title (the witch, the Puritan, the prophet), the chapter is nevertheless not so much concerned with dismissing the drive behind historical fiction writing as with raising problems over what such novels 'can or should do' (p. 22).

Sarah Gamble's chapter on Angela Carter's posthumous short-story collection *American Ghosts and Old World Wonders* (1993) is connected to Hodgkin's approach in that she too is interested in the places where slippages occur in the nature of the writing of historical fiction. As Gamble argues, Carter's narratives do not allow for the possibility for an escape from one's past because it is in one's (hi)stories that the core of identity is formed and found. This, rather than 'politics or culture', is the essential barrier which prevents New World settlers escaping from the individual pasts that tie them to the Old World.

'Falling Off the Edge of the World' by Sherry Booth explores the novel *Ana Historic* (1988) by the Australian-born Canadian author Daphne Marlatt. The novel, Booth argues, raises questions about the nature of historical truth and fiction as much as about the nature of literary texts themselves. Interestingly, Booth reads Marlatt's exploration of identity and individual history, documentation and (in)authenticity as also partly a challenge to a postmodern world in which the concept of 'History' rests uneasily. Theory and its focus on group mentality rather than individual identity are critiqued both in the novel and in Booth's discussion, an approach which opens up new questions about the study of story in relation to history.

One of the more influential feminist and theoretical approaches to the relationship between women and history is Julia Kristeva's 'Women's Time' (1979). This essay also provides an important way into historical fiction for Julia Tofantšuk's contribution on Eva Figes's fiction. Tofantšuk's argument centres round the idea that Figes's female characters are part of a 'movement ... from or towards history' (p. 61). Reading Figes's three novels *Days* (1974), *Nelly's Version* (1977) and *The Tree of Knowledge* (1990) as a single text and the female characters as aspects of an individual woman, the chapter argues that the female protagonist is 'frozen in the static no-time that Kristeva describes, but she also inhabits the "real time" of history, or *her* story, the story of betrayal, seduction, and loss, which embraces three generations of women and makes them one' (p. 63). Perceiving women as trapped in an inescapable eternity of 'herstories', Figes plays with the idea of the female as surviving, like Scheherazade, through the telling of tales.

The fact that Figes uses real historical personages in her texts, such as Milton's daughter in *The Tree of Knowledge*, connects her work to other writers who blur the boundaries between the factual individual and their fictionally reclaimed voice. Rachel Morley's chapter, 'From Demidenko to Darville', which concludes this section, shares this theme but is distinctly different from the other contributions to this volume in that the public blurring of fiction and reality, truth and fabrication, lie at its very heart. Exploring the case of Helen Demidenko/Helen Darville/Helen D, an Australian writer who 'faked' her supposed family history as a descendant of a Ukranian Holocaust survivor, the chapter highlights how aspects of the public furore surrounding Darville's attempt to market her vivid imaginings as oral history reveal important elements of wider social and cultural factors in Australians' sense of a collective and shared past.

Part II, 'Historiographic Re-visionings', engages in more depth than the chapters in Part I with Linda Hutcheon's influential concept of 'historiographic metafictions' in conjunction with Adrienne Rich's notion of feminist cultural 're-vision'.[19] The chapters in this section investigate Angela Carter's, Caryl Churchill's and Michèle Roberts's rewritings of W. B. Yeats, Joanna Baillie, Gustave Flaubert and William Wordsworth, as well as Jeanette Winterson's and A. S. Byatt's de/reconstructions of 'masculinity' and 'romance'.

Christine Colón's opening discussion, 'Historicizing Witchcraft Throughout the Ages', deals with the relationship between two dramatists whose lives and works are separated by over a century. While not arguing that the relationship between Caryl Churchill and Joanna Baillie can be seen as clearly as that of rewriter and original, Colón's chapter suggests interesting ways in which such cross-cultural and cross-temporal literary relationships might be explored. Indeed, in underlining the fact that feminist literary criticism has by no means comprehensively recovered lost female works, especially in the case of plays (p. 90), Colón provides a corrective to assumptions that the most dynamic theatrical works by women in recent years are entirely new in outlook and fresh in perspective. Colón's argument is that individuals like Caryl Churchill may not be 'breaking new ground' but are rather 'unaware' of a longer tradition to which they nevertheless belong (p. 90). Modern texts by women writers, it might then be argued, are haunted almost unknowingly by precursor works.

Where Churchill may be unconsciously engaging with past literature, Michael Sinowitz's chapter on Angela Carter's fiction demonstrates the ways in which other women writers are eager to rewrite older, male-authored texts. Taking on board Carter's own assertion that she considered herself to be 'in the demythologizing business' (p. 102), Sinowitz argues that in works like *Nights at the Circus* (1984) Carter holds an internal dialogue with Modernists such as Yeats, with the Modernists providing the myths which she 'seeks to debunk' (p. 103).

A similar sense of engagement between masculinist and feminist discourses is suggested by George Letissier's chapter on Jeanette Winterson's and A. S. Byatt's explorations of the ideas of 'passion' and 'possession' as opposed to a monolithic (and misogynistic) 'cosmic' masculinity. Letissier suggests that both novelists are consciously intent on playing with readerly expectations of narrative technique and approach because the very titles of their works, *The Passion* and *Possession*, suggest an intensely personal and emotional response to the past. In doing so, both novels, Letissier argues, undermine not only historical processes but also the expectations surrounding what historical fiction 'should' do.

Michèle Roberts's work, the subject of the next chapter by Sarah Falcus, also displays a concern with the role of the personal in remembering the past, whether through individual memory or through shared cultural experience. Like Byatt and Winterson, however, and particularly the latter, Roberts has frequently sought to push the boundaries of the historical in terms of its relationship to truth and fiction, reason and the irrational. As Falcus notes, a recurring theme in Roberts's historical fiction is the textual nature of re-visionism and the impossibility of either 'truth' telling or retelling. This does not make the (re)creation of women's stories any easier, as the chapter demonstrates; although the events which are absent from the recording processes of history are offered prominence and even priority in the fictional space, there remains the struggle to find a voice and a reliable language through which the tale can be told.

The final section of the book deals with 'Generic Experimentations: Gender and Genre'. While questions and discussion about the nature of historical fiction as a genre play a part in the previous two sections of the book, it is here that sustained attention is given to the ways in which recent women's fiction and criticism has made more conscious play with the relationship between gender, genre and the process of a feminist reclaiming of historical narratives. Johanna M. Smith's chapter on 'Rewriting *The Rover*' uses Aphra Behn's Restoration drama and some of its later rewritings, in particular Susan Kenney's campus detective novel *Graves in Academe* (1985), to explore how the original's status as a canonical work has fluctuated. Smith argues that in the history of *The Rover* there are at least two types of historical recovery in progress: first, the recovery of a (female) literary tradition via Behn and second, the reclamation of a literary genre itself. In a thoroughly contextualized piece, Smith provides an illuminating narrative of both *The Rover*'s history and the academic and popular moment of its resurrection in 1979. Although the chapter seeks to challenge some of the often naïve assumptions behind the problematic feminist 'restoration' of women writers from the past to the canon, Smith concludes with a 'reminder of the potential, and above all the necessity, of women's historical fictions' (p. 156).

While Smith takes a single text example, Diana Wallace explores an entire genre in her chapter on the convent novel. Beginning with a contrast between Julian of Norwich and Geoffrey Chaucer and treating them as representatives of differing historical (and gendered) positions on the representation of the past, Wallace moves from this long view of history to a very precise examination of the ways in which twentieth-century novelists have used the convent as a fictional site wherein the fundamental issue of historical recuperation and representation can be debated.

In the context of women reclaiming the past, Wallace writes: 'If history is dangerous for women, to have no history is a kind of death' (p. 168), and in her chapter on 'Re-Writing the History of the Gothic Heroine in Alice Thompson's *Justine*', Maria Vara demonstrates how the deathly silencing of Gothic literature's women also poses dangers for women readers and writers. Exploring how the trope of the suffering heroine has been sidelined in much rewriting of the Gothic in favour of the figure of the madwoman in the attic, Vara argues that it is the nature of the narrative device of passivity to be found in the Gothic genre which has precluded sustained discussion of attempts to 're-vision' or recover female figures who do not fit the pattern of the oppressed or 'mad' woman. Vara's critical engagement with issues of pornography, sexual exploitation and its narratalogical and historiographic equivalents in her discussion of Alice Thompson's 1996 novel *Justine* serves to heighten awareness of the problems of the attempt to reclaim fictional female figures who sit uncomfortably in our stereotyped versions of the 'woman victim'.

From the Gothic canon to the American canon may be a significant leap, but the imperative found in the work of contemporary women writers and the desire to rewrite a male-centred *his*tory are also the subject of Jeannette King's chapter on *Ahab's Wife* (1999) by Sena Jeter Naslund, a reworking of Herman Melville's *Moby Dick*. King's chapter begins by both aligning itself with the second wave of feminist criticism as figured in the work of Judith Fetterley and yet distancing itself from this same criticism's attempt to place too neat a reading onto the relationship between male and female fiction. While we might agree with Fetterley's arresting statement that 'American literature is male' (p. 182), it does not follow, King argues, that women cannot rewrite male-authored fiction and make it part of a female reality in the process. The novel King explores represents just such an attempt to take on a high-canonical author in order to provide not only a new, female-authored and woman-centred vision of the narrative but also a sensitive, critical engagement with the precursor text.

The book concludes with a chapter by Mark Llewellyn on the work of the novelist Sarah Waters. This final chapter serves to draw together some of the key themes and discussion points of our book as a whole and points to a possible new way of thinking about women's historical writing in the early twenty-first century. The question of 'historical fiction' is, Llewellyn argues, one of Waters's key themes as she deals with issues around (sexual) categorization, outsiders, 'deviancy' and her characters' growing awareness of their identity. Importantly, it is through acts of reading and, in some cases, acts of writing that such awakenings occur; Llewellyn's discussion of 'historical fiction in action' is therefore as much concerned with exploring Waters's metafictional devices as it is with the idea that she might be rewriting a wider historical narrative. Providing an overview of Waters's four novels, the chapter suggests that their subject is in part exactly the concern with the reading of history, which is also present at the margins of many of the other works discussed in this volume. Far from enacting a break with a literary tradition, Waters's work might be considered the most recent fulfilment of it.

And this tradition is itself important, especially in its openness to a multiplicity of literary and historical experiences. The authors and texts discussed in this volume should not be seen as innovative in the sense that they have created a new way of approaching history. Rather, they have developed and progressed from a tradition which existed prior to their work, albeit in a less prominent form, opening it up to new, postmodern, feminist-inflected possibilities. Although concerned with looking backwards, women's historical fiction is also, crucially, about moving forwards. We hope that readers of this book will take away from it a sense of the vibrant possibilities and futures which lie ahead for women's historical fiction.

Notes

1. Patricia Waugh, *Metafiction: The Theory and Practice of Self-Conscious Fiction* (London: Routledge, 1984), p. 6.
2. Hayden White, *Metahistory: The Historical Imagination in Nineteenth-Century Europe* (Baltimore, MD and London: Johns Hopkins University Press, 1973), p. ix. See also White's 'The Question of Narrative in Contemporary Historical Theory' in *The Content of the Form: Narrative Discourse and Historical Representation* (Baltimore, MD and London: Johns Hopkins University Press, 1987), pp. 26–57.
3. A. S. Byatt, *On Histories and Stories: Selected Essays* (London: Chatto & Windus, 2000), p. 11.
4. Diana Wallace, *The Woman's Historical Novel: British Women Writers, 1900–2000* (Basingstoke: Palgrave Macmillan, 2005), p. 204.
5. See Hayden White, *Tropics of Discourse: Essays in Cultural Criticism* (Baltimore, MD: Johns Hopkins University Press, 1978) and *The Content of the Form*.
6. Linda Hutcheon, *A Poetics of Postmodernism: History, Theory, Fiction* (New York: Routledge, 1988).
7. Steven Connor, *The English Novel in History 1950–1995* (London: Routledge, 1996).
8. Peter Middleton and Tim Woods, *Literatures of Memory: History, Time and Space in Postwar Writing* (Manchester: Manchester University Press, 2000).

9. Jürgen Pieters, *Speaking with the Dead: Explorations in Literature and History* (Edinburgh: Edinburgh University Press, 2005).
10. Hutcheon, *A Poetics of Postmodernism*, p. 93.
11. Ibid., p. 110.
12. For a more detailed exploration of the relationship between Hutcheon's analysis and postmodern women's writing see Ann Heilmann and Mark Llewellyn, 'Women (Re)Writing and (Re)Reading History', Introduction to special *Hystorical Fictions* issue of *Women: A Cultural Review*, 15, 2 (Summer 2004), 137–52.
13. Hayden White, 'The Fictions of Factual Representation' in *Tropics of Discourse*, p. 121.
14. Middleton and Woods, *Literatures of Memory*, p. 1.
15. David Leon Higdon, *Shadows of the Past in Contemporary British Fiction* (London: Macmillan, 1984).
16. John Kucich and Dianne F. Sadoff (eds), *Victorian Afterlife: Postmodern Culture Rewrites the Nineteenth Century* (Minneapolis, MN: University of Minnesota Press, 2000).
17. Jeannette King, *The Victorian Woman Question in Contemporary Feminist Fiction* (Basingstoke: Palgrave Macmillan, 2005).
18. Wallace, *The Woman's Historical Novel*, p. 2.
19. In her essay 'When We Dead Awaken: Writing as Re-Vision' (1971), Adrienne Rich conceptualized a culturally and historically sensitive 'Re-vision' as an 'act of looking back, of seeing with fresh eyes, of entering an old text from a new critical direction' and ultimately as tantamount to 'an act of survival' for women, who as a gender had been written out of history. The essay is reproduced in Barbara Charlesworth Gelpi and Albert Gelpi (eds) *Adrienne Rich's Poetry* (New York: Norton, 1975), p. 90.

Part I

Towards a Reconceptualization of History and Identity

1
The Witch, the Puritan and the Prophet: Historical Novels and Seventeenth-Century History

Katharine Hodgkin

In the historical fiction of the last two or three decades, the sixteenth and seventeenth centuries seem to be a particularly favoured period, providing the setting for a wide range of both literary and genre novels. The starting point for this chapter is curiosity about why that should be so. For me, as a historian of the seventeenth century, the interaction between fictional and historical versions of this period is of particular interest: how do the political and cultural concerns of the present shape this fictional past? This chapter offers some thoughts about that question, by way of a discussion of some aspects of recent historical fiction about early modern England.[1] The discussion is inevitably a speculative and general one; in focusing on a few issues, there is much about historical novels in general and these novels in particular that will be left aside. But to explore the choice of specific historical moments or events in historical fiction offers an opportunity to examine in more detail the truism that historical novels are always about the present, the time of writing, as well as the past; and I hope here at least to raise some questions about history, story and the relations between them.[2]

This is not simply a discussion about historical truth, although that is one way of thinking about what is at stake when a historian reads historical fiction. Historical novels are indeed always threatened by anachronism and error, and criticism includes among its yardsticks a variety of ways of measuring the notion of truth: are there mistakes of fact, of diction, of probability? Do people speak, think, behave plausibly? Praise may focus on the successful recreation of imagined otherness, measured especially through the detail of everyday life (food, clothes, pastimes, preoccupations), and also through the idea of the accuracy and verifiability of the content. The implicit assumption in making such judgements is that history is knowable and factual, and that fiction, while it operates on another level of truth, nonetheless has certain responsibilities to those knowable facts. Novelists may choose to transgress the historical record, but they should do so knowingly, not out of ignorance.[3]

But the notion of historical truth, as a straightforward opposite to fiction, can hardly go unchallenged. Most historians would now be uncomfortable with the kind of unproblematic absolutism that goes with a phrase such as 'the historical record'. Historiography over the last couple of decades has increasingly acknowledged the 'story' component of history and the problematic nature of the 'historical fact', as well as the need to engage with the forces of emotion and the irrational in history, traditionally the territory of the fictional.[4] So although this discussion is concerned with the relationship between history and fiction, my aim is less to measure texts for historical accuracy than to revisit the question of what it means to write authentically about the past. What kinds of accuracy or authenticity can the historical novel provide? Should it even try to provide any? If history is itself discursive, textual, fragmentary and uncertain, and, like fiction, driven in unrecognized ways by our own individual and cultural preoccupations and desires (as several chapters in this book note), then to set up the debate on the presumption that history is true and fiction must obey its rules would be naïve in relation to both.[5] But as a reader I am unable not to think about times when the history in a novel seems to me wrong, just as I am unable not to disagree with historians' accounts that seem to me wrong; and I am also interested in when and why that might matter.

The main part of my discussion is organized around the three figures identified in the title, the witch, the Puritan and the prophet, exemplifying particular problems in relation to the idea of historical truth and/or authenticity. But the framing questions are larger and have to do with our own investments as historical (and gendered) subjects – as readers, writers and researchers – in particular periods and particular themes and in the making of the subject (or subjects) of history. The point that we are ourselves historically located is underlined by the striking prominence in contemporary historical fiction of dual temporalities, in which the relationship between past and present is self-consciously and self-reflexively foregrounded through interlocking stories – one historical, one contemporary. (Frequently the link between the narratives is made through women, and the association of femininity with possession, fluidity and channelling is clearly significant; the dialogue between past and present is set up on the basis of a physical similarity, a possession or obsession affecting the modern woman in the partnership and an eventually disclosed blood lineage.[6]) The popularity of this structure emphasizes these novels' overt concern with connections between past and present, and the continuing salience of figures such as those I focus on here.

Twentieth-century fiction and seventeenth-century culture

The Tudor and Stuart period has long been popular with both adult and children's novelists. But earlier historical novels set in this period give a different and generally more romantic picture. Novelists like Daphne du Maurier and Elizabeth Goudge represent it as a time of organic wholeness, invoking an England of passionate and loyal aristocrats, households of productive labour and rosy children, and enduring local loyalties, in which both sides in the Civil War could in different ways be right.[7] Early modern Englishness, for writers of the mid-twentieth century, is something to be celebrated.[8] Historical novels in the 1940s, Diana Wallace notes, 'at least on the surface, stressed continuity and unity', evoking preindustrial England as 'a pastoral Eden'.[9] More recent historical fiction, by contrast, identifies this as a period of trouble, change and instability; of new science, new explorations, new politics, new philosophies. The notion of the seventeenth century as a crucial transitional stage in the development of capitalism and imperialism reinforces the underlying narrative of conflict and insecurity. The period is characterized by violent and arbitrarily exercised power (class, gender and national or colonial violence all figure); casual war and bloodshed; dirt and disease, though also flourishing herb gardens (a survival from the earlier fictions); and widespread (though not universal) religious fervour.

With this perspective on the century, it is perhaps not surprising that the decade of the 1660s, with its atmosphere of crushed revolutionary hopes, materialism, scientific experiment and sexual adventurism, is attractive to many authors. Rose Tremain's *Restoration*, first published in 1989, is a prime example of this; and rereading it today, it is impossible not to be struck by what a very 1980s version of the period it is. Tremain's unattractive hero is a man on the make in a new world of materialism, greed and egotism, in which people of insatiable appetites circle around the corrupt court and its hollow values – except the Quakers, who try to separate themselves out from their lustful and mercenary culture by establishing forlorn lunatic asylums, and die. Part of what Tremain sees in the Restoration, it seems, is the disillusionment and ineffectiveness of a revolutionary generation, echoing the disillusionment of the Thatcherite 1980s.[10]

This is not to say that Tremain offers a 'wrong' picture of the Restoration era, but merely to make the obvious point that novelists use the past more or less consciously, and more or less explicitly, to reflect on what they see in their own time: precisely because Tremain was writing in the 1980s, particular aspects of the Restoration were resonant for her. At the same time, of course, 'right' and 'wrong' cannot be entirely neutered by inverted commas. In using the past as a lens through which to explore aspects of the present, we are in certain ways denying it its pastness – treating it as a commentary, that is, on something that does not belong in the past at all. And the question of what it means to engage with the difference of the past is one I want to explore now in more detail.

The Puritan

When I first read Jeanette Winterson's 1989 novel *Sexing the Cherry*, soon after it was published, I was taken aback by its evident hostility to Puritanism. For many of us involved at that time in research on radical religious groups in the seventeenth century, and especially on women in those groups, Puritanism had history and the angels on its side. Puritans invoked the language of individual conscience against the feudal insistence on the duties of a subject. They were precursors of the new world of political debate, of civil society, even though for them the debate was framed in theological terms. Moreover, religious radicalism was the context in which women, like lower-class men, were able for the first time in any numbers to find a political voice, publish their opinions, engage in debates, argue over the meaning of life and good government. In the conflict between absolutist hereditary power and the spiritual equality of all believers (male and female), I had a clear preference for the second.[11]

For Winterson, however, Puritanism has a very different meaning. In *Sexing the Cherry*, it is a narrow, repressive, hypocritical thing, characterized above all by its refusal to acknowledge human desire:

> The Puritans, who wanted a rule of saints on earth and no king but Jesus, forgot that we are flesh and in flesh must remain. Their women bind their breasts and cook plain food without salt, and the men are so afraid of their member uprising that they keep it strapped between their legs with bandages.[12]

Winterson's Puritans are self-interested hypocrites; they are seething with repressed desire; and they are male. The two main Puritan characters are peculiarly unredeemable; driven throughout the novel by avarice, lust and lies, they come to a particularly violent and revolting end in a brothel (naturally). Women and the poor, by contrast, are depicted resenting and despising these oppressive (though ineffective) male authority figures. Even Parson Firebrace's meek and compliant wife, on hearing of the death of her husband, thanks God for his mercy and takes off to live with her sister. The idea that a Puritan might actually *be* a woman, or poor, finds no place in the novel's ferociously scurrilous depiction of radical religion. And while Winterson's polemic authentically echoes seventeenth-century anti-Puritan rhetoric, it remains puzzling that in this text there is no counter-discourse, no alternative view of what the years of revolution might have meant; only Dogwoman the royalist proclaiming her preference for sins of excess over sins of denial.

One might suppose that Winterson's venomous antipathy to Puritanism is given particular force by her own growing up in a repressively evangelical household; or (to take a more complex view than the biographical) that the novel presents Puritanism not as historical phenomenon, but as a transhistorical opposition to life, something which, oversatisfied with its own unquestionable rightness (or righteousness), exploits and degrades and will lead to death.[13] It is interesting to compare Winterson's Puritans with Angela Carter's, discussed in Chapter 2, who are similarly life-denying, but allowed more in the way of intelligence and dreams: 'The greatest genius of the Puritans lay in their ability to sniff out a pagan survival...they were the stuff of which social anthropologists would be made!'[14] But the aspect I want to highlight here is one particular feature of Winterson's stereotypical Puritan which is repeated with variations in a great many novels, and that is the denial of sexuality.

The figure of the Puritan driven by repressed sexual desire is a strangely insistent one. In one novel after another, men (and the occasional similarly motivated woman) are suffused by erotic fantasy, which they transform into persecutory rage. Men stare at the breasts of the women they will go on to accuse of witchcraft; they dream about them and pray desperately to be rescued from filth; they are obsessed with and repelled by sexuality. This is not necessarily psychologically implausible as one account of Puritan mentality. What is perturbing, though, is that this account is almost the only version of Puritanism offered; and in consequence, that it becomes implicitly the *cause* of Puritanism. If not for their hideous repressed lusts, the model seems to imply, these would be normal people, not given to religious excess, ready to live quietly cultivating their gardens, eating cakes and ale and having regular sex.

Sexual repression becomes in effect the motor of history, the underlying explanatory narrative for the history of the Puritan movement. And this is a disturbingly narrow view of a complex phenomenon.

It is of course a view with a long history: early modern anti-Puritan polemic drew on very similar images of erotic desire denied, though generally in the language of hypocrisy rather than of repression. However, its centrality to modern discourses on Puritanism indicates a more general problem around how we conceptualize the human psyche historically. As Foucault famously pointed out, sexuality in modern Western discourse has come to occupy the place of the hidden truth of our being; to tell the truth about desire is the great imperative of the post-Freudian subject.[15] The very modern problem afflicting these fictional Puritans is that they cannot speak their desire, and therefore they are repressed and neurotic. Now it may well be the case that many Puritans were sexually unhappy; but it would be a mistake to reduce Puritanism as a historical movement to a side effect of sexual neurosis. The stereotype is not intrinsically and always wrong, but it is founded on a quite historically specific – and modern – notion of subjectivity and its relation to sexuality. And in fiction as in history, we need to be cautious about mapping the early modern psyche after the models we are familiar with.

The witch

If the Puritan has been fictionally represented as a misguided and self-deceiving neurotic, the wicked witch has followed an opposite trajectory, re-emerging as protofeminist ecological heroine. The witch is a powerfully alluring presence in contemporary culture, both for feminist (and postfeminist) politics and for new age and Wiccan histories (and as Christine Colón's discussion in this book of Joanna Baillie's work makes clear, the witch is a source of meaning for earlier generations of women writers as well). Modern witchcraft folklore has as its reference points not only traditional fairy-tale versions of the witch, but more recent accounts: the witch as remnant of an ancient cult, as repository of ancient female knowledge, as persecuted independent woman, as an exemplary case in the unending history of misogyny, frequently burned at the stake (by sexually repressed Puritans, of course).[16] And the fictional witch draws substantially on these cultural narratives.

Fictional witches are overwhelmingly herbalists and midwives. Whether good or bad, whether their powers are real or not (and it is startling how often the fictional witch has real powers in historical novels), it is their healing skills that identify them as witches within their communities and to the reader. They generally live in cottages, where they make healing salves, tend the locals and pop out to deliver babies (like their magic, their herbal remedies tend to be surprisingly efficacious); but these very skills may lead the ungrateful locals to turn on them and accuse them of evil deeds.[17] 'The practice of witchcraft is common amongst those of her trade', remarks a magistrate of a suspected midwife in Betsy Tobin's *Bone House*, voicing the opinion of writers of the time as well as of contemporary novelists.[18] But while intuitively, for many people, this picture is very persuasive, historically it simply is not. Extensive archival searches have not come up with any indication that healers and midwives were disproportionately likely to be targeted in witchcraft accusations; as a proportion of women accused of witchcraft, their number is not significant.[19] (Midwives, on the contrary, are more likely to be involved on the other side, using their expertise in women's bodies to search for the devil's mark.[20]) Nor is there any evidence that witches were participating in an underground female-centred religion or preserving ancient pagan rites.[21] And yet despite the well-established and extensive historical literature on the subject, this version of witch-craft has come to occupy a dominant place, with little to support it beyond the feeling that this is how it should have been.

A related issue has to do not so much with the typical witch as with the untypical one – in particular the defiant and argumentative young woman. In the fictional world of the seventeenth century, it makes perfectly good sense for a woman accused of sexual or spir-itual disorder to be accused of witchcraft too.[22] To the modern writer these are all acts of female transgression or defiance, and to the extent that the witch is seen as a symbol of generalized patriarchal oppres-sion, witchcraft accusation can function as a general way of disciplining unruly females, a threat hanging over the heads of all women all the time. (Caryl Churchill's play *Vinegar Tom*, also discussed in Chapter 6, is another example of this pattern, in dramatic rather than fictional form.) To those who brought accusations of witchcraft in early modern villages, however, that correspondence simply does not work in the same way. Historically witchcraft is not a random accusation, though at certain times and places it could spill out to encompass untypical victims (including the young, the rich and the male); it is an accusation directed in the first instance against people regarded as witches, rather than a catch-all to be directed against any woman for any transgressive act. Laws and sanctions in early modern England regulated women's activities in all kinds of ways. Scolding, sexual misconduct of all kinds, heresy, giving birth to illegitimate children, disobeying your husband or father and a host of other offences against the early modern patriarchal social order were all subject to punishment. If a woman was accused of witchcraft, as a rule, it was because that was what she was thought to be doing.

Gender remains of course a critical issue in the study of witchcraft; the fact that the vast majority of those accused were women undoubtedly requires comment and analysis. But it is not the only issue. The reshaping and re-imagining of the witch in fiction makes me uneasy because it appeals too blatantly to the fantasies and preoccupations of the present.[23] If the repressed-Puritan stereotype registers our tendency to individualize social movements into personal neurosis and to assume the essential historical continuity of the sexual self, then the witch as protofeminist or ecofeminist icon might be said to go in the opposite direction, tending to flatten out the complicated particularities of individual lives into a generalized history of patriarchal oppression and female resistance. But both stereotypes involve a reduction and simplification of the complexity of the past.

The prophet

Witches and Puritans are not uncommon in historical fiction; prophets are rather rarer.[24] In the last part of this chapter, I turn to a novel about a female prophet, Stevie Davies's *Impassioned Clay*. This novel in a sense sparked off for me the question of the stories we tell about the seventeenth century, not least because Davies is in the relatively unusual position of having written both historical and fictional accounts of the women of the revolutionary period; and as a novel it is very directly concerned with the areas I would identify as issues for historical fiction.[25] The relations between the researcher and the object of research, the problems of identification and fantasy and the need to establish difference, the relation between fictional and historical writings, are among the questions the novel is grappling with; and my reservations about how these problems are addressed may be read as at least in part open questions about what historical novels can or should do, rather than simply as criticisms. I focus here on two aspects of the novel: the question of historical voice and pastiche, and the figure of the female prophet.

The novel takes place in two time frames: the first-person narrative of Olivia, a twentieth-century academic, and the story of the seventeenth-century religious radical Hannah, whose life she is researching. Hannah's narrative is presented through the documents uncovered by Olivia – diary, memoir and testimony – written variously by Hannah, her companion Isabel and other characters in their story, and underpinned by the apparatus of authenticity: explanations of provenance, details about paper and handwriting, appropriate language (imitation seventeenth-century prose). They are woven into the story in a way that invites us to read them as genuine seventeenth-century documents. And this raises the first question. To write convincing pastiche is difficult. For many readers of *Impassioned Clay* the mock seventeenth-century prose would be indistinguishable from the real thing, but inevitably there are phrases that jar a specialist reader. That is not necessarily important; what is more interesting is the question of what jars and why.

Historical fiction as a rule assumes certain fictional elements as part of the story: physical description and locatedness, emotional depth and interiority, dialogue, for instance. In the case of Davies's pastiche documents, however, these fictional needs are at odds with the conventions of the forms through which the story of Hannah is supposedly being told. Seventeenth-century religious writing – whether diary, spiritual narrative or other form – aims to hold the reader differently to fiction; it is primarily concerned with the drama of relations with the divine, not the human, and its material is organized in accordance with that imperative. The overall effect of spiritual writing, indeed, is destabilizing in its abstraction and imprecision. Names of both people and places, even close connections and home towns, are often left out as irrelevant. Time is telescoped in order to focus on significant spiritual experiences; ordinary questions of eating and sleeping and earning a living and seeing friends and family and falling in love are almost entirely absent. There may be the odd patch of dialogue or more detailed account of a particular encounter or episode, but it would never be enough to fulfil the expectations of a modern novel-reader.

Thus when Davies's (repressed) Puritan clergyman writes in his diary, describing the prophet Hannah,

> *Because her habit was grey, modest & becoming (except where the kerchief strayed adrift), those green eyes struck me to the heart & the chestnut brightness of her hair . . .* [26]

it is to me an inconceivable sentence for this context. In all the material of this kind I have read, I have practically never known the colour of anybody's hair or eyes, still less the state of their dress.[27] Even a diarist as alert to the material world as Samuel Pepys is vague and imprecise on such details; and Puritan diaries, as a general rule, do not do description. It would be too much even to say that these writers consciously exclude the material and concrete in order to focus on the spiritual world; the conventions that might direct them to consider writing about interiority, appearance, lifestyle, simply do not yet exist. The difficulties of writing convincing pastiche thus go much further than the issue of anachronistic language. An entire mode of thought, or even of subjectivity, is in question.[28]

On the other hand, the question of whether it matters remains a valid one. There are very few historical novels which do not at some point irritate a specialist; this does not necessarily make them poor accounts of the period, or indeed unsuccessful as novels, notwithstanding historians' pedantry. Fiction necessarily requires readers to subscribe to generic conventions even if the forms of writing produced are intrinsically implausible. Diarists do not in general record great swathes of conversation, accompanied by well-observed and constructed physical descriptions; autobiographers do not remember sequence, dialogue, thoughts with the precision required in a first-person novel. Pastiche documents should in theory be subject to the same rules: if we know they are fictions, we should not require them to be exactly true to the language and style they are imitating. In the specific case of Davies's novel, it becomes a problem in part because of the juxtaposition of the early modern and modern texts, with its implicit claim that reading these documents is in some sense *like* the experience of reading the real thing. But it is at least an arguable point that this is not a problem; fiction, in the end, is subject to other rules.

The problem with the prophet Hannah, however, is not only her writing, but herself. Hannah is the prophet all feminist scholars working on the period would have liked to find. She has an egalitarian female-centred spirituality, a happy and intimate sexual relationship with a same-sex partner, and a sort of primitive communalist politics. She speaks for the poor and the oppressed. She also demonstrates the range and scope of patriarchal power in early modern England by being subjected to all the gender-specific accusations and punishments that in a modern analysis might be directed against transgressive women: she is called a witch, a whore, a scold, and is punished with the scold's bridle. She is a walking demonstration of women's resistance and men's oppression.

Now it is clearly possible to find among seventeenth-century sectarians comparable ideas, and indeed sufferings; Davies gives historical notes suggesting analogues and parallels for all the features she attributes to Hannah. So it is not so much that the figure of Hannah is unthinkable, but rather that she is excessive. When every trait of interest to feminist historians is encapsulated in this single imagined prophet, it makes me uneasy. Hannah, it seems to me, is a prophet generated by a wish that the opaque, complicated, irritatingly religious and inexplicitly feminist women of this period would only give up their meanings more clearly, speak more directly, in language more recognizable to us; and to that extent she represents not so much a fictional recreation following different rules as a failure of historical imagination. Like the fictional witch, she is a creature of twentieth-century desire, a wish fulfilled, rather than a full engagement with the otherness and difficulty of the past.

The history of the self, or the impossibility of historical fiction

Historical fiction has the great advantage over history that it can invent sources that do not exist. The poor, the illiterate, the insignificant actors of history, who seldom leave their mark on formal records and who for centuries were of minimal interest to historians, can be given voices and points of view; the traditional view of history as the story of the dominant classes and nations can be subverted. This agenda, several chapters in this book suggest, is a significant one for women's historical fiction in particular, through which those hidden from history can be brought to light. But the risk, of course, is that we write our own wishes into the silence of the oppressed. If it is a mistake to write as if all servants in the past were happy folks who knew their place, it is equally a mistake to fill the novel with implausibly tolerant, sceptical, liberal-minded characters, who appreciate the injustice of hereditary hierarchies and patriarchal power.

From the point of view of historical fiction, the simplest way of thinking about the difference of people in the past is to ignore it: people are always the same, but they used to wear different clothes and do different work, and medical treatments were grim. Or the idea can be constructed in a slightly more elaborate way: fundamentally people are the same, but the culture they live in gives them some odd opinions (about religion, women's rights, race, democracy). For fictional purposes, such opinions are detachable add-ons to the character rather than constitutive. It is a more complex fictional project to try and engage not just with different views and lifestyles, but with the concept of truly different subjectivities.

In discussions about the history of the self, this period is one that has been identified as in some way transformative; the modern self, many would argue, has its origins here, traceable precisely in the emergence of new forms of writing – diary, autobiography, the novel. But it is still at the point of origins; and we cannot necessarily suppose that the forms of subjectivity at this time are truly familiar to us. One might therefore argue that all attempts to write from inside a real seventeenth-century consciousness must be doomed, simply because seventeenth-century consciousness was not characterized by this specific kind of self-narrative. The first-person narrative voice by its nature cannot but defeat the aim of expressing subjectivity as something radically unfamiliar.

I would be reluctant to conclude, however, with an argument that historical fiction is impossible for any period before some specified point at which the subject enters into its modern form (whatever that might be). Equally, my aim is not to suggest that all novels should be vetted by a historian before publication. As the wide range of texts discussed in this book demonstrates, historical fiction is a capacious category, which can take many forms besides the traditional model of a fictional narrative set in a realistically portrayed past time. Novels with multiple temporalities, involving magic and fantasy as well as gritty social realism, and novels that appropriate and rewrite past texts and past histories can all be included as studies in how fiction represents the past; and a narrow insistence on literal accuracy is not generally the most productive way of approaching these fictions.

At the same time, though, to recognize that the notion of historical truth is complex, contradictory and riddled with power relations should not lead us to assume that there is no such thing as getting history wrong. Successful fiction does not necessarily follow from a serious effort to engage with historical subjectivities; there are other ways to acknowledge the difference of history. In historical fiction as in history we have to be alert to the possibility of other ways of being; the truth of historical fiction is to be measured imaginatively rather than literally. The challenge is in how far we are able to apprehend difference and think ourselves into other modes of selfhood, whether at the level of attitude or more intimately at the level of what it means to be a self. If we allow identification with what is like, and a wish for it to be more like, to get in the way of hearing other versions that may be more difficult and less likeable, then however careful we may be about dates, we are refusing really to hear and engage with the voices of other times.

Notes

1. The following indicative list gives a sense of the range and quantity of historical novels by women set in this period (some of these are referred to directly, others not): Jeanette Winterson, *Sexing the Cherry* (London: Bloomsbury, 1989); Rose Tremain, *Restoration* (London: Hamish Hamilton, 1989) and *Music and Silence* (London: Chatto & Windus, 1999); Stevie Davies, *Impassioned Clay* (London: Women's Press, 1999); Deborah Moggach, *Tulip Fever* (London: Heinemann, 1999); Tracy Chevalier, *The Virgin Blue* (1997) and *The Pearl Earring* (London: HarperCollins, 1999); Geraldine Brooks, *A Year of Wonders* (London: Fourth Estate, 2001); Maria McCann, *As Meat Loves Salt* (London: Flamingo, 2001); Betsy Tobin, *Bone House* (London: Review, 2001); Jane Stevenson's trilogy *Astraea* (London: Jonathan Cape, 2001), *The Pretender* (London: Jonathan Cape, 2002) and *The Empress of the Last Days* (London: Jonathan Cape, 2003). In genre fiction (though the distinction is unstable): Philippa Gregory, *The Wise Woman* (London: HarperCollins, 1992), *Earthly Joys* (London: HarperCollins, 1998), *Virgin Earth* (London: HarperCollins, 1999), *The Other Boleyn Girl* (London: HarperCollins, 2001) and *The Queen's Fool* (London: HarperCollins, 2003); Joanna Hines, *The Cornish Girl* (London: Hodder and Stoughton, 1994) and *The Puritan's Wife* (London: Hodder and Stoughton, 1996); Barbara Erskine, *Hiding from the Light* (London: HarperCollins, 2002); Christie Dickason, *The Lady Tree* (London: HarperCollins, 1999), *Quicksilver* (London: HarperCollins, 1999) and *The Memory Palace* (London: HarperCollins, 2003).
2. For an illuminating recent survey of the issues in historical fiction, see Diana Wallace, *The Woman's Historical Novel: British Women Writers, 1900–2000* (Basingstoke: Palgrave Macmillan, 2005); for a historian's view of the relationship, see Anna Davin, 'Historical Novels for Children', *History Workshop Journal*, 1 (1976), 154–65. In this chapter, I am dealing with historical novels by women only; there are interesting questions about the ways in which similar issues arise in some novels by men, but for reasons of space it is not possible to explore the question of authorial gender here.
3. See Wallace, *The Woman's Historical Novel*, p. 88, for further discussion of the question of 'accuracy'.
4. For an introduction to a large and complex debate, see Keith Jenkins, *Rethinking History* (London: Routledge, 1991); on history as narrative, see Hayden White's influential essay 'The Historical Text as Literary Artifact' in his *Tropics of Discourse: Essays in Cultural Criticism* (Baltimore, MD: Johns Hopkins University Press, 1978). Linda Anderson also discusses the destabilization of historical knowledge in relation to historical fiction, in 'The Re-imagining of History in Contemporary Women's Fiction', in Linda Anderson (ed.) *Plotting Change: Contemporary Women's Fiction* (Sevenoaks, Kent: Edward Arnold, 1990), pp. 129–41.
5. On the instability of the notion of historical truth, see Chapters 4, 8 and 9.
6. For example, Davies, *Impassioned Clay*; Erskine, *Hiding from the Light*; Chevalier, *Virgin Blue*. The trope is a long-standing and familiar one in children's fiction too, with Alison Uttley's *A Traveller in Time* (London: Faber & Faber, 1939) a famous early example.

7. For example, Daphne du Maurier, *The King's General* (1946); Elizabeth Goudge, *Towers in the Mist* (1938); see also Rosemary Sutcliff's early novels of the sixteenth and seventeenth centuries, *The Armourer's House* (1951), *Brother Dusty-Feet* (1952) and *Simon* (1953).

8. See Alison Light, *Forever England: Femininity, Literature, and Conservatism between the Wars* (London: Routledge, 1991), who describes England in this period as a country in love with itself.

9. Wallace, *The Woman's Historical Novel*, p. 81.

10. Compare the Christopher Hill of *The World Turned Upside Down: Radical Ideas during the English Revolution* (London: Maurice Temple Smith, 1972) with the Hill of the 1980s, in *The Experience of Defeat: Milton and Some Contemporaries* (London: Faber, 1984).

11. There is a considerable body of work now published on radical women in particular in this period. See for example Phyllis Mack, *Visionary Women: Ecstatic Prophecy in Seventeenth-Century England* (University of California Press, 1992); Hilary Hinds, *God's Englishwomen: Seventeenth-Century Women's Writing and Feminist Literary Criticism* (Manchester: Manchester University Press, 1996).

12. Winterson, *Sexing the Cherry*, p. 70.

13. For Winterson's fictional account of her upbringing, see her *Oranges Are Not the Only Fruit* (London: Pandora, 1985). For the broader view, thanks to Jeni Williams, who made this point in discussion at the original conference version of this chapter.

14. Angela Carter, 'The Ghost Ships', *American Ghosts and Old World Wonders* (London: Vintage, 1994), p. 90.

15. Michel Foucault, *The History of Sexuality* vol. I: *The Will to Know*, trans. Robert Hurley (London: Allen Lane, 1979).

16. For a lively account of these various strands, see Diane Purkiss, The *Witch in History: Early Modern and Twentieth-Century Representations* (London: Routledge, 1996).

17. This tradition is perhaps even more powerful in children's novels, but elements of it are found very widely. Adult examples include Gregory, *The Wise Woman*, and Erskine, *Hiding from the Light*; in children's fiction, Celia Rees's very successful *Witch Child* (2000) and *Sorceress* (2002), and Julie Hearn's *The Merrybegot* (2005). In fact it is a pattern that goes back some way and is found in novels about many other periods besides the seventeenth century; see for example Margaret Reisert's *The Third Witch* (2001), *The Witch of Blackbird Pond* (1959) and Rosemary Sutcliff's *The Witch's Brat* (1970).

18. Tobin, *Bone House*, p. 215. The *Malleus Maleficarum* ('Hammer of Witches'), a famous fifteenth-century treatise on witchcraft, is particularly inclined to insist that witchcraft is especially common amongst midwives.

19. See James Sharpe, *Instruments of Darkness: Witchcraft in England, 1550–1750* (London: Hamish Hamilton, 1996), pp. 106–24. Robin Briggs, *Witches and Neighbours* (London: HarperCollins, 1996); Lyndal Roper, *Witch Craze: Terror and Fantasy in Baroque Germany* (New Haven, CT and London: Yale University Press, 2003). On midwives in particular, see David Harley, 'Historians as Demonologists: The Myth of the Midwife-Witch', *Journal of the Society for the Social History of Medicine*, 3 (1990), 1–26.

20. See Jim Sharpe, 'Women, Witchcraft and the Legal Process', in Jenny Kermode and Garthine Walker (eds) *Women, Crime and the Courts in Early Modern England* (London: UCL Press, 1994), pp. 106–24.
21. For a comprehensive debunking of the theory that witches belonged to an ancient pagan cult, see Norman Cohn, *Europe's Inner Demons* (2nd edn, London: Pimlico, 1993); for further discussion see Purkiss, *The Witch in History*. Traces of pagan beliefs in early modern magical practice have been identified by some historians (see for example Carlo Ginzburg, *The Night Battles: Witchcraft and Agrarian Cults in the Sixteenth and Seventeenth Centuries* [London: Routledge and Kegan Paul, 1983]); but not in the form of a coherent belief system.
22. For example, the heroines of Dickason, *The Memory Palace*; Hines, *The Puritan's Wife*; and Davies, *Impassioned Clay*.
23. See also Wallace's discussion of Ellen Galford's 1984 novel *Moll Cutpurse: Her True History*; as she comments, 'This is history as lesbian feminist fantasy... it clearly reflects the desires of 1980s feminists rather than offering a realistic picture' (*The Woman's Historical Novel*, p. 177).
24. An interesting comparison is with the female prophet in Iain Pears's *An Instance of the Fingerpost* (London: Jonathan Cape, 1997), who is the only major character in the novel not to tell her own story; much more might be said about this novel and its strategies.
25. See Stevie Davies, *Unbridled Spirits: Women of the English Revolution, 1640–1660* (London: Women's Press, 1998).
26. Davies, *Impassioned Clay*, p. 83 (emphasis in original).
27. I can think of two cases where men describe the appearance of women they know, neither in the form of a diary nor with anything like the physical intimacy of the language here. Goodwin Wharton, in his very long manuscript journal/autobiography, describes in novelistic terms (long black hair; astonishingly small waist considering her 20 children) the physical appearance of Mrs Parish, who was initially his contact with the spirit world, and subsequently his mistress ('Autobiography of the Hon. Goodwin Wharton', BL Add. MSS. 20006–20007, 1686–1704; the late date puts it in the same time frame as the novel). And an account of the life and death of Mrs Drake, who suffered from melancholy, describes her as 'of a low well compacted stature, of a lovely browne complexion, having a full nimble quick Sparrow-hawke eye'; this is part of a general account of her constitution, which seeks to explain her malady through an analysis of her physical and mental humours. See Hart On-Hi (John Hart), *Trodden Down Strength, by the God of Strength, or, Mrs Drake Revived...* (London: n.p., 1647), pp. 6–7.
28. For a polemical approach to the relations between autobiography, interiority, individualism and narrative, see Michael Mascuch, *Origins of the Individualist Self: Autobiography and Self-Identity in England, 1591–1791* (Cambridge: Polity Press, 1997).

2
History as Story in Angela Carter's *American Ghosts and Old World Wonders*

Sarah Gamble

Angela Carter's last collection of short stories, *American Ghosts and Old World Wonders*, was published posthumously in 1993, the year following her death from lung cancer. When it appeared it was dismissed by one reviewer as 'a book of fragments', which should be regarded as nothing more significant than 'a kind homage from a loyal publisher'.[1] This is an assessment which carries with it the faint suggestion that *American Ghosts* might be nothing more than an over-hasty attempt on the part of Carter's publishers to capitalize on the extra publicity surrounding the death of a well-known author, but this was actually far from the case. On the contrary, it was a book that Carter herself had planned, and for which she had assembled the material and chosen the title. Most of the stories included in this book had previously been published elsewhere between 1987 and 1992, and only two – 'Gun for the Devil' and 'The Ghost Ships' – were discovered among Carter's papers after her death and added by her editor, Susannah Clapp.

American Ghosts and Old World Wonders cannot be allowed the unified coherence it might have had if, over a limited period of time and in full knowledge of her illness and its outcome, Carter had written a group of stories which she knew would be her last. Nevertheless, this collection does have a loose structure which, while it may at times seem a little strained, does create a kind of overall pattern. It is divided up into two sections: four stories about America, followed by five stories about Europe, which, in its juxtaposition of narratives of the New and Old Worlds, sets up the opposition conveyed by the title.

This chapter will explore the nature of that opposition by charting a journey from the Old World to the New and back again. Concentrating particularly on the stories which are set in America, it intends to argue that the common purpose which links them is Carter's concern to problematize the very concept of 'newness' to which America lays claim. In these narratives, far from constituting a chance to start afresh individual lives, or even the historical process itself, America remains (however reluctantly) bound to its European antecedents. This is where the concept of 'story' comes in, for Carter does not envisage the hold that the Old World retains over the New as one that has its origins in either politics or culture. Instead, in these texts it is manifested at what, for Carter at least, is a much more fundamental level – the level of the imagination, which is steeped in the forms and patterns of narrative structures.

'Story' was a concept which assumed an increasing importance in Carter's later work – her last two books, *Nights at the Circus* and *Wise Children*, are both structured as autobiographical narratives, where the self-evident enjoyment with which the narrator tells her tall tale serves to draw the reader's attention to the manner in which the story is told, thus foregrounding the decisions which dictate its structure. By being rendered opaque in this way, the narrative acquires an artefactual solidity: it is not merely a transparent frame through which the reader can view the contents of the text.

The stories in *American Ghosts and Old World Wonders* function as good examples of Carter's generally metafictional narrative approach. These are not stories which masquerade as reality, nor are they the kind of fantasy which Todorov terms the 'pure marvellous',[2] where an imagined world is rendered unproblematically coherent by functioning according to its own internal logic. Instead, they are characteristically mannered and artificial, so that one is never allowed to forget that one is listening to a story, and the voice of the narrator – whether it issues from a character or from an anonymous commentator whom the reader cannot help identifying with Carter herself – tends to be an emphatic presence, who is always too well aware of the existence of an audience.

An oppositional parallel could perhaps be drawn here between Carter and the case of Helen Demidenko discussed elsewhere in this book by Rachel Morley. The revelation that Demidenko was herself a created persona delegitimized her supposed autobiography, creating the same tension between authenticity and invention which Angela Carter both played on and played up throughout her career. And while, in the case of *American Ghosts and Old World Wonders*, we are dealing with a literal and authentic 'Death of the Author', Carter's use of the intrusive narrative voice ensures that she remains a presence behind the text which, through her ostentatious storytelling practice, works to simultaneously legitimize and illegitimize its origins.

However, in the context of the texts that are going to be discussed here, 'story' also acquires an authority which dissolves the boundaries we tend to assume divide 'real life' from 'fiction'. In this sense, Carter's attitude is reminiscent of Lyotard's idea of the 'grand' or 'meta' narrative, which legitimizes certain ways of seeing, and thus of shaping, the world.[3] Like Lyotard, Carter evidently regards us as beings who conceptualize experience through narrative structures; and this is the principal means by which she forges the link between the Old World and the New, whereby America is shown in the process of struggling to formulate an independent metanarrative through which it will be empowered to construct a uniquely American identity. It is certainly tempting to reinforce the link with Lyotard further and to argue that these stories show America, founded out of a belief in the 'little narrative' of human individualism, fighting to break away from the prohibitive influence of an all-encompassing European metanarrative. However, neat though it might sound, can such an idea really be sustained? As Carter portrays it, America is not born out of the desire to pursue freedom at all, but out of rigid conformity to a particularly powerful and pervasive belief system which is firmly rooted in biblical narrative. Its European inheritance, because it includes more than just religious fanaticism, can therefore also be regarded as providing America with beneficial ways to counteract the kind of myths which are, in Carter's own words, 'designed to make people unfree'.[4]

Yet these short narratives bear out a point also stressed by Michael Sinowitz with reference to Carter's use of Yeats in *Nights at the Circus*: 'that simply overturning these constructions is ... much more complicated a process than this might seem, and that such reversals do not simply restore or grant the freedom that Carter implies myths take away' (see Chapter 7, p. 103). By the time we reach the stories about Europe, the relationship between Old and New Worlds has become a complicated tangle of influence and counterinfluence, with neither necessarily any more free of the entangling tendrils of myth than the other.

In terms of both context and content, 'The Ghost Ships' exemplifies the concepts which hold the collection as a whole together. In its position as the first story of the second section of the text, and the fifth story out of a total of nine, it quite literally forms a bridge between the Old World and the New, a function which is reinforced by the action of the narrative itself. It imagines the first Christmas Eve in America, and the way in which, despite the Puritans' desire to make a new start on a new continent, uncluttered by the legends and traditions of the

England they have left behind, the pagan memories of the Old World persist through memory, dream and story.

The Puritans conceptualize America as a definitive break in history – it is a 'new leaf they have just turned over',[5] 'a blank page' (p. 89) just waiting for their god-fearing inscription. But in Angela Carter's fiction, moments of calendrical change are significant and dangerous. The ancient festival of Christmas marks the occasion of the Winter Solstice, a time when 'the hinge on which the year turns' (p. 96) creaks open just enough to allow the past to slip through and make its bid to regain a position in the minds and imaginations of the colonists of the New World. Three 'ghost ships of Christmas past' (p. 91) come sailing into Boston Bay, each containing the paraphernalia of seasonal celebration – holly and mistletoe; roast swan and Christmas pudding; and, finally, the festival's presiding spirit, the Lord of Misrule himself. Yet each ship in its turn fails to land, blown, quite literally, out of the water by the censorious minds of the Puritan sleepers: 'the immigration officials at the front of the brain, the port of entry for memory, sensed contraband in the incoming cargo and snapped: "Permission to land refused!" ' (pp. 92–3).

The conflict portrayed here is one which is already thoroughly familiar to any reader who knows Carter's work, which has always persistently eroded the authority of law and order, logic and rationalism, by exposing its repressed oppositional Other – the playful, anarchic and grotesque forces of the carnivalesque. Somewhat surprisingly, Carter claimed that she did not actually read Bakhtin's writing until after the publication of *Nights at the Circus* in 1984 because, she found, 'he was invoked so often by readers'.[6] Nevertheless, their visions of the form and function of carnival are uncannily similar, for, like Bakhtin, Carter portrays it as a form which exists to

> consecrate inventive freedom, to permit the combination of a variety of different elements and their rapprochement, to liberate from the prevailing point of view of the world, from conventions and established truths, from clichés, from all that is humdrum and universally accepted. The carnival spirit offers the chance to have a new outlook on the world, to realize the relative nature of all that exists, and to enter a completely new order of things.[7]

This quotation from Bakhtin demonstrates an aspect of carnival which is crucial to the story. While the Puritans dismiss celebration as 'gross', 'heathenish' and 'lewd' (p. 90), they have actually missed the point.

During the 12 days of Christmas, nothing may be forbidden, but precisely because anything is permissible, 'everything is forgiven' (p. 96), thus enabling the participants to make a new start of the coming year. The crowning irony of this story, therefore, is that the New England Puritans are clearly mistaken in their belief that they are starting afresh. In fact, labouring under a burden of ancestral sin that requires them to regulate their every thought and action, they have rejected the very rich and lively customs which have traditionally enabled the community to put the actions of the past behind them. What they have not grasped is that in temporarily condoning the community's desire to indulge in excess and disorder, such festivals have also purged it.

Thankfully, however, the past is not exiled as easily as all that. Although none of the metaphorical ghost ships reach the shore, in the very act of sinking the Lord of Misrule throws a well-aimed Christmas pudding towards the land. In the morning, each child finds a juicy raisin in their shoe; a comic indication that the separation between the Old World and the New is not as absolute as the Puritans would wish it to be. Fragments of the folklore, customs and stories of the past have found a toehold in America – so what does America make of them?

In at least two of the other stories in the collection – 'John Ford's *'Tis Pity She's a Whore'* and 'Gun for the Devil' – the relationship between the Old World and the New is no less uneasy, for, as in 'The Ghost Ships', Carter is concerned with problematizing notions of America as the land of the free, the home of the brave and a place of limitless possibility. Here, however, that critique is not counterbalanced by the stories of the Old World, to which the liberatory effects of the carnivalesque are no longer attached. Shorn of their pagan origins, they carry with them echoes of biblical narratives and are thus imbued with the same notions of transgression and retribution that burdened the Puritans in 'The Ghost Ships'. The recurring Old World narrative referent in both these short stories is Jacobean tragedy, whose tragic vision is itself predicated on the violent repercussions surrounding a refusal to forget the misdeeds or mistakes of the past.

'John Ford's *'Tis Pity She's a Whore'* takes place on the prairies of the American West. It is a landscape on which an enduring myth of American identity has been founded, an identity defined by reference to a macho code of hardy individualism and pioneering spirit. But what is truly startling about this story is the thoroughness with which it recontextualizes such concepts by reinscribing them within a framework formed exclusively by Old World texts.

As the title suggests – and which, just in case the reader neglects to pick up the reference, the detailed notes at the bottom of the first page make absolutely clear – this entire story is a narrative pun on the name 'John Ford', one which is shared by a sixteenth-century Jacobean dramatist and a twentieth-century American film-maker. It is this conceit which influences the construction of a multilayered text which masquerades as a John Ford movie adaptation of a John Ford play: as envisaged, of course, by Angela Carter. Long passages of prose, dominated by a deliberately intrusive narrative voice which frequently speaks in the first person, are interspersed with quotations from an imaginary film script and an actual play.

Beneath the mannered progression of the narrative, Carter's intentions are nevertheless clear. The great plains of the New World, rather than signifying freedom and an escape from the restrictions of the past, become a stifling enclosure which serves merely as the latest setting for the playing out of tragedies which are so well worn as to be archetypal. The ease with which the narrative elides drama into screenplay suggests that America is almost wholly the construct of an imagination which cannot eradicate its European origins.

This intimation of restriction, be it cultural or imaginative, is thematically introduced through the figure of the absent mother. This is another familiar Carter trope – throughout her fiction she specialized in the creation of motherless children – but in this story the mother's death is an important element in her undercutting of the myth of the American dream. This woman dies not of homesickness nor simple loneliness, but only 'of the pressure of that vast sky, that weighed down upon her and crushed her lungs until she could not breathe any more, as if the prairies were the bedrock of an ocean in which she drowned' (p. 20). The constriction of her grave, where she is described as lying in the ground 'with all the prairies and all that careless sky upon her breast' (p. 21), therefore constitutes no more than an intensification of the already intense claustrophobia she experienced while living.

Any individual identity this woman might have had is squashed out of existence by the weight of the prairie's emptiness, and her essential anonymity is underlined by the fact that her tombstone has no space for her name, commemorating her only as 'Beloved wife of . . . Mother of . . .' (p. 21). Yet her very absence is in itself significant. In a narrative sense, her death constitutes a metafictional gesture which binds this particular text ever more firmly onto the wheel of perpetual story, for as Carter notes elsewhere in *American Ghosts and Old World Wonders*, in a story which is both a meditation on and a speculative rewrite of the fairy tale 'Ashputtle' ('Ashputtle or The Mother's Ghost'), the death of the mother is a recurrent motif in traditional tales, where it becomes the crucial event which sets the story-line in motion.

The way in which the maternal presence accumulates meaning through the very fact of its absence (thus constituting a kind of *inverted* presence) has, however, another function in this story. By drawing attention to the way in which the mother's identity is constituted through her relation to other people – husband, children – Carter points to another problematic aspect of the notion of America as a radically new world; the fact that the subject it constructs is implicitly male. In this way, this world's claims to newness is placed in question, for, after all, what has changed for the woman who has to cook, sew, clean and bear children, wherever she happens to be?

In the first four paragraphs of the story, therefore, in which Carter no sooner evokes the presence of the mother than she banishes her, the notion of America as 'space' has been replaced with a notion of America as 'emptiness' or 'absence'. In this sense, the mother's death has set her children adrift in a vacancy which is as much actual as it is emotional or moral. When, a few pages later on, Carter ponders on 'those enormous territories! That green vastness, in which anything is possible' (p. 24), the reader is meant to pick up on the irony, especially when it is immediately followed by a scene from the imaginary John Ford screenplay which is rendered in terms which point up its stale familiarity:

EXTERIOR. PRAIRIE. DAY.
(Close up) Johnny and Annie-Belle kiss.
'Love Theme' up.
Dissolve. (p. 24)

It could be a love scene from any one of a million films – but there is one crucial difference here, of course, and that is the fact that the motherless Johnny and Annie-Belle are brother and sister. However, there is nothing new about this either. Not only is the theme of incest an essential part of the original Ford play, *'Tis Pity She's a Whore'*, on which this story is modelled, it is also the last manifestation of Carter's long-standing fascination with the subject. From *The Magic Toyshop* onwards, sexual relationships further complicate the already convoluted familial relations, both biological and constructed, within her fiction. It is certainly not being suggested that Carter was promoting incest as a valid lifestyle choice for her readers, but as one of the last great cultural taboos it retains a connection with a moral code which, once again, is founded in an overarching metanarrative.

The tragic tale of these related lovers, in which Annie-Belle tries to atone for what she comes to see as sin by marrying the son of the local minister, only to be killed (along with her husband and unborn child) by Johnny in a fit of drunken jealousy, thus has antecedents which go further back than John Ford's play. The introduction of the theme of incest evokes associations of biblical sanctions, which enable America's claim to be a new beginning to be presented in terms which, while they may be parodically exaggerated, are also thoroughly familiar. Johnny, his 'intelligence nourished only by the black book of the father', imagines 'himself as a kind of Adam', with Annie-Belle 'his unavoidable and irreplaceable Eve, the unique companion of the wilderness' (p. 26). The care with which Carter subsequently points out that 'he knows they do not live in Eden' does not alter the fact that the parallel has been drawn: a parallel which, in the context of this argument, brings us back to the Puritanical code out of which the concept of this continent as the New World was born, based all too securely on the tales to be found in the (founding) father's black book.

The incestuous relationship of Johnny and Annie-Belle is therefore doomed to fail, not because it is morally 'wrong' from the author's point of view, but because it cannot break out of the multilayered cycle of story in which it is so firmly embedded. Elsewhere in Carter's fiction, incest is presented as a dramatic and effective act of rebellion against the codes which seek to regulate propriety and morality. But this is not the case here, where it constitutes nothing more than a failure of the imagination, a self-absorbed narcissism which enables the protagonists to evade the possibility – and the dangers – of change. Precisely because the 'vast margin' of silence and space with which these children are surrounded is indicative of 'an unimaginable freedom which they dare not imagine' (p. 22), they turn to an image of the other which is, comfortingly, also an image of the self, since they regard 'the other's face as if it were their own' (p. 25). And, as the following passage makes clear, Johnny and Annie-Belle are meant to be regarded as emblematic of America as a whole, which is similarly born, not of difference, but of essential sameness:

In the fragments of the mirror, they kneel to see their round, blond, innocent faces that, superimposed upon one another, would fit at every feature, their faces, all at once the same face, the face that never existed until now, the pure face of America. (p. 24)

It is this notion of American identity as essentially incestuous which lies at the heart of Carter's critique. America is a country which, for all its claims to newness, has been born out of an imagination steeped in the patterns and associations of Old World narratives, be they Christian or pagan, censorious or carnivalesque, and thus retains a tendency to focus inwards on sameness, rather than outwards on difference. And this foregrounds another characteristic of story, which is that it is inherently repressive, colonizing the narrative space available to it by suppressing all other possible versions of itself.

Carter, therefore, is also concerned about demonstrating that what may be a New World from a European point of view may already be an Old World from someone else's. Both 'John Ford's *'Tis Pity She's a Whore*' and 'Gun for the Devil' are haunted by what in 'Gun for the Devil' Carter terms 'the banned daemonology' of the 'unknown continent' (p. 58). Death stalks through the narrative of both stories, with 'high cheekbones' and wearing 'his hair in braids' (p. 20). He is a figure who is symbolic of another, banished, version of the story of America which, while never quite being able to take it over, retains the ability to exercise a disruptive power from the margins of the dominant narrative.

The kind of postcolonial sensibility at work here is, however, somewhat convoluted, for Carter, appearing not to want to leave anybody out, also shows that the opposition between Old and New America is not a simple dualism between white man and Indian. This New World exists in many possible versions. In 'John Ford's *'Tis Pity She's a Whore*' she evokes an image of the continent as fundamentally divided and exiled from itself; in which 'the top half doesn't know what the bottom half is doing'.

While 'John Ford's *'Tis Pity She's a Whore*' plays games with the heroic myth of the American Wild West, 'Gun for the Devil' is set more firmly in a chaotic world of multiple, fundamentally incompatible, American identities, for it is a story where a number of different borderlines cross. Not only, chronologically speaking, does it take place 'about the turn of the century' (p. 45), its setting is a Mexican border town, the point where white, blond, English-speaking North America is confronted with its despised darker-skinned, Spanish-speaking South. The characters, too, form a jumble of racial and cultural identities, Mexicans rubbing shoulders with North Americans and Europeans, and all of them haunted by the spectre of Death in his Indian guise.

The most significant character in this story is known only as the Count. An 'ageing, drunken, consumptive . . . aristocrat' (p. 45), he is the distilled personification of European decadence. In his habitual dress of 'soiled, ruffled shirts and threadbare suits of dandified black' (p. 46), he seems a figure more suited to the turn of the eighteenth century than the nineteenth, and thus out of context historically as well as geographically. The Count is the possessor of secrets and the focus of rumour and speculation.

He is, therefore, to this narrative what the ghost ships were to the story discussed earlier in this chapter, for by his very foreignness he functions as an insistent reminder of the very past from which America wishes to disassociate itself. But while the Puritans attempt to deny the folklore and customs of their native land, the Count stands, spider-like, at the centre of an ever-proliferating web of stories. It does not matter that he himself is never too explicit about the reasons for his presence in this 'flyblown town' (p. 52): the very fact of his alienness generates conjecture of the most imaginative kind. It is whispered, for example, that he was once so accurate a shot,

> they said only that the devil himself – it's best not to pay atten-
> tion to such stories, even if Maddalena once worked in a house in
> San Francisco where Roxana used to work and somebody told her –
> but the Count's shadow falls across the wall; they hush, even if
> Maddalena furtively crosses herself. (p. 46)

A figure who trails rumours of wickedness and past misdeeds, the Count, like the absent mother and the incestuous siblings of 'John Ford's '*Tis Pity She's a Whore*', has appeared in Carter's fiction before, and under the same name too. In a novel published in 1972, *The Infernal Desire Machines of Doctor Hoffman*, the Count is a blasphemous and perverted monstrosity who is the embodiment of Carter's interest in the work of the eighteenth-century French pornographer, the Marquis de Sade. The character in 'Gun for the Devil' is a heavily diluted version – de Sade in shabby retirement, as it were. The Count's cynicism and general world-weariness stands him in good stead here, for it allows him to see through the fantasy of the American dream and satirize it in terms that remind us of his author's narrative intentions:

> 'We must leave the Old World and its mysteries behind us,' says the
> Count. 'The old, weary, exhausted world. Leave it behind! This is a
> new country, full of hope . . .'

He is heavily ironic. The ancient rocks of the desert lour down in the sunset.

'But the landscape of this country is more ancient by far than we are, strange gods brood over it. I shall never be friends with it, never.' (p. 51)

While he may function as the representative of the moral exhaustion of the Old World, therefore, the Count echoes Carter in his refusal to see America as representing a new start. Instead he regards it as a country with its own memories, history and, most significantly, ancient vendettas. When another foreigner appears in the town, a piano player called Johnny, a drama is initiated which is at once another replay of Jacobean tragedy and the retribution of America's exiled and forgotten past on its colonizers.

Johnny is a man hell-bent on wreaking 'operatic revenge' (p. 52) on the bandit family who rule the town, whom he accuses of having killed his parents; but he is also the Count's double, with whom he shares a 'crazy, black-clad dignity' (p. 51) and an ability to speak German. Together – 'eyes the same shape, hands the same shape' (p. 51) – they function as the other's shadow self, the Count the master and Johnny the acolyte in what becomes another oft-told tale of Faustian bargains and acts of self-destructive vengeance. For Johnny wants the Count's secret: that of the bullet which, through demonic agency, cannot miss its target.

It does not work, of course – or rather it works too well, for Johnny, carried away by 'the sudden ease with which he can kill' (p. 64), shoots not only the matriarch and patriarch of the hated Mendoza clan, but also their daughter, his fiancée, Teresa. Horrified, Johnny flees into the desert, looking for all the world like 'a man with the devil pursuing him' (p. 64). The story's final twist, however, is that the Devil is not running after Johnny at all. Instead, because the Faustian narrative *always* ends with the sorcerer being claimed by the forces he has attempted to enslave, all the Devil has to do is wait for Johnny to run to him. So in the end, it is the Devil, even more than the Count, who is revealed to have the greatest knowledge about the nature of story: that is, that it is inescapable.

The image with which 'Gun for the Devil' concludes – that of the figure speeding towards an inevitable fate – is one picked up again at the beginning of the story which follows it, 'The Merchant of Shadows'. This narrative reconfigures the clash between the Old World and the New in terms which give their relationship a slant which is quite different from either the two stories which precede it or the one which follows it.

Like the Count in 'Gun for the Devil', the unnamed male narrator of 'The Merchant of Shadows' is a stranger in a strange land. But while it is implied that the Count left Europe through pressing necessity and thus lives the life of an exile who, however much he might wish it, can never return to his native land, this young man regards America through very different eyes: 'I don't intend to go native, I'm not here for good, I'm here upon a pilgrimage' (p. 66). However, although he is admittedly approaching the New World in a somewhat different spirit, his attitude at the beginning of the story is not all that dissimilar from that of his Puritan predecessors. Dismissing Britain as 'a foggy, three-cornered island' (p. 66), he enthusiastically embraces America as a place full of magical possibility, and experiences a pleasurable, and self-consciously dramatic, frisson in imagining it as utterly different:

The first time I saw the Pacific, I'd had a vision of sea gods, but not the one *I* knew, oh, no. Not even Botticelli's prime 36B cup blonde ever came in on *this* surf. My entire European mythology capsized under the crash of waves Britannia never ruled. (p. 67)

The question is, is the narrator's 'European mythology' really as defunct as he imagines it to be? The answer is that it both is and is not. It is not, because the narrator has come to America to study film, and this story is most emphatic in the manner in which it stresses the European antecedents of 'the Great Art of Light and Shade', which, claims the author, was born out of alchemical research 'four centuries ago in the Gothic north' (p. 68). Furthermore, the specific object of the narrator's research is a German director, Heinrich Mannheim, thus emphasizing still further that cinema is not an American invention.

But as the story proceeds the narrator's alienation, which is initially at least half-imaginary, becomes wholly genuine. Antecedents quite apart, it is only in the 'white light' (p. 68) of the Californian sun that cinema attains its apotheosis, becoming Hollywood, the quint-essential dream factory. And it is in Hollywood, the narrator's 'Holy Grail' (p. 66), that America finds its own mythology, and out of which it creates a past which, while it may be almost wholly the work of imagination, is rendered in such larger-than-life terms that it acquires a self-authenticating force which puts it on an equal footing with history.

In 'The Merchant of Shadows' the relationship between the Old and the New Worlds is thus significantly altered. In 'The Ghost Ships', the New World is portrayed as quite consciously attempting to ignore the way in which it is ineradicably structured through an imagination which has its roots in the Old World. 'John Ford's *'Tis Pity She's a Whore'* and 'Gun for the Devil', by combining Old World themes with New World settings, both emphasize that America is still in thrall to its European antecedents, because it cannot conceptualize an American identity which is not, somehow, indebted to them. But 'The Merchant of Shadows' is different. Here, cinema is portrayed as an art form which enables the New World to finally turn tables on the Old. Through a medium which America has made its own, Europe gets its dreams and myths mass-produced and reflected back to it – larger than life and twice as unnatural.

Through Hollywood, therefore, the American dream is made, not flesh, but celluloid – and precisely because it is manufactured, it can look more authentic than the real thing. The object of the narrator's quest is Mannheim's supposed widow, who is a legendary film star in her own right – 'far, far more than a Hollywood widow; she was the Star of Stars, no less, the greatest of them all . . . dubbed by *Time* magazine the "Spirit of the Cinema" ' (p. 69). When he meets her, however, this self-dramatic, almost terminally self-conscious, young man is reduced to abject discomposure and firmly dislodged from the elite perspective of the professional researcher.

From the first moment of their meeting, the Spirit exerts a compulsive fascination over him. In spite of her age, which thick layers of make-up – that 'one hundred per cent Max Factor look' (p. 76), as he observes at one point – cannot disguise, she nevertheless has what he can only describe as '*star quality*':

I'd never before, nor am I likely to again, encountered such psychic force as streamed out of that frail little old lady in her antique lingerie and her wheelchair. And, yes, there was something undeniably erotic about it, although she was old as the hills; it was as though she got the most extraordinary sexual charge from being looked at and this charge bounced back on the looker, as though some mechanism inside herself converted your regard into sexual energy. (p. 77)

The 'ghastly sense of incipient humiliation, of impending erotic doom' (p. 79) this arouses in the narrator is, however, only the beginning, for he has yet to realize exactly *how* artificial this figure is. Far from being Mannheim's widow, the Spirit turns out to be, of course, Mannheim himself.

The Spirit, like the Count, has her antecedents in Carter's earlier fiction. *The Passion of New Eve*, published in 1977, features not only a narrator who has undergone a sex-change from male to female, but a man who has become the iconic female movie star of her generation: Tristessa de St Ange. Both Tristessa and the Spirit fulfil the same function, which is to exemplify the *constructed* nature of femininity. They are both men who make more perfect women than women themselves are ever able to be, because what they enact upon the blank canvas of their own bodies becomes the distilled essence of the male fantasy of femininity. They are also figures born out of Carter's fondness for the cinematic *femme fatale*, most particularly with Marlene Dietrich, whose ability to function as an object of desire was directly related to the extent to which her appearance was stylized: in Carter's words, 'invented, like a piece of cookery, really, a piece of *haute cuisine*'.[8]

The Spirit, therefore, for the precise reason that she 'exist[s] almost and only in the eye of the beholder' (p. 82), is indeed the genuine Spirit of Cinema. Characterized by Carter elsewhere as 'the apotheosis of the fake',[9] the essence of the cinematic effect is to render the illusory real, and the real, in its turn, curiously insubstantial. In this role, the Spirit becomes the symbol of America's triumphant transformation of its Old World inheritance, and the means by which the ancient stories contained within the Puritans' black book are finally displaced. Against her burning, fanatical self-conviction, the narrator has no defence. Desperate to believe that 'there was more to flesh than light and illusion' (p. 85) and finding it a wish that America cannot satisfy, he finally flees home to England. It is an act which brings the journey between Old World and New full circle back to where it once began, but with the power balance between the two significantly altered. America, now, is the myth-maker.

However, we are also back to Carter's original definition of myths: that they are stories designed to make people unfree. As 'John Ford's *'Tis Pity She's a Whore*' has already implied, there may be nothing much that is truly liberatory about the myth-making apparatus of the dream machine. Instead, one metanarrative (Puritanism) has been replaced by another (Hollywood), and the net result is much the same. The Spirit, indeed, possesses the madness of the fundamentalist, believing with absolute assurance that the making of movies is analogous to a religious mission, in which her role is to function as the conduit through which 'the transmission of divine light' can be conveyed to feed the desires of 'the congregation of the faithful, the company of the blessed' (p. 80). Carter loved cinema for the very reason that it constituted nothing more than a sophisticated con trick, but she was all too well aware that it is a con trick with serious repercussions. The potential for change and renewal signified by the carnivalesque has become debased currency in cinematic context, where the individual has the chance to change all right, but it is a change wrought by plastic surgery, the judicious application of cosmetics and artful camera angles, rather than by any optimistic assertion of communal spirit.

In *American Ghosts and Old World Wonders*, therefore, the past is presented as something that should not be discarded altogether; but neither should it be endlessly reiterated. For Carter this conundrum is symbolized in America, a country born out of the wish to make a new start, yet also inescapably indebted to a European moral tradition which obscures all alternative histories and identities. Yet envisaging the past narratologically allows Carter to posit an alternative. Stories may codify and confine, but they can also be rewritten. Carter's own favourite narrative technique was to conduct a kind of artistic smash and grab on other texts and to use the fragments as elements of new, dramatically different, narratives, thus giving the concept of story a dynamic immediacy in which all kinds of opportunities can be glimpsed, if we only dare to be creative enough.

Notes

1. Neil Paraday, 'Easily Missed', *The Guardian* (23 March 1993), p. 8.
2. See Rosemary Jackson, *Fantasy: The Literature of Subversion* (London: Methuen, 1981), p. 32.
3. See Jean-François Lyotard, *The Postmodern Condition: A Report on Knowledge*, trans. Geoff Bennington and Brian Massumi, foreword by Frederic Jameson (Manchester: Manchester University Press, 1984).
4. Angela Carter, 'Notes from the Front Line', in Michelene Wandor (ed.) *On Gender and Writing* (London: Pandora Press, 1983), p. 71.
5. Angela Carter, *American Ghosts and Old World Wonders* (London: Chatto, 1993), p. 90. Further references appear in the text.
6. 'Angela Carter interviewed by Lorna Sage', in Malcom Bradbury and Judy Cooke (eds) *New Writing* (London: Minerva, 1992), p. 188.
7. Mikhail Bakhtin, *Rabelais and His World*, trans. Hélène Iswolsky (Bloomington, IN: Indiana University Press, 1984), p. 34.
8. Angela Carter quoted in 'Angela Carter's Curious Room', *Omnibus*, BBC (15 September 1992).
9. Ibid.

3
Falling Off the Edge of the World: History and Gender in Daphne Marlatt's *Ana Historic*

Sherry Booth

Most feminist scholars in both history and literature would agree that the historical record has consistently written women out of history, or when they are present these women serve most often as adjuncts to men or as anomalies. Little wonder, then, that contemporary women writers, whether they write history, fiction, poetry or literary criticism, are drawn to the past and to past histories. History and fiction come together in ways both problematic and promising in much fiction by women, not surprisingly as the novel has been linked to history since its inception in the seventeenth century. Australian-born Canadian author Daphne Marlatt's novel *Ana Historic* brings together questions about the truth (and fictiveness) of history, the fictiveness (and truth) of literary texts and the role of imagination in the creation of true stories, of accurate histories.

Ana Historic fits well the category of novel Linda Hutcheon has defined as 'historiographic metafictions', which 'are intensely self-reflexive but that also reintroduce historical context into metafiction and problematize the entire question of historical knowledge'.[1] But Marlatt's novel critiques more than historical knowledge; the intertwined narratives of the three major characters propose that many categories, including gender and identity, are much more fluid and varied than the normative narratives about them suggest. Following the line of queer theory, which deconstructs the ideologies that shape and control sexuality as stable categories,[2] the novel stretches our notions of how history, identity and sexuality come into being. Judith Butler explains that queer 'make[s] us consider at what expense and for what purpose the terms are used, and through what relations of power such categories have been wrought'.[3] Marlatt constantly questions any number of disciplinary structures and institutions that shape minds and bodies. The novel blurs the line between traditional classifications of fiction and history in order to assert the limitations of and gaps within history and the necessity for and truth of the fictive. Perhaps the most apt metaphor to describe the nexus of history, body, gender, identity and writing in this text is the labyrinth: all the strands are interconnected, but finding one's way through it proves difficult.

These difficulties stem in part from the connectedness of the topics as well as their contested nature. History is a concept that lives uneasily in a postmodern world; the postmodern novel is equally unsettled. Yet another complication is the presence of theory; while we cannot interpret texts in the absence of a theory or theories, the consequence of theory is to move the focus from the individual to the group or from the particular character or event to what it exemplifies. Jonathan Culler articulates the conflict between theory and specific works of literature:

> Literary works characteristically represent individuals, so struggles about identity are struggles within the individual and between individual and group ... In theoretical writings, arguments about social identity tend to focus ... on group identities ... Thus there are tensions between literary explorations and critical or theoretical claims.[4]

Just as any interpretation of a literary work must move back and forth between the theoretical and the specific, a work like Marlatt's must also negotiate the spaces between the general/theoretical and the particularities of her characters and her plots, using her characters as both singular and exemplary. She brings together her chosen strands to expose history's power to shape who we are as well as to show the ways that history has, and continues to, impact on the material and emotional lives of women – their bodies, their ideas about their bodies, their gendering and the results of that gendering. These are not topics with which history has been concerned, an attitude and practice that Marlatt critiques in her novel because the past, as the character Zoe says, is never past. The story in 'history' must be reimagined and rewritten if a different – more open and expansive – future can result. For we are born into and shaped by discourses: the discourses of traditional histories, literature, families and, in this novel in particular, discourses about women.

The problem of history

We might begin by asking two related questions of history: what kind and whose? Marlatt's narrator Annie is married to a historian and serves as his research assistant, so she knows well the nature of historical documents and the facts they contain. She also comes to know just how elusive and inaccurate both the documents and the facts of history can be. The problematic relationship between history and story is addressed by Chapters 1 and 4. Tofantšuk calls our attention to stories that have been suppressed as 'marginal' and cites histories of women in particular; and Hodgkin stresses that 'the notions of historical truth, as a straight-forward opposite to fiction, can hardly go unchallenged' (p. 16). Annie's current project, which is to explore archival texts relating to the early history of Vancouver, gets derailed by two events, unrelated in time but linked by effect: her mother's recent death and a brief mention 'in the pages of history' of a woman, 'Mrs. Richards, a young and pretty widow' who comes to teach in the school at Hastings Mill.[5] As she searches for other references to her, finding few, Annie begins to write a journal for Mrs Richards, whom she names Ana. The almost complete absence of 'facts' about Ana's life seems a blank page that needs to be composed, because while history may offer a great deal of information, where women are concerned it tells us very little beyond descriptions of their roles. As Annie's attention moves from searching out the facts for her husband to imagining in detail what Ana's life might have been like – how she spent her days, what she felt, what she desired – Annie connects the absences in Ana's history with her own mother, Ina. Annie says, 'I'm no longer doing my part looking for missing pieces, at least not missing facts. Not when there are missing persons in all this rubble' (p. 134).

The choice of their names is a critical key to understanding Marlatt's enterprise. 'Ana' is of course a palindrome, its roots from the Greek meaning running back again, recurring, and but for one letter – the assertive 'I' of the first person pronoun – is Annie's mother's name, which is Ina. Ana and Ina may be separated in time but they share a number of important characteristics; Ina's life in many aspects 'runs back' into Ana's. To solidify further the shared identities, Annie's own name is a version of theirs. Annie's question, 'Ana/Ina/Whose story is this? (the difference of a single letter)/(the sharing of a not)' (p. 67), fore-grounds the link between Ana's absent historical story and the absent/dead mother. These strategies of naming create what Michael Riffaterre calls a 'worklike' text, a narrative that has a subtext resulting from 'superfluous details' that induce truth.[6] Kalle Pihlainen, drawing from Riffaterre's assertion that this superfluous detail gives fiction its verisimilitude, argues that this is a key textual difference that separates history from fiction.[7] The constraints on traditional history in effect 'limit the narratives . . . to events and situations that [the historian] knows . . . have occurred', and thus 'stories don't exist in reality'.[8] Whereas we might question in a historical narrative additional details that have not been directly recorded and that move beyond events to less 'factual' matters, we do not question their presence in fiction – in large part, Pihlainen argues, because of the generic conventions governing history and fiction. Riffatere's description of how the details function illuminates Marlatt's 'play' with names and events. Not all signs in the text can be read or explained mimetically; they are, in Riffaterre's terms, 'ungrammatical',[9] and to understand them we must recognize the ambiguity and then find a way to make them make sense. When we connect the variants of the names with issues of identity and history, the overlapping connections become clearer. We see how Ana is Ina is Annie as well as how they differ, and we begin to see how the 'historically' absent Ana/Ina is also Everywoman. Even surnames resonate, as 'Ana Richards' suggests 'Richard's Annie'.

Central to Marlatt's enterprise is the notion of what history is and where we can find the truth. Annie learned 'that history is the real story the city fathers tell of the only important events in the world, a tale of their exploits' (p. 28), 'history, the story . . . of dominance. mastery. the bold line of it' (p. 25).

History is gendered as masculine in Marlatt's text while story is gendered as feminine; the few historical facts recorded about Ana 'are not facts but skeletal bones of a suppressed body the story is. there is a story here, Ina, i keep trying to get to' (p. 29).

It is interesting that Marlatt has Annie address Ina here, once more merging the characters and the issues. In part, Annie addresses her mother because Annie is responding, after the fact, to her mother's accusation that she 'grew up' and 'learned the difference between story and history' (p. 28). It is not clear why Ina dislikes the distinction her daughter has drawn, but a possible answer rests in Ina's intuitive understanding that women's lives – her life – is not history but story, and her story only lives in her daughter's memory. Annie, at the moment of accusation, subscribed to traditional understanding of both history and story, so the likelihood of Ina's story surviving is small. No genre yet exists in Annie's imagination that could give Ana's and Ina's stories permanence, and thus Ana and Ina share the negative state or 'not' of being ahistoric: women without a history. The story Annie 'keeps trying to get to' will, once achieved, make Ana and Ina 'historic', but Annie 'doesn't want history's voice. I want . . . something is wanting in me, and it all goes blank on a word. Want' (p. 48). What is 'wanted' is a way to rectify the past – for Annie to somehow have understood her mother and what she needed, to 'have stopped [Ina's] dying' and 'provoked [Ina] into a torrent of speech' that was 'dammed up' by the shock therapy Ina suffered as treatment for her mental illness (p. 49).

This merging of story and history raises questions about the nature of history and suggests that there should be multiple types. Traditional history is too narrow in what it allows to be included. In her astute analysis of how patriarchy was created and why women participated in their own subordination, Gerda Lerner explains the effects of keeping women from theory-making by depriving them of education and 'the conditions under which to develop abstract thought'.[10] To create 'new conceptual models – theory formation' requires not just education and the stimulus of other thinkers but '[i]t depends on having private time . . . [and] individual thinkers making a *creative leap into a new ordering*'.[11] Women's exclusion from knowledge of their own history was a crucial component in maintaining patriarchy, and women's lack of confidence in themselves as symbol makers continues today. It is extremely difficult 'to step outside of patriarchal thought' and to do so requires 'overcoming the deep-seated resistance within ourselves toward accepting ourselves and our knowledge as valid'.[12] Annie's individual condition mirrors Lerner's depiction of women generally, but Annie, unlike her foremothers, has the advantages of some 'private time' and education that allow her to begin to think outside of the parameters of both history and patriarchy. She stubbornly refuses to give in to male definitions of what counts as history.

A good example is one of the documents Annie discovers in the archives, a journal of a nineteenth-century woman named Alice Patterson. The archivists view it as 'inauthentic' because while it is a document, it is 'not history . . . not factual' (p. 31). Thus even when written, the personal story is not a history according to those in control of the definitions. The only way Annie can imagine to make a truer 'history' from the available facts is to write a new story, create a document and/or change the definition of history, expanding history's generic parameters. Annie does all of these: she tells Ana's and Ina's stories, creates 'Ana's' journal and brings to the reader's attention the idea of what counts as history through her comments on it. Such work is creative and imaginative, but imagination is suspect, the enemy of history. As she writes, Annie hears her mother's and Richard's critical voices telling her that she is 'indulging in outright speculation. This isn't history, it's pure invention' (p. 55) because it is 'cut loose from history and its relentless progress towards some end' (p. 81). Annie does not trust herself as a woman or a historian's assistant or a writer; she disparages her writing as 'scribbling' and sees her work as 'undefined territory, unaccountable' (p. 81). And it is, as she works in the borderland between history and facts and imagination, unsure what it is she is trying to write or to do. The reader, however, disagrees with this assessment of her endeavour. We are drawn in by the imagining of these women's lives in a time we think is past, but which we recognize in small shocks as part of our own and mothers' and grandmothers' lives. We are reminded too of Virginia's Woolf's famous dictum in *A Room of One's Own* that 'we think back through our mothers if we are women'[13] and Woolf's anger when she realizes 'that nothing is known about women before the eighteenth century'.[14] Marlatt's novel suggests that this condition is largely unchanged and that women – ordinary women – are ahistoric. The historical texts that exist have not represented women's lives in its rich complexity, and like Woolf, Annie realizes how little we know about women from history.

Only the deconstruction of traditional histories and the creation of new ones that break normative categories will provide ways to understand the past in a richer, more comprehensive manner, and the facts alone are never enough. Fact comes under scrutiny in the novel, not just in commentary but in the very language of the text. Marlatt's wordplay forces the reader to stop and reconsider that which has been rendered invisible through custom. The word *fact*, for example, is broken apart as '(f)act' and described as the 'f stop of act', and she highlights the distinction between the factual and the actual with '(f)actual' (p. 31). The facts of Ana's and Ina's lives are not their actual stories; imagining the spaces between them is required. Events may give us a starting point, but until they are made into stories with the wealth of 'superfluous details' to embody person and place and emotion, they have little chance of shaping a wider future; and history, which is supposed to teach us about ourselves – how we got where we are and where we might go – loses its knowledge-making function. History as epistemic, Marlatt's novel suggests, will only transpire when we move to and imagine in story that territory which has been undefined, unarticulated or on the margins of the master narrative. So we get not just the history of Vancouver as the historical record presents it, but the imagined story of Ana Richard's life, the reconstructed story of Ina's life and Annie's own 'history' composed of personal memory.

The women: personal histories

Personal memory and facts coalesce in Ina. Annie can put flesh on the 'bones' of fact of her mother's life only when she grapples simultaneously with the difficulties of writing Ana's story. The absence of Ana's history brings the absence of her mother's forward, inextricably linking them. The key fact of her mother's life from Annie's perspective was Ina's mental illness, diagnosed as schizophrenia. In the depiction of the mother's life, that of a traditional 1950s housewife with too much energy and no place to put it except in painting walls and preparing a public persona through the clothes she buys and wears, Marlatt makes manifest the conditions that led to Ina's deterioration. Ina is a 'perfect' example of what happens within Betty Friedan's 'feminine mystique'.[15] On the surface, her life seems ideal: good husband, healthy normal children, a home, money to spend and none of the stresses of working outside the home. But the reality Annie reconstructs is of a mother who threatened to poison her children, a wife who screamed at her husband, a woman never satisfied and pathologically unfulfilled and unhappy. Annie remembers the *hysteria* of her mother's episodes and builds from the word, moving from the individual hysteric to 'hystery', which she defines as 'the excision of women (who do not act but are acted upon)' (p. 88). Ina's condition is both individual and representative; Annie writes that 'they removed your uterus, they pulled your rotten teeth, they put electrodes on your misbehaving brain' (p. 88), and the mother she got back from the doctors was a shell, disoriented, gutted like a burned-out house. When the father brought Ina home after her electric shock treatments, Annie says he 'brought home a new fear (who's there?) that no one was there at all' (p. 148).

In her dawning understanding of her mother's deep unhappiness and the 'historical' causes of it, Annie begins to comprehend the complex factors that have shaped her own identity. It is at this crossroads of writing history (Ana's) and thinking about history that the key issue of identity emerges for Annie herself: How do we come to be who we are? Who gets to name us? How much control might we have over our sense of who we are? Annie's research has made it clear that what small portion of Ana's identity is known is one assigned to her by the historical record: she came to Hastings Mill, taught school, bought a piano and married Ben Springer. But the bare facts of her life do not begin to represent who she was beyond her roles. What was her inner life like? How did she relate to friends? Did she have friends? What did she think of the wilderness that surrounded her? Of her students? History has no answers to these questions, so for Annie the only recourse is to write Ana's life from a perspective that answers them. Ina's identity, too, is fraught with contradictions that tantalize the adult Annie – the person who was 'mother' was of course much more complex than the child's perception allowed for. We as readers come to understand Ina as Annie herself does – in bits and pieces, fragments of memory, snatches of conversation. It is from these pieces, woven into story, that Ina's identity becomes more visible and she is rendered more fully human, but the process of remembering puts Annie's own identity in flux, a key to which is the consistent use of the lower case 'i' instead of the upright and assertive capital 'I'.

The monstrous: self and history

Another important textual clue that signals the instability of Annie's identity is a repeated question: the novel opens with the child Annie's whispered question 'Who's There?' (p. 9) This question echoes throughout the novel, repeated sometimes verbatim and sometimes in other forms. Its first appearance is linked to a nightmare memory of unidentified night noises in the basement. Annie as the eldest feels responsible for her sisters on the nights when she is left to baby-sit, and when she hears those noises, she takes the carving knife in one hand and her fear in the other to see who is hiding in the frightening ward-robes – ones 'big enough to hide Frankenstein'. The figure she imagines there is 'monstrous' and male: 'what if he were hungry, starved even, and so desperately from outside he would kill to get what he wanted' (p. 10). As this sequence develops, the blurring of point of view suggests a divided self, as the speaker moves from 'i' to 'you' to 'she', all in the same passage with the same speaker, Annie. She continues to refer to herself in both third and first person:

> the boys in Never-Never Land . . . (fought the enemy, that's what boys did) and what i did when i was she who did not feel separated or split, her whole body trembling with one intent behind the knife . . . it was trespassing across an old boundary, exposing my fear before it could paralyse me – before i would end up as girls were meant to be. (pp. 11–12)

The sense of fragmentation, the fear of some monstrous male, and the binary boy/girl split signals a deep psychological division.

These gender concerns, as well as the mention of 'monstrous' things, maintain a visible presence, from Annie's description of herself as tomboy ('tom, the male of the species plus boy, double masculine, as if girl were completely erased' [p. 13]) to her memory of a girlfriend's body in the water one summer. Her memories of childhood move back and forth between her mother's actions and remembered words and the moments when her own body, with its emerging sexuality, was the focus of her attention. The gendering of a girl in 1950s Canada was a mix of messages – first, to be girlish, to grow into 'another shape, finding a waist, gaining curves', but her mother's response was to tell her she was boy-crazy (p. 52). And Annie writes that as she and her friends sauntered past boys on street corners and on the beach, their 'head[s were] full of advertising images, converting all action into the passive: to be seen' (p. 34). Annie says, 'i ended up doing what i was meant to, i followed the plot through, the story you had me enact' (p. 17). The move from the active voice and agency of the tomboy to the passive recipient of the male gaze characterizes Annie's ambivalence about what she wants to be and what she is told she should be. But to escape from the passive and become an agent is linked to monstrosity, and Marlatt's numerous references to Frankenstein underscore just how unnatural it is to link agency with the female.

This same monstrous agency is present also in Ana: Annie has Ana write in her journal an address to her (Ana's) father: 'I cannot but think that I am failed somehow as a woman. Perhaps I am the monster you feared I would become – Is it that I want what womanhood must content itself without?' (p. 72)

The answer, of course, is yes, at least in her historical moment; she had already moved far beyond the normal boundaries of a Victorian woman by leaving her father's home, travelling to Canada, finding work and representing herself as a widow. In a related moment in the text, Annie imagines her mother asking, 'and i suppose you see me as the monster hidden at the heart of it?' (p. 24). Annie's immediate response is that 'there is a monster, there is something monstrous here, but it's not you' (p. 24), signalling a shift in her understanding of the source of the monstrous: it does not rest in women's actions but in society's messages to women. Women, Ina included, were 'suspended out of the swift race of the world' and 'the monstrous lie' (p. 24) functions to make them blame themselves for their restlessness and dissatisfaction.

The many direct allusions to Frankenstein and thus indirectly to Mary Shelley lead us to the 'Introduction' Shelley wrote for the 1831 edition of *Frankenstein*, where she describes the genesis of the story from one of her dreams and writes the ambiguous line, 'I bid my hideous progeny go forth and prosper'.[16] The 'hideous progeny' can be the Creature, the Creature's creator or the novel itself as a monstrous act. Women, conditioned to believe that agency and authorship are monstrous, suffer profound ambivalence when they persist. But the real 'monstrous lie', conveyed and enforced by history, is that it is a natural condition of women to be passive, absent, silent and heterosexual. The sexual desire women feel, almost all of history tells us, is the desire for men. Annie asks 'what does Soul, what does a woman do with her unexpressed preferences, her own desires?' when 'history' has commodified and controlled her sexuality, misrepresented her real body and denied her intellectual potential (p. 35). The force of history is not aimed at the integration of body and mind in woman but to split them apart. Annie's writing, which like Shelley she thinks might be monstrous in the belief that it can do what history cannot, is a way to mend past blindness, but writing and 'scribbling', she tells us, have the same origin: 'scribe is from the same root, *skeri*, to cut the ties that bind us to something recognizable – the "facts" ' (p. 81).

Writing, in Annie's formulation metaphorized as a weapon, has the potential to simultaneously sever and heal. Women's writing severs historical representations of women from a monstrous patriarchal hegemony and cures by giving women new plots – in this case, a lesbian plot as both Ana and Annie find relationships with other women. In her book *Writing Beyond the Ending*, Rachel DuPlessis argues that what women need after the realist novels of the nineteenth century with their finales of marriage are new plots for women that open up possibilities.[17] But thinking of the new, whether in terms of what constitutes history or what constitutes sexuality, is a perilous enterprise because the power of the status quo works effectively to repress that which threatens it. In the queering of the major relationships in the text, Marlatt also unsettles other comfortable categories, not just history but sexuality and identity. Her questions about history illuminate the ways this disciplinary structure shapes minds and bodies, revealing the power inherent in history. The historical texts Annie is examining, in their focus on men and events, present a version of an era that leaves out more than it includes.

Omission and repression are corollaries. Repression, Foucault has taught us, works through a 'triple edict of taboo, nonexistence and silence';[18] history has consistently enacted this triumvirate. Women were silenced, their existence and achievements virtually ignored, and essential aspects of their lives – sexuality, self-actualization, agency – were taboo. To provide new 'plots' requires new writing because we are beings constructed in, by and through language, and Annie's journal for Ana takes part in this process. Reflecting on Ana's life in the journal Annie is writing for her, Annie says, 'She should have been born a man . . . She wanted to be free', and adds that Ana is 'in the gap between two versions' (pp. 105–6), the historical version and the imagined. Writing something new is not easy, for it demands that the writer convey the truth, and when there are only the recorded historical facts, where does the truth come from?

One of the truths Annie comes to through her writing is the knowledge that her identity – as daughter, wife, mother, research assistant – is largely false, based on what she was expected to be as a good girl, good wife, good mother. Particularly false is her sexual identity, which she only comes to identify as she imagines a new sexual identity for Ana. The historical record tells us that Mrs Richards bought a piano and married Ben Springer: 'that was her, summed up. Ana Historic' (p. 48). But as she discusses with her friend Zoe the impasse she has reached in writing the novel, dissatisfied with Ana's 'end' and feeling Ana had no choice, Zoe asks a key question: 'so what is it you want from her?' (p. 91). What Annie wants is other choices for Ana: not to be forced by lack of options to marry Ben Springer but perhaps to 'live in hotel rooms where you [Ana] give lessons . . . a secret friend perhaps to Birdie Stewart' (p. 108). But her answer to herself immediately following this independent and lesbian possibility is 'you can't even imagine?', a blurred sentence that is at once both declarative and interrogative, a perfect representation of Annie's state: wanting to declare but not sure what it is she wants to declare and which, until imagined, cannot come into being. The end of Annie's novel of Ana places her in Birdie's room, but even as she writes Ana into this scenario, Annie cannot quite believe or understand what has happened:

> Ana, what are you doing? . . . you've moved beyond what i can tell of you, you've taken a leap into this new possibility and i can't imagine what you would say. which means history wins again? as if it were a race – one wins, the other has to lose . . . but what if they balance each other . . . and we live in history *and* imagination. (p. 139)

Annie's distress and confusion, while apparently focused on Ana, actually represent her own confusion. Zoe's comment on the use of imagination – 'well, you could say you've imagined your way into what [Ana] really wants' – is followed by another of Zoe's insights, because she asks Annie 'who are [your characters] if they aren't you?' (p. 140).

Naming again is important, as *Zoe*, from the Greek, means life, and Annie's new life rests with Zoe. Annie has traversed the territory of gender and sexuality from Ana/Ina to Zoe, from A to Z. But still Annie is shocked by the idea that Ana might be a lesbian because it is, Annie says, 'a monstrous leap of imagination' (p. 135), but it is a necessary leap. Until such a relationship is constructed in language, Annie cannot move to an acknowledgment of her own sexual orientation; writing Ana into a lesbian relationship – and queering history – is the necessary ground for Annie's (lesbian) desire to exist. It must be imagined before it can be written, and until written, cannot come into being.

The conclusion of Marlatt's novel places Annie in Zoe's room, a mirror image of Ana's presence in Birdie's, and the placement signifies the movement from subject to agent, from heterosexuality to a more diverse sexuality, from wife to lover, from history's trap to a story that is grounded in desire, a 'desire reading us into the page ahead'.[19] At the end Annie is awakened, the opposite state she was in the beginning of the novel, when she was asleep and dreaming 'Who's There?' In a radical reworking of Sleeping Beauty, Marlatt has moved Annie from sleep to the awakening with a kiss – but the kiss of a woman, thus queering the story. Significantly, the grammar of pronouns has shifted too; whereas the novel opens with Annie's references to herself as 'she' and 'i', creating a divided self, the last pronouns in the novel move from the plural 'we' of Annie, Zoe, Ina and Ana to the 'You' of the reader and finally the 'us' of women: 'we give place, giving words, giving birth, to each other . . . it isn't dark but the luxury of being has woken you, the reach of your desire, reading us into the page ahead' (p. 153). What we are reading is the result of imagination, even if 'only' in discourse. The novel closes with bodies rendered in language through Zoe and Annie's lovemaking.

The vehement critique of history that Annie has waged in the pages of the novel – and that others in this book have also waged through their examination of women's fiction (Gamble, Tofantšuk, Morley and Hodgkin in particular) – testifies to its power to determine the 'true' story of human's lives, from origins beginning with Adam and Eve to sexuality. History, Marlatt writes, 'Call [us back], to the solid ground of fact. You don't want to fall off the edge of the world' (p. 111). Yet ironically, history has had little to say about bodies in any kind of detail, except perhaps the heroic. Peter Brooks suggests that the body in modern narrative, particularly the erotic body, is an 'epistemophilic' project that brings together 'the body, the drive to know, and narrative'. The body, then, is a 'site of signification – the place for the inscription of stories – and itself a signifier, a prime agent in narrative plot and meaning'.[20] The bodies in *Ana Historic* are indeed sites of signification, spaces on which history has written its dictates. But (some) bodies escape the strictures of history, as Annie and Zoe demonstrate. Annie's writing of a different kind of history serves an epistemic function: it opens a path to understanding outside the traditional structures – a path along the margins. In giving Annie (and her readers) an alternate plot, it works cognitively as well as emotionally and narratively. The closure of the novel in the bodies of women is not a final answer, however, and to imply so does a disservice to Marlatt's text. The ending does, however, raise new questions about women and history, how we come into being and how we might change the beings that we are.

Notes

1. Linda Hutcheon, ' "The Past Time of Past Time": Fiction, History, Historiography, Metafiction', in Michael J. Hoffman and Patrick D. Murphy (eds) *Essentials of the Theory of Fiction* (Durham, NC: Duke University Press, 1996), p. 474.
2. Colleen Lamos, 'The Ethics of Queer Theory', in Dominic Rainsford and Tim Woods (eds) *Critical Ethics: Text, Theory, and Responsibility* (New York: St Martin's Press, 1999), p. 144.
3. Judith Butler, *Bodies that Matter: On the Discursive Limits of 'Sex'* (New York: Routledge, 1999), p. 229.
4. Jonathan Culler, *Literary Theory: A Very Short Introduction* (Oxford: Oxford University Press, 1997), p. 111.
5. Daphne Marlatt, *Ana Historic* (Concord, ON: Anansi Press, 1988), p. 21. Further references appear in the text.
6. Michael Riffaterre, *Fictional Truth* (Baltimore, MD: Johns Hopkins University Press, 1990).
7. Kalle Pihlainen, 'The Moral of the Historical Story: Textual Differences in Fact and Fiction', *New Literary History*, 33, 1 (2002), 46.
8. Anthony Savile, 'Imagination and the Content of Fiction', *British Journal of Aesthetics*, 38 (1998), 138.
9. Riffaterre, *Fictional Truth*, p. 233.
10. Gerda Lerner, *The Creation of Patriarchy* (New York: Oxford University Press, 1986), p. 223.
11. Ibid., p. 233; emphasis mine.
12. Ibid., p. 228.
13. Virginia Woolf, *A Room of One's Own*, in Jon Stallworthy (ed.) *The Norton Anthology of English Literature*, vol. 2C, seventh edition (New York: W. W. Norton, 2000), pp. 2193–4.
14. Ibid., p. 2177.
15. Betty Friedan, *The Feminine Mystique* (New York: W. W. Norton, 1963).
16. Mary Shelley, *Frankenstein*, Norton Critical Edition, J. Paul Hunter (ed.) (New York: W. W. Norton, 1996), p. 173.

17. Rachel Blau Du Plessis, *Writing Beyond the Ending: Narrative Strategies of Twentieth-Century Women Writers* (Bloomington, IN: Indiana University Press, 1985).

18. Michel Foucault, *The History of Sexuality: An Introduction* (New York: Vintage Books, 1990), vol. 1, p. 5.

19. Heather Zwicker, 'Daphne Marlatt's "Ana Historic": Queering the Postcolonial Nation', *Ariel: A Review of International English Literature*, 30, 2 (April 1999), 161–74. Zwicker provides a fascinating reading of this passage in her postcolonial analysis of the novel, seeing in the wardrobe/wordrobe that Annie fears in the beginning of the story an inversion of a coming-out story: 'The empty closet – initially a puzzling trope – stages Marlatt's complicated vision. Whereas conventions of the coming-out narrative posit a stable closet out of which emerges a homosexual Self, Marlatt turns the closet inside out around homophobic fear.' Zwicker sees the Frankenstein metaphor not as the 'inassimilable Other' but as 'a free-floating signifier for the terror that keeps women inside the bound of propriety – in other words, homophobia' (p. 171).

20. Peter Brooks, *Body Work: Objects of Desire in Modern Narrative* (Cambridge, MA: Harvard University Press, 1993), pp. 5–6.

4
Time, Space and (*Her*)Story in the Fiction of Eva Figes

Julia Tofantšuk

The period from 1975 to 2005 has witnessed a decline of interest in large-scale, abstract theories of universal historical development and at the same time an increasing interest in, as Ursula Heise observes, the articulation of 'other stories that had been repressed, or had seemed too marginal or too deviant to find an audience before'.[1] Among these 'deviations' are histories of non-Western cultures, women, ethnic, racial and sexual minorities, which emerged from under the veil after Jean-François Lyotard expressed his 'incredulity towards meta-narratives'.[2] Lyotard's distrust of grand narratives as 'official' History accompanied the bankruptcy of the humanist idea of progress as promising liberation and emancipation of the individual. It is the 'little narrative' that is credible now, or simply *Story*, as most of the chapters in this book illustrate. In terms of literary theory, there is currently a great deal of scepticism concerning the stability of such customary notions as time and space, the materiality of the body found within these notions and the stability of identity the body accommodates. It has already become a cliché to speak of (his)story: feminist theory has long distinguished between history and *her*story – one the official account of wars, conquests and achievements (which, as Sherry Booth points out in Chapter 3, 'has consistently written women out' [p. 45]), and the second a parallel course of obscure existence, reproduction, nurturing and serving. It is this historical position as instrumental in shaping the feminine identity that this chapter proposes to explore, drawing on the example of the 'eternal woman' as portrayed in three novels by Eva Figes – *Days* (1974), *Nelly's Version* (1977) and *The Tree of Knowledge* (1990).

History and time

Etymologically, the word *history* is related to the Old French *historie* (fourteenth century) and the Latin *historia*, both meaning 'narrative, account, tale, story', the Greek *historia*, 'a learning or knowing by inquiry, history, record, narrative', as well as *historein*, 'inquire' and *histor*, 'wise man, judge'.[3] Thus the meaning of *history* as 'account of events' comes before *history* as 'events', which suggests that what appears to be stable and objective is in fact a subjective representation of events constructed post-factum, the authenticity of which is highly arguable. What the *histor* – wise man, judge – continues to tell us is that there is a stable object shaped by time, which is logical, linear and measurable. On the other hand, theorists like Julia Kristeva have argued that temporality as we know it is only one possible way to organize the world. In 'Women's Time' (1979), Kristeva's aim is to emphasize the multiplicity of female experience and argue against the construction of a homogeneous, universal woman. She speaks of different kinds of time – *cyclical* (repetition) and *monumental* (eternity) – which are related to motherhood, reproduction and female *jouissance* and opposed to the *linear* time of history, which she describes as a 'time of project, teleology, departure, progression and arrival'.[4] It is the latter kind of time that we traditionally associate with history, politics, official records and the symbolic order – for the symbolic order is the order of verbal communication; it consists in enunciations of sentences, each being *a sequence of words*, having a purpose, message, beginning and ending. Personified as an aged, bald man carrying a scythe and an hourglass, the time of history for Kristeva is patriarchal, 'the paternal order of genealogy', as she refers to it in *Des Chinoises*.[5]

For Kristeva, there is an obvious connection between the ideas of time, history and identity. The 'genealogy' in which a subject emerges is sustained by a rigid temporal structure organized around a past, present, and future or, as she puts it, 'a before, a now, and an after'.[6] But if the past, present and future are being constructed in the act of communication, so too is identity, and this undermines the stability of the subject, which only exists as long as the structure is stable. For Kristeva, the subject exists only in the speech addressed to another or 'in the moment of that communication'.[7] Furthermore, a subject is part of its family lineage, but this is no less arbitrary because it is also 'placed in that before and after, the number of ancestors and future generations'.[8] Kristeva calls the whole construct, which is a system of inhibitions, constraints and taboos, the *socio-symbolic order*[9] and envisages two ways in which a woman can deal with patriarchal symbolic temporality: by inserting herself into the symbolic order, embracing the masculine model for femininity and identifying with the father, or by refusing to identify with the father and thus staying 'outside' the symbolic order, politics and history.[10] The former approach can be associated with the attempts of the First Wave feminists to actively participate in political and social processes and contrasts with the French Second Wave women's movement's distancing itself from the symbolic order and the realm of the Father. Interested in the specificity of female psychology, these 'new' women sought to give a language to the intra-subjective and corporeal experiences 'left mute by culture in the past'.[11] In 'Women's Time' Kristeva criticized both approaches as dead ends and conceptualized a third way between the unconscious and the social – 'a *demand* for a new ethics' and a third generation of feminism.[12]

Post-war women writers have tried to explore these temporalities in different ways: from Angela Carter and her fierce Melanie (*The Magic Toyshop*), Marianne (*Heroes and Villains*) and Amazons/Juliettes[13] to Jeanette Winterson who repaints time as *tide*[14] without past, present or future, history instead being viewed as 'coiled' in 'this battered room';[15] indeed, as George Letisser puts it in Chapter 8, time becomes 'an undefined zone of instability where memory can have free play' (p. 125). Carter and Winterson's experimentations with time are explored elsewhere in this book; this chapter concentrates on the writings of Eva Figes and the movement of her female characters from or towards history. My approach consists in treating the selected novels as a single entity and the women within them as variations of the same woman: *woman in time*.

Space and *Days*

Figes, author of 13 novels to date, has described her own sense of an emergent identity in her autobiography *Little Eden* as 'a secret, solitary nucleus inside which nobody could reach. It held pain, but also dreams, and I needed to be withdrawn to allow it to grow'.[16] Withdrawal meant finding a private place to retreat from the crowd, an urge she experienced as a boarding school pupil starting her love affair with reading and writing poetry. In a larger sense, it means the rejection of imposed labels and assigned roles. Her fictional explorations present both types of withdrawal as necessary for preserving the 'inner nucleus' that cannot be attained in a world shaped by the habitual spatial and temporal dimensions into which women are constantly cast. The three novels under discussion here place this recognizable 'Woman' into various temporal settings, from the ambiguity of *Days*, the (possible) 1970s of *Nelly's Version* to the seventeenth century in *The Tree of Knowledge*. Yet it must be emphasized that the physical setting is always the same and very restricted: at best a small town, and within that usually a room, four walls, a garden and a bed. The woman's story is reduced to uneventful days in which time is spent without regard for the big history outside. The beginnings of these texts all contain the same claustrophobic overtones introducing *her*story:

> Pray be seated, sir, and pardon such *humble surroundings*. This *room* must serve both as schoolroom and for living in, and I fear it is but a shabby place to receive visitors. You see how *bare* it is . . . (*The Tree of Knowledge*)[17]

> I recognise the *room*: . . . it simply took a moment for . . . me to disentangle who I was, this *body* in which *I am possessed*, a particular body lying in one *room*, a specific *bed*, the *walls* surrounding me. (*Days*)[18]

> He watched my hand slide across the page as I signed a false name and address in the *hotel* register . . . The porter arrived to show me to my *room*. (*Nelly's Version*)[19]

The female character's role in these suffocating surroundings is to reconcile herself to her position in a story told to her by someone she will never identify. Thus, in addition to Marlatt's questions concerning history ('what kind and whose?' [p. 47]), as discussed in Chapter 3, Figes' protagonists seem to ask for the 'when and where?'

In *Days*, history is reduced to one room and complete darkness, the woman is lying in bed 'alone with her thoughts' in the 'womb of the dark' (*D*, p. 8). This room in a vast, anonymous hospital becomes like a womb into which she has been inserted, but by whom? 'My arrival has been blotted out. I suppose I have been pushed through the door by *somebody*' (*D*, p. 7, emphasis mine). This is precisely the way she has arrived into the world, pushed into it, 'from one darkness only to find another' (*D*, p. 7). The latter quotation is taken from the description of her waking, of passing from the 'darkness' of the unconscious, the place of the mother, the no-time that the womb imagery symbolizes, to the 'darkness' of the room that is indeed the only space allotted to her in life. The woman is motionless because her lower body is paralysed, but the physical paralysis is less alarming than the one she has been living with all her life, having to pull herself through the domestic lies, marital disappointments and hardships that brought her to this miserable state. She wakes up to reconstruct herself, but is only capable of doing so once she can see the walls surrounding her person, which she sarcastically calls 'the knot of nerve ends looking out from the bedclothes' (*D*, p. 9). At night, she is surrounded by darkness and cannot see the walls. She feels insecure, exposed and alone in the world, not defined by anything, and is thus overcome by panic: 'I do not know where I am, or who' (*D*, p. 8). In this novel, identity and existence are modified by space, time and the role an individual plays in them. Without these coordinates, one is nothing, one does not exist: 'The walls, so carefully constructed to protect me, fade away, leaving me exposed, disoriented, in incalculable dimensions of darkness' (*D*, p. 8). She feels that she exists only once she has placed the walls, in her vision or imagination, 'back where they belonged' – round her person (*D*, p. 9).

It is interesting to note that the seemingly stable, physical objects (the walls) are described as something elusive, something of a change-able nature, capable of fading away and reappearing once reconstructed. Thus the 'I' lying within the walls is even less stable, given that it is defined by the surroundings and the days that exist only in the mind, that is, in memory. Yet in this fluctuating landscape, there is a specific body in a specific room, and the body is paralysed. It is impossible to identify whose body this is, for the narrating voice is alternately (or simultaneously) that of the protagonist, her mother and daughter, or possibly all three assembled in one body, the collective female body paralysed in history. The woman is frozen in the static no-time that Kristeva describes, but she also inhabits the 'real time' of history, or *her*story, the story of betrayal, seduction and loss, which embraces three generations of women and makes them one. The ambiguity of the identity of the three women suggests a perpetual cycle that ends and begins simultaneously and no longer distinguishes between individual women, mothers, daughters and grandmothers. In the past that only exists in their minds they had no voice and no choice except submission. Now they are all lying silent in the same bed.

' "*Cherchez la femme*" – we always know that means: you'll find her in bed', says Hélène Cixous in her classic *Le Sexe ou la Tête?*,[20] using bed imagery to illustrate the silencing of the feminine subject in history. Cixous regards Sleeping Beauty as archetypal of all women: she falls asleep and is laid on a bed, to stay there, inactive. 'Woman, if you look for her, has a strong chance of always being found in one position: in bed. In bed and asleep – "laid (out)"'.[21] Drawing on the fairy tale she suggests that its subsequent events are a standard patriarchal script for a woman: Prince Charming appears to wake up the Princess, only to transport her into the next bed – his own. And so she will continue her trajectory through several functional beds – marriage bed, birth bed, sickbed, deathbed – 'so that she may be confined to bed ever after, just as the fairy tales say'.[22] Although Cixous highlights the role of the man in confining the woman to a certain place, it is the entire culture that determines her trajectory 'from bed to bed', as is suggested by Cixous's juxtaposition of the archetype of Sleeping Beauty and that of Red Riding Hood, the rebellious woman who endeavours to 'make a detour' and 'travel through her own forest' – only to be brought back to bed, in the stomach of her own grandmother, who turns out to be the Big Bad Wolf of the patriarchal order.[23]

It is important that Cixous turns to folklore in order to explore the issues raised in a variety of texts written by women about women. Folklore can be regarded as the unofficial history of (wo)mankind in that it reflects the collective unconscious, the whole 'pattern' that 'has so many heads' and 'strangles so',[24] as Charlotte Perkins Gilman puts it in her portrait of hysteria, *The Yellow Wallpaper* (1892) – another text exploring the effects of confining a woman to a particular place. As in *Days*, the events of Gilman's short story happen in the protagonist's troubled imagination and revolve around a particular room, her bed and the paper on the wall, the paper that at first appears simply an instance of poor decoration with a sickening colour and repulsive smell and later becomes a symbol of the unfreedom of all women, including the protagonist (and author) herself. In this room the woman is denied a voice and a pen, is supervised by the female guardian (Prince Charming's sister) and Prince Charming himself, the narrator's husband John, who is a physician and a loving man, yet is only able to express his 'love' by fixing his wife in the bed of his choice: 'And so dear John gathered me up in his arms, and just carried me upstairs and *laid me on the bed*, and sat by me and read to me till it tired my head'.[25]

In her theoretical *Patriarchal Attitudes*[26] Figes turns the historically unrooted Prince Charming into the twentieth-century icon Charlie Chaplin, and vice versa. This kind of play with history and time makes the protagonist of *Days* suspect that her present 'lying alone in a small white room' will continue forever, for 'there is no way of leaving it . . . Unless I pass through the door. In which case I shall carry it with me, in my head' (*D*, p. 105). Wife, mother and daughter, she has been secluded in the room by her father, husband, lover, the young hospital doctor, but mostly by her own understanding of her function, which is 'to give comfort' (*D*, p. 119). In order to 'give comfort', she had to 'twist her body' to 'accommodate the lies' (*D*, p. 118). Her paralysis is like Cixous' decapitation – the speechless, powerless, vegetative state of existence in a world that tells a (his)story to her, for her and about her. It is only when she realizes that 'A person must be strong enough to inhabit his or her own story' (*D*, p. 118) that the protagonist is able to get out of bed and sit in the chair that has been unoccupied throughout the narrative. For the first time, she can see the bed as an object, and not an extension of herself, shaping and controlling her person. In this sense, she is in a much more favourable position than Gilman's protagonist. Despite her serious physical disability, Figes' woman progresses rather than regresses. Through the strength of her mind, she does leave her bed, while the prisoner of the yellow wallpaper gradually loses her ability to walk and finally resorts to crawling around the room.

Identity and *Nelly's Version*

If in *Days* it is a growing awareness of the past that allows the protagonist to cope with her present position, then in *Nelly's Version* the heroine is caught in the net of her past which precludes any free choice and drags her back into the imposed identity she once miraculously escaped. The novel opens with a middle-aged woman signing herself into a hotel in a small town. The false name she has invented – (Emily Brontë's?) Nelly Dean – may or may not be her own, for she has no recollections of who or what she used to be until that day. This ingenuous thriller about an identity crisis explores whether it is possible to live outside any historical placement, thus leaving the precious 'inner nucleus' intact and enjoying the delirious freedom Nelly experienced during the first days at the hotel. *Nelly's Version* is a first-person narrative structured as a personal account recorded in two notebooks that, respectively, modify the two parts of the novel. The Nelly of the *First Notebook* is a blank sheet devoid of memories, yet endowed with a strong and opinionated mind that people who used to know her found rebellious and alarming. It will not be long, however, before the past will come to claim her – the past represented by a former school friend with photographic documentation of Nelly's lost self, a detective, a husband, a son and a psychoanalyst. She sends them away at first, but gradually comes to accept their company and thus reverts to what she used to be – the 'David's mother' of the *Second Notebook*. The Nelly at the beginning of the novel is contrasted to the shop assistant, who claims to be her classmate and whom Nelly accuses of desperately clutching onto all the 'trash' like old photographs and school essays. The past acquires a defining meaning: 'If you don't hold on to something, all these bits of the distant past . . . If you don't keep a hold on these things, how do you know who you are?' (*NV*, p. 43). Nelly, who does not want to know 'who she is' in the eyes of the others, catches a glimpse of the shop assistant from the street and registers an image of her 'framed in the doorway to her inner sanctum' (*NV*, p. 45). The choice of words is important here: the woman is *framed* by the story she has created for herself and that she does not dare to leave, as Nelly's accusation suggests: 'There you are then – what kept you? Were you afraid of getting lost in another town, that you wouldn't be able to find your way around?' (*NV*, p. 39). She goes on to suggest that her meek classmate had every choice in her time, but she never used the opportunity: she could not find her own way around because it had never occurred to her to buy a map, she never asked anyone for the way because she was always afraid of asking, she had been working in the shop for so long because she never dared say 'no' to her father and, to sum it up, she had never consciously wanted anything: 'You gave in along the line, didn't you? The good girl, afraid of blotting her copybook, irritating the teacher. You were always resigned, obedient, terrified of being noticed. And you mistook it all for duty' (*NV*, p. 39).

Nelly, who is not afraid of 'getting lost in another town', is Cixous' Red Riding Hood allowing herself 'a little detour', or a degree of 'trespassing', as Figes puts it elsewhere.[27] Unfortunately, the attempt is rendered futile after her son appears with a psychoanalyst who, though rejected by her, instills discomfort in the heroine. In Cixous' discourse, the psychoanalyst represents 'that great Superego' that punishes the Red Riding Hoods of this world for having the nerve to 'go out and explore their forest'.[28] Cixous insists that the famous Freudian question – 'What do women want?' – is rhetorical, for the answer would always be 'She wants nothing',[29] because either the woman in history is passive and confined to bed or, if she does want something, she cannot utter her desires, cannot speak.[30] That is why the shop assistant is 'afraid of asking' for what she wants, mistaking cowardice for duty – a common misconception, one that makes the woman in *Days*, for instance, believe that life consists in 'giving comfort' (*D*, p. 119). In the same way, despite the earlier attempt to discard her role as 'David's mother' and retreat from all imposed identifications into a world of her own and a no-time of freedom in order to read, contemplate and enjoy her present amorphous state, Nelly is safely placed back into history and all its attributes. David, who comes to claim her, represents the outside world as well as social institutions (family) adopting her and thus imposing a 'correct' lifestyle on her. The son's presence indicates all the other roles Nelly must play:

mother, mother-in-law, grandmother; thus, she enters Kristeva's linear temporality and the ready-made scripts that leave little for her to invent. 'If you don't like the script, change it' can hardly work in this context, as she was captured precisely when she was for once trying to change the script; withdrawn from the path she had tried to follow she is placed back into the house, in which she feels imprisoned. The only thing she can do is wonder who is to blame, David or somebody else (*NV*, p. 208).

Although he clearly represents patriarchy as he assumes the role of the 'Man' and thus the responsibility of controlling Nelly in the absence of a father/husband, David cannot be really held culpable for imprisoning her, for he, too, is only fulfilling an assigned role. This Gothic nightmare of living in a strange house, alone but never really alone, with the invisible presence of authorities who have even closed down the railway station, hypothetical lawyers whose irresistible logic she can already foresee (can she prove she is *not* David's mother?) is typical of Figes' books, in which women progress along a ready-made path or regress into depression, paralysis, amnesia or insanity. Nelly, who finds her brain becoming 'fuddled' (*NV*, p. 209), has an uncanny sense of having been 'brainwashed in some hospital ward and then set free, apparently free, to wander the face of the earth, but really programmed in advance to do just what I had gone on to do . . . to participate in some pre-arranged plan' (*NV*, p. 214).

The 'pre-arranged plan' is of course the whole development of history, and women find themselves in it, some without wondering who they are or what they are for, who do not want to escape, and behave like the mysterious female voice on the phone, promising to meet Nelly and 'catch up' on everything. Conversation is the easier the more meaningless it is; all one has to do is to fill the gaps with standard phrases and it makes sense and the act of communication becomes possible. The phone conversation is an example of *talking* in Cixous' terms, the meaningless parrot-work woman has always been doing in history. Although Nelly fails to *speak* or construct her own version, she is vindicated in *The Tree of Knowledge*, which goes further into history than Figes' other novels in search of wisdom for women.

History and her voice: *The Tree of Knowledge*

The Tree of Knowledge can be regarded as a historical novel. It has a clear historical setting, England in the second half of the seventeenth century, mainly during the Restoration (1660–1688). Flashbacks and the narrator's meditations extend the setting to the time of the Revolution

(1642–1649) and the reign of Oliver Cromwell (1653–1658). The protagonist and narrator is a daughter of John Milton, who is presented
as powerless and obscure. It is through her comments, however, that
we learn the story of her father and his involvement in the political
and ecclesiastical controversy of the day; his forceful pamphlets cham-
pioning individual freedoms and even the right to divorce; his mastery
of Latin, which earned him the position of Cromwell's Latin Secretary;
his imprisonment during the Restoration; his blindness and eventual
withdrawal from public affairs to produce his masterpieces, *Paradise Lost*
(1667) and *Paradise Regained* (1671). There is, however, an unofficial,
underlying history that presents another vision of the father: a tyrant
culpable of oppression no less than his contemporaries were though
never admitting it, as particular about tradition as he was articulate
against it, leaving his daughter to the charity of the curious because her
grandfather, who perished in the Civil War, had never paid his wife's
dowry. It is telling her own story that makes the daughter breathe again;
and as the narrative of *The Tree of Knowledge* unfolds, she emerges as
more alive and vocal than her father, having enough wisdom to arrive
at a conclusion with a universal resonance:

> It is ever thus . . . that some would open the door for their own liberty,
> but slam it shut before the rest can follow. I am born free, they say,
> but thou, being born to serve me, that is, being born a woman, are
> not so. (*TK*, pp. 43–4)

The narrative is a monologue addressed to a 'sir', who is obviously a
scholar from Cambridge or Oxford, one of the many who come to 'test
her', listen to her recite Latin and Greek as proof that it was really her
eyes and her quill that Milton adopted after going completely blind.
The gentleman is a scholar – a wise man, *histor*, who comes to write
his version of *historia*, an account of Milton's life, and as such is a *judge*
entrusted with the authenticity of the record. The woman's dilemma
is thus whether to tell the *histor* how it was or to reproduce what he
wants to hear. Fortunately, she is subject to a double gaze, the second
belonging to her daughter, which enables her to present *her*story and
her vision of events, of hardship, neglect, falling victim to hypocrisy
despite her father's public preachings. 'Divorce is but for men', she sighs
(*TK*, p. 8) and acknowledges that her father, 'for all his years of study,
learnt not this. Whether in things domestic or political, or in his version
of the classic mode, he ever put the blame on lesser men and, if he
could, on women, these being least of all' (*TK*, p. 83). The narrator's

story is a continuation of the endless *her*stories of other women, her mother and stepmother who died in childbirth[31] as pre-*her*story of her own daughter's recent bereavement and present pregnancy. Neither the narrator nor the daughter has a name – they are the same no-name motionless women of *Days*, who accommodate three generations and are at once mother and daughter; and all of them are Eve, the eternal woman, and Scheherazade, the eternal storyteller who survives as long as the narrative unfolds.[32] They are all frozen in the mother-time of eternal stories, piling up stories that go back to the story of the Fall and the curse God cast upon Eve, 'In sorrow shalt thou bring forth children' (*TK*, p. 37).

The introduction of the image of Eve here, however, is problematic. Like Cixous, Figes questions mythological (in this case, biblical) archetypes in order to vindicate them and perhaps rewrite *her*story. 'Or so they tell us' (*TK*, p. 44), adds Milton's daughter, addressing the inculcated notions that originate from the Bible, but which men have been in a position to turn around, interpret, deconstruct and reconstruct, in order to arrive at the conclusion they want to see. She recalls how in writing pamphlets on divorce, Milton ventured to 'twist and turn the Bible to his ends, and say it meant by this some other thing, being ill translated or interpreted' (*TK*, p. 23). The ultimate end to this pseudo-hermeneutics is, according to the protagonist, 'seeking to use women like discarded garments to be thrown out at pleasure' (*TK*, p. 23). It appears that women learnt obedience from the same book that taught men about freedom and active participation in grand historical events; women were 'bred for household tasks, hard labour and child-bearing and all we could read was our Bible' (*TK*, p. 24). She recalls how she suddenly became wild and rebellious at 14, and her stepmother said there was the Devil in her, because she would be 'brooding in thoughts' and 'speak to nobody' (*TK*, p. 148). Now that she is old, she re-evaluates that time employing biblical imagery: 'Was it the serpent spoke to me? . . . If so, then I have had a lifetime to repent, in bitterness and in sorrow' (*TK*, p. 148).

Milton's daughter as depicted in *The Tree of Knowledge* is not simply a woman. On the one hand, she is reminiscent of the heroines of Katherine Mansfield's *Daughters of the Late Colonel*, who feel the forbidding power of the patriarch long after he is gone.[33] On the other hand, she follows her father in his late-humanist reading of the Fall story, in which he presents Eve as not the mother of all evil, but as an advanced woman. The Serpent seduces Eve into seeking a new identity for herself, not one imposed by God, but one determined by 'intellectual food'[34] that would allow her to 'reject/Envious commands, invented with design/To keep them low . . . '[35] In the same manner, Figes' heroine comes up with the bold idea that 'though they speak of two . . . the tree of knowledge and the tree of life are but one and the same, and in eating the fruit of one we must taste the other' (*TK*, p. 153), meaning that no tradition or indoctrination will keep her silent. She affirms her right to think, speak and live.

This is why in the end she is able to transcend all physical and metaphoric limits and go out into the orchard (leaving the room she occupies throughout the narrative time) to taste the apple of awareness and in so doing discover who she is and why. What is more, she invites her daughter to taste it too. Although the daughter has just begun her apprenticeship in real life – the loss of a child – her mother teaches her to bear hardships with dignity, not to be crushed inside the gloomy house where the dead child is, but follow her mother into the orchard, look up and 'see daylight' (*TK*, p. 154). Thus, the mother is *both* Eve *and* Serpent who is empowered by continuously telling Her Story; who said that the Serpent has to be male?

Chronologically, Figes moves from the claustrophobic no-time of *Days* through *Nelly's Version* towards the historically set *The Tree of Knowledge* in order to suggest that the silent, paralysed position of woman is an enduring one. Kristeva's monumental temporality and cyclic time manifest themselves in the recurrence of recognizable female types and voices, which are stifled and silenced, and confided to typical, bare, closed rooms. It is interesting to observe, however, that on the *linear* level, Figes' narratives progress *towards* history and against the real time of the author's life (the most 'historical' novel is also the most recent, published in 1990, while the earlier ones have a more contemporary setting). Although the female protagonist becomes older by the time of *The Tree of Knowledge*, she is younger in her mind and spirit, and more willing to take control over her identity and herstory, by *telling* it, however difficult that may be.

Notes

1. Ursula K. Heise, *Chronoschisms: Time, Narrative, and Postmodernism* (Cambridge: Cambridge University Press, 1997), p. 16.
2. Jean-François Lyotard, *The Postmodern Condition: A Report on Knowledge*, trans. Geoff Bennington and Brian Massumi, foreword by Frederic Jameson (Manchester: Manchester University Press, 1984), p. xxiv.
3. Eric Patridge, *Origins: A Short Etymological Dictionary of Modern English* (London and Henly: Routledge & Kegan Paul, 1977), p. 289.

4. Julia Kristeva, 'Women's Time' (1979), trans. Alice Jardine and Harry Blake, in Toril Moi (ed.) *The Kristeva Reader* (New York: Columbia University Press, 1986), p. 192.
5. Julia Kristeva, 'About Chinese Women' (1977), trans. Seán Hand, in Moi (ed.) *The Kristeva Reader*, p. 153.
6. Ibid., p. 153.
7. Ibid.
8. Ibid.
9. Ibid.
10. Kristeva, 'Women's Time', p. 194.
11. Ibid.
12. Ibid., p. 211 (emphasis in original).
13. Representatives of the fantastic female community of Beulah in *The Passion of New Eve* are modelled on the Marquis de Sade's Juliette, analysed by Angela Carter in *The Sadeian Woman*; the figure is an example of an early feminist radical fighting against her involuntary historical placement.
14. Jeanette Winterson, *The PowerBook* (London: Vintage, 2001), p. 242.
15. Jeanette Winterson, *Written on the Body* (London: Vintage, 1996), p. 192.
16. Eva Figes, *Little Eden: A Child at War* (New York: Persea Books, 1978), p. 91. Subsequent references will appear in the body of the text as *LE*.
17. Eva Figes, *The Tree of Knowledge* (London: Sinclair-Stevenson, 1990), p. 1 (emphases mine). Subsequent references to this novel will appear in the body of the text as *TK*.
18. Eva Figes, *Days* (London: Faber, 1974), p. 7 (emphases mine). Subsequent references to this novel will appear in the body of the text as *D*.
19. Eva Figes, *Nelly's Version* (London: Secker and Warburg, 1977), p. 9 (emphases mine). Subsequent references to this novel will appear in the body of the text as *NV*.
20. Hélène Cixous, 'Castration or Decapitation?' trans. Annette Kuhn, in Robert Con Davis and Ronald Schleifer (eds) *Contemporary Literary Criticism: Literary and Cultural Studies* (London: Longman, 1989), pp. 482–3.
21. Ibid., p. 481.
22. Ibid.
23. Ibid.
24. Charlotte Perkins Gilman, 'The Yellow Wallpaper', in Nina Baym et al. (ed.) *The Norton Anthology of American Literature*, vol. 2, 2nd edn (New York: W. W. Norton, 1985), p. 654.
25. Ibid., p. 650 (emphasis mine).
26. Eva Figes, *Patriachal Attitudes* (London: Panther, 1972).
27. Figes, *Nelly's Version*, p. 207. The term seems to be of special concern to Figes, representing as it does an attempt to be 'more than' one is permitted to be. Eva and her mother are 'trespassing' in *Little Eden* when they enter the forbidden territory of Englishness, as immigrants, Germans, Jews, others (*LE*, p. 31).
28. Cixous, 'Castration or Decapitation?', p. 482.
29. Ibid., p. 483.
30. This brings us back to the issue of hysteria and silencing discussed in connection with *Days* and 'The Yellow Wallpaper'. According to Cixous, 'silence is the mark of hysteria'. The 'great hysterics' have not only lost speech, but any

rudiments of willpower, desire and language; 'they are pushed to the point of choking' (Cixous, 'Castration or Decapitation', p. 486) – or 'suffocating', which is the synonym used by Gilman ('The Yellow Wallpaper', p. 654).

31. Milton's wife Mary Powell, presumably the mother of Figes' heroine, died while giving birth to their only son, having previously delivered three daughters.

32. See Angela Carter's belief in the life-keeping power of the Story, particularly for women, collected in the archetype of Scheherazade, as explored in *Expletives Deleted* (London: Chatto & Windus, 1992), p. 2 and throughout her writings.

33. Katherine Mansfield, *The Daughters of the Late Colonel*, in Sandra M. Gilbert and Susan Gubar (eds) *The Norton Anthology of Literature by Women*, 2nd edn (New York: W. W. Norton, 1996), pp. 1463–77.

34. John Milton, *Paradise Lost*, in Gordon Campbell (ed.) *The Complete English Poems* (London: David Campbell, 1992), p. 354.

35. Ibid., p. 236.

5
From Demidenko to Darville: Behind the Scenes of a Literary Carnival

Rachel Morley

> I'm telling a story you've seen over and over again. We're going to follow the oldest set-ups in the world, but then we're going to the moon.
>
> (Quentin Tarantino)[1]

The day 19 August 1995 marked an infamous day in Australia's literary and cultural history. A day where newspapers bled similar headlines, radio stations overflowed with interviews from suddenly famous academics, and talkback shows fed the chattering thousands desperate to do battle with their suburban counterparts over the cultural 'scam' that was leaking its way across the country. For it was on this day that multi-award winning writer Helen Demidenko was revealed as an impostor – a confidence trickster on par with the Felix Krulls of the world. As journalist David Bentley revealed in Brisbane's *Courier Mail*, the author of *The Hand that Signed the Paper* was not Helen Demidenko, daughter of Ukrainian and Gaelic migrants, as she had told the Australian public, but Helen Darville, daughter of English-born couple Harry and Grace.[2] The novel about the 'other side of the Holocaust' had not been based on family oral histories as its author had argued, but had instead evolved out of a vivid imagination, propped up by a carefully selected pseudonym. In signing her name as Demidenko and not Darville, Helen D – as she was later referred to in true postmodern style[3] – had concocted an elaborate hoax, fooling Australia's cultural elite and bringing three of the nation's top literary prizes into serious disrepute.[4]

Helen D's novel, however, had a contentious history long before the Bentley revelation, beginning in 1993 when the then 22-year-old 'Australian-Ukrainian' won The Australian/Vogel Literary Award for her 'part fact, part fiction' story about the tragic circumstances surrounding the 1930s Ukrainian famine and the atrocities committed by the Nazis during the Second World War.[5] Set in contemporary Queensland and war-time Europe, *The Hand that Signed the Paper* tells the story of Fiona Kovalenko who, as a 23-year-old female university student of Australian-Ukrainian heritage, learns that her father and uncle are to be prosecuted for war crimes for their roles in the Nazi death camps.

For Fiona, the problem is not so much the realization that her family committed the crimes – early in the novel she reveals how as a child she discovered photographs connecting her father and uncle with the SS involved in the mass genocide of the Jewish people at Treblinka. Rather it is with the personal ramifications of the family history in the face of the trials as Fiona tries to understand how the people she loves could have such horrific pasts.

The Hand represents Fiona's auto/biographical attempt to 'understand' the reasons for her family's actions and the brutality that followed. She returns to the past via the first-hand stories of her father Evheny, his brother Vitaly and their sister Kateryna who each tell of their experiences as peasants under Stalinist Soviet rule during the artificially induced 1930s Ukrainian famine and later in the death camps at Treblinka.

The story primarily focuses on Vitaly and Evheny who, after witnessing the devastation of their village and family by what they believe to be the 'Jewish Bolsheviks', readily embrace the German inva-sion and enthusiastically 'sign the paper' that inevitably sees them parti-cipating in the slaughter of Jews and Communists.[6] It is here, in this historical moment, that most of the action takes place. Interspersed with scenes depicting Vitaly falling in love with a Polish woman, Kateryna marrying an SS officer, and drunken rampages marked by singing, dancing and sex, are killings and starvation in the Ukraine and mass shootings at Babi Yar and Treblinka, the latter of which are recounted with an almost cool, passionless detachment. The novel ends in contem-porary Australia as the family prepares for the war trials; however, Vitaly dies before taking the stand. He dies, as the novel's narrator writes, while 'trying. To be sorry'.[7]

Upon receiving the Vogel, the then-Demidenko claimed the book had been inspired by war crime trials and by her family's first-hand experiences in the Ukraine during the German occupation of Eastern Europe. Speaking to Rosemary Sorenson on radio 3RN she said,

This is from my own experience . . . The reaction from my family has been, 'Yes, you have it right' in the sense that you face the history

honestly and face the past honestly. A lot of Ukrainians don't want
to own up to their pasts . . . [8]

Indeed, Demidenko argued that she had access to the stories because of
her birthright. When confronted with claims of inaccuracy, she returned
to her family history in self-defence, claiming her grandfather had been
murdered by Jewish Bolsheviks during the Ukrainian famine: 'most of
my father's family, including my grandfather, were killed by Jewish
Communist Party officials in Vynntsya', lending veracity to the implication that her tale was authentic because her family had observed it.[9]
Her supporters contended that although the history was not necessarily
'factual', according to mainstream history, it was a courageous historical
tale that needed to be heard.[10]

Certainly Helen Demidenko enjoyed provoking debate. She was ideal
media fodder, eagerly jumping on the interview bandwagon to cross-
pollinate views and stories in a variety of media outlets. To counteract
the growing negativity surrounding her novel, she spoke enthusiastically
about her family, her Ukrainian ancestry and what it meant to be Helen
Demidenko. It was a tale that many Australians, desperate to make up
for a stained unicultural past, were keen to embrace.

And it *was* a good story. Helen, daughter of Markov – an illiterate
Ukrainian taxi driver with flat feet and an old valiant – and a scullery
maid Gaelic mother, had 'done good'. Helen, who was raised in a
housing commission, whose family embarrassed her at school functions as 'a bedraggled pack of scrappy people talking too loudly and
gesticulating wildly at each other', who 'cheered and drank and poured
vodka over my head', was 'one of us'.[11] Helen, who was young, female,
ethnic and a victim of her people's history, had made 'us' proud.
Helen, with her long blonde hair, her peasant blouses, Ukrainian dances
and idiosyncrasies, was Australia's multicultural success story, sentiments that she herself echoed in a speech given at the Sydney Writers'
Festival (later reprinted in *Southerly* in an essay titled 'Writing After
Winning'):

So my father who can read and write neither English nor Ukrainian
flew to Brisbane to see me after I'd won a prize for writing . . . words.
So my mother, who left school at the age of twelve to go out and work
as a domestic (it was fashionable to have servants with Irish accents)
read her first book . . . So I learned to take pride in my scrappy pack
of people and to reclaim my Effie accent.[12]

By creating Helen Demidenko in the early years of Australia's decision to celebrate rather than continuing to denigrate its multicultural land-scape, Helen Darville gave readers exactly what they wanted – a home-grown, safely white success story on which to hang the bulging bag of community-owned guilt, pride and horror about the Holocaust and Australia's own mottled past. Helen Darville, of course, could not offer the same satisfaction and it was here that the bulk of debate began.

The issues at stake

In the 1990s, Demidenko was big news in Australia. From talkback radio to the letters pages of the dailies, the Demidenko debate, and the issue of authorship and history, moved swiftly through the kitchens and workstations of everyday Australians. 'Doing a Demidenko' became part of the Australian vernacular.[13] Yet, one decade later, the Demidenko debate has become little more than an embarrassing stain on the nation's literary landscape. Few critics refer to either Darville or her alter ego, except in occasional sideway snipes. Yet the story, as I will argue, presents critics with an opportunity to explore more broadly a range of interdisciplinary issues that continue to dog practitioners of historical fiction as well as literary and cultural studies. These include the shadowy boundaries between author and text, fact and fiction, and literature and history. This is notwithstanding, of course, the politics of reading and the social, ethical and political function of the writer as textual effect.

The questions I consider in this chapter then are very particular to the issue of authorial identity and inevitably bring to the fore the ambi-guities that exist between these apparent polarities as I ask, why did it matter that Helen Demidenko was not who she said she was? What effect did the performative change in authorial identity from Demidenko to Darville have on the (re)definition and (re)interpretation of the text? And what is the responsibility of the writer who works in historical fiction to readers and to cultural history?

Bodies with meaning/bodies with intent

In her 'Author's Note', which appears on the front page of the 1994 Demidenko version of *The Hand* (later recalled following the Bentley article and reprinted under the name Darville), the author wrote:

What follows is a work of fiction. The Kovalenko family depicted in this novel has no counterpart in reality. Nonetheless, it would be

ridiculous to pretend that this book is unhistorical. I have used historical events and people where necessary throughout the text. (p. i)

In making this statement, in alignment with comments that the novel
stemmed from her 'own experience' and her knowledge of the dreadful
'things done to her own family', Demidenko positioned herself as the
book's central authority and as a quasi-mouthpiece for the story behind
the stories.[14] In this way, she encouraged readers to rediscover the philosophical contractual links which constitute the unspoken agreement
between the author and the text, linking what Sean Burke has referred
to as the six 'cardinal intersections': that is, authenticity, autobiography,
biography, intention, accountability and oeuvre.[15]

When Barthes described 'writing [as] the destruction of every voice, of
every point of origin . . . that neutral, oblique space' where subjectivity
slips away, 'starting with the very identity of the body writing', he did
not take into account the social and ethical configurations of authorial
identity.[16] Nor did he validate a diminution in the author's responsibility for what he or she has written.[17] One of the main problems with
authorless criticism is that while it is an ideal practice in theory (i.e. in its
agenda of uncovering individual meanings in texts by refuting universal
narratives and avoiding personal biographical details in analysis), it does
not translate into the actuality of reading or the act of interpretation.
As postcolonial theorist Maire Ni Fhlathuin asserts, 'it is, in practice,
impossible to separate the author as literary force from the author as
legal entity or human being'.[18] Ni Fhlathuin is referring to the 'Salman
Rushdie Affair', yet the same can be said of the authorial problems of
Australia's own literary scandal.

Like Rushdie, the debate over Demidenko emphasized the change
imposed by publication on the relations between the author and the
text by focusing on reception or the way an author's biographical details
shape and alter a text's social production. One of the axioms of 'The
Death of the Author' is that a text can be liberated only by 'refusing to
assign a "secret", an ultimate meaning to the text' and that it is only
through this negation that 'anti-theological activity' can be 'liberated'.[19]
With Demidenko, Paul de Man and Rushdie, the opposite occurred with
the meaning identified not in the text or through other literary devices,
as the poststructuralists envisaged, but through the authority thought to
be speaking – the 'arche' or the traditional origins of the structure, reconstituted in the body of the author.[20] The signatory and performative
practices represented by the names Demidenko and Darville gave *The
Hand* particular essences, with the names providing bodies of evidence

in the extrapolation of information about the novel's intent and the author's personal convictions.[21]

Put simply, Darville invented an identity for the 'live' signature that, in turn, lent her book veracity and authority. As Demidenko, Darville embodied particular tropes of ethnicity, not only through Ukrainian costuming and her long blonde hair, but also with anecdotal stories about her 'flat-footed peasant parents who can neither read nor write';[22] the liberal use of Ukrainian words and gestures, which she constantly referred to as 'typically Ukrainian'; and through the stances she took to promote multiculturalism.

Indeed, the parallels drawn between Fiona Kovalenko and Helen Demidenko/Darville became a central feature for those who argued that the novel was an apologia for the Holocaust, with critics drawing connections between Demidenko – daughter of persecutors or, at the very least, the secondary link between the prejudices driving the Holocaust – and the viewpoints elucidated in the novel. It did not matter that Darville claimed not to be speaking her 'truth', but rather the 'truth' of her characters. As critics like Louise Adler argued, the ultimate problem lay in the lack of responsibility the author had shown to readers and to historical and cultural memory:

> Authors are responsible for the views they propagate . . . I now understand the world to be divided into those who believe in the banality of evil and those who believe evil is decidedly not ordinary and that collaboration should be viewed as an act of monstrous complicity.[23]

While the Demidenko debate does little to ease the problem of the shadowy realities of fiction, it calls close attention to the way readers instinctively draw parallels between the acts of writing and speaking and between the body of the text and the body of the writer. *The Hand* was judged not by the words on the page, but rather by the similarities between the writer and the critic's implied reading.

As Derrida states in 'Structure, Sign and Play', when a centre is dislodged, it inevitably recourses into the location of yet another 'centre; in this case the combination of reader and author, creating a new reading polemic'.[24] Thus, while Helen Demidenko argued that 'it is not the writer's job to pass moral judgements or to do the reader's thinking for him' – effectively dislodging herself from the structure's centre – by inventing Demidenko, she encouraged her readers to apply her personal narrative not only to the broad historical background of her fiction, but also to her own perceived sympathies and prejudices, showing how the author remains a central feature of the text.[25] The causal link that the novel attempted to establish between the famine of the 1930s and the Ukrainian complicity in the Holocaust was seen as a major indicator of the writer's own prejudices, encouraging, whether unwittingly or not, the conversion of fiction into a manifesto or 'anti-Semitic tract'[26] in what Gerard Henderson called a 'loathsome book'.[27]

Conversely, the Demidenko identity was also used to support complimentary readings of the book, first as testimony to the author's 'courage'[28] and then, when the identity was revealed, as further evidence of her 'extraordinary imagination and literary abilities'.[29] For many others her identity was irrelevant; as novelist and literary critic Gerard Windsor asserted: 'I have no idea of Helen Demidenko's personal feelings, how many of her best friends are Jewish etc – and the matter is irrelevant to her book. This is how people saw it, goes her story . . . '[30]

Some critics did look to literary theory. Andrew Riemer argued that the 'outing' of Darville should have alerted readers and critics to the importance of judging fictional work purely on its imaginative merits. In *The Demidenko Debate* Riemer wrote that the revelation of Helen Darville ought to 'have made it mandatory to return to the novel, and examine it as a work of fiction governed by the laws and conventions of imaginative writing':[31]

> Precisely because the strong ethnic and perhaps even familial bond between the author and the subject matter had been broken, it could no longer be assumed that the characters' sentiments are also the author's or her novel's. In other words, once Helen Demidenko was revealed to be a fictional character in a sense, *The Hand* should have been read and discussed as a work that employs literary techniques . . . whatever claims of its 'fictional' status the author might have made during her masquerade as a Ukrainian.[32]

But while it is admirable to try to (re)read the novel for its literary value (as Barthes himself would have hoped), any argument which suggests that little has changed in the politics of the reading space cannot be sustained. Even though the text has not changed on the page, the signs *behind* the words have, making any informed reading preinformed. Darville's book is substantially different to Demidenko's. To argue that the book should stand alone on its own merits is to simplify the issue and to ignore the ethicopoliticization of the novel by readers and the impact of the author on the book's interpretation. We cannot read Ern Malley as Max Harris first did – as the work of a young genius staring death in the eye.[33] For those aware of the history behind the name, we can only read him as a fabrication and system of literary effects designed to create a particular impression. Similarly, *The Hand* will always be remembered first as the story of a hoaxer and secondly as the story about evil or the other side of the Holocaust.

Spaces: real and imagined

Two months before David Bentley exposed the fraud of Helen Darville, Helen Demidenko was asked to respond to claims that her book was a 'racist apologia for the Holocaust' which advocated an amoral 'savagery begets savagery' agenda.[34] In defending her work, Darville had this to say about author–text relations:

> Of course, revengeful attitudes are morally wrong. However, for those who feel the need for ethical signposting, the fictional form I've employed clearly doesn't provide enough in the way of didactism. I've always maintained it is not the writer's task to do the thinking for him. I don't provide a neat moral.[35]

Helen Darville is right in saying it is not the writer's task to do the thinking on the reader's behalf. To do so is, as Barthes himself said, 'to impose a limit on that text, to furnish it with a final signified, to close the writing'.[36] Yet both statements fail to appreciate the way novels take effect *and* come to affect, as well as the way readers construct authors to suit their interpretation of the speaking subject, particularly in texts that lack an authoritative voice or which disagree with conventional cultural/historical narratives. While the Demidenko debate complicates many of the unresolved problems of authorship, it also highlights the reason why the author will always continue to matter in cultural theory, and the fact that textuality – whether fictional or not – is rarely considered in solitary isolation. Rather, as Darville asserts, it is often read as a slice of didactics.

As Sherry Booth argues in this volume, '[h]istory is a concept that lives uneasily in a postmodern world' (p. 46); it is a concept that is complicated by theory. Booth writes that 'while we can't interpret texts in absence of a theory or theories, the consequence of theory is to move the focus from the individual to the group, or from the particular character or event to what it exemplifies' (p. 46). The Demidenko debate similarly reasserts and reminds critical theorists and the reading public that while discursive anonymity is acceptable for nontrouble-some texts, in the event of an ethical discursive crisis, the desire to locate and connect the speaking subject to the broader issue of signification is very much alive. A reader might well support discursive anonymity for 'experimental gain' in a novel like Jeanette Winterson's *Written on the Body* (1993) – a love story in which the narrator's gender is masked throughout, causing some readers to seek solace in the author's own sexual identity for narrative reference – while declaring a social and polit-ical 'right' to locate the speaking subject in a more 'contentious' novel like *The Hand*.[37] While Beardsley and Wimsatt's 'Intentional Fallacy' states that a work of literature is 'not the author's (it is detached from the author at birth and goes about the world beyond its power to intend or control it)', it seems that the ethical concerns which motivated Plato are still of the highest importance.[38]

As a general principle, the necessity of assigning a text a signatory is generally related to principles of copyright and to ward off imitation.[39] Yet since the time of Plato, the signature has refused deposition in direct relation to what Burke identifies as the perceived 'gravity of the ethico-political issues raised by the text';[40] that is, the direct and causal links between what is interpreted by readers and any perceptions, real or otherwise, about the author's own personal/political/ethical stand. In an essay titled 'The Ethics of the Signature' Burke writes, 'the profound interrelation of ethics and the signature is borne out by the fact that questions of the signature are among the first to be raised in the context of an ethically troublesome text'.[41]

The Hand is one such novel where the desire to locate a speaking subject reinforced not an absence in the relevance of authorial identity, but rather a perfect example of the 'return to the subject'.[42] In this instance, the processes of rewriting, interpreting and interrogating both the author and the work in search of a 'body of evidence' revealed an effort to validate or refute the viewpoints of both the characters in the novel and the subsequent criticisms of readers about any implied textual meanings and the nature of the author herself.

In Demidenko, we find a confusing blur between the real and the imagined, a problem emphasized by the author's own conflation of fact and fiction, and further complicated by the tendencies of author-centred criticism to seek out biographical detail as evidence rather than as another interpretative function.[43] It is here, at this junction, that some of the inconsistencies between the two extremes of author-theory can be found. While on the one hand the polemics of 'the death of the author' do not adequately account for a reader's (re)creation of the authorial figure, the practice of author-centred criticism on the other – particularly in fiction – tends to conflate the real with the imagined, leading to a halfway house of fictionalized reality.

The approach that allows writing to give way to reading is admirable in its attempts to give interpretive power to the reader, however, in my opinion, fails in three key areas. It fails because it does not account for the significance of the author's biography in the act of interpretation; because it does not account for the fact that disposing of the author, in effect, opens up the hierarchical 'Author–God' space to the critic; and because it does not recognize the way an author can open up *other* possibilities for interpretation. Ideally, both the author and the critic would function, as Foucault had hoped, as only two of a number of tools for interpretation, with neither closing the act of writing. If that cannot occur in the act of reading, rather than denying the presence of these subjects in the text, we need to examine the way in which they impact on the text's relationship with readers. The interesting question in the Demidenko debate, then, is not why Darville did what she did but why critics and readers chose to respond to the text and author(s) as two interconnecting works. To answer this question would be to unravel the philosophical links that continue to inform society's approach to literature as an act of responsibility and accountability. In making the author matter, Darville showed, whether consciously or not, that the graphic sign of the signature stands in for more than a mark of originality. Rather, as Burke asserts,

the signature binds the text respectively to the still-living author, to the legacy and estates of the dead author, to whatever traditions might have been established *in nomine auctoris* and to the posthumous reconstructions of *authorial intention, biography, and any system of oeuvre effects which might influence the ethical rereading of the text in question.*[44]

A poststructuralist culture – where texts interact with the world independently of their creator's control – forfeits what Burke calls 'the dialectical structure of response and counter-response which supposedly ensures that discourses will not be misprised or irresponsibly interpreted'.[45] As Barthes, Derrida and Foucault have variously argued, such approaches open up new possibilities for reading and interpretation by instantiating the text as an independent body, free of its controlling ruler. However, as Burke goes on to argue, a culture governed by 'external signs' also 'opens up an ethical abyss in which no system of responsible discursive transmission can be instated in terms of a text's reception, appropriation, legacies, or the pedagogic relations between its subject and audience'.[46] In attempting to mediate between the two poles, then, we cannot help but ask who reads? Who interprets?

Conclusions

While the plurality of meanings (or in Barthes' terminology, the polysemy) advocated by authorless criticism is to be admired, it cannot be sustained once the text enters the speaking space. Once the text becomes recognizable in that sea of textuality and that clash of 'multiplicities', the very same as Barthes proposed, it is exposed to a 'galaxy of signifiers' which, in the case of a 'troublesome' text, can (will) signal the end of that text's ability to allow the very 'identity of the body writing' to slip away and evade 'every point of origin'.[47] For as we have seen with the Demidenko debate, once a text begins to partake in the weave of other textual fabrics, the text, whether fictional or not, can be called upon to speak of its intent. It is here, in that pursuit for understanding (no matter how misguided), that readers will almost always return to the most prominent and accessible point of origin; that of the speaking voice and physical body of the signature – the author. While a critical overview of the author successfully argues against the use of biographicisms in *evaluating* a text, the same cannot be said for the way these components are used in the act of interpreting and analysing the way a text operates in cultural practice; that is, the way it is read and the way in which the author, along with a range of other devices (and this is the key), is used in the circulation of the discourse. As I have argued throughout this chapter, whether critical theorists like it or not, meaning (even when it is determined by the reader deploying the rules of language), once assigned, will reveal the presence of the author in the text (whether or not that author wishes it).

Critical theorist Wayne Booth, whose work on the author has not been mentioned here but who has commented widely on the subject, writes:

> Even if we eliminate all . . . explicit judgements, the author's presence will be obvious on every occasion when he moves into or out of the character's mind – when he shifts his 'point of view' as we have come to put it . . . The author's judgement is always present, is always evident to anyone who knows how to look for it . . . *Though*

*the author can to some extent choose his disguises, he can never choose to
disappear...*[48]

While it is acceptable for some writings to be 'unauthored', cases such
as Demidenko indicate a need for other considerations of authorship in
order to make way for those practices where knowledge of the original
is demanded. Better work will be done not by denying the existence and
actuality of the process, but by examining the reasons why the author
cannot altogether disappear from the cultural space.

As Derrida purports, texts like language are marked by instability
and interdeterminancy, yet they are also marked by a reader's desire
to implicate a point of origin or position of address.[49] Fracturing the
spaces that once held the author in that state of 'theological' command
will not automatically ensure that the 'position' will not, in turn, be
(re)stated. If the author is dead, who is it that speaks and who is it that
controls the text?

The (post)postmodern age has yet to resolve the cultural and social
ambiguities of the artist, and the past thirty years remain chequered by a
failure on behalf of the academy to move beyond ideology and into the
realities of reading. The Demidenko debate, I would like to suggest, offers
a strong case study through which to explore these issues – namely the
problematic line between imaginative freedom and ethical constraint,
between fact and fiction, history and creativity and the relationships
between author and text.

The Demidenko debate is a debate 'we had to have' and is one we
should continue to explore. It exposes flaws in critical theory and reveals
that certain forms of thinking cannot be sustained where there is vari-
ation and incongruity. It also reminds us that literature does not just
involve aesthetical appreciation. Texts *affect* different people in very
different ways, creating a multitude of *effects*. The Helen Demidenko
debate is but one example.

Notes

1. Quentin Tarantino, *Shooting from the Hip* (London: Judy Piatkus, 1995), p. 1.
2. On 19 August 1995 journalist David Bentley uncovered one of the biggest
   literary scoops since the Ern Malley affair of the 1940s. His article 'Questions
   Posed on Author's Past' in *The Courier Mail* (p. 1) revealed Helen Demidenko's
   real identity as the Australian-born daughter of English migrants. The story
   was picked up by every metropolitan and national news source.
3. In a letter to the editor of a metropolitan daily Mark Butler of Woy Woy
   suggested that Darville be referred to as Helen D, calling her 'the first truly

postmodern, deconstructed author, the first real product of critical theory'. See Mark Butler in John Jost and Gianna Totaro (eds) *The Demidenko File* (Victoria: Penguin, 1996), pp. 193–4.

4. *The Hand* won three major literary awards – The Australian/Vogel in 1993 and both the Miles Franklin and the ALAS in 1995.

5. In his book *The Demidenko Debate* (Sydney: Allen & Unwin, 1996), Andrew Riemer cites Marjory Bennett's 1993 *Sun-Herald* article on Demidenko where she described the novel as 'part fact, part fiction' (p. 23).

6. Many critics objected to Darville's use of the term 'Jewish Bolshevik'. See Alan Dershowitz, 'Holocaust "abuse excuse" fails to disguise murder most foul', in *The Australian Financial Review*, 29 June 1995, p. 16.

7. Helen Darville, *The Hand that Signed the Paper* (Sydney: Allen & Unwin, 1994), p. 154. Subsequent references will appear in the text.

8. Helen Demidenko, 'Books and Writing', interviewed by Rosemary Sorensen, *Radio National*, Radio 3RN (4 September 1994), quoted in Jost and Totaro, *The Demidenko File*, p. 7.

9. Helen Demidenko, 'All Peoples are Capable of Atrocities', *The Sydney Morning Herald*, 27 June 1995, p. 11.

10. Demidenko's supporters included Frank O'Shea, Jill Kitson, David Marr and Roger McDonald.

11. Helen Demidenko, 'Writing After Winning', *Southerly*, 55, 3 (Spring 1995), 157.

12. Ibid.

13. To do a Demidenko meant, to use another Australian term, to 'pull a swiftie', to try to dupe someone or to behave fraudulently.

14. Demidenko, 'Books and Writing', pp. 7–8.

15. Sean Burke, *The Death and Return of the Author: Criticism and Subjectivity in Barthes, Foucault and Derrida* (Edinburgh: Edinburgh University Press, 1992), pp. 4–5.

16. Roland Barthes, 'The Death of the Author', *Image–Music–Text*, trans. S. Heath (London: Fontana, 1977), p. 142.

17. Ibid.

18. Marie Ni Fhlathuin, 'Postcolonialism and the Author: The Case of Salman Rushdie', in Sean Burke (ed.) *Authorship: From Plato to Postmodernism. A Reader* (Edinburgh: Edinburgh University Press, 1995), p. 277.

19. Barthes, 'The Death of the Author', *Image–Music–Text*, trans. S. Heath (London: Fontana, 1977), p. 147.

20. Sean Burke, 'The Ethics of Signature', in Sean Burke (ed.) *Authorship: From Plato to Postmodernism* (Edinburgh: Edinburgh University Press, 1995), pp. 285–91.

21. Michel Foucault, 'What is an Author?' *Language, Counter-Memory, Practice: Selected Essays and Interviews*, trans. Donald F. Bouchard and Sherry Simon (Ithaca, NY: Cornell University Press, 1977), p. 123.

22. Demidenko, 'Writing After Winning', p. 157.

23. Louise Adler, Pamela Bone, Gerard Henderson, Robert Manne and Gerard Windsor, 'Forum on the Demidenko Controversy', *The Australian Book Review*, 173 (August 1995), 14–18.

24. Jacques Derrida, quoted in Raman Seldon and Peter Widdowson, *A Reader's Guide to Literary Theory* (New York: Harvester Wheatsheaf, 1993), p. 144.

25. Demidenko, 'Morning Program', interviewed by Terry Lane, *Radio National,* Radio 3RN (11 June 1994), in Jost and Totaro, *The Demidenko File,* p. 45.
26. Manne, 'Forum on the Demidenko Controversy', p. 15.
27. Henderson, 'Forum on the Demidenko Controversy', p. 15.
28. Judith Armstrong, 'Sword Cross Over the Terror', *The Age,* 17 June 1995, p. 9.
29. Jill Kitson, 'Morning Program', interviewed by Peter Thompson, *Radio National,* Radio 3RN (21 August 1995), in Jost and Totaro, *The Demidenko File,* p. 116.
30. Windsor, 'Forum on the Demidenko Controversy', p. 17.
31. Riemer, *The Demidenko Debate,* p. 26.
32. Ibid., p. 175.
33. Known as one of Australia's most infamous literary hoaxes, the Ern Malley affair erupted in the 1940s when two writers, James McAuley and Harold Stewart, invented the 'poet' genius Ern Malley along with a grieving sister Ethel. The hoax intended to disrupt the literary establishment and in particular literary editor Max Harris. For further readings on the Ern Malley affair, see Michael Heyward's 1991 book *The Ern Malley Affair* (London: Faber & Faber, 1993).
34. Manne, 'Forum on the Demidenko Controversy', p. 15.
35. Demidenko, 'All People are Capable of Atrocities', p. 11.
36. Barthes, 'The Death of the Author', p. 147.
37. Burke, 'The Ethics of Signature', p. 287.
38. Monroe C. Beardsley and W. K. Wimsatt, 'The Intentional Fallacy', in W. K. Wimsatt, Jr., *The Verbal Icon: Studies in the Meaning of Poetry* (London: Methuen, 1954), p. 5.
39. Molly Nesbit, 'What is an Author?', in Sean Burke (ed.) *Authorship: From Plato to Postmodernism* (Edinburgh: Edinburgh University Press, 1995), pp. 247–62.
40. Burke, 'The Ethics of Signature', p. 289.
41. Ibid.
42. Burke, *The Death and Return of the Author,* pp. 1–7.
43. Ni Fhlatuin, 'Postcolonialism and the Author', p. 283.
44. Burke, 'The Ethics of Signature', p. 289 (emphases mine).
45. Ibid., p. 286.
46. Ibid.
47. Barthes, 'The Death of the Author', p. 142.
48. Wayne Booth, *The Rhetoric of Fiction* (Chicago, IL: Chicago University Press, 1961), p. 20 (emphasis mine).
49. Jacques Derrida, 'Signature–Event–Context', repr. in Samuel Weber and Henry Sussman (eds) *Glyph 1* (Baltimore, MD: John Hopkins University Press, 1971), pp. 172–97.

Part II
Historiographic Re-visionings

6
Historicizing Witchcraft Throughout the Ages: Joanna Baillie and Caryl Churchill

Christine A. Colón

In the introduction to the American edition of her book, *Hidden from History*, published in 1974, Sheila Rowbotham discusses the influence that the women's movement had on her study of history and remarks, 'it is evident that the rediscovery of our history is an essential aspect of the creation of a feminist critique of male culture'.[1] Caryl Churchill echoes these sentiments in the introduction to her play *Vinegar Tom*, first produced in 1976, as she explains her motivations for writing about seventeenth-century witchcraft trials. While she had always imagined 'burnings, hysteria, and sexual orgies',[2] her research, as well as the research by the feminist theatre group Monstrous Regiment with whom she created the play, revealed a very different picture: a picture that she wished to capture in her play as a way of exposing the oppression of women that still occurs. She declares, 'I wanted to write a play about witches with no witches in it; a play not about evil, hysteria and possession by the devil but about poverty, humiliation and prejudice, and how the women accused of witchcraft saw themselves' (*VT*, p. 130). For both Rowbotham and Churchill, the women's movement provided a means of reconstructing the history they thought they already knew as a way to critique the inequities of their own society. As Rowbotham remarks, 'the women's movement has made many of us ask different questions of our past'.[3]

But what about women who wrote before the women's movement? Were they doomed to see the past simply through the lenses of male culture? Rowbotham may be correct that the women's movement has created unique possibilities for women to expand their critiques of history and society. This issue, however, needs to be placed in a more complex context, for much of our discussion has often been based on extremely limited information. While the rise of feminist literary criticism has allowed many women writers to be rediscovered, large gaps still remain, particularly for playwrights. In their introduction to *Women and Playwrighting in Nineteenth-Century Britain*, Tracy C. Davis and Ellen Donkin remark, 'Historians and critics have consistently leapt over the nineteenth century (and sometimes the entire eighteenth century too), forgetting all the generations between Aphra Behn and Caryl Churchill.'[4] This gap is problematic not only because it allows us to ignore the work of many female playwrights but also because it calls into question many assertions about contemporary female playwrights. For instance, in her discussion of Churchill, Aemilia Howe Kritzer remarks, 'In her application of socialist-feminist analysis to contemporary power relationships and socio-economic institutions, Churchill has revealed herself as not only an original playwright, but also an original thinker.'[5] Kritzer assumes that Churchill's originality as a playwright stems from her ability to infuse both the themes and the forms of her plays with her contemporary socialist-feminist perspective in order to provoke change in her audience; and, using Toril Moi's definition of the historical text,[6] she argues that '[Churchill's] work signals a rejection of the traditional function of the history play as a "passive, 'feminine' reflection of an unproblematically 'given', masculine world"'.[7] But is Churchill truly breaking new ground here? Or is there actually a longer tradition of which both Kritzer and Churchill might be unaware?

What happens, for instance, if we look at someone like Joanna Baillie (1762–1851), an early nineteenth-century Scottish playwright, who had virtually disappeared from critical discussion until the 1990s? In the preface to her play *Witchcraft* (1836), published 140 years before *Vinegar Tom* (1976), she also counters established history, questioning whether women confessed to witchcraft to 'have an end put to their wretched existence' and arguing instead that

> [i]t is more reasonable to suppose that some of those unhappy creatures, from the state of their minds, and from real circumstances leading to it, actually did believe themselves to have had intercourse with the Evil One, consequently to be witches.[8]

She creates her play to 'illustrate this curious condition of nature' (*W*, p. 613). Like Churchill, Baillie rejects the tradition she has been taught and crafts her play in order to present a new understanding of history. (In this way, Baillie and Churchill are similar to several of the writers Diana Wallace discusses in this volume as they discover that 'one of the uses of history is to undo "History"' [p. 169].) What, then, might we learn by comparing Baillie's impulse to historicize with Churchill's?

At first glance, Baillie and Churchill would appear to have very little in common. The seemingly conservative nineteenth-century woman described by John Francis Waller as 'small, prim, and Quaker-like'[9] who crafted a series of plays designed to improve the morality of her audience certainly appears to be very different from the radical, twentieth-century, feminist-socialist playwright who provokes her audiences with overtly political plays. Their approaches to historical drama seem to emphasize these differences. While both set their plays during the time of witchcraft trials in Britain (late seventeenth-century England for Churchill and early eighteenth-century Scotland for Baillie), Baillie follows nineteenth-century dramatic conventions, using language appropriate to the time period of her play and carefully keeping it within the narrow confines allowed by nineteenth-century censors. The most 'radical' aspect of her language is her use of realistic Scottish dialect. Churchill, however, rejects realism and deliberately chooses anachronistic language designed to shock even her twentieth-century audience. She not only freely discusses sexual desire, menstruation and menopause but also talks about these issues in very graphic terms. While Baillie seemingly accepts the constraints placed on her in the early nineteenth century, Churchill takes advantage of the freedom of expression available in the late twentieth century, pushes the boundaries even further and explores the radical potential of language, creating a surprising portrait of the seventeenth century. Their styles of historical drama may seem very different, but, as we examine their plays in more depth, we discover that both playwrights ultimately use the context of witchcraft in surprisingly similar ways to critique gender and class constraints and to argue for change. (See Chapter 1 for a discussion of why the seventeenth century in particular is ripe for this type of consideration.)

Baillie and Churchill believe strongly in the transformative power of theatre, and they craft their plays in order to maximize the type of audience reaction that they believe will lead to social change. Baillie embraces moral philosophy derived from the Scottish enlightenment while Churchill turns to Bertolt Brecht. In the Introductory Discourse to her first volume of plays, Baillie builds upon Adam Smith's *The Theory of Moral Sentiments* and carefully outlines a process of transforming society through drama in which individuals will learn to reform themselves by observing the struggles of characters on stage. She believes that drama enhances reality by allowing audiences access to 'those exclamations of the soul which heaven alone may hear'.[10] This access, Baillie argues, will then allow individuals to reflect upon their own passions and learn to control them, for '[i]n examining others we know ourselves . . . [and] we cannot well exercise this disposition without becoming more just, more merciful, more compassionate'.[11] With her plays, Baillie desires to create a connection between the audience and the characters so that the audience members may more easily transfer what they are learning in the play to their own lives.

This theory compelled her to critique the theatrical conventions of her day. While most playwrights were busy creating lavish spectacles to entertain the huge audiences at Covent Garden and Drury Lane, Baillie argued for more realistic acting so that audiences could recognize the humanity of the characters they observed on stage. She realized that this connection rarely happened in the huge theatres of her day, so in the preface to her third volume of plays she proposed smaller theatres and lights from above rather than below so that the nuances of the dramatic moments could be displayed more effectively.[12] She also wished to expand the audience for plays to the lower classes, declaring that

> a play, but of small poetical merit, that is suited to strike and interest the spectator, to catch the attention of him who will not, and of him who cannot read, is a more valuable and useful production than one whose elegant and harmonious pages are admired in the libraries of the tasteful and refined.[13]

Here, she is arguing not for simple spectacle that will entertain but for meaningful drama that will be accessible to all. Baillie's goal is to transform her society, and her philosophy of theatre reveals just how passionate she is about it.

In *Witchcraft*, Baillie develops her ideas in interesting ways. As Susan Bennett relates, 'In very many ways, *Witchcraft* is a startling text, not so much revising the category of tragedy as reinventing it. The scope of Baillie's ambition to do things differently is perhaps no better realized anywhere than in this text.'[14] In her *Plays on the Passions*, Baillie concentrates on a single character (usually male) who struggles with a single passion, and she uses this character to demonstrate to her audience members the dangers of allowing themselves to be overcome with a particular passion. In *Witchcraft*, she broadens her scope, moving from exploring the passions within an individual that may cause his or her downfall to revealing the larger problems within a society that may also destroy individuals. The main character the audience is asked to identify with is Violet, a young, innocent, middle-class girl who, through her loyalty to her father, becomes vulnerable to the charge of witchcraft. When Violet's father (a convicted murderer who is supposedly dead) secretly reveals himself to her and compels her to keep his secret, she leaves the safety of her middle-class cottage for visits with him on the moor that is thought to be a haven for witches. Annabella, who is jealous of Violet's relationship with Dungarren (the man they both love), takes advantage of the situation by stealing one of Violet's dresses, tearing a piece from it, and placing that piece in a room where a little girl claims she is being tormented by witches. Despite her good reputation, Violet cannot overcome this 'evidence' against her, and the audience is asked to wonder what is wrong with a community in which even an honourable girl cannot withstand these accusations. By identifying with Violet's plight, the audience gradually comes to see how vulnerable women are in this society when they lack a man's protection.

Baillie, however, does not focus entirely on Violet, for she also asks her audience to sympathize with Mary Macmurren, a lower-class woman who is tempted by witchcraft because she is hungry and desperate to provide for her child. With the character of Mary, Baillie challenges her audience members to move beyond simply identifying with the character in the play who is most like them to identifying with the predicament of a woman entirely different from them. As Mary waits on the moor for Grizeld Bane to arrive and supposedly initiate her into the ways of witchcraft, she reveals her plight and the bitterness that has arisen from her destitution. Mary condemns her neighbours for their unconcern and looks to witchcraft to provide her with the power she lacks, crying, 'Ay; the hated anes will pay the cost, I trow' (*W*, p. 616). Relating to Mary may not be as easy as empathizing with Violet, particularly as Mary contemplates what she will do to her neighbours once she has the power of witchcraft behind her, but Baillie still asks her audience to understand her motivation and recognize the dangers in society that make her vulnerable to these temptations. Like Violet, Mary has no place of refuge within this community, and she tries to survive the only way she knows how. By focusing on the motivation behind the actions, Baillie asks the audience to sympathize with her plight and to critique the social structures that have made her so desperate.

This critique does not end with Mary, however, for Baillie compels her audience to sympathize with one more character: Grizeld Bane, the 'true' witch who seemingly conjures storms and speaks with the devil. Throughout most of the play, Grizeld Bane has been the hated villainess who tempts other women to evil, and the audience begins to accept the fact that while other women may resort to witchcraft out of desperation, Grizeld Bane is truly evil. At the conclusion of the play, however, Baillie reveals just how wrong the audience has been. Rather than being a witch, Grizeld Bane is simply '[a] miserable woman whose husband was hanged for murder... and who thereupon became distracted' (*W*, p. 642). While she was once cared for, she has now escaped from keepers 'who may not be very anxious to reclaim her' (*W*, p. 642). Society no longer has room for Grizeld Bane, so she imagines herself a witch in order to achieve some control over her life and the lives of those around her. In addition, she gains recognition from the society that once ignored her. While the community may overlook a poor, 'distracted' woman, it cannot disregard a witch. Once again the audience is asked to think about the social structures that have compelled this woman to act the way that she does. Even further, they are asked to think about their own judgements of the situation, for they, too, have easily condemned a desperate woman who deserves pity rather than scorn. By the conclusion of this play, then, Baillie has asked her audience to identify with three very different women, both middle class and lower class, and by revealing how quickly the community (and the audience) may turn against them, she compels her audience to recognize the social inequities then and now that have made women so vulnerable.

Like Baillie, Churchill wishes to draw her audience's attention to these social inequities. She, however, approaches this task from a very different perspective. Rather than creating a realistic play, which she fears may lull her audience into complacency, Churchill uses Brechtian techniques to make the ideology of the play clear and to compel her audience members to reflect upon it.[15] Like Baillie, Churchill creates several different women from various classes to illustrate that the problems she is exploring are social rather than individual. She takes this technique even further, however, by using an epic structure in which no one character takes precedence. We are introduced to Alice, a sexually active, single mother from the village; Susan, her young married friend who is pregnant with yet another child; Joan, a poor widow who continually beseeches her neighbours for help; Ellen, a 'cunning' woman who dispenses herbs and advice to the community; and Betty, a landowner's daughter who cannot bear the thought of marriage. All of these characters will eventually face charges of witchcraft, but rather than presenting a continuous narrative that allows her audience to get lost in the story of any one of these women's lives, Churchill fragments the tale, giving her audience only isolated scenes that represent pivotal moments in these characters' lives. And within several of these scenes, she uses what Brecht called a 'social gest' to focus the audience's attention even more strongly on the power dynamics that are oppressing these women.[16] As we watch Betty tied to a chair and about to be bled to cure her of her 'hysteria' or as we watch Goody and Packer lift Joan's skirts and begin pricking her with a needle to discover the 'devil's spot' that will prove her a witch, we can clearly see within these images the dangers that awaited any woman (rich or poor) who overstepped the bounds of this society.

In addition to the epic structure and social gests that Churchill borrows from Brecht, Churchill also uses songs in a manner similar to the way Brecht employs them in plays such as *The Threepenny Opera*.[17] The songs create an alienation effect, disrupting the action and compelling the audience members to think about the significance of what they are seeing. In *Vinegar Tom*, they also encourage the audience to draw parallels between the seventeenth and the twentieth centuries. In the production note at the beginning of the play, Churchill states, 'The songs, which are contemporary, should if possible be sung by actors in modern dress. They are not part of the action and not sung by the characters in the scenes before them' (*VT*, p. 133). The seven songs that are interspersed throughout the twenty-one scenes of this play jar the audience members out of the seventeenth-century world and ask them to consider the implications of the power dynamics they are observing. In the song that follows the hanging of Joan and Ellen, for instance, the audience is asked to '[l]ook in the mirror tonight./Would they have hanged you then?/Ask how they're stopping you now' (*VT*, p. 176). With all of these techniques, Churchill asks her audience members to reflect upon the images they are viewing, question how they relate to their own lives and then consider how they can transform their own worlds in reaction to the critical dialogue in which they have just participated.

On the surface, Baillie's and Churchill's techniques are very different. Baillie longs to create a connection between her audience members and her characters while Churchill tries to distance her audience members from the play so that they do not become lost in the story. The results they desire, however, are the same. Both wish their audiences to be transformed by drama so that they may work to change the rest of the society. In these two plays, then, they historicize the witchcraft trials not simply to illustrate how easily women were vilified in a world that denied them access to power but also to argue for transformation of the dangerous power dynamics that are still evident in their own societies. Baillie and Churchill illustrate how the charge of witchcraft could endanger women on all levels of society, pointing to a pervasive social problem that stretches far beyond the seventeenth and the eighteenth centuries.[18] The similarities between their representations of witchcraft, however, extend much further, for even without the benefit of the women's movement, Baillie crafts a play that may implicitly be as radical as Churchill's.

No real witchcraft occurs in either of these plays. While the accusations abound, the authors show that they are a result of a flawed social system that works to oppress any women who transgress its boundaries. Interestingly, Baillie and Churchill reveal that this discrimination is based not simply on gender but also on class, for in both plays the lower-class women are in the most danger. Mary Macmurren in *Witchcraft* and Joan in *Vinegar Tom* represent the lowest class, and they are the first to be accused of witchcraft. As poor widows, they have become dependent upon their neighbours who are reluctant to grant them the aid that they require, and they resent their position. Mary vigorously condemns her neighbours, declaring, 'They refused us a han'fu in our greatest need, but now it wull be our turn to ha' fou sacks and baith cakes and kebbucks at command, while their aumery is bare' (*W*, p. 617). Joan, as well, resorts to cursing her neighbours, Jack and Margery, for their refusal to aid her, crying to Margery, 'Devil take you and your man and your fields and your cows and your butter and your yeast and your beer and your bread and your cider and your cold face...' (*VT*, p. 144). Their neighbours have become tired of extending charity, so Mary and Joan respond the only way that they can – with curses, and these curses make them vulnerable to charges of witchcraft. Both are perceived as draining society's resources without contributing to them and are therefore susceptible to the accusations of their neighbours who will use any excuse to relieve themselves of the obligations they have towards these women.

Economic distress, however, is not the only danger, for Baillie and Churchill reveal that any lower-class woman who is in any way different from the norm is at risk. As was mentioned previously, Baillie, through the character of Grizeld Bane, reveals that society ignores the plight not only of the poor but also of the mentally ill. Churchill similarly explores the plight of lower-class characters who are 'different' and are, therefore, vulnerable. Alice's sexual activity outside of marriage, Ellen's knowledge of healing potions and Susan's desire to rid herself of an unwanted pregnancy all allow their neighbours to accuse them of witchcraft. Any lower-class woman who does not remain within the narrow confines of 'proper' behaviour is in danger. Churchill emphasizes this fact in the first scene. After his sexual encounter with Alice, the man calls her a whore. When she rejects this characterization, he responds, 'What are you then? What name would you put to yourself? You're not a wife or a widow. You're not a virgin. Tell me a name for what you are' (*VT*, p. 137). Alice cannot respond, but eventually her community gives her a name: witch.

The dangers for women who do not conform are extreme, for Baillie's character Violet and Churchill's character Betty reveal that even 'respectable' middle-class girls may be vulnerable to accusations if they leave the confines of the middle-class home. Violet becomes an easy target when she wanders the moors in search of her father, and Betty places herself in danger with her rebellious rejection of marriage and her frequent visits to Ellen, the 'cunning' woman, for advice. In her final visit to Ellen, Betty reveals, 'I am afraid to come here any more. They'll say I'm a witch... They say because I screamed that was the devil in me. And when I ran out of the house they say where was I going if not to meet other witches' (*VT*, p. 169). She escapes being tried as a witch only because her family has enough money to call a doctor who claims that he will make her well through bleeding her and because she finally takes Ellen's advice. While Betty longs to be 'left alone', Ellen reminds her of the realities she is attempting to ignore, asking, 'Left alone for what? To be like me? There's no doctor going to save me from being called a witch. Your best chance of being left alone is to marry a rich man' (*VT*, p. 169). Through Violet and Betty, as well as the other women in these plays, Baillie and Churchill illustrate the dangers of a society in which women who do not conform are condemned as witches.

These inequities in society are not only dangerous for the women accused as witches, however. They also create a world in which women are compelled to act against each other in order to gain power. In addition to showing the victimization of women within society, Baillie and Churchill also reveal how women, themselves, may become complicit in the social structures that allow rebellious or outcast women be accused of witchcraft. Annabella in *Witchcraft* and Goody in *Vinegar Tom* try to use the existing social structures to their advantage. While Annabella originally goes to Grizeld Bane for a charm to relieve her of her passion for Dungarren, she soon recognizes that she can gain more control over the situation by framing Violet for witchcraft. In her desire for revenge, she becomes the most powerful 'witch' of them all. Even Grizeld Bane acknowledges, 'There is not a cloven foot, nor a horned head of them all, wickeder and bolder than [she is]' (*W*, p. 638). By attempting to use the accusation of witchcraft to remove her rival for Dungarren's affections, Annabella not only supports this dangerous power structure but also enhances it.

In *Vinegar Tom*, Goody also works within the existing social constructs by helping Packer, the witchfinder, in his 'examinations'. Her position gives her power within this society, and she clearly recognizes the dangers that she avoids by having this vocation. After discussing the benefits of her job and the power it bestows on her, she remarks, 'Yes, it's interesting work being a searcher and nice to do good at the same time as earning a living. Better than staying home a widow. I'd end up like the old women you see, soft in the head and full of spite with their muttering and spells. I keep healthy keeping the country healthy' (*VT*, p. 168). Both Annabella and Goody victimize other women as they use the accusations of witchcraft to try to gain power for themselves in a world that allows women little power.

The women in these plays are either corrupted by the social structures as they attempt to gain power or accused as witches for their nonconformity, and in their conclusions Baillie and Churchill emphasize just how pervasive these problems are. As Violet and Mary await execution at the conclusion of *Witchcraft*, Baillie reveals that while the inequities of this society are seen most clearly through the witchcraft trials, they extend much further. As a woman, Violet has no legal voice. She is dependent upon her exiled father hearing of her plight, deciding to risk his life for hers and arriving before she is burned at the stake. And even this is not enough, for she still faces execution until the servant boy escapes from Annabella and discounts the rest of the evidence against her. Violet's life depends entirely upon the honour of the men who have the power to rescue her, but salvation by honourable men seems to be only a matter of chance. This point is emphasized with the character of Mary Macmurren, who only escapes execution because the decree repealing punishment for the crime of witchcraft arrives seconds before her death. Unlike the many women before her who were executed for what is now called 'an imaginary crime' (*W*, p. 642), Mary escapes. But her salvation, as well as the salvation of the other accused witches, comes purely by chance. By ending the play with the decree, Baillie could have emphasized that the problem of witchcraft is now over, but she does not. She focuses, instead, on the continuing inequity of power that still makes women vulnerable. The punishment for witchcraft may have been repealed, but the women still live in a world where the laws that control them are all drafted by men.

For the accused witches in *Vinegar Tom*, salvation never comes. Joan and Ellen are hanged while Susan and Alice look on awaiting their own deaths, and in the final scene Kramer and Sprenger, two fifteenth-century theologians who wrote *Malleus Maleficarum* (the most influential treatise on witchcraft), appear as Edwardian music hall comics to remind the audience of the 'truths' of the weaknesses of the female sex that make them vulnerable to witchcraft: they are more wicked, 'more credulous', 'more impressionable' and, most importantly, 'more carnal' (*VT*, p. 177). While the audience members might like to dismiss these ideas as stereotypes of the past, Churchill will not allow them to, for in the final song she reminds them that even if '[w]e earn our own money/And buy our own drink', we may still be condemned as 'evil women' who bring about the downfall of men (*VT*, p. 179). With her use of the contemporary song, Churchill explicitly connects this past treatment with the current oppression of women that she still sees in society.

In the conclusions to their plays, Baillie and Churchill present a clear critique of the ways women have been treated in the past and the power dynamics that still make them susceptible to this treatment. True, Churchill is allowed a broader canvas for her story as she discusses issues that would never have been allowed on the stage in the nineteenth century and creates many different types of 'transgressive' women. She is also able to draw far clearer connections between the witchcraft trials and the continued oppression of women in the twentieth century through her innovative stage techniques. Baillie's critique is much more subtle, but it is still a compelling analysis of the history she is representing and an insightful assessment of the power dynamics that are evident within her own society. Even though she does not draw explicit connections between the past and the present as Churchill does, Baillie gives audience members the opportunity to relate to the characters and hopes that they will then draw their own conclusions about what still needs to be transformed in society.

Despite writing in very different time periods that allow women very different freedoms, Baillie and Churchill create remarkably similar versions of history. Is Churchill, then, in the words of Kritzer, 'not only an original playwright, but also an original thinker'?[19] Yes, she is, for her plays demonstrate a remarkable ability to capture contemporary power struggles and to shock her audiences into action, and the stage techniques that she uses to accomplish this are revolutionary. Her originality, however, needs to be placed in the context of the many female playwrights who have come before her. The twentieth-century feminist movement may have allowed women to present their case for equality much more directly and may have compelled all of us to see the past in different ways from some of our foremothers, but the similarities between *Witchcraft* and *Vinegar Tom* illustrate that the need to historicize women's experience must be placed within a long tradition and the complexities of this task throughout the ages must be addressed. We must not simply assume that the tradition of women's literature is an evolutionary narrative in which women writers gradually become more radical and thereby ignore early writers whom we often presume to be more conservative.[20] Nor must we only discuss early writers who easily fit our conception of what it means to be radical, for Baillie, herself, has a seemingly conservative project of improving the morality of her audience. Instead, we must strive to create a more complex tradition in which we begin to break down this dichotomy of conservative versus radical and focus instead on the intricate conversations that women writers have with each other throughout time.

Notes

1. Sheila Rowbotham, *Hidden from History: Rediscovering Women in History from the 17th Century to the Present* (New York: Pantheon, 1974), p. xvii.
2. Caryl Churchill, 'Vinegar Tom', in *Churchill Plays: One* (New York: Routledge, 1985), p. 130. All further references will be given in the body of the text using the abbreviation VT.
3. Rowbotham, *Hidden from History*, p. xxxvi.
4. Tracy C. Davis and Ellen Donkin, 'Introduction' to Tracy C. Davis and Ellen Donkin (eds) *Women and Playwriting in Nineteenth-Century Britain* (New York: Cambridge University Press, 1999), p. 3.
5. Aemilia Howe Kritzer, *The Plays of Caryl Churchill: Theatre of Empowerment* (London: Macmillan, 1991), p. 194.
6. Toril Moi, *Sexual/Textual Politics: Feminist Literary Theory* (London: Methuen, 1985), p. 8.
7. Ibid., pp. 84–5.
8. Joanna Baillie, 'Witchcraft', in *The Dramatic and Poetical Works* (New York: Georg Olms, 1976), pp. 613–43. All further references will be given in the body of the text using the abbreviation W.
9. John Francis Waller, 'Joanna Baillie', *The Dublin University Magazine*, 37 (1851), 529.
10. Baillie, 'Introductory Discourse', in *The Dramatic and Poetical Works* (New York: Georg Olms, 1976), p. 8.
11. Ibid., p. 4.
12. Baillie, 'To the Readers', in *The Dramatic and Poetical Works* (New York: Georg Olms, 1976), pp. 232–5.
13. Baillie, 'Introductory Discourse', p. 16.
14. Susan Bennett, 'Genre Trouble: Joanna Baillie, Elizabeth Polack – Tragic Subjects, Melodramatic Subjects', in Davis and Donkin (eds) *Women and Playwriting in Nineteenth-Century Britain*, p. 227.
15. See Janelle Reinelt, 'Beyond Brecht: Britain's New Feminist Drama', *Theatre Journal*, 38, 2 (1986), 154–63 and Kritzer, *The Plays of Caryl Churchill*, for detailed discussions of Churchill's use of Brechtian techniques in *Vinegar Tom*.

16. See Bertolt Brecht's definition of social gest in 'On Gestic Music', in John Willett (ed. and trans.) *Brecht on Theatre: The Development of an Aesthetic* (New York: Hill and Wang, 1992), pp. 104–6.

17. See Bertolt Brecht's 'On the Use of Music in an Epic Theatre', in Willett (ed.) *Brecht on Theatre*, pp. 84–90.

18. While I agree with Katharine Hodgkin that using witchcraft 'as a symbol of generalized patriarchal oppression' (p. 21) can be problematic because it oversimplifies historical reality, I find it interesting that when we explore this impulse in writers as different as Baillie and Churchill, we discover that it may not be as embedded in twentieth-century ideals as we thought. I also think that Baillie and Churchill both acknowledge a few more of the complexities of witchcraft than the writers Hodgkin discusses, for their characters are not simply the traditional midwives or herbalists, nor are they symbols of a feminine pagan tradition. Instead, both Baillie and Churchill explore a variety of ways women could be implicated in witchcraft.

19. Kritzer, *The Plays of Caryl Churchill*, p. 194.

20. See Margaret J. M. Ezell, *Writing Women's Literary History* (Baltimore, MD: Johns Hopkins University Press, 1993), especially pp. 1–13 and 14–38.

7
The Benefits of Watching the Circus Animals Desert: Myth, Yeats and Patriarchy in Angela Carter's *Nights at the Circus*

Michael Sinowitz

Angela Carter wrote an essay 'Notes from the Frontline' (1983) for a collection entitled *Gender and Writing*, a relatively short while before one of her most acclaimed novels, *Nights at the Circus* (1984),[1] appeared to the public. While many critics, clued in by some of Carter's own interviews, have looked to understand Carter's novel by reading it through *The Sadeian Woman*, which she had published in 1979, it seems clear to me that Carter, while thinking through her own career as an author in this essay, anticipated the issues she was to take on in the forthcoming novel. In particular, Carter discusses the relationship between her own writing and myths and folklore, conceding that she 'become[s] mildly irritated... when people... ask me about the "mythic quality" of my work', since she 'believe[s] that all myths are products of the human mind and reflect only aspects of material practice'.[2] The implication seems to be that while myths purport to a kind of timelessness, they cannot and should not be seen as transcendent of the material conditions of their own creation, and they are dangerous: myths 'are extraordinary lies designed to make people unfree'.[3] In fact, rather than seeing herself as a writer who perpetuates myths by incorporating them in her work, she considers herself to be 'in the demythologizing business'.[4]

In this same essay, Carter expresses some anxiety about the power writing has to change these very conditions she seems to be challenging; in fact, she says writers are 'not the unacknowledged legislators of mankind' and she wishes to demythologize the greatness and importance of writers themselves, saying that 'most of the great male geniuses of Western European culture have been either depraved egomaniacs or people who led the most distressing lives'.[5] Although this path of discussion began with Baudelaire, we might identify William Butler Yeats as someone who might be called both a 'genius' and an 'egomaniac'. In fact, if Carter sees herself as a demythologizer, we might say that Yeats appears to have been in the mythologizing business, drawing upon a complex – sometimes self-invented, perhaps an ultimate sign of ego – system of symbols to construct his myths. Critics have argued that Yeats' particular spiritualism and its mythology grew out of his desire to create a poetics that would contravene the rationalism he saw rising into prominence in the late nineteenth century.[6] From this perspective, Yeats seems a perfect foil for Carter. He and his fellow Modernists provide the myths, if you will, that Carter in works like *Nights at the Circus* seeks to debunk. That Yeats began to emerge as a prominent poet at the same period in which Carter set her novel makes the connections to him that much more appropriate. This would suggest that one could read Carter's novel then as a fairly straightforward critique of figures who perpetuated myths – imprisoning lies, in Carter's phrase – and an attempt to debunk those myths. However, while I believe that my discussions of the significant connections between Yeats' poetry and Carter's novel reveal her subversion of his symbolism and ideas, Carter's novel also reveals that simply overturning these constructions is, first of all, much more complicated a process than this might seem and that such reversals do not simply restore or grant the freedom that Carter implies myths take away. Sarah Gamble in Chapter 2 on *American Ghosts and Old World Wonders* suggests that this pattern of treating myths and the past gets reiterated throughout Carter's oeuvre.

Some of the earliest reviewers of *Nights at the Circus* have made mention of Yeats.[7] Elaine Jordan has noted that '*Nights at the Circus* rewrites Yeats'[8] but stops short of explaining exactly what this 'rewriting' entails and to what ends Carter intends to use such re-vision. The Yeats connection most often discussed at some length is the novel's invocation of Leda and the Swan, and the reason for this observation seems largely tied up in the fact that Carter had alluded to this myth before. In her earlier novel, *The Magic Toyshop* (1967),[9] Melanie, the young heroine of that novel, is forced to be the human actor in a puppet show re-enactment of Zeus' visit to Leda in the form of the Swan. Jean Wyatt reads Carter's depiction of Leda and the Swan in *The Magic Toyshop* as a re-vision of Yeats' own rendering of the myth in 'Leda and the Swan' (1928):[10] 'Yeats mystifies rape as a moment of divine transcendence...Carter shows it to be an act of brute force.'[11] As we examine Carter's use of this myth in *Nights at the Circus*, we can see that the allusion is much more complicated, as critics have noted, because Carter gives the 'swan-like' qualities to a woman, the novel's main character, Fevvers, rather than to a man, and thus Carter appears no longer to be simply 'rewriting' that myth so as to expose the violation and rape masked as transcendence as Wyatt perceives to be the case in Yeats' poem. Some see the depiction of Leda and the Swan in *Nights at the Circus* in terms of a reversal of roles – with Fevvers becoming the swan and Walser becoming Leda – however, its presentation here is ultimately ambiguous.[12] While Walser may give himself over to Fevvers, it is quite difficult to read that scene as a rape (although Walser's perspective on events at the end is somewhat removed). In fact, Walser's commentary reveals itself as typically ambiguous as he recalls the path of his life over the course of the novel:

> All that seemed to happen to me in the third person as though, most of my life, I watched it but did not live it. And now, hatched out of the shell of unknowing by a combination of a blow on the head and a sharp spasm of erotic ecstasy, I shall have to start all over again . . . (p. 294)

Here, clearly some of the language – 'blow', for instance, derived from the first line of the poem, 'A sudden blow' – clearly picks up that of Yeats; however, Walser is 'hatched', as Fevvers is supposed to have been (and which Zeus' swan was certainly not!). Even Walser's rebirth cannot be entirely attributed to this encounter with Fevvers, as she notes earlier that 'some other hen had hatched him out' (p. 290), a phrase representing her own play on his role as a chicken in the clown routine, which he continues to act out even after he loses his memory, as well as conceding that she had not succeeded in her own previously stated desire to 'hatch him out' as 'the New Man' (p. 281). Aidan Day argues that 'The relationship between Walser and Fevvers is based not on the principle of dominator and dominated but on the idea of love between equals.'[13] Perhaps Lorna Sage's contention that Fevvers is both 'Leda *and* the Swan' is more accurate,[14] which suggests the way in which individuals seek to give birth to themselves, to be their own forgers of knowledge and identity. (See also Chapter 8 for a discussion of how both Jeanette Winterson and A. S. Byatt construct similar situations where gender role hierarchies are reversed and ultimately called into question.)

Although any of these attempts to smoothly translate the myth – even in an inverted fashion – is likely to fall apart (a concept I will return to later), it is worth reading this novel's relation to this myth (and Yeats' poem) in terms of the key moments of danger for Fevvers, such as the closing scene of the novel's first section. In the scene with Rosencreutz, we witness a different kind of inversion. If we might typically view the long neck and beak of the swan as emphasizing the phallus, we can see that construction as divided apart and complicated in this scene. While Rosencreutz worships the phallus – his Rosicrucian cross has been literalized into a phallus with a rose wrapped around it – Fevvers possesses her own blade to defend against his. After his phallic spear leaves only a 'flesh wound' on her foot, her wings give her freedom, as she 'soared up and away from that vile place, over the maypole on the front lawn' (p. 83). Even in this description, we do not have a simple reversal. The Swan and Leda are taken apart, if you will, and reconfigured. Rosencreutz cannot be viewed as simply an ineffectual Swan, since Fevvers cannot be read as simply an empowered Leda.

In terms of considering Yeats' relationship with Carter's novel, one must explore the figure of Rosencreutz a bit further. As Brian Finney has pointed out, as a potential destroyer/violator of Fevvers, he is difficult to take seriously in part because even in the retelling Fevvers never really does so.[15] After deducing the significance of his rather unsubtle medallion, Fevvers concludes that 'This is some kind of heretical possibly Manichean version of neo-Platonic Rosicrucianism, thinks I to myself; tread carefully, Girlie!' (p. 77). Yeats himself, after being expelled from the Theosophists, joined an offshoot of the Rosicrucians, the Hermetic Students of the Golden Dawn, and its influence can be seen in his use of Rosicrucian symbolism. In and of itself, this may be a minor connection; however, the spiritualism that Yeats embraced certainly influenced his poetics. His essay 'Magic', for example, makes direct comparisons between the work of the Magician and the artist.[16] Richard Ellmann concludes that 'Magic offered to the symbolists, many of whom studied it, a reinforcement of their belief in the power of the word or symbol to evoke a reality otherwise inaccessible.'[17] Carter, the materialist, deliberately floods her novel with symbols in an exaggeration of these Symbolist techniques. Fevvers, most notably, is constantly made a symbol of something or described as resembling pre-existing figures – the New Woman, Winged Victory, Leda, Helen, Venus – and the novel is preoccupied with this process of reading the world through symbols, of seeing people as symbols and, as Carter suggests through Fevvers, ideas.

Lorna Sage has argued that Fevvers is in fact a 'symbol come to life as a character'.[18] To a certain extent, this may be a matter of perspective. In other words, who is telling the story, who is doing the 'gazing' seems to become integral to whether we read Fevvers as a character/human first or, as Sage suggests, a symbol who comes to transcend that status and escape those Sage aptly calls the 'symbol hunters' of the novel. As Walser seeks to categorize Fevvers early on and relate her to Leda and the Swan, he wonders 'who turned this girl into a piece of artifice, who had made her a marvelous machine and equipped her with her story?' (p. 29).[19] Sage reminds us that Yeats 'circles around [Fevvers] in some of his most urgently visionary moments' and in particular in ' "Sailing to Byzantium" and "Byzantium", where a golden bird symbolizes "the artifice of eternity" '.[20] Walser seems to perceive Fevvers as already constructed into an artifice, albeit a farting, belching, voracious and pungent one. However, what is fantasy for Yeats in 'Sailing to Byzantium' (1928) and 'the bird or golden handiwork' (line 17) which is 'in glory of changeless metal' (line 21) in 'Byzantium' (1933) is clearly a trap for Fevvers. I have already noted that the Rosicrucian tries to name her as symbol – he seems to run through names for her as if all he can do is perceive the world in terms of representation, but all fail in his attempt to name her precisely – like the formation of a Lacanian 'chain of signifiers': 'Welcome Azrael . . . Azrael, Azrail, Ashriel, Azriel, Azaril, Gabriel; dark angel of many names' (p. 75). Similarly, Sage notes that, in Fevvers' second significant encounter with danger, the Grand Duke almost succeeds in transforming her to a 'Yeatsian golden bird'.[21] For most of this episode with the Grand Duke, he, too, is nothing but a symbol, a figure written out of myths. Consider this description: 'the Grand Duke surveyed his clockwork orchestra with a satisfied air. A bored Emperor commissioned them long ago, in China' (p. 188). The Grand Duke's eggs resemble Yeats' 'artifices', aesthetic objects that transcended history, things that cannot fall apart. They are 'inward things' (p. 189) that seem to open up to more and more internal 'surprises' (p. 189). As Fevvers witnesses her own self in miniature and begins to feel 'less and less her own mistress', her salvation lies somewhat ironically in the Grand Duke becoming more human and less symbolic. First, 'she realized he was a man of quite exceptional strength', a strength to hold her but that of a 'man' nonetheless (p. 191). While she has lost her own 'sword' that saved her against the Rosicrucian, she turns the phallus against the Grand Duke as she, how shall we say, manipulates her way to freedom, exchanging his quite literal phallus for the modern mechanical, albeit still phallic, train, which provides her escape. Lizzie's comments upon her return mark the collapse of the elaborately symbolic and mechanical world of enchantment that almost imprisoned Fevvers once again: 'Look what a mess he's made of your dress, the pig' (p. 192). As Sage suggests in her reading of the novel, Fevvers again and again uses her 'knowledge' of the low to undermine the traps of the high, an ironic path considering her role as aerialiste.[22] In this moment, as in many throughout the novel, we see a resistance to the purely fantastic. The stains on Fevvers' dress suggest that what appeared to be a moment of the fantastic had real, physical and material consequences. While Fevvers may be a 'symbol come to life', that very life faces genuine, physical dangers.

At the end of each section of the novel, after facing one of these dangers, Fevvers is seemingly reborn or restored, a process that fascinated Modernists. Perhaps none of Yeats' poems demonstrates the Modernist interest in both apocalypse and mythic cycles of rebirth more than 'The Second Coming' (1921).[23] Here, Yeats draws heavily on mythic symbolism, which he alludes to as 'a vast image out of Spiritus Mundi' (line 12). In the world of the *Nights at the Circus*, this apocalyptic poem is connected with clowns, in particular, the undisputed king of the clowns, Buffo. We are told that 'Things fall apart at the very shiver of his tread on the ground' and that Buffo 'is himself the center that does not hold' (p. 117). Like Yeats' poem, which suggests that history is itself a series of cycles, Buffo, despite being the catalyst of chaos, notes that 'The beauty of clowning is, nothing ever changes' (p. 117). In fact, he performs a mock ritual of rebirth as a part of the 'Clown's Funeral' routine and is also compared to Jesus (p. 116). Carter's clowns satirically live out the cycle of violence, death and rebirth that Yeats observes in his poem.

The clowns take on an important role in relation to the novel's other Yeatsian themes. Buffo tells the story of all clowns, saying that 'this story is not precisely true but has the poetic truth of myth and so attaches itself to each and every laughmaker' (p. 121). In retelling this myth, he becomes complicit in its perpetuation. In this way and in the more obvious construction of his clown face, he is overshadowed by his symbolic mask. Buffo's story demonstrates the restrictive nature of donning masks, of letting a symbol replace the person.[24] However, he also points out the ironic power granted to the clown because they 'can invent [their] own faces! We *make* ourselves' (p. 121, emphasis in original). Buffo, despite being a drunkard and something of a homicidal maniac, does take this opportunity – Walser's introduction to life in clown alley – to elaborate on the paradox of these masks and identity in general: 'I have become the face that is not mine, and yet I chose it freely' (p. 122). Buffo's somewhat Lacanian musings do not entirely leaven the mood of Yeats' poem – despite his being a 'clown'. Perhaps most importantly, his discussion sheds light on Fevvers' own crisis, the temptation to give oneself over to the world of outer signs, of the comfort of identity – however limited – they offer, of the path into a place, even if it is mythic in nature, that allows for a kind of order, sense and meaning.

In the first section of the novel, we find a direct reference to Yeats' famous late poem, 'The Circus Animals' Desertion' (1939)[25] that puts the novel – and its 'menagerie' of circus animals and performers – into a more metaphoric context. Yeats' speaker in 'The Circus Animals' Desertion' decries his loss of power and proclaims himself 'a broken man' (line 3). This poem offers a retrospective not only on Yeats' career, but also on the poetics he developed throughout his lifetime. Yeats' attitude towards his own work and his methods fluctuates between ironic distance and pride. Noting that his 'circus animals were all on show' from 'winter and summer to old age began' (lines 5–6) suggests both his longevity as an artist and a somewhat surprising self-deprecating view of the poet as a kind of P. T. Barnum, who trots out symbols and myths to entertain and amuse the literati. Yeats' speaker notes that 'Players and painted stage took all of my love/And not those things they were emblems of' (lines 31–2). He appears to confess that 'those masterful images because complete' obscured, for him, the larger ideas and emotions that they were to represent (line 33). In terms of Carter's novel, Yeats' speaker apparently acknowledges that he fell in love with the masks while forsaking what they were meant to evoke.

Here, it is worth recalling how Yeats understood Symbolism. Yeats' introduction to this largely French poetic movement came from his fellow Rhymer's Club member Arthur Symons, who dedicated his 1899 book, *The Symbolist Movement in Literature*, to Yeats. In this text, Symons notes that Symbolism 'has now become conscious of itself' – a point that becomes very clear when one considers Yeats' work – and that within its 'literature' 'the visible world is no longer a reality, and the unseen world no longer a dream'.[26] Essentially, Symons argues that Symbolism is an attempt to move away from 'a materialistic tradition' or what Yeats called in 'The Symbolism of Poetry' the consequences of the 'scientific movement',[27] from art that seeks to document the world: for Symons, then, Symbolism 'is all an attempt to spiritualize literature, to evade the old bondage of rhetoric, the old bondage of exteriority. Description is banished that beautiful things may be evoked, magically; the regular beat of verse is broken in order that words may fly, upon subtler wings.'[28] In Yeats' own essay on Symbolism published within a year of Symons' book, he argues along the same lines and goes so far as to see such poetry as 'foreshadower of the new sacred book, of which all arts, as somebody has said, are begging to dream'.[29] Symbolism appears to fall in line with many of Yeats' interests in a kind of transcendence of the material – a process depicted as a struggle revealed in much of Yeats' own poetry.

Yeats' late poem, then, seems to suggest both the continuing power of these earlier ideas regarding Symbolism, and also how, to at least some extent, the means may have eclipsed the ends. Richard Ellmann says that, in this poem, Yeats 'calls all his characters together as if to say, here is the universe which I have created and peopled and made as real as anything in the world'.[30] However, Ellmann suggests that Yeats – like Buffo the clown – recognizes that humans cannot necessarily shed their masks or elude the masks they put on: 'Not only are the symbols like men, but conversely the men are like symbols or actors.'[31] He reads this poem as a kind of admission that 'Yeats does not escape his own symbols, but is caught up into them also'.[32] In his essay on 'Magic', Yeats suggests that 'all men, certainly all imaginative men, must be for ever casting forth enchantments, glamours, illusions',[33] and one can read his response to his 'circus animals' as an admission that he fell under his own spell. At the least, we see that Yeats has struggled with his desire to transcend the material throughout his entire poetic career, and this very struggle reveals a kind of acknowledgement of the difficulty of escaping from the material, as Carter's novel might be read as an acknowledgment of the difficulties of escaping the symbolic.

Since these 'circus animals' form the core of Yeats symbology, they would seem to stand largely in opposition to Carter's materialism. Nonetheless, one initial question to ask is if Carter's novel puts her own 'circus animals' on display. The novel does bring forth an almost overwhelming array of symbols, motifs and ideas, such as Leda and the Swan, and the various Gothic motifs and plotlines, many of which are familiar to the reader of Carter's work. While I would hesitate to say that Carter is fully reflecting back on her writing in the same manner as Yeats – and if she is, it is certainly with a great deal more irony – there is certainly a sense that this novel brings together many of Carter's central concerns as well as many of the techniques for representing those concerns that Carter had developed by this point in her career.

However, unlike Yeats, Carter brings circus animals directly to our attention as beings not always seen in relation to their creator/orchestrator. The novel does have its very own disciple of P. T. Barnum, Colonel Kearney, who relies heavily on the prescience of his pet pig to guide his choices. If he is an artist, it is of the most crass, capitalist sort. His red, white and blue uniforms reinforce the sense that he is a representative of emerging American Imperialism. He makes an odd figure to compare with Yeats – perhaps Yeats literalized as a low-brow, fairly selfish, entertainer.

Yet, what of the circus animals themselves? The novel features essentially four distinct groups of circus animals: the elephants, the tigers, Lamark's Educated Apes and arguably Fevvers herself. Yeats' title emphasizes the 'circus animals' desertion, of symbols taking on a life of their own and leaving their creator behind and powerless, a desertion that is clearly negative from the creator's perspective – another instance of things falling apart. However, in Carter's novel, the only 'circus animals' that desert of their own volition are Lamark's Educated Apes. When we first encounter these apes, they appear to be conducting a class run by their leader, who is known as the Professor. As Walser approaches, however, 'the lesson immediately stopped' and the apes quickly revert to slapstick as one of the pupils 'struck the Professor full in the face with a juicy ink-pellet' (p. 108). These Apes, then, resemble the clowns, locked into a perceived low, comedic position. However, the Apes shed the drunken Lamark, the Ape-Man, whose role appears to have been to give legitimacy to their routines. The gradual rise of the apes is not about desertion *per se*, but a desire to improve their lot; as the narrator notes, 'their dedication to self-improvement . . . was boundless' (p. 147). Towards the end of the St Petersburg section of the novel, after the wildly chaotic night that saw Buffo taken away to an institution and the death of a particularly jealous tiger, the Professor leads the only true desertion on the part of the 'circus animals', and they leave in a contract dispute based on a clause the Professor negotiated. Yeats' 'circus animals' here are both satirically elevated and lowered; they seek their own freedom – they want to be improved and no longer exploited – yet they are also tied up in the material world of contract negotiations.

While one would certainly hesitate to consider the fate of the elephants' desertion, they offer a poignant alternative to those ambitious apes. Here is the initial description of the elephants early in the St Petersburg section:

> The only sounds drifting from the menagerie, the continuous murmuring purr of the great cats, like a distant sea, and the faint jingling of Colonel Kearney's elephants of flesh and blood as they rattled the chains on their legs as they did continually, all their waking hours, since in their millennial and long lived patience they knew quite well how, in a hundred years, or a thousand years' time, or else, perhaps tomorrow, in an hour's time, for it was all a gamble,

a million to one chance, but all the same there *was* a chance that if they kept on shaking their chains, one day, some day, the clasps on the shackles would part. (p. 106)

In this characteristic duality of the novel, these elephants are 'flesh and blood'; they are real and not symbols or representations. However, they are also a kind of 'eternal' elephant – an eternal oppressed (and recalled in their symbolic connections to colonialism), who hopes for freedom through the smallest resistance, the smallest friction against the 'chains' that imprison. They lack the autonomy of the apes; outright desertion seems beyond them. Yet they are the largest and most powerful of the 'circus animals'. They seem to stand in for any number of repressed groups, such as the women held in check by the exploitive male figure of Colonel Kearney, for example. Their fate, too, gets bound up in the dreams of others, for they are the central figures in the Colonel's fantasy to 'best' Hannibal (p. 201). As the train makes its way across Siberia, however, the elephants are 'weakening, succumbing' (p. 201). When their train wrecks, somewhat ironically, at the hands of the 'brotherhood of free men', both the tigers and the elephants are released from capture. However, neither can 'desert' or escape their situation. As Fevvers observes, the elephants reach 'the moment of destiny, when indeed their chains all parted and they were free! Yet free for what? They achieve their longed-for liberty at just the moment when it won't do them any good!' (p. 207). Fevvers views this incident as 'a lesson to us all' (p. 207), as she might also view the fate of the tigers, who 'had frozen into their own reflections and been shattered, too, when the mirrors broke' (p. 206). The death of the final elephant, however, coincides with the approach of the female prisoners who have escaped the panopticon – a prison of the gaze as well – and who will 'need no more fathers' (p. 221).

The fates of the elephants and the apes in particular lead to a consideration of how Fevvers might be placed in relation to these other 'circus animals'. The novel's overt allusion to Yeats' poem appears during Fevver's recounting of her time at the brothel of Madame Schreck, which 'catered for those who were troubled in their... souls' (p. 57) and offers some insight into how Fevvers' story relates to those of the other circus animals. Fevvers describes a place for 'dispossessed creatures, for whom there was no earthly use, in this lumber room of femininity, this rag and bone shop of the heart' (p. 69). Here, we see Yeats' language (a passage that includes 'the raving slut at the till') appropriated by Fevvers. Linda Hutcheon reads this allusion as an 'ironic feminization...of traditional or canonic male representations of the so-called generic human – "Man" '.[34] This passage is not about the poet relinquishing some of his dreams of transcendence and enlightenment ('now that my ladder's gone'). Instead, the perspective has shifted; these figures have not deserted, but have instead been deserted by the larger community, dispossessed, as Fevvers says.

Throughout *Nights at the Circus*, Carter uses the autobiography of the be-winged Fevvers as part of an allegory about women's aspirations to soar over the nets and restraints of a strongly patriarchal world, a world illustrated by Yeats and his 'circus animals'. The novel, then, charts her growing ability to step away from controlling systems while exposing the complexity of these systems (for instance, while the gaze of the audience imprisons Fevvers, it also feeds her sense of her own reality and importance; to step outside this gaze means reconfiguring and examining how one forms one's sense of self). As Carter imagines the path towards emancipation for her magical heroine, she confronts and rewrites the myths of Yeats, which symbolize illusionary stability that ultimately seeks to restrain and imprison. While looking at Leda and the Swan tempts readers to invert and deconstruct Yeatsian mythology, just as much is at stake by looking at another Yeats connection: how things fall apart. On the one hand, Carter seems to say that things, at their most basic, cannot fall apart in the Yeatsian sense (and always do), because material and material conditions do not simply disappear. Systems of oppression, however, must be made to disappear, but they will not do that on their own. The diverse fates of the colonial symbols, the apes and elephants, emphasize this dilemma. After the loss of Buffo, the literal centre that could not hold, the clowns themselves fall apart: 'and [of] the clowns themselves, not one sight, as if all together had been blown off the face of the earth' (p. 243). The chaotic dance that the clowns conduct which leads to this 'fantastic' disappearance recalls the various debilitating processes of mythologizing:

They danced the whirling apart of everything, the end of love, the end of hope; they danced tomorrows into yesterdays; they danced the exhaustion of the implacable present; they danced the deadly dance of the past perfect which fixes everything fast so it can't move again; they danced the dance of Old Adam who destroys the world because we believe he lives forever. (p. 243)

From these sequences, then, we can conclude that materializing concepts is for Carter a step in dismantling oppressive mythologies and the systems that result from them in the material world. At the end of the novel, we have no definitive answers to whether Fevvers will avoid ultimately falling into the traps laid out by symbols and the roles patriarchy ascribes. The problem of how Fevvers can reconcile what Lizzie calls the 'custom' of the 'happy ending' (p. 281), namely marriage, remains uncertain even as we witness Fevvers and Walser together in bed – or on a straw mat – at the end of the novel. We know that Fevvers has no navel, but we might, like Walser, hesitate in reaching 'any definite conclusions from that fact' (p. 292). When Lizzie and Fevvers argue over the path the plot of Fevvers' life – and the novel for that matter – appears to be headed, Fevvers defends her choice to seek out Walser by saying that she intends to transform Walser into the New Man. Like Lizzie, most readers can only mutter, 'Perhaps so, perhaps not' (p. 281). Therefore, we are left feeling that the ending of the novel cannot be read as purely Utopian.[35] Even the very end of the novel, with the wonderfully infectious laughter emanating from Fevvers – that 'spiraling tornado' that spreads itself across Siberia – leaves us wondering whether Walser and Fevvers are simply acting out one of the comedic plots Lizzie warned her about.

I began this chapter with a discussion of 'Notes from the Frontline', an essay in which Carter had the task of explaining 'how feminism has affected my work'.[36] In that essay, she talks of how the 'sense of limitless freedom that I, as a woman, sometimes feel *is* that of a new kind of being'.[37] Such phrases lead us to consider that this novel, *Nights at the Circus*, written quite close in time to this essay, contains a character very much modelled upon Carter, as it features a kind of artist who also was very much a 'new kind of being'.[38] In 'Notes from the Frontline', Carter says that she feels herself more and more sharing the mission of 'certain Third World Writers', those 'who are transforming actual fiction forms to both reflect and to precipitate changes in the way people feel about themselves – putting new wine in old bottles, and in some cases, old wine in new bottles'.[39] We can view Yeatsian symbolism as part of the pattern of old bottles surely – or what Carter calls elsewhere in that essay 'the vast repository of outmoded lies'[40] – and Yeats himself as one of the figures and artists from which Carter tried to see herself as throwing off, as an 'egomaniac' and controlling presence. Indeed, Carter surely reinforced her observations from that essay – namely, that 'language is power, life and the instrument of culture, the instrument of domination and liberation'.[41] However, when asked to consider the way in which Carter herself had been 'affected' by 'feminism' she says, 'I don't know'.[42] So we, too, find ourselves asking, has Fevvers managed to fly above the nets of patriarchy and emerge the new woman? Has Carter managed to expose the dangers of Yeats' symbols and liberate those imprisoned by them? 'Perhaps so, perhaps not'.

Notes

1. Angela Carter, *Nights at the Circus* (New York: Penguin, 1984). Page references to the novel will appear in the text.
2. Angela Carter, 'Notes from the Frontline', in Jenny Uglow (ed.) *Angela Carter: Shaking a Leg. Journalism and Writings* (New York: Penguin, 1997), p. 38.
3. Ibid.
4. Ibid.
5. Ibid., p. 41.
6. In *The Gaity of Language: An Essay on the Radical Poetics of W. B. Yeats and Wallace Stevens* (Berkeley, CA: University of California Press, 1968), Frank Lentricchia suggests Yeats believed that 'Anything that the mind conjured up was real; nothing existed outside our perception of it' (p. 80).
7. See Adam Mars-Jones, 'From Wonders to Prodigies', *Times Literary Supplement*, 28 September 1984, p. 1083.
8. This allusion is largely in passing in what is Jordan's defence of Carter in 'The Dangers of Angela Carter', in Lindsey Tucker (ed.) *Critical Essays on Angela Carter* (New York: G. K. Hall & Co., 1998), p. 42.
9. Angela Carter, *The Magic Toyshop* (New York: Penguin, 1967).
10. W. B. Yeats, 'Leda and the Swan', in M. L. Rosenthal (ed.) *Selected Poems and Three Plays of William Butler Yeats* (New York: Collier Books, 1986), p. 121.
11. Jean Wyatt, 'The Violence of Gendering: Castration Images in Angela Carter's *The Magic Toyshop, The Passion of New Eve*, and "Peter and the Wolf" ', in Alison Easton (ed.) *Angela Carter* (New York: St Martin's Press, 2000), p. 68.
12. For one such argument, see 'The Ravished Reader: Angela Carter's Allegory in *Nights at the Circus*' by Marita Kristiansen (Department of English, University of Bergen, 2000), http://www.ub.uib.no/elpub/2000/h/501001/.
13. Aidan Day, *Angela Carter: The Rational Glass* (Manchester: Manchester University Press, 1998), p. 192.
14. Lorna Sage, *Angela Carter* (Plymouth: Northcote House, 1994), p. 47.
15. See Brian Finney, 'Tall Tales and Brief Lives: Angela Carter's *Nights at the Circus*' (1998), http://www.csulb.edu/~bhfinney/AngelaCarter.html.
16. W. B. Yeats, 'Magic', *Ideas of Good and Evil* (New York: Russell & Russell, 1903), pp. 29–69.
17. Richard Ellman, *Yeats: The Man and the Masks* (New York: E. P. Dutton & Co., Inc., 1948), p. 88.
18. Sage, *Angela Carter*, p. 48.
19. In *Angela Carter: Writing from the Front Line* (Edinburgh: Edinburgh University Press, 1997), Sarah Gamble reminds us that Walser's goal of categorizing

Fevvers 'is incapable of resolution if one can't distinguish between fact and fiction in the first place' (p. 162).

20. Sage, *Angela Carter*, p. 47. W. B. Yeats, 'Byzantium' and 'Sailing to Byzantium', in M. L. Rosenthal (ed.) *Selected Poems and Three Plays of William Butler Yeats* (New York: Collier Books, 1986), pp. 102–3, 138–40.

21. Sage, *Angela Carter*, p. 48.

22. Along these same lines, Gamble notes that 'Fevvers is a wonderful amalgam of the transcendent and the earthly' (*Angela Carter: Writing from the Front Line*, p. 159).

23. W. B. Yeats, 'The Second Coming', in M. L. Rosenthal (ed.) *Selected Poems and Three Plays of William Butler Yeats* (New York: Collier Books, 1986), pp. 89–90.

24. Gamble points out that 'Fevvers is concerned [that] the clowns are her dark mirror image for there is always the risk that she may share their complete submersion in performance' (*Angela Carter: Writing from the Front Line*, p. 164).

25. W. B. Yeats, 'The Circus Animals' Desertion', in M. L. Rosenthal (ed.) *Selected Poems and Three Plays of William Butler Yeats* (New York: Collier Books, 1986), pp. 198–9.

26. Arthur Symons, *The Symbolist Movement in Literature* (New York: E. P. Dutton & Co., 1908), pp. 3–4.

27. W. B. Yeats, 'The Symbolism of Poetry', *Ideas of Good and Evil* (New York: Russell & Russell, 1903), p. 240.

28. Symons, *The Symbolist Movement in Literature*, p. 8.

29. W. B. Yeats, 'The Symbolism of Poetry', p. 253.

30. Ellman, *Yeats*, p. 280.

31. Ibid., p. 281.

32. Ibid.

33. Quoted in Ellman, *Yeats*, p. 90.

34. Linda Hutcheon, *The Politics of Postmodernism* (London: Routledge, 1989), p. 98.

35. Readers of Carter's novel have tended to fall into two camps, those who see the novel as utopian in nature and those who feel that Carter suggests that the issues of the novel are too complicated to be resolved easily by the novel's conclusion. My discussion clearly falls into the latter camp. In 'Revamping Spectacle: Angela Carter's *Nights at the Circus*', Mary Russo (in Alison Easton [ed.] *Angela Carter* [New York: St Martin's Press, 2000], pp. 136–60) uses this exchange between Lizzie and Fevvers to extensively argue for the latter position. Gamble takes a similar position and notes that 'Fevvers . . . is inherently contradictory' (*Angela Carter: Writing from the Front Line*, p. 162).

36. Carter, 'Notes from the Frontline', p. 43.

37. Ibid., p. 40.

38. In this same essay, Carter comments on how 'the women's movement tends to overlook' the kind of performing artist that Fevvers represents (p. 40).

39. Carter, 'Notes from the Frontline', p. 42.

40. Ibid., p. 41.

41. Ibid., p. 43.

42. Ibid.

8
Passion and Possession as Alternatives to 'Cosmic Masculinity' in 'Herstorical Romances'

Georges Letissier

In both *The Passion* and *Possession*,[1] two women novelists set out to venture into a past that has been extensively covered by institutional historiography, often by male academics. However, the titles of both novels do not really call to mind either the manly Napoleonic wars or the patriarchal Victorian Age, which has more recently come in for radical re-vision in Sarah Waters' novels (see Chapter 14). So, right from the paratext, it would seem that the punning metaphors conveyed by both the terms *Passion* and *Possession* open the way for a personal return to a past that might be called into question. Indeed, in the epigraph to her third novel *Sexing the Cherry*, Winterson, alluding to the Hopi Indian tribe, points out that '[they] have a language as sophisticated as ours, but no tenses for past, present and future',[2] and in *The Passion*, she has one of the two narrators state that 'All time is eternally present and so all time is ours' (*TP*, p. 62). Byatt, for her part, in her own *Passions of the Mind* explains that in *Possession* she meant to 'find a narrative shape which would explore the continuities and discontinuities between the forms of nineteenth- and twentieth-century art and thought'.[3] So, paradoxically, here are two women writers who immerse themselves unreservedly in history, while suggesting that time should not be envisaged as linear, as prospective unfolding and teleology. Rather than pointing to any temporal succession, like *War and Peace* or *Remembrance of Things Past*, both *Possession* and *Passion* express forcefully a notion of intensity belonging to the Here and Now; to quote Winterson, they are superconductors: 'Passion, delirium, meditation, even out-of-body, are words we use to describe the heightened condition of superconductivity'.[4]

My concern in this chapter is to show how Winterson and Byatt, alongside other women writers such as Roberts and Waters whose works are analysed in this book, invite their readers to reconsider their relation to time by foregrounding emotion and the affects of the heart, at the expense of the pure intellect. The two novels under discussion demonstrate that subjectivity is no longer suspected of being a potential pitfall in the writers' attempt to make sense of the past. If the common denominator between possession and passion is the conflation of the active and the passive, suggesting that the subject is as much acted on by history as she/he acts upon it, one should be wary, however, of not assimilating the two novelists. They relate to the past in different ways. For Winterson, revisiting *his*tory is a direct experience in writing, in which desires and the body are central, in so far as only 'through the flesh we are set free' (*TP*, p. 154). Byatt's approach, on the other hand, is probably at once more mental and more formal, as she resorts to a tradition of history-writing to rehabilitate the corporeal element as a mediating agent between past and present. By referring insistently to Michelet, the French historian, she introduces a sensual, quasi-physiological relation to history, occasionally verging on necrophilia. As Hilary Schor observes,

the form of writing she [Byatt] invokes is ghostwriting, which she reads in a double sense: first, that of the 'borrowings' ('writing like . . . ') that seem to approach the postmodern forms of pastiche, and second, a ghostwriting that is speaking with the dead, not so much as writers but as moldering bodies, decaying forms.[5]

In his attempt to revive the past, Randolph Henry Ash, the Victorian poet, lends his voice to the literary forebears who literally possess his thoughts. As for Roland Mitchell and Maud Bailey, the two contemporary scholars, they show an unwonted concern for the haunting presence of Victorian objects.

The Passion and *Possession* are two fictions exhibiting their historical contents, and yet, they are markedly different from the paradigm of the historical novel studied by Lukács.[6] If, on the surface, some similarities can be noticed, such as the inclusion of real historical figures – Bonaparte in *The Passion* and a host of Victorian celebrities in *Possession* – differences soon transpire. In Winterson's novel, dates are mentioned and provide a sort of narrative frame, ranging from 20 July, with Napoleon's attempt to invade England from Boulogne, to the Emperor's death on the island of Saint Helena, some twenty years later. Yet, it would seem that historical chronology is peripheral more than it is intrinsic to the novel's structure because, as Falcus and Llewellyn also show in their essays, traditional historiography imposes an arbitrary structure, artificially creating a time, instead of merely recording it. What is immediately perceptible is a network of thematic oppositions that are not meant to be dialectically overcome through any Hegelian progress towards a final resolution. For example, the first part, entitled 'The Emperor', highlights a masculine, predatory thirst for power that is fated never to be quenched as 'there's no such thing as a limited victory' (*TP*, p. 133); and the third part, 'The Zero Winter', snidely underscores the tyrant's will to cut reality down to arithmetics and geometric order: 'When Bonaparte goes, straight roads follow, buildings are rationalised' (*TP*, p. 112). However, by choosing to close her Napoleonic novel in an open-ended way, by featuring Venice, a 'mercurial city' (*TP*, p. 49) or 'a city of madmen' (*TP*, p. 112), the novelist signifies clearly her intention not to get her story tailored to fit the requirements of the historical novel by precluding any sense of finality.

For all its circumstantial details about the Victorian age, *Possession* does not match the format of the historical novel either. Indeed, it aims less at achieving historical faithfulness than at questioning cliché-ridden views, and at rescuing all the complexities of an epoch, which according to Byatt had been unfairly belittled through diminishing parodies. The literary quest central to the plot illustrates the hermeneutic process at work in any attempt to come to grips with the past. The female literary tradition is of course high on Byatt's agenda since it is of paramount importance to reconsider the Victorian Age from a new angle (see Chapter 14 on how Waters' novels are, similarly, engagements with other literary works). Paradoxically, the era that was emblemized by a female icon, in turn Queen and Empress, was to confirm the position of women as 'Angels of the House'. As a matter of fact, Victoria may be seen as the passive object of a system of representation that only comforted patriarchal domination: 'Victoria was seen at once to symbolize and to embody a mythology of private experience . . . even as she was held, and held herself, to the exacting standards of impersonality'.[7] *Possession* provides several instances of woman's subordination, from the self-effacing spouse of the famous poet Randolph Henry Ash, or the marginalized Blanche Glover, to the self-ostracized Christabel LaMotte, ending her life like 'a Witch in a Turret' (*P*, p. 451) or a Madwoman in the Attic, in some remote corner of rural England. Threatened to be erased from the text and written out of history, the plight of these female figures is epitomized by the precarious, liminal condition of the Cumean Sybil:

Who are you?
Here on a high shelf
In webbed flask I
Hook up my folded self
Bat-leather dry. (*P*, p. 54, emphasis in original)

This marginal positioning is in sharp contrast with the centripetal approach to history-writing of such eminent Victorians as Froude or Carlyle, whom Byatt quotes in passing. In *Possession*, fictional characters like Isidore LaMotte, with his *Key to All Mythologies*, and of course Ash, with his poetry propounding a comprehensive, all-encompassing vision of the past, are illustrations of this 'cosmic masculinity' (*P*, p. 42) that is both monolithic and homogenizing. In *The Politics of Postmodernism*, Linda Hutcheon argues that postmodernist historical narratives (historiographic metafictions) value personal or life narratives: journals, confessions, biographies and self-portraits.[8] So *her*story, in opposition to what Maud Bailey dismisses as 'cosmic masculinity' in *Possession*, substitutes the particularity of plural histories for the universality of enlightened historiography. The supposedly objective historical studies, flaunting their scientific pretensions, are short-circuited by dissident voices from the margin, and to quote Elaine Showalter: 'We realize that the land promised to us is not the serenely undifferentiated universality of texts but the tumultuous and intriguing wildness of difference itself.'[9]

The Passion and *Possession* do not offer any smoothed out, unified representation of the past, but rather differing perspectives. History is filtered through private, individualized consciousnesses. By introducing two narrative voices, that of Henri, the French soldier, and then of Villanelle, the Venice-born *vivandière*, Winterson's fiction presents a relativistic approach, preventing the possibility of any definitive truth. Henri himself signals, metafictionally as it were, what differentiates his own version of events from Villanelle's: 'She was all primary colour . . . she was not equivocal in her thinking' (*TP*, p. 109). As a gambler, Villanelle is fascinated by the sheer intensity of the present, whereas Henri is constantly preoccupied by what is to come next (*TP*, p. 23). Thus each character's relation to time has its idiosyncrasies; one is diachronic and reflects the *post hoc ergo propter hoc* stance, whereas the other favours synchronicity and the *hic et nunc*. *Possession*'s narrative technique emphasizes the individualized viewpoints to the detriment of generalized, universal ideas. It consists in gradually bringing to the fore a perspective that had been either obfuscated or plainly obliterated and, as a result, in reaching the past through untrodden paths. Byatt's novel provides many instances of mislaid documents which, once they have been retrieved, shed a different light on facts and contribute to filling in the silences of history. Blanche Glover's letter to Ellen Ash, for example, a concealed and long-forgotten piece of correspondence between the estranged lover and the deserted wife, provides in a minor key an alternative version of the events of the past (*P*, p. 233). So, Byatt and Winterson both imply that side by side with the well-known explanations of mainstream history, there is room for re-vision, and thus advocate a centrifugal conception of history, allowing different angles to coexist.

In her essay on 'Women's Time', Julia Kristeva insists on the predominance of space over time in women's experience of the real: 'When evoking the name and destiny of women, one thinks more of the space generating and forming the human species than of time, becoming or history.'[10] In both *The Passion* and *Possession*, the linear, teleological representation of time is counterbalanced by an emphasis on space as the site of the novel's tensions and oppositions. Thus, even if *The Passion* is less daring than *Sexing the Cherry* in its attempt to spatialize time, it nonetheless manages to highlight the peripatetic dynamism inherent in storytelling. Temporal shifts are somehow eclipsed by geographic itinerancy, and a sense of nomadic displacement, in order to offer an updated version of the picaresque. By showing in turn an unspecified country area in France, then Boulogne and Paris with the Tuileries, and by subsequently embarking on peregrinations across vast expanses of Eastern Europe, with constantly shifting borders, before ending up on the labyrinthine canals of Venice, itself a tiered city ('I . . . discovered the city within the city that is the knowledge of a few' [*TP*, p. 53]), Winterson's fiction plays on the *mapping* of fictional events. Besides, the sense of textual spatialization is further reinforced by the mobility and instability of signifiers. For instance, Domino, the flash rider, proleptically points to the double-speed dominoes of the Casino in a tale that capitalizes on the breakneck speed of the diegesis. A play between ontological levels is thus subtly orchestrated. The narrative is not so much built on linear temporal destiny, or Providence, as it is open to a free play of seemingly random associations. From the very beginning, the priest's Bible is hollow, with a pack of cards inside (*TP*, p. 12), and between the Queen of Spades (a wild card) and the Queen of Heaven (the Virgin Mary) Winterson's fiction follows the chance moves of characters on a wide geographic scale. The passing of time is decided by a throw of the dice, with all the passion that goes with gambling: 'Dicing from one year to the next with the things you love, what you risk reveals what you value' (*TP*, p. 43).

Any notion of a progressive arrow of time is equally absent from *Possession*, and several critics, like André Brink, have repeatedly emphasized that 'chronology, historicity is not only suspended but inverted, and Ash and LaMotte [the Victorian poets] are determined as much by their successors [Maud Bailey and Roland Michell] as vice versa'.[11] Whereas the game metaphor is seminal in *The Passion*, in *Possession* mirroring effects bring in patterns of reversals that are conducive to a spatialization of time.

The choice of narrative strategies to render the past is instrumental in deconstructing pseudoscientific historiography. As a cognitive discipline, history posits the neutrality and transparency of the enunciator, as if a series of concatenated events needed no mediation whatsoever to be recorded. This illusion of the possibility of an objectified history, in which facts could be arranged of their own accord, in a way, without any external 'emplotment' (Hayden White),[12] and by means of a transitive language, was defended by the upholders of scientific historiography. *The Passion* and *Possession* both underline, through their enunciative process, the constructedness of the past: the first by inscribing the biological and the organic within the fiction, the second through textual polymorphy; the layering of fictional levels, which Byatt also refers to as laminations.[13]

Winterson's novel bears witness to the presence, within the symbolic, of these semiotic pulsions which Kristeva associates with the *chora*: 'the *chora* precedes and underlies figuration and thus specularization, and is analogous only to vocal or kinetic rhythm ... this receptacle or *chora* [is] nourishing and maternal, not yet unified in an ordered whole'.[14] The tempo of *The Passion* defies the logical rules of a progressive, rational demonstration by allowing manifestations of a bodily presence to surface. The text seems to betray physical symptoms of a pulsating or breathing life. Not only do medium-sized sentences constantly alternate with brief clauses (often a pronoun and a verb), but aphoristic statements keep recurring at unpredictable intervals: 'I'm telling you stories. Trust me' (*TP*, p. 5, p. 13). Variations on a given expression are also to be found: 'It's somewhere between fear and sex. Passion. I suppose' (*TP*, p. 55). The name Villanelle itself, given to one of the two narrators, explicitly points to this play on fixed forms, through a polyphonic construction. And the same statements are disseminated throughout the fiction, regardless of the narrators. The accumulation of these verbal effects (repetition, circularity) contributes to undermining the linear time of language 'considered as the enunciation of sentences (noun + verb; topic–comment; beginning–ending)',[15] to open out onto other temporal modalities such as the cyclical of biological rhythm or Nietzsche's monumental time, that is 'all-encompassing and infinite like imaginary space'.[16] Significantly enough, in the last part of the book, Henri alone in his cell at the madhouse on the island of San Servolo hears, and lives with, the voices of his former war-comrades, and so unwittingly retells fragments of the former narrative.

In *Possession* too, it is the return into the present of the voices of the dead that evokes time reversibility. Byatt indulges in ghostwriting through the extensive use of pastiche. The séance is obviously one way of short-circuiting the arrow of time. In a way, the novelist is a medium who ventriloquizes poems that are akin to their Victorian hypotexts. Ash's lines, for instance, are strongly reminiscent of Browning's dramatic monologues, which through prosopopœia themselves revived the speeches of notorious historical figures. The whole fiction then is a vast echo chamber, where all the various discourses, in their different guises, ultimately all refer to what Byatt, quoting Podmore, calls 'that protoplasm of human speech' (*P*, p. 393), a sort of linguistic equivalent for Lydgate's primary tissue in Eliot's *Middlemarch*. The many tales in *Possession* are said to stem from a common matrix, so that the embedded fairy narratives do not so much propel the plot forward as they provide modulations on the main themes in a minor key: chiefly, the initiatory quest in 'The Threshold' (*P*, pp. 150–6) or death and resurrection in 'The Glass Coffin' (*P*, pp. 58–67). As Sabine de Kercoz, LaMotte's French cousin, is keen to stress, tales are expansions and improvisations from a common framework, and consequently, do not significantly alter the original story:

My father told the tale of Merlin and Vivien. The two characters are never the same in successive years . . . The end is always the same. So is the essence of the tale . . . But my father, within this framework, has many stories. (*P*, p. 353)

Tales are not progressive, but digressive or derivative. So, by inserting legends and myths, Byatt means to inscribe the corporeal within the text so as to initiate a relation to the past, eschewing the strictures of linear history or cursive time: 'Myths, like *organic* life, are shape-shifters, metamorphic, endlessly reconstituted and reformed.'[17]

Folklore and the supernatural are also central to Winterson's rewriting of history. History is mythologized and almost all the characters can be read through the grid of the fairy tale. Bonaparte features as the ogre, Henri as the young peasant tested through a succession of ordeals and Villanelle is known for her metamorphoses. Like Melusina in *Possession*, she is androgynous, and her webbed feet, invested with magic power, call to mind the fairy's muscular tail. Even the lesser characters are endowed with fairy-tale attributes, for instance Patrick, the de-frocked Irish priest has an eagle eye (*TP*, p. 15). Yet, the demarcation line between the realm of magic and the mimesis of the real is not as visible in Winterson's fiction as it is in *Possession*. Byatt plays on the juxtaposition of different genres, whereas Winterson deconstructs forms of representation of the real, by playing on the fluidity between realistic elements and the irrational. In *The Passion* the supernatural never provides any escape from the hard, tangible facts of history ('Bonaparte the Corsican. Born in 1769' [*TP*, p. 12]) but is there as a reminder that what happens is one possibility that is actualized among many others: 'every mapped-out journey contains another journey in its lines'.[18] Conversely, Winterson also suggests that even the most objective historical facts may encounter the irrational at unexpected turns, as when George III – the notorious mad King George – addressed the members of the Upper Chamber as 'My Lords and peacocks' (*TP*, p. 142).

Another way of challenging historiography's authority is to shift the place generally attributed to woman in the Western philosophical tradition. In *Spéculum de l'autre femme*, Luce Irigaray argues that from Plato to Freud, femininity has always been conceived of as an absence, or as a negation of the male, and in a chapter devoted to Irigaray, Toril Moi coined the portmanteau term *specul(ariz)ation*, a combination of speculation and specular (mirror reflection), to claim that the tradition of Western philosophical thinking has produced a narcissistic image of masculinity, making femininity the blindspot.[19] Patriarchal discourse thus situates woman outside representation. Woman is, according to Freud's well-known remark, the 'dark continent' and can only attain to a degree of ontological existence as man's specularized Other. In *The Passion* and *Possession*, it could be asserted that mirror games come as a response to specul(ariz)ation.

Byatt introduces the mirror theme to destabilize its symbolic value. First, the allusion to the Lady of Shalott confirms Irigaray's theory. Christabel LaMotte identifies with the famous Lady of Astolat who, cursed to weave her tapestry from what she sees refracted in her mirror,

is both forbidden any direct access to the outside world and condemned
to invisibility:

> *Think of me if you will as the Lady of*
> *Shalott . . . who chooses not the Gulp of outside Air and the*
> *chilly river-journey deathwards – but who chooses to watch*
> *diligently the bright colours of her Web – to ply an*
> *industrious shuttle – to make-something – to close the*
> *Shutters and the Peephole too . . . (P,* p. 187, emphasis in
> original)

Yet, her initial declaration proves to be a boast, as she too breaks the
spell, by committing herself in an adulterous affair which is disclosed,
more than a century later, through the novel. Furthermore, far from
being a byword for woman's negation, the looking glass is also used in
the fiction to boldly assert woman's presence, at least on two occasions.
When Maud Bailey, the contemporary lecturer, sees her image reflected
in her mirror, she starts speculating in an existentialist way on the
definition of woman's identity:

> She slipped on her nightdress . . . and considered her perfectly regular
> features in the mirror. A beautiful woman, Simone Weil said, seeing
> herself in the mirror, knows 'This is I'. An ugly woman knows, with
> equal certainty, 'This is not I'. Maud knew this neat division repres-
> ented an over-simplification. (*P,* p. 57)

Later on, the story seems to turn the specul(ariza)tion concept upside
down, by condemning Roland Michell, the *male* protagonist, to a condition of invisibility. This happens when his own reflection is partly erased
by his mental projection of the image of the woman he is falling in love
with: 'There was a gilt mirror over the washbasin in which he imagined
Maud examining her perfection; *his own furry darkness was only a shadow
on it'* (*P,* pp. 148–9, emphasis mine). Winterson, for her part, goes even
further in this parodic reversal of the specular motif by making of Henri,
in his San Servolo cell, at the end, a sort of transgendered reincarnation
of the Lady of Shalott: 'I have a mirror and I stand slightly to one side
of the window when she passes and if the sun is shining I can catch the
reflection of her hair' (*TP,* p. 52).

In both *The Passion* and *Possession,* a reflection on the *aporia,* or contradictions, linked to the experience of time, is at the heart of fiction
writing. Although the text is shown to be the guardian of time, time

remains the central enigma. The relation between the story's time and the time of writing is riddling and problematic. In Winterson's novel, Henri jots down notes in diaries for fear of forgetting something. Yet, it is clearly mentioned on several occasions that he is writing the final version, years later with the benefit of hindsight, from his San Servolo's cell. The fiction is therefore the result of a double writing process that can never really coincide with what actually happened. Time does not provide any firm grounding since, anyway, there is no such thing as an absolute calendar. Villanelle reminds the reader that the Venetians had their own system for measuring time, and 'began the days at night' (*TP*, p. 56). Time, therefore, is an undefined zone of instability where memory can have free play. Between Henri's notebooks and the memoirs he is subsequently writing there is the possibility of memory tricks. And, as Domino remarks, one version of the past is no truer than the other: 'The way you see it now is no more real than the way you'll see it then' (*TP*, p. 28). For Villanelle who, incidentally, is never described as writing, time is sheer immediacy and instantaneousness. It is broad daylight as opposed to night-time. Indeed, night is a muted, toned down version of day (*TP*, pp. 57–8). All the intensity of existence lies in the present which, on top of being at the crossroads between past and future, offers the possibility of dreaming and, therefore, of unfolding life as a fan, to think up any number of alternative scripts: 'Perhaps our lives spread out around us like a fan and we can only know one life, but by mistake sense others' (*TP*, p. 144).

Possession tackles the *aporia* of time from another angle. Right from the epigraph, which Byatt borrows from Hawthorne's preface to *The House of the Seven Gables*, it is unambiguously asserted that the fiction, which is advertised as a romance, is the privileged locus to fashion time or be shaped by it: 'The point of view in which this tale comes under the Romantic definition lies in the attempt to connect a bygone time with the very present that is flitting away from us' (*P*, Epigraph). Yet, paradoxically, concerned as it is with the role of temporality, *Possession* cannot help alluding to ways of reaching beyond time, through the evocation of the origins, the absolute alpha, or the opposite, the end. The fascinated quest for the beginnings takes on different forms, from the allusions to the cosmogony in the Nordic Eddas, through Ash's rewriting of *Ragnarök* (*P*, pp. 239–42), to LaMotte's pert and perky egg riddle (*P*, p. 137). In either case, what is illustrated is the possibility of escaping the confining boundaries of time. LaMotte's metaphoric description of the egg in particular conjures up a snug haven, shut off from the demands of temporal life. It is an abode, beyond the reach of time, where woman can devote herself fully to her artistic creation, without having to be preoccupied with motherhood (*P*, p. 137). The ending is, for its part, called up through references to eschatology and, in particular, to the final deflagration in *Ragnarök*. However, more interestingly, it is also the subject of an insect poem by Ash. In it, the reader's urge to reach the story's denouement is compared to the mating instinct of the male wasp. After consummation there is no reprieve and death inevitably follows. Likewise *finis*, the End, signals that the pleasure of the text, to quote Roland Barthes,[20] is to be brought to a close, since any re-reading is liable to lose the initial excitement of the first discovery.

Having demonstrated how *The Passion* and *Possession* substitute a poetics of temporality for chronological time, while nonetheless purporting to treat of the historical past, one question still has to be raised. What do the concepts of passion and possession contribute to a definition of *herstorical* romance?

Possession and passion are two ways of relating to the past, emphasizing emotions, impulses and affects; in short, all that historiography, as a field of study, rejects as obstacles in any attempt to establish objective, reliable knowledge. Cognitive processes are premised on the necessity to dismiss as misleading what is provided by sense perception or may be suspected of irrationality. According to Derrida, Western thought is erroneously based on the notion of an originary 'logos', a concept taken from the Greek, which the French philosopher glosses as truth, reason, meaning, thought and speech. Since intellectual pursuits have historically been a masculine prerogative, Derrida coined the term 'phallogocentrism' to underscore the indissociable link between phallus and logos.[21] By giving the names of passion and possession respectively to two fictions exploring the past, Winterson and Byatt claimed that some degree of historical truth may be achieved without necessarily resorting exclusively to reason and the intellect.

There is no doubt that even though Winterson is writing a book about early nineteenth-century Europe, she means to distinguish her work from a certain official, serious historiography. When Henri strongly disapproves of the fact that 'Nowadays people talk about the things he [Napoleon] did as though they made sense' (*TP*, p. 5) he is clearly taking to task some historians who impose rational frames on the flux of life and are eager to control and subjugate passion. Such scholars endeavour, at all costs, to come up with logical explanations to account for even the most aberrant facts of the past. Explaining away Napoleon's quirks, and the disasters to which they ultimately led, through notions such as 'hubris' (*TP*, p. 5) or nemesis, boils down to forcing meaning upon what is essentially beyond the pale of the rational. It amounts to writing history as tragedy, the way de Tocqueville did according to Hayden White.[22] Winterson's intention is thus to start off from a notion that is poles apart from what historians might envisage. She picks out the poly-semic concept of passion and, by so doing, states unambiguously that drives and impulses may write history. What comes directly from the body should not be spurned as a hindrance, because any investigation of the past is bound to be an inner exploration: 'Explorers are prepared. But for us, who travel along the blood vessels, who come to the cities of the interior by chance, there is no preparation. We who were fluent find life is a foreign language' (*TP*, p. 68). If for Napoleon politics was destiny, for Freud it was *anatomy*, Winterson, for her part, eschews both power-wielding and biologic determinism as a shaping force for history, by propounding a third possibility: 'Passion is not so much an emotion as a destiny' (*TP*, p. 62).[23] How then can passion intervene in a rewriting of history that forgoes the well-oiled mechanisms of rational history: causality, intellectual clarifications and the notion of *telos*? The force that pushes Henri to join up in Bonaparte's army is not Gallic patriotism, let alone a warlike desire to conquer. It is rather a thirst for an absolute that is not met by the lukewarm religion of his forefathers. In Roman Catholicism, confession is totally devoid of the kind of fervour Henri is hankering after, and God remains aloof. The young man's need to transcend his condition is unanswered by a kind of religion that cannot meet passion with passion. Henri's decision to become a soldier is an act of love, prompted by irrational idolatry, by his worship of a man who, though far above his station, is nevertheless approachable: 'He was my passion and when we go to war we feel we are not a lukewarm people any more' (*TP*, p. 108). Love, of course, leads to the worst excesses, and it is Henri's unflinching commitment to Napoleon that permits him to countenance the most abominable by staying in the Grande Armée: 'I've seen soldiers, mad with hunger and cold, chop off their own arms and cook them . . . You could chop yourself down to the very end and leave the heart to beat in its ransacked palace' (*TP*, p. 82). In the most tragic circumstances, face to face with death, Henri's words are imbued with Christ-like symbolism; passion is the ultimate passive surrender to suffering and pains: 'Were these my stigmata then? Would I bleed for every death and living death? If a soldier did, there would be no soldiers left' (*TP*, p. 42). But passion is also at the core of a constellation of meanings. It can take a debased form too. In the case of Napoleon, it is synonymous with lust, greed and appetite. Synecdochically, it is Napoleon's passion for 'chicken' (*TP*, p. 3) that turns Europe into a huge battlefield and eggs him on to make mincemeat of all his enemies. The carnage goes on till passion gradually gives way to obsession. Passion indeed is inebriating and infectious, it is what pushes 'a people who love the grape and the sun' (*TP*, p. 108) to let itself be carried away by the ego trip of a megalomaniac. The story of Napoleon the conqueror, and probably that of conquerors in general, is a narcissistic romance. It is self-love or the idealization of the ego that nurtures the wildest dreams of self-aggrandizement. Winterson redefines romance by alluding to the most horrendous pages of history:

> Perhaps all romance is like that; not a contract between equal parties but an explosion of dreams and desires that can find no outlet in everyday life. Only a drama will do and while the fireworks last the sky is a different colour. He became an Emperor. (*TP*, p. 13)

Winterson, however, may not be suspected of falling in the trap of what Hélène Cixous in an influential essay diagnosed as 'patriarchal binary thought'.[24] In the wake of Derrida's work, Cixous contended that Western philosophy and literary thought are caught up in a set of opposites, in which one term is hierarchically defined against what is deemed as its other. Thus, applying passion to the Napoleonic butchery does not entail that it can have no ideal, uplifting value. For example, Winterson is not dismissive of Courtly Love which she hints at in passing: 'Here, without women, with only our imaginations and a handful of whores, we can't remember what it is about women that can turn a man through passion into something holy' (*TP*, p. 27). Courtliness, as the possibility of an ennobling form of love, is not radically thrown into question, it is its contextualization and the likelihood of its ever happening in real life that are problematic. Because Winterson's line of reasoning is not based upon mutually exclusive binary opposites, she tends to link together elements from different fields of experience. The profane and the sacred can be jarringly mingled to suggest all the polysemy contained in the term 'passion'. For instance, crucifixion may be parodically used in relation to a scene of lovemaking: 'We went to his room and he was a man who liked his women face down, arms outstretched like the crucified Christ' (*TP*, p. 70). Obviously, here passion is tautologically doubled over, but with different meanings. A woman is led, more or less willingly, to undergo a toned-down form of Christ-like passion, by being subjected to the passionate ardour of her lover. By searching to situate within the body itself the possibility of attaining to a form of release and liberation, through carnal exultation, as it were, Winterson is hyperbolically rewriting history.

For Byatt, too, the body is the mediator between past and present. *Possession* is, to some extent, a metahistorical novel; it deals with the issue of history writing. Not surprisingly, it is Michelet, a nineteenth-century historian who 'emplots his history of France up to the Revolution in the mode of romance', whom Byatt is repeatedly alluding to.[25] Bodily metaphors and organicism – particularly the cycle of life – inform Michelet's historiography. Indeed, the historian must come as close as possible to the experience of death. He is supposed to live death vicariously and to form an attachment to the departed ones by letting himself be possessed by their memory. Michelet's relation to the past is both compulsive and irrational; for example, he has been described by Barthes as physically suffering from the illness of history: 'Michelet malade d'histoire'.[26] When writing, he could be overcome by nausea and a splitting headache. But these ailments were also what fed him as a historian. *Possession* is also much about this yearning to be physically close to the past. The moment of the discovery of the two Victorian poets' correspondence is evoked unequivocally as 'being uselessly urged on by some violent emotion of curiosity – not greed, curiosity, more fundamental even than sex, the desire for knowledge' (*P*, p. 82). In other passages of the novel, Byatt is in a necrophiliac proximity to the dead, for instance, when the text refers at some length to the mourning brooches and plaited watch-chains made of hair cut off at the death bed (*P*, p. 258), objects much in fashion after the death of Prince Albert. When all is said and done, for Michelet, all history rests on the commemoration of the dead and on palingenesis: their resurrection. (This is the reason why the historian considers that historical documents are not so much objects to study, as relics that are still haunted by the voices of the dead.) Likewise, Ash speaks about his being possessed by Shakespeare, Browne, Donne or Keats, with whom he finds himself conversing in the process of writing. Finally, for Michelet, the historian's duty is to make up for the wrongs that were done to the dead while they were alive. The historian is a sort of Oedipus, who retrospectively solves human riddles; he has a duty towards the dead, which is to do them justice, by permitting their deeds and sacrifices to be rescued from oblivion and passed on to posterity. In *Possession*, by painstakingly reconstructing the secret and long-forgotten love story between two Victorian poets, the contemporary scholars pay homage to the couple by restoring a central episode that was to shape their destinies.

The Passion and *Possession* are not just fictional texts calling up a historical vision of their own. They are deeply committed to questioning ways of representing the past. According to Fredric Jameson,

> history is not so much a text, as rather a text-to-be-(re)constructed. Better still, it is an obligation to do so, whose means and techniques are historically irreversible, so that we are not at liberty to construct any historical narrative at all . . . [27]

Bearing this in mind, it may be argued that these two novels offer an alternative version to mainstream, male-controlled historiography. Instead of privileging the analogical method, by reading the present into the past, both Winterson and Byatt start from the assumption that, in a sense, the past cannot be known. This does not entail that it should not be written about, in fact just the opposite. Creating imaginary pasts from a total experience, blending daydreams, erotic fantasies, allegories and the fairy tale: this is Winterson's contribution to herstory. Byatt, without relinquishing analysis altogether, favours the close, physical proximity with the dead, through ventriloquism in particular, as a way of doing justice to the elusive past.[28] In both cases, what the two highly poly-semic terms of passion and possession convey is a plural, polygeneric approach, spurning the body and mind dichotomy.

Notes

1. Jeanette Winterson, *The Passion* (London: Vintage, 1996; first published 1987) and A. S. Byatt, *Possession* (London: Vintage, 1991; first published 1990). All further references will be given in the body of the text using the abbreviations *TP* and *P*.
2. Jeanette Winterson, *Sexing the Cherry* (London: Vintage, 1996; first published 1989).
3. A. S. Byatt, *Passions of the Mind* (London: Vintage, 1993; first published 1991), p. 6.
4. Winterson, *Sexing the Cherry*, p. 91.
5. Hilary M. Schor, 'Sorting, Morphing, and Mourning', in John Kucich and Dianne F. Sadoff (eds) *Victorian Afterlife: Postmodern Culture Rewrites the Nineteenth Century* (Minneapolis, MN: University of Minnesota Press, 2000), p. 237.
6. Georg Lukács, *The Historical Novel*, trans. Hannah and Stanley Mitchell (London: Merlin, 1962).
7. Karen Chase and Michael Levinson, ' "I Never Saw a Man So Frightened": The Young Queen and the Parliamentary Bedchamber', in Margaret Homans and Adrienne Munich (eds) *Remaking Queen Victoria* (New York: Cambridge University Press, 1998), p. 201.

8. Linda Hutcheon, *The Politics of Postmodernism* (London and New York: Routledge, 1989), p. 160.
9. Elaine Showalter, 'Feminist Criticism in the Wilderness', in Elaine Showalter (ed.) *The New Feminist Criticism* (London: Virago, 1986), pp. 266–7.
10. Julia Kristeva, 'Women's Time' (1979), trans. Alice Jardine and Harry Blake, in Toril Moi (ed.) *The Kristeva Reader* (Oxford: Blackwell, 1986), p. 190.
11. André Brink, *The Novel: Language and Narrative from Cervantes to Calvino* (London: Macmillan, 1998), p. 300.
12. Hayden White, *Metahistory: The Historical Imagination in Nineteenth Century Europe* (Baltimore, MD and London: The Johns Hopkins University Press, 1973).
13. 'She thinks of Forster and Lawrence, only connect, the mystic Oneness, and her word comes back to her again, more insistently: laminations. Laminations. Keeping things separate. . . . She has the first vague premonition of an art-form of fragments, juxtaposed, not interwoven, not 'organically' spiralling up like a tree or a shell, but constructed brick by brick, layer by layer, like the Post Office Tower', A. S. Byatt, *Babel Tower* (London: Chatto & Windus, 1996), p. 359.
14. Julia Kristeva, 'Revolution in the Poetic Language' (1979), in Moi (ed.) *The Kristeva Reader*, p. 94.
15. Kristeva, 'Women's Time', p. 192.
16. Ibid., p. 191.
17. A. S. Byatt, *On Histories and Stories: Selected Essays* (London: Chatto & Windus, 2000), p. 125 (emphasis mine). See in Michael Sinowitz's essay how, by contrast, Angela Carter claims to be in the demythologizing business, even if her works have often been regarded as reviving myths and legends.
18. Winterson, *Sexing the Cherry*, p. 23.
19. Luce Irigaray, *Spéculum de l'autre femme* (Paris: Minuit, 1974) and Toril Moi, *Sexual/Textual Politics: Feminist Literary Theory* (London and New York: Routledge, 1990; first published 1985), pp. 132–46.
20. Roland Barthes, *The Pleasure of the Text*, trans. Richard Miller (New York: Hill and Wang, 1973).
21. Jacques Derrida, 'The Purveyor of Truth', *The Post-Card: From Socrates to Freud*, trans. Alan Bass (Chicago, IL: University of Chicago Press, 1987). The term is also commented on by Gayatri Chakravorty Spivak in the preface to her translation of Derrida's *Of Grammatology* (Baltimore, MD and London: The Johns Hopkins University Press, 1976), p. lxix.
22. White, *Metahistory*, pp. 199–229.
23. See Toril Moi, *What is a Woman?* (Oxford: Oxford University Press, 2001; first published 1999), pp. 374–8.
24. Toril Moi, *Sexual/Textual Politics: Feminist Literary Theory* (London and New York: Routledge, 1990), p. 104. Moi's analysis takes up Cixous' analysis in Hélène Cixous, 'Sorties: Out and Out: Attacks/Ways Out/Forays', in Hélène Cixous and with Catherine Clément, *The Newly Born Woman*, trans. Betsy Wing (Minneapolis, MN: University of Minnesota Press, 1986; first published 1975), pp. 63–132.
25. See Hayden White, 'Interpretation in History', *Tropics of Discourse: Essays in Cultural Criticism* (Baltimore, MD and London: The Johns Hopkins University Press, 1990; first published 1978), p. 69.

26. Roland Barthes, *Michelet* (Paris: Points Seuil, 1995; first published 1954), p. 21.
27. Fredric Jameson, 'Imaginary and the Symbolic in Lacan: Marxism, Psycho-analytic Criticism, and the Problem of the Subject', *Yale French Studies*, 55–7 (1978), repr. in Shoshana Felman (ed.) *Literature and Psychoanalysis: The Question of Reading. Otherwise* (Baltimore, MD: John Hopkins University Press, 1982), p. 388.
28. In *On Histories and Stories*, Byatt confesses her intention to turn away from purely intellectual preoccupations when she started writing *Possession*: 'By the time I wrote *Possession* in the 1980s my interest in both character and narration had undergone a change – I felt a need *to feel and analyse* less, to tell more flatly, which is sometimes more mysteriously' (p. 131).

9
Michèle Roberts: Histories and Herstories in *In the Red Kitchen, Fair Exchange* and *The Looking Glass*

Sarah Falcus

Michèle Roberts's work has always displayed a concern for the past, whether this is in the form of personal memory and a subsequent sense of subjectivity or shared cultural experiences. From *The Wild Girl* (1984) to *The Mistressclass* (2003), Roberts's novels engage creatively with the contemporary debate about the place of women in history and the ways in which women can tell their own histories. Julia Tofantšuk argues in Chapter 4 of this book that 'feminist theory has long distinguished between history and *her*story' (p. 59), and Roberts's work can clearly be defined using the latter term. In line with Linda Anderson's argument that any attempt by women to reclaim history must make clear the way that 'existence is textually mediated', in order to avoid 'simply reconstituting reality as it is', Roberts's engagements with history refuse to work within the confines of traditional historical binaries of truth and lies, reason and irrationality.[1] All of Roberts's historical and mythical reconfigurations are notable for their insistence upon the textual nature of any remake and the inability to 'tell the truth' in any narrative, questioning the processes of both history and historical retelling. In *In the Red Kitchen* (1990), *Fair Exchange* (1999) and *The Looking Glass* (2000), Roberts takes such disparate figures as an Egyptian pharaoh, William Wordsworth and Gustave Flaubert and produces versions of people and events which revise and question historical record, destabilizing the notions of authority and truth, and encouraging instability in narrative, and therefore in history.[2]

Fair Exchange, The Looking Glass and *In the Red Kitchen* all have some basis in historical report and record, but use this creatively, altering events, times and perspectives, and refusing to respect the historical tradition of reason, proof and authority in narrative. *In the Red Kitchen* brings together five women from Ancient Egypt, Victorian London and contemporary London. Connected by narrative and visual and nonlinguistic communication, these women struggle to tell competing stories, voicing the lives often overlooked in historical report. Hat's narrative is based upon records of Hatshepsut, reputedly the only female pharaoh to rule Egypt, and this tale makes explicit the importance of language and storytelling. Obviously drawing on psychoanalytic paradigms, Hat's story links language and the pen to manhood and authority. She must learn to write in order to be powerful in Ancient Egypt; language allows her to deny her womanhood and her mortality, making death and not the mother the place of birth: 'The tomb is the first book; the house of life; the body that does not decay because it is written' (*RK*, p. 24). The erasure of the hieroglyphs from Hat's tomb in her dream signals the absence of language, turning Hat into a woman again, 'a lack . . . a poor dead body that lacks the signs of life' (*RK*, p. 133). Hat's final narrative suggests the fulfilment of this dream as her name is deconstructed to the cyclical and absent 'O':

> KING HAT.
> HAT KING
> HATTIE KING
> HATTIE NOT KING
> HATTIE NOTHING
> HATTIE NOT
> HATTIE
> HAT
> HA
> H
> O (*RK*, p. 146)

This suggests the failure of this position of male authority, which erases the feminine in order to speak. And so Hat tries to find a scribe down through the ages, someone who will write her name and thereby allow her to live. It is this desire which connects her with two of the other women in the novel: Hattie, a contemporary woman, and Flora, a nineteenth-century medium. The narratives of these women also explore issues of language and history, making up the multilayered and unstable text of *In the Red Kitchen*.

The story of the nineteenth-century medium Florence Cook is mined in the narratives of Flora and Rosina Milk, providing a good example of the way that Roberts presents an alternative view of historical figures and events. Florence Cook was one of the first mediums of her period to produce full-form materializations and was involved in a psychical investigation undertaken by William Crookes, an eminent scientist of the time. Crookes's defence of Florence in *Spiritualist* magazine frames many narratives about the young medium and in most historical sources Florence is cited only in relation to Crookes's research and the rumours of sexual relations between Crookes and his subjects.[3] In Roberts's text, however, William's voice is refracted through the stories of his wife, Minny, and Flora Milk (based largely upon Florence Cook). In Minny's narrative, William is presented as a loving and attentive husband, 'all that is most considerate' (*RK*, p. 5). But he is also a Victorian patriarch, spending little time in the family home and refusing to discuss 'intellectual' matters with his wife for fear of 'over-stimulating [her] nerves' (*RK*, p. 5). Flora's tale suggests a sexual relationship with William but, like so much else in this novel, the exact nature of this relationship is unclear. What is certain, however, is that William becomes a shadowy and distorted figure, denied his own voice in the text. The novel also refuses to engage with issues of true or false, which confine most historical studies of mediumship, where it is situated in empirical terms, as exemplified by Crookes's original studies of Florence Cook. The issue of Flora's reliability as medium is not solved in the text; indeed, her potential unreliability is exploited to prevent any one narrative dominating the others.

William's wife, Minny, relates an epistolary narrative of serial childbirth and possible infanticide, a story rescued from beneath the veils of respectable Victorian womanhood, bringing with it overtones of Charlotte Perkins Gilman's *The Yellow Wallpaper*.[4] Minny's own voice is limited in the novel to the letters she writes to her mother as she lies either recovering from, or preparing for, childbirth. In these epistles, she tells of her grief for her recently deceased newborn daughter, Rosalie, who is apparently the reason for Minny's interest in the spiritual, something which brings her close to Flora, the medium. But this is not a simple tale of love and loss. Flora's narrative provides another perspective on events, suggesting that Minny herself may be implicated in her daughter's untimely end. Whilst Flora is living with Minny and her family, she hears the keening sounds of a child in distress and during a private séance, when only Minny and Flora are present, the child makes explicit its message: '*Mother. Smother. Mother, you smothered me*' (*RK*, p. 94). The violence of this maternal relationship cannot be openly expressed in the novel. Minny, as mother, cannot admit to the harm she may have done her child, releasing her anger only briefly at Flora. But

In the Red Kitchen tells the story of the very real difficulty of numerous childbirths for women, where maternal anger and exhaustion are treated only with rest and lack of stimulus, as nervous, female complaints. In this way, the novel explores the dark underside of the maternal, and of history, presenting a complex narrative where competing versions of the truth prevent one story from dominating.

Fair Exchange similarly draws upon the lives of historical figures and situations, in this case William Wordsworth; his lover and the mother of their child, Annette Vallon; Mary Wollstonecraft; and her lover, Gilbert Imlay. And again this text underlines the impossibility of any accurate or reliable version of historical events and figures. Roberts explicitly removes any claim to authenticity or truth in the novel by insisting in her Author's Note upon the creativity of the text and its use of historical sources and figures:

> It [*Fair Exchange*] turned into a historical romance which is *not* about William Wordsworth but about his compatriot and friend William Saygood, a wholly fictional character. Similarly, although Mary Wollstonecraft appears in the novel, I have plundered various aspects of her life for my character Jemima Boote. (*FE*, n.p.)

Even cursory research into biographies and letters of Wollstonecraft and Wordsworth supports this claim.[5] The novel brings together Vallon and Wollstonecraft at the time of the Terror in France, despite the fact that the two women did not come together in this way, and concentrates on their experiences of maternity and childbirth, events passed over quickly in historical texts. Once again the stories and experiences omitted or reduced in historical record are given the most textual space. Through its depiction of Annette Villon and Jemima Boote, *Fair Exchange* investigates the 'other side' of the public faces of Wollstonecraft and Wordsworth. It is the birth of Wollstonecraft's daughter, Fanny, that is represented by Jemima and her child, Maria. Significantly, Maria and Jemima are the names of two of Wollstonecraft's fictional 'children', the protagonist and her working-class keeper-turned-friend in *Maria: or the Wrongs of Woman*. The novel creatively reinscribes the voice of the young mother here and investigates the difficulties experienced by the advocate of women's rights in surrendering to her body through childbirth and negotiating a relationship with a man. In the same way, Annette Vallon's pregnancy is portrayed through the experiences of Annette Villon. Despite the interest generated by the twentieth-century discovery of Wordsworth's affair with Vallon, little space has been given to her experience, with most texts concentrating on the relationship between Wordsworth's poetic development and his sexual and romantic exploits during the Revolution. Roberts imagines the experiences of Annette during this time, evoking the anger and dismay of her family on the discovery of her condition, and Annette's own suffering when Wordsworth remained absent during and after her pregnancy. *Fair Exchange* does not pretend to be an accurate portrayal of historical events; rather, it underlines the impossibility of any such portrayal. In this way the novel engages with the past, but does not claim to represent reality as it is, or was, allowing the text a freedom to concentrate on marginalized stories and to refuse to authenticate these. Setting the novel in the time of Romanticism emphasizes the importance of this storytelling role and is particularly appropriate for a text that deals with the issue of women's stories, since many women writers were struggling to find voices at this time, dominated as it was by the now canonical male writers.[6]

Fair Exchange is framed by the narrative of Louise, who is initially a servant to the Villon (Vallon) family and takes Annette into her rural family home after the discovery of Annette's pregnancy. Giving the servant, a traditionally silenced historical figure, the narrative voice in this story emphasizes the concentration on marginal figures in this text, as in the others addressed in this paper. Louise is an important figure in the narrative, present during the pregnancies of both Jemima and Annette, but even her tale is not left in an authoritative position. She depends upon hearsay and overheard conversations to make up her narrative, relating Jemima's childhood, 'as she had heard Jemima tell it to Annette almost twenty years ago' (*FE*, p. 7). Struggling to come to terms with her part in events, Louise finds the production of linear narrative very difficult:

To admit to the crime she had committed was difficult. She could not state it baldly. It had to be surrounded with other facts, but then these demanded to be arranged in a row seemingly as logical as those begettings of wise men and prophets. (*FE*, p. 7)

As Georges Letissier argues in Chapter 8, with reference to *The Passion* and *Possession*, the 'enunciative process' therefore emphasizes 'the constructedness of the past' (p. 121). But Louise is not the only woman in *Fair Exchange* who finds that language must be manipulated in order to communicate the past. Annette, too, 'test[s] out versions of the story' of her relationship with Saygood on Louise, in preparation for telling her father of her pregnancy (*FE*, p. 69). And to her father she will emphasize her own confusion, applying for his sympathy. There is no reliable language, nor version of truth, in this novel. Language and expression are subject to negotiation, and truth must be fabricated according to audience and need. This applies also to history and treatment of the past: memories and events must be ordered into logical sequences, to obey the dictates of linear time and to satisfy the audience. History imposes an arbitrary structure, a beginning and an end, creating a time, rather than simply recording it.

The Looking Glass uses a similar braiding of stories to that found in *In the Red Kitchen*, drawing on the lives of Gustave Flaubert and Stephane Mallarmé to tell the story of the women who surround a writer, Gérard Colbert, in early twentieth-century France. It is Flaubert's life that provides the model for the relationships and many of the events in the text. Gérard is largely based on Flaubert, with a similar home life, an affair with a married woman, and a career as a writer. The links with Mallarmé's life are less obvious, but include the fact that Gérard is a poet and not a novelist, and that Marie-Louise's discussion of Gérard's work in her narrative suggests a style reminiscent of Mallarmé and not Flaubert. What is significant here in terms of Roberts's use of historical sources is that once again this use is creative and not bound to an ideology of truth and authority. A good example of this is the fact that, despite some use of the lives of Mallarmé and Flaubert in the figure of Gérard, both authors are actually mentioned in the novel as significant artists. This refusal to respect the binary of fact/fiction is further exploited by the indiscriminate use of historical report alongside fictional and mythical sources, such as Flaubert's *Madame Bovary* and fairy tales of mermaids.[7]

One narrative is interwoven throughout this novel: the story of Geneviève, a servant based on the shadowy historical figure of Miss Julie, servant to the Flaubert family for many years. She told Flaubert many of the mythical tales he later used in his writing, as does Geneviève here, and she also served as the model for Félicité in *Un Coeur Simple*.[8] But in this text Geneviève is not the silenced servant; it is she who is given the most textual space, as her narrative weaves around those of the other women. *The Looking Glass*, like *Fair Exchange*, concentrates on stories that are not given space in traditional historical narrative, those stories which are suppressed or lost. In this novel, it is the male poet who becomes the muse for women, reversing the traditional situation of the male poet/artist objectifying the female muse. Millicent describes Gérard in typically Romantic terms, praising his creativity and need for freedom and seeing Madame Colbert as a negative influence on her son:

Artists must be free, and unshackled by the normal petty conventions of domestic life. I know this because I have the passionate soul of an artist myself. Gérard suffers terribly from the restrictions imposed on him by the need to live with his mother and take care of her. (*LG*, p. 133)

Isabelle, on the other hand, describes Gérard in more sexual terms, as an adept lover who is experienced in the ways of the world (*LG*, pp. 170–3). Gérard is the 'devoted son' to Madame Colbert, the caring uncle to Marie-Louise, the employer of Geneviève. In all of these roles Gérard is a malleable figure, who exists only in relation to the narrators and their points of view, and whose voice, like that of William in *In the Red Kitchen*, is heard solely in a ventriloquized form, as when Isabelle describes Gérard's bedtime conversation:

Sex was like writing poetry, he informed me: you didn't expect to get it right the first time but took it through many drafts; you had to listen to your lover/muse; practise; discover and refine the techniques that produced your artless, spontaneous effect. (*LG*, p. 170)

But here, Gérard is the muse, as the women of the text make him the voiceless lover, uncle, son, neighbour and employer.

The five narratives of *The Looking Glass* also suggest the complexity of historical remaking in their various forms: diaries, letters, memoirs, interviews. Geneviève is telling the story of her life, providing an account of events which took place during the spring and summer of 1914. Millicent's diary offers a similarly detailed version of the summer period. The narratives of Isabelle, Yvonne and Marie-Louise, however, cover longer periods of time, as Isabelle's letter brings together the sixteen months of her affair with Gérard; Marie-Louise, Gérard's niece, narrates her memories of her uncle; and Yvonne, a contemporary of Marie-Louise, speaks to a researcher about her memories of Gérard, Marie-Louise and Madame Colbert. These narratives represent many of the sources from which conventional history is cobbled, and all of these tales are partial, recording certain details and omitting others, highlighting the fragmented nature of memory and history. Numerous perspectives are therefore provided upon the same people and the same incidents, and these perspectives are sometimes contradictory. Millicent's diary represents the outpourings of a romantic governess, naïve and judgemental. She sees Geneviève as a 'very simple character' (*LG*, p. 100), a servant with little learning and no intellectual worth: 'She is a very ordinary sort of girl, of course; she spends her days head down working for the Colberts, and has no time for anything else' (*LG*, pp. 111–12). This is of course ironic in the light of Geneviève's narrative, which precedes that of Millicent and shows a complex and thoughtful character with finely tuned emotional sensibilities. And, as Geneviève's later narratives show, she is very much aware of Millicent's naivety and romanticism, recognizing in her childish blushes her desire for Gérard (*LG*, p. 158). This process of multifaceted characterization prevents the identification of one authoritative narrator. Geneviève's tale takes up the most textual space, and begins and ends the book, but it is undermined in various ways by those of the other women. The descriptions of events in the novel are also various and sometimes contradictory, as the diverse representations of Isabelle's visit to Gérard's home demonstrate. Roberts is undoubtedly indebted here to the structure and theoretical basis of Julian Barnes's *Flaubert's Parrot*, a source mentioned in her Author's Note. As in Barnes's text, *The Looking Glass* internalizes the debate about the reliability and subjectivity of history, highlighting the constructed nature of historical account and record.

As these points suggest, these texts are taking creative approaches to history and historical figures, encouraging instability and uncertainty, and refusing any attempt at ultimate verification of one truth of the past. In this way, as Georges Letissier argues in this volume, herstory promotes 'dissident voices from the margins', with their 'plural histories' (p. 119). This allows the novels to tell hypothetical herstories, without falling into the trap of which Anderson warns, the danger of 'reconstituting reality as it is'.[9] By creatively interpreting and rearranging the historical narratives of the lives of these famous figures, these texts question the authority not only of their own representations, but also of the historical texts themselves.

Part of the questioning of history undertaken in these three texts is of course the stress on the absence of women in history and an attempt to tell women's stories. As I have already suggested, these novels insist upon giving voice to those marginalized by history: women, particularly servants. But telling herstories is not unproblematic and the women in these texts struggle to find voices and order their tales, emphasizing the unreliability of language and narrative. As already demonstrated, in *Fair Exchange* Louise admits to finding the truth an elusive thing, which is difficult to express, since facts have to be 'arranged in a row' and her story 'arrange[d] in her head as a line of incidents' before being told (*FE*, p. 7). This statement very neatly encapsulates the whole project of historical narrative, which must arrange incidents 'in a row', in linear narrative, in order to communicate them. And just as Louise struggles to express herself, so all of the narrators in *The Looking Glass* confront the difficulty of presenting themselves in language. Inhibited by Gérard's literary success, Isabelle struggles to communicate her feelings fully in the written word, resorting to scribbled notes and hasty messages, and writing long letters to the absent Gérard only in her imagination. Only this narrative gives Isabelle a voice, allowing her to express herself without restraint in 'language that can flow and does not have to stop' (*LG*, p. 187). For Geneviève, the battle for language is intimately connected to a battle for her sense of self, her subjectivity. She struggles throughout *The Looking Glass* to find a voice to express her needs and desires, but generally ends up acting as the role of confidante for the various men in the text. The only stories she can express are those told to her by Madame Patin, which she repeats to Gérard and which he later uses in his own works. Just as the men in *Fair Exchange* efface the maternal experience by translating it into poetry, so Gérard effaces his servant as he appropriates the tales passed down to her from her surrogate mother. It is only at the end of the text that Geneviève learns to find a voice, and she expresses, like Louise, the difficulty of ordering her memories into linear narrative:

> When you smoothed and flattened and straightened the story out, made it exist word by word in speech, you lost that heavenly possession of everything at once . . . Perhaps Eve's punishment, thrust forth from paradise, was to become a storyteller. (*LG*, pp. 274–5)

These novels are therefore all intimately concerned with the need to tell herstories, and in different ways they all question the authority and dominance of a strictly linear time and history. Like Julia Tofantšuk and Georges Letissier, I am drawing on Julia Kristeva's three times, linear, cyclical and monumental, from 'Women's Time', in order to provide a lexis which can describe different times and spaces. It is possible to see in these texts aspects of the cyclical and monumental, times which disturb the linear timescale of history. Kristeva argues that women are linked closely to cyclical and monumental (eternal) time by virtue of their reproductive capacities. This is exemplified in her discussion of European women, who belong to the linear time of Europe, but can also be linked synchronically to a greater, monumental time of women, from China, India, North America and so on. The cyclical time of reproduction to which women are related is connected explicitly to the problematic of women as space, the traditional maternal space of Plato's chora.

Therefore, women's time is that of repetition and eternity, rather than linearity and history, which is of course problematic since linear time is 'inherent in the logical and ontological values of any given civilization'.[10] Kristeva does, however, insist that women cannot escape linear time altogether, and this inter-relation of different times is demonstrated in *In the Red Kitchen*, *Fair Exchange* and *The Looking Glass*. Letissier argues that Winterson's *The Passion* and Byatt's *Possession* 'spatialize time' in various ways (p. 120), and a similar argument can be made about Roberts's three novels, which offer times and spaces which could be categorized as cyclical or monumental, but are of course dependent upon the linearity of narrative and language.

In *Fair Exchange* and to a lesser extent *The Looking Glass*, the domestic arena provides a textual representation of a different system of time, one based on seasons, nature and the repetition of domestic labour, suggesting the cyclical time described by Kristeva. This labour records an aspect of generations of women's time that has gone largely undocumented and forgotten. And these domestic and seasonal tasks also afford a forum for women to connect with each other and build up relationships of support. Annette shares with Louise the tale of her affair with William as Louise is dusting the furniture in the salon. The bond that forms between Louise and Annette is sealed during the time of Annette's pregnancy, as they share a variety of tasks, from folding laundry to peeling vegetables for their daily soup. The close links made in *Fair Exchange* between language and women's labour, both domestic and biological, underline the use of the domestic as an arena for expression, rather than the traditional silencing of women through their domestic role. This is not to say that the confines of the domestic role are not acknowledged; Daisy's experience in the Villon household and her awareness of her powerlessness as a servant make clear the difficulties of the domestic position. Daisy uses housework as a form of control over her life, allowing her to 'feel she [has] achieved something' (*FE*, p. 30). However, after being found in a compromising position with her lover Billy, Daisy realizes that as a servant she has less power than the family she serves, and the son of the household sees that 'where Billy had been, George could follow' (*FE*, p. 55). In *The Looking Glass*, Madame Patin and Geneviève find the space and time for talking as they cook, clean and garden, but the tales Madame Patin relates are of 'cunning and malignity and doom . . . hidden under beauty', peopled with 'enchantresses and witches and wicked queens' (*LG*, pp. 26–7). These are fairytales where, as Marina Warner's *From the Beast to the Blonde* demonstrates, women are introduced into the patriarchal order of associations between their sexuality and sin, their silence and virtue.[11] This is the ambiguous nature of the communication between Madame Patin and Geneviève, which not only brings about a loving bond, but also prepares Geneviève for the pain of adulthood in a patriarchal order. Nevertheless, it is clear that in both of these novels the domestic space provides a time and place for communication between women. This is not a utopian answer to the exclusion of women from linear time and history, but a space in which women's experiences can be communicated and valued, something underlined by the pregnancies of Annette and Jemima. As these women share a domestic space they are aware of the different timescale to which they are anchored by virtue of their bodies, and the domestic tasks which they undertake allow them time to communicate their fears and hopes about their situations.

The plane of communication between women in *In the Red Kitchen* is one which stretches both space and time, as ancient Egypt, Victorian and contemporary London are brought together through the experience of spiritualism. This suggests an approach to history that is not strictly linear, as the women of the text are linked through history and across geography by voice, visuals and even colour associations, from Hattie's vision of Flora in the basement to the white which connects Hat and Hattie. These connections between the women often offer support and aid, as Hattie is comforted after the death of her unborn child by a vision of the young Flora, and Hattie helps Flora to escape from the mental hospital in France. But the spiritual plane shared by Flora, Hat and Hattie, and to an extent Minny, is also a space in which the validity and boundaries of self and subject are tested and found wanting. Flora experiences this in her sense of dispossession of self, something echoed by Hattie, who feels herself dissolving as a subject in the face of the monumental time space in which she encounters the spirit of Flora: 'I was transparent and I dissolved; "I" no longer existed; "I" was just a linguistic convenience, not any kind of truth' (*RK*, p. 104). Using Kristeva's terms, it can be argued that the women sharing the spiritual plane in this novel have found a means of communication in a monumental timespace that does not force them to conform to the rigidity of linear time, which is predicated upon notions of authority and truth. This timespace calls into question not only history, but the very nature of the self, as the previous quotation suggests.

However, like the domestic arena, the space offered by spiritual communication is not unproblematic and not always a positive force. Flora, as practising medium, is caught in the ambivalent position described by Alex Owen in *The Darkened Room*, whereby a medium can move into the public sphere and, significantly, gain an authoritative voice, but only by the abdication of voice, and often of self, to another.[12] In *In the Red Kitchen*, Flora undoubtedly gains in a material sense from her mediumship, in terms of patronage and increased status, but she also experiences an almost schizophrenic dispossession of her own body during some séances, in a similar way to Hattie during her experience of spiritual communication. This can suggest a sense of powerlessness, something emphasized when Flora is taken by William to see Charcot and she performs in one of his hypnotic sessions. Drawing on Charcot's nineteenth-century work on hysteria, Roberts exploits the controversial link between the medium and the hysteric, a link made by Owen in her work, as Flora dances for the audience.[13] Objectifying herself by the use of the third person, Flora acts as a spectator to her own performance, an othering she also experiences as a medium:

> Flora is the little girl in the white nightdress who sits on her father's knee. He tickles her and she tickles him back. She laughs so much she is almost sick. Flora twirls and dances for her daddy . . . Flora dances for Dr Charcot and for William just like she dances for her daddy. (*RK*, p. 127)

As hysteric, or as medium, Flora is able to suggest a space and 'voice' for which the symbolic cannot cater. Yet, this marginal position also forces her to translate her anger and her actions into a form sanctioned by the male symbolic, signified by the doctors, where she is ultimately a dumb show. Both options offer the opportunity for women to speak sideways, from an alternative position, but both are premised upon traditional associations of women with madness, passivity and marginality. However, this is mediated to an extent in this novel because it is Flora who relates her own tale in the text, preventing her from becoming simply another mute display for the gratification of empirical reasoning.

In the Red Kitchen begins with a letter written by Flora's sister which vilifies Flora's mediumship and concludes with another such epistle, again raising questions of empiricism and reason. Yet, this only serves to highlight the instability of this blend of narratives. There are no answers to so many questions even at the end of this text, from the 'reality' of Hat to the 'truth' of Flora's performances. Roberts has not closed down Flora/Florence's tale, but opened it up to further possibility and appropriation. *Fair Exchange* similarly leaves a host of unanswered questions, ending, as do all of Roberts's novels, with a new beginning, as Louise looks forward to telling her story again and again to new audiences: history, or herstory, as process. And *The Looking Glass* sees Geneviève returning to Madame Patin, the place of the start of her narrative. This idea of return is important and suggests the need for repetition and a different notion of time and space from that ordained by linear history, a need to retell and retrace histories and herstories endlessly and not close them down into one interpretation, one linear account. This is underlined at the end of the text as Geneviève watches the waves on the shore:

> that soft crash, crash of water, the salt foam tracing filigree lines of script onto the loose shingle and then erasing them, repeatedly, the sea endlessly writing its life into ours and into our stories... (*LG*, p. 277)

This cyclical pattern marks many of Roberts's novels, from Caroline's return to her mother in *Fair Exchange* to Hatty's symbolic return to motherlove as she nurtures her unborn child. All of these retraversals attempt to weave the past into the present, suggesting that history and memory are necessary and yet dangerous aspects of both shared and individual subjectivity, and things that defy temporality in their constant influence on the present. Geneviève in *The Looking Glass* expresses this at the beginning of her narrative:

> But the past walks with us, shoulder to shoulder, like an invisible enemy or friend; it kicks inside us like an unborn child; it embraces us like a lover; it will outlive us and lay us out, like a wise woman, when we die. The past has lodged in my brain and cannot be pried loose. It is my country and my prison and my home. (*LG*, p. 3)

The need to return is linked to the project of rewriting and renegotiating the past, historical, mythical, religious, engaged in by these novels. This awareness of history does not, however, mean an unquestioning acceptance of one version of events, as Roberts's work demonstrates.

Notes

1. Linda Anderson, 'The Re-imagining of History in Contemporary Women's Writing', in *Plotting Change: Contemporary Women's Fiction* (London: Edward Arnold, 1990), p. 134.
2. Michèle Roberts, *In the Red Kitchen* (London: Vintage, 1999; first published 1990), *Fair Exchange* (London: Virago, 2000; first published 1999) and *The*

Looking Glass (London: Little Brown, 2000). All further references will be given in the body of the text using the abbreviations *RK*, *FE* and *LG*.

3. This is the case in John Beloff's *Parapsychology: A Concise History* (London: Athlone, 1993). For more information on Florence Cook, see Alex Owen, *The Darkened Room: Women, Power and Spiritualism in Late Nineteenth Century England* (London: Virago, 1989) and Janet Oppenheim,*The Other World: Spiritualism and Psychical Research in England, 1850–1914* (Cambridge: Cambridge University Press, 1985).

4. Charlotte Perkins Gilman, *The Yellow Wallpaper* (London: Virago, 1981).

5. Sources I have consulted include the following: Meena Alexander, *Women in Romanticism: Mary Wollstonecraft, Dorothy Wordsworth and Mary Shelley* (Hampshire and London: Macmillan, 1989); Robert Gittings and Jo Manton, *Dorothy Wordsworth* (Oxford: Clarendon, 1985); Margaret Tims, *Mary Wollstonecraft: A Social Pioneer* (London: Millington, 1976); John Williams, *William Wordsworth: A Literary Life* (Hampshire and London: Macmillan, 1996); *Journals of Dorothy Wordsworth*, Mary Moorman (ed.) (Oxford: Oxford University Press, 1971). See Sarah Falcus, 'The Odyssey, Herstory in Michèle Roberts's *Fair Exchange*', *Critique: Studies in Contemporary Fiction,* 44 (2003), 237–50 for an extended discussion of the use of historical sources in this text.

6. See Margaret Homans, *Women Writers and Poetic Identity* (Princeton, NJ: Princeton University Press, 1980).

7. See Sarah Falcus, 'Truth and Lies, History and Fiction, in Michèle Roberts's *The Looking Glass*', *Ecloga*, 2 (2002), http://www.strath.ac.uk/ecloga for an extended discussion of the use of historical sources in this text.

8. Hermia Oliver, *Flaubert and an English Governess* (Oxford: Clarendon, 1980), p. 25.

9. Anderson, 'The Re-imagining of History', p. 134.

10. Julia Kristeva, 'Women's Time', in Toril Moi (ed.) *The Kristeva Reader* (Oxford: Blackwell, 1986), p. 192.

11. Marina Warner, *From the Beast to the Blonde* (London: Chatto & Windus, 1994), pp. 398–400.

12. Owen, *The Darkened Room,* p. 12.

13. Ibid., p. 236.

Part III
Generic Experimentations with Gender and Genre

10
Rewriting *The Rover*
Johanna M. Smith

Aphra Behn's play *The Rover* was among the first of her works to be 'discovered' in the twentieth century and reconstituted as an important, indeed originary, component of a canon of women's literature. This canonical status has extended from literature into popular culture and back again, as evidenced in the rewritings of the play I will examine in this chapter. I begin by briefly discussing the play's production history and then move on to the functions *The Rover* serves in Susan Kenney's mystery novel *Graves in Academe* (1985). I hope to show that, in the fortunes of this play and the narrative of this novel, two kinds of historical recovery are being played out. In the modern recovery of *The Rover*, we can see the construction of an 'Aphra Behn' according to a particular brand of liberal-humanist feminism. In Susan Kenney's recovery of *The Rover*, we see an academic and – like Aphra Behn – a professional writer, reclaiming a genre of popular fiction for liberal-humanist-feminist purposes.

To begin with Aphra Behn's comedy, *The Rover: Part I* was first performed in 1677 and *Part II* in 1681. Thereafter *Part II* was performed only twice; *Part I*, in contrast, was performed frequently, if somewhat intermittently, until *circa* 1760. Although no portion of my task here, it is worth speculating *en passant* why the rest of Aphra Behn's plays dropped out of production altogether in the eighteenth century, and why there were no productions of *The Rover I* between 1691 and 1703, only one between 1743 and 1757, and none after 1760.[1] Jane Spencer points out that this pattern – popularity in the first half of the eighteenth century, 'steep decline' in the second[2] – holds true for the performance history of Restoration comedy in general. More recently, however, Spencer has complicated that pattern by charting the adaptability of *The Rover I*. While a Restoration audience might have appreciated Willmore as part of the play's royalist 'celebration of cavalier life,[3] a 1690s audience might instead have found 'dangerously Jacobite connotations' in Willmore,[4] and in eighteenth-century productions the character's politics were as variable as his oft-changed uniform. *The Rover I*'s fortunes follow another pattern in eighteenth-century theatre too, the tendency towards sanitized and revised versions of older plays. Judging from a promptbook for a 1720s production of *The Rover I*, both Edward Langhans and W. R. Owens claim that cuts to the script were designed to 'clean it up'.[5] And *Love in Many Masks*, a comedy 'altered from Mrs. Behn's *Rover*' (n.p.) by inveterate reviser John Philip Kemble, was performed as late as 1790.[6] *The Rover I* itself, however, was not performed again until 1979, and the context was academic rather than popular. That 1979 revival, at the University of Illinois at Chicago Circle (US), and a 1982 revival, at the Theatre Centre of the Folger Shakespeare Library (US), indicate that 'scholarly interest [in the play] preceded and stimulated interest among theatrical practitioners'.[7] This theatrical interest resulted in a fringe production at London's Upstream Theatre Club in 1984, and *The Rover I* 'achieved canonical status' in 1986 with a production directed by John Barton at RSC's prestigious Swan Theatre.[8]

Both Nancy Copeland and Jessica Munns critique this production in terms that suggest the problematic of liberal-humanist feminism I indicated above. Very briefly, by 'liberal-humanist feminism' I mean a Wollstonecraftian belief in the primacy of reason, in the equality of men and women in the capacity to exercise reason, and hence in their potential equality in social and sexual relations. In the first and second waves of academic feminism, this set of beliefs translated into an assertion of equality in literary relations as well, an equality demonstrated by the recovery of hitherto ignored texts by women and the re-evaluation of such 'women's' genres as sentimental fiction. The recovery of women's writing also initiated a re-visioning of 'masculine' genres and standards of literary excellence, and Aphra Behn can be seen as '*the* figure for the volatility of the marketplace in women's literature'.[9] It is these elements of academic feminism that Copeland explores in the RSC's production of *The Rover I*. Analysing the programme/text provided for the audience, Copeland finds an Aphra Behn constructed in the same 'authoritative, yet contemporary, image' as the RSC's Shakespeare:[10] her play is both historical (better than Killigrew's *Thomaso*, from which it was adapted) and contemporary (entertaining, indeed something of a star-vehicle for Jeremy Irons as Willmore); and Behn herself is represented as both a historical figure (the first professional woman writer) and a contemporary (a 'sexually liberated protofeminist').[11] For Jessica

Munns, however, Barton leant too far in the direction of the contemporary. In his effort to create a *Rover* of relevance to the 1980s, says Munns, Barton obscured what was historically specific to Restoration England. In particular, he 'blithely ignores' the elements of Behn's play that stress 'an imbalance in male–female relations which is experienced as economic and political subordination as well as sexual control'.[12] Thus, his more-feminist-than-thou alterations to Behn's text are both 'patronizing and anachronistic', for they 'substitute an easy and uncontroversial modern approval of female sexual liberation and aggression for [Behn's] more complex and alien attempt to balance male and female needs'.[13]

I am more struck by this critique because Susan Kenney's use of *The Rover I* is indebted to Munns: in a prefatory note to *Graves in Academe*, Kenney thanked Munns for 'bringing to my attention the splendid possibilities of Aphra Behn's play'.[14] Specifically, a performance of *The Rover I* becomes part of the novel's exploration of sexual/textual politics in the English department of a US college. For Kenney, herself a university professor, Aphra Behn's play offers a way to examine not only the construction of a masculinist literary canon but also the persistence of 'hystorical' ideas about women's literacy and sexuality. Yet one could argue that Kenney's reworking of *The Rover I* is no less 'patronizing and anachronistic' than Barton's. In the remainder of this chapter, I want to explore the problematics of Kenney's academic project of historical recovery, her construction of women's literary history.

Graves in Academe was published in 1985, and it is much concerned with two issues of canonicity current in critical debates of the period. The first is not explicit in the novel, but as a writer of crime fiction Kenney can hardly have been unaware of it: I refer to the ways in which women writers were joining, challenging and in general altering the canon of detective fiction. By 1985, P. D. James had published *An Unsuitable Job for a Woman* (1972) and *The Skull Beneath the Skin* (1982), her books about private detective Cordelia Gray; Liza Cody had begun her series about private eye Anna Lee with *Dupe* in 1982; also in that year, Sue Grafton had commenced her alphabet series featuring private investigator Kinsey Millhone. While these women were regendering the hard-boiled school of detective fiction, other women writers were rethinking the 'amateur woman sleuth' tradition of Agatha Christie and her ilk. Among the most successful of these was the academic and theorist of androgyny Carolyn Heilbron: writing as Amanda Cross, in 1979 she published *The Theban Mysteries*, which introduced her series heroine, English professor and mystery solver Kate Fansler. It is this updating of the Christie tradition, rather than the more radical re-visioning of the hard-boiled masculine school, to which Kenney's Roz Howard mysteries belong.

The first of these books, 1983's *Garden of Malice*, sets the tone that will be developed in *Graves in Academe*. Roz Howard, assistant professor of literature at Vassar College, takes on the editing of a well-known British woman writer's papers as a tenure project but finds herself instead enmeshed in country-house skulduggery. While the presence of a closet transsexual adds a contemporary element to the plot, in most ways the novel is a throwback to the had-I-but-known tradition of hapless damsels involving themselves in distress by their innocence, inexperience, naiveté or general gormlessness. Certainly, it is possible to recuperate this kind of plot for feminist purposes: in the late 1970s, re-visionist studies of the Gothic were already doing so, as were writers of the Gothic (Chapter 12 of this book astutely analyses some workings of this 'revenge of the stereotype'). And it is true that Kenney makes her heroine's naiveté a problematic of the novel. Roz 'wants to believe the best of people' and to 'think that everyone acted from the best of motives'; while such a person may be 'gullible', says Kenney, those 'who always believe the worst' may be 'peculiarly evil', because a 'supreme arrogance' leads them to treat 'the rest of the world' as 'gullible [and] open to manipulation'.[15] The villain of *Garden of Malice* is a sociopath of this sort, and despite her naiveté Roz manages to save herself from his murderous attack. If Roz is a damsel in distress, then her ability to, as she frequently says, 'take care of [her]self'[16] nevertheless serves to validate her naiveté.

It is therefore striking that *Graves in Academe* presents a Roz still naïve but almost totally unable to take care of herself. And here I turn to the second issue of canonicity current when the novel was published, namely the re-visioning of a male-dominant literary canon. Roz's vulnerability includes her position as visiting professor in a traditional, male-dominated English department, and the department's hidebound nature is indicated by the novel's thematic of canon formation. Some of the allusions to canonical texts are comic: the name of the institution is Canterbury College; the English department is housed in Tabard Hall; one of the student protagonists is named Squires, one of the faculty wives is called Griselda, and the male faculty rejoice in such names as Manciple, Franklin, Shipman, Huberd, and Parry (short for Parfit) Knight. But the novel also offers a feminist critique of the male-dominated canon that readers are meant to take more seriously. When Roz first encounters quondam English professor and current Dean of Liberal Arts Luke Runyon, they engage in a kind of witty combat – familiar from Restoration comedy – which sets out this critique. Luke, who is characterized as 'a swashbuckling cavalier' (p. 10) and 'a gentleman of the old school' (p. 19), shows himself also as an academic of the old school in his 'suspicion' of the feminist 'new wave in literary history' (p. 43). Roz counters with an exposition of antifeminist writing through the ages, clearly intended by Kenney to demonstrate a continuum between such texts and those men 'in the groves of academe who still believed in keeping women down' (p. 44). Yet Roz herself seems unable to take the point. Believing throughout the novel that she is 'as good a judge of character as anyone' (p. 71), that 'most people acted for the best according to their lights' (p. 245), and that 'she could take care of herself' (p. 99), she does not suspect that Luke is the killer.

This thematic of the male-dominated canon takes on rather darker overtones with the growing prominence in the plot of the *Norton Anthology of English Literature*. The young student whose death is at the centre of the mystery, Alison Nelson, was found dead with a copy of the *Norton* in her lap, and we learn that she had previously been a victim of 'academic terrorism' (p. 206) at the hands of the English professor teaching the survey course for which the *Norton* was the text. When a number of English professors with some connection to Alison are attacked, Roz develops a theory that the attacker is following a syllabus based on the *Norton* in order to avenge Alison's death. While this turns out to be an elaborate red herring, the exposition of the theory makes obvious the amount of masculine violence and vengeance enshrined in the male-authored canon – some of it, as in the case of *Othello*, violence against women. In other words, a parallel is being drawn between the *content* of the literature canon and the *conduct* of those who teach and maintain that canon. And the atmosphere of Canterbury College as a whole becomes ever more poisonous for women as the novel progresses: we learn of date rapes, gang bangs and attempted assaults; women students are menaced by an unknown 'Grabber'; and there is the day-to-day sexual harassment by fraternities.

Where does *The Rover I* fit into all this? Derek Hughes is the most recent of many critics to point out that while the play 'glamorise[s]' the Cavalier world, it also anatomizes the damage done to women by the Cavalier 'culture of rank, male heroism and male loyalties'.[17] The tyranny of fathers and brothers, the amorality of the 'hero' Willmore, and especially the ubiquity of attempted rape and near-incest – all these elements of *The Rover I* point to a masculine world of subtle and implicit but real danger for women, a world very like that of Canterbury College's professors and fraternities. This connection between *Graves in Academe* and *The Rover I* is particularly evident in the role that Carnival plays in both texts. Granted, in good Bakhtinian fashion the licence and disguises of Carnival enable *The Rover*'s women of quality to display and pursue their desires. But the carnivalesque also serves to regenerate the corrupt economies of 'property marriage and aristocratic libertinism' in the play,[18] and Joanne Akalaitas's 1994 production of *The Rover I* emphasized that Carnival is 'unpredictable and thus especially threatening for women'.[19] *Graves in Academe* picks up this threatening element in its depiction of a carnivalesque Halloween at Canterbury College. During this *'Walpurgisnacht'* (p. 166) of Miltonic 'Pandemonium', the Women's Association's antiharassment and antifraternity 'Bring Back the Light' rally is interrupted by the Interfraternity Council's 'Screech Out and Clutch Somebody' party, and Roz is half-smothered and kicked in the head by an unknown assailant. I have already noted the general atmosphere of menace at Canterbury, and another element of that menace lies in the omnipresence of carnivalesque disguise. The 'Grabber' is always masked, as is the figure who thrice attacks Roz, and the group of fraternity boys who roam the campus playing misogynist pranks disguise themselves as Ninjas.

This Fraternity Ninja Brigade also disrupts a student production of *The Rover I*, and I want to turn now to Kenney's uses of that play. To some extent, as I have said, she is patronizing: according to Roz, as a playwright 'poor Aphra' is guilty of 'an excess of complication, not to mention language' (p. 117). But Kenney also recuperates Behn for a feminist literary canon: the playwright once thought to be 'slavishly copying the male dramatists of her time', says Roz, is 'now being re-evaluated as a feminist heroine and radical' (p. 115), and *The Rover I* can thus be read as 'subversive' (a term omnipresent in second-wave feminist criticism). The play's cavaliers, for example, are all 'lecherous, opportunistic, and irresponsible miscreants' (p. 115), and Willmore is dismissed as a 'twit' (p. 115). For Kenney, then, Willmore is certainly not the swashbuckler played by Jeremy Irons in the RSC production. But neither is he the mirror image of Blunt, the buffoon or loose cannon that Jones DeRitter and Lizbeth Goodman have proposed.[20] Rather, while Kenney namechecks the pervasiveness of *The Rover I*'s critique of libertines, in fact she flattens out that critique. In *Graves in Academe*, Behn's play becomes not an analysis of sexual exploitation but 'a send-up of anti-feminism' (p. 117), and its villain becomes the 'arch-antifeminist' Blunt. Behn's critique of libertines is further weakened by Kenney's alterations to the play. She does include Blunt's infamous 'kiss and beat thee' speech to Florinda and thus maintains the miasma of sexual violence that hangs over both the play and the novel. But she moves the speech from Act 4 Scene 5 to the end of Act 3, so that Blunt is threatening not the virtuous Florinda, as in the play, but the whore Lucetta. What is lost by this change is the point that Behn repeatedly makes through the many near-rapes of Florinda: all the Cavaliers insist on the difference between whores like Lucetta and 'women of quality' like Florinda, but in practice they seldom recognize the distinction. In the cynical words of the cavalier Frederick about Blunt's attempt on Florinda, ' 'twould anger us vilely to be trussed up for a rape upon a maid of quality, when we only believe we ruffle a harlot'.[21] It can be argued, in other words, that Behn's critique is not so much of (twentieth-century) 'antifeminism' as of the 'rape culture'[22] of cavalier masculinity.

Both Behn's play and Kenney's novel are comedies in the sense that both conclude with generically conventional romantic pairings. But in both texts, the happy endings are problematic. Just as the angry-woman, revenge-tragedy figure of Angellica Bianca has disrupted the comedy conventions of *The Rover I* throughout, so her exclusion from the concluding dance signals the limits of restored social and romantic harmony. Her 'isolation' at the end of the play contributes to a 'lack of closure',[23] and the happy ending of *Graves in Academe* is similarly, indeed more, anomalous. The novel too has an angry woman: Iris LeBeau, the English department's sole senior woman, 'glowering', 'forbidding' (p. 15), often heard 'muttering under her breath about the male power structure, seniority, and Title Nine [a US federal Act prohibiting discrim-ination against women]' (p. 66). Dark suspicions of such feminism in an academic spinster (read 'lesbian'?) appear in clues that lead the reader to suspect Iris of the revenge murders, and Roz is worryingly wrong to think that her friend Iris is the murderer. Perhaps readers are meant to confront their own preconceptions about academic spinsters: it is Iris who saves Roz from Luke's final murderous attack, and Iris's 'resentment' at the 'years of being put down [and] passed over for the [department] chairmanship' is clearly meant to be justifiable (p. 253). So the fact that Iris is included in the celebratory dinner which is the novel's equivalent of the play's concluding dance indicates, I think, an acceptance of a feminism far more radical than Roz's.

The character who *is* shown off at the novel's end is its potential romantic lead: young Patrick Squires, for whom Roz has developed a *tendresse*. Although she is reunited with her boyfriend Alan in the novel's last pages, that romantic reunion is somewhat undercut by her continuing attraction to Squires. And it is pertinent too that Roz has been attracted throughout the novel to swashbuckling cavalier villain

Luke Runyon, because he reminds her 'disturbingly' of Alan (p. 189). An inability to tell the villain from the hero is another convention of the had-I-but-known school of detective fiction, so this slippage calls into question Roz's detective as well as romantic acuity. Most telling is the comparison between Roz, attracted to a man whose antifeminism leads to murder, and Hellena, attracted to the drunken skirt-chasing Willmore in *The Rover I*, for Luke is to Kenney's novel what Willmore is to Behn's play, namely a 'signifier for [its] phallic logic'.[24] Unlike Hellena, of course, Roz is not paired with her phallic signifier; yet perhaps the instability of her desire may be compared with Hellena's naming herself 'Hellena the Inconstant',[25] as an open-endedness that, however faintly, disturbs the phallic economy of a heterosexual happy ending.

I want to close by pointing to a few other texts that take historical fictions of Aphra Behn and *The Rover I* in directions different from Susan Kenney's. In the Open University film of *The Rover* directed by Tony Coe (1995),[26] the contemporary setting and the casting of black actors both update and interrogate the play's representation of Restoration sexualities. The film is thus doubly a historical fiction – as a production of Behn's play and also as a representation of contemporary views of that play. Several contemporary women writers are turning not to *The Rover I* but to Aphra Behn. A 1995 novel, *Invitation to a Funeral*, draws on Behn's time in Surinam and her work as a spy to make her a sort of amateur woman sleuth in Charles II's London.[27] Codpieces, cod history and Restoration-speak make this Aphra Behn a disappointment, but others are more promising. Two plays by Canadian dramatists, one by Nancy Jo Cullen, Alexandria Patience and Rose Scollard entitled *Aphra* and Beth Herst's very interesting *A Woman's Comedy*, suggest that feminist playwrights in particular are beginning to write metadrama about women dramatists.[28] So, although I have been stressing some of the problematics of feminist projects of recuperation, I want to conclude by naming these plays as a reminder of the potential, and above all the necessity, of women's historical fictions.

Notes

1. Jane Spencer, '*The Rover* and the Eighteenth Century', in Janet Todd (ed.) *Aphra Behn Studies* (Cambridge: Cambridge University Press, 1996), p. 85.
2. Ibid., pp. 84–106.
3. Jane Spencer, *Aphra Behn's Afterlife* (Oxford: Oxford University Press, 2000), p. 187.
4. Ibid., p. 188.
5. Edward A. Langhans, 'Three Early Eighteenth-Century Promptbooks', *Theatre Notebook*, 20, 4 (Summer 1966), 144. See also W. R. Owens, 'Remaking the

Canon: Aphra Behn's *The Rover*', in W. R. Owens and Lizbeth Goodman (eds) *Shakespeare, Aphra Behn, and the Canon* (London: Routledge, in association with the Open University, 1996), pp. 131–91.

6. *Love in Many Masks: As Altered by J. P. Kemble from Mrs. Behn's Rover* (London: T. & J. Egerton, 1790), n.p.

7. Nancy Copeland, 'Re-producing *The Rover*: John Barton's *Rover* at the Swan', *Essays in Theatre*, 9, 1 (November 1990), 45.

8. Ibid.

9. Catherine Gallagher, *Nobody's Story: The Vanishing Acts of Women Writers in the Marketplace, 1670–1820* (Oxford: Clarendon, 1994), p. 4 (emphasis in original).

10. Copeland, 'Re-producing *The Rover*', p. 48.

11. Ibid., p. 49.

12. Jessica Munns, 'Barton and Behn's *The Rover*: or, the Text Transpos'd', *Restoration and Eighteenth-Century Theatre Research*, 3, 2 (Winter 1989), 16–17.

13. Ibid., p. 19.

14. Susan Kenney, *Graves in Academe* (New York: Putnam, 1985), n.p. Further references appear in the text.

15. Susan Kenney, *Garden of Malice* (New York: Putnam, 1983), p. 48, p. 201, p. 175.

16. Ibid., p. 178.

17. Derek Hughes, *The Theatre of Aphra Behn* (Basingstoke: Palgrave, 2001), pp. 83–4.

18. Linda R. Payne, 'The Carnivalesque Regeneration of Corrupt Economies in *The Rover*', *Restoration*, 22, 1 (1998), 47.

19. Susan Carlson, 'Cannibalizing and Carnivalizing: Reviving Aphra Behn's *The Rover*', *Theatre Journal*, 47, 4 (December 1995), 527.

20. Lizbeth Goodman, 'The Idea of the Canon,' in W. R. Owens and Lizbeth Goodman (eds) *Shakespeare, Aphra Behn, and the Canon* (London: Routledge in association with the Open University, 1996), pp. 3–19; Jones DeRitther, 'The Gypsy, *The Rover*, and the Wanderer: Aphra Behn's Revision of Thomas Killigrew', *Restoration*, 10, 2 (Fall 1986), 82–92.

21. Aphra Behn, *The Rover, or, The Banished Cavaliers*, ed. Anne Russell, 2nd edn (Peterborough, Canada: Broadview, 2002), Act 4, Scene 5: 123–5.

22. Anita Pacheco, 'Rape and the Female Subject in Aphra Behn's *The Rover*', *ELH*, 65, 2 (1998), 341.

23. Nancy Copeland, ' "Once a Whore and Ever"? Whore and Virgin in *The Rover* and its Antecedents', in Anita Pacheco (ed.) *Early Women Writers 1600–1720* (Harlow, UK: Addison Wesley Longman, 1998), p. 158.

24. Elin Diamond, 'Gestus and Signature in Aphra Behn's *The Rover*', *ELH*, 56, 3 (Fall 1989), 519–41; repr. in Anita Pacheco (ed.) *Early Women Writers 1600–1720* (Harlow, UK: Addison Wesley Longman, 1998), p. 169.

25. Behn, *The Rover I*, Act 5, Scene 1: 470.

26. *The Rover*, by Aphra Behn. Directed by Tony Coe, BBC, 1995.

27. Molly Brown, *Invitation to a Funeral* (London: Gollancz, 1995).

28. Nancy Jo Cullen, Alexandria Patience and Rose Scollard, *Aphra* (Toronto: Playwrights Union of Canada, 1997); Beth Herst, 'A Woman's Comedy', in Tony Hamill (ed.) *Big-Time Women from Way Back When* (Toronto: Playwrights Canada Press, 1993), pp. 150–236.

11
The Convent Novel and the Uses of History
Diana Wallace

The first Englishwoman of letters is commonly accepted to be the medieval mystic Julian of Norwich, an anchoress living in a cell attached to the church of St Julian in Norwich.[1] Born around 1342 or 1343, she was a contemporary of Geoffrey Chaucer but the contrast between these two figures, the anchoress and the court poet, can be seen as emblematic of the differences between men and women's relationships to both writing and history. *The Canterbury Tales* is a worldly text, looking outward to depict a cross-section of people on a pilgrimage, while Julian's *Revelations of Divine Love* looks inward to explicate a series of mystical visions granted to her when she was believed to be dying.[2] Other than this, we know very little about Julian of Norwich – even her name may have come from the church to which her anchorage was attached. In her sequestered partially recorded life, Julian seems in many ways to represent the shadowy figure of women, who have, as Simone de Beauvoir put it, 'no past, no history, no religion of their own' because 'throughout history they have always been subordinated to men'.[3]

I have begun with this brief glance back along what Mary Beard called 'long history' because Beard and, following her, Gerda Lerner have argued that a view of 'long history' (across different histories and cultures) is essential to understanding 'the major developmental patterns and essential differences in the way historical events affect women and men'.[4] Only by taking such a 'long' view can we understand the ways in which, in Beard's words, 'woman *is* and *makes* history'.[5]

In looking at women's writing, I want to argue that we also need to look at 'long history'. The recent critical focus on an apparent renaissance in women writers using history in contemporary fiction, and particularly the attention given to historiographic metafictions, has obscured the fact that these contemporary texts can usefully be read as a continuation of a tradition of women's historical fiction throughout the twentieth century.[6] In this chapter I want to explore the uses made of history in a group of historical novels by women, all centred in or around convents, but written at points spanning the twentieth century: Florence Barclay's *The White Ladies of Worcester: A Romance of the Twelfth Century* (1917), Sylvia Townsend Warner's *The Corner That Held Them* (1948), H. F. M. Prescott's *The Man on a Donkey* (1952), Julia O'Faolain's *Women in the Wall* (1975), Moy McCrory's *The Fading Shrine* (1991) and Philippa Gregory's *The Wise Woman* (1992).[7] Set in a variety of periods, these novels represent a range of the fictional forms within which history has been represented in the twentieth century, including romance, socialist realism, the chronicle, historiographic metafiction and the popular blockbuster.[8]

What these novels share is an interest in women's relationship with history and the ways in which women have both used and been used by history. In these novels the convent, both prison and refuge, womb and tomb, acts as a figure for the specificity and difference of women's relationship to history, symbolizing their marginality and/or exclusion from history both as events in the past and their representation as 'History'. These texts show that it is in the historical novel that some of the most interesting and important thinking about women's relationship to history and its uses have taken place. *Pace* Beauvoir's argument that women have 'no history', they show that women have both taken part in the events which make up history and written historical narratives, although they have not been regarded as 'serious' or 'proper' history. In fact, women scholars such as H. F. M. Prescott, Bonnie G. Smith has argued, often chose to write historical novels because they could not adequately narrate 'private experience' (for which we can read 'women's experience') in traditional historiographic forms.[9] With the exception of Barclay's *The White Ladies of Worcester*, the novels on which I am focusing are serious attempts to use fiction (often based on original documentary research) to explore women's problematic relationship with history.

The question 'What is the use of history?' somewhat anxiously debated by historians,[10] raises particular issues for women. Whatever answer is offered by the historian – metahistory which can offer us guidance to the future, or antiquarianism which offers history for its own sake – looks different to those 'outside' history. A. L. Rowse's *The Use of History* (1946), the key volume for the popular 'Teach Yourself History Library' series, illustrates particularly neatly the ways in which 'History' as a discipline has been constructed in ways that exclude women. Writing with an urgency inspired by the Second World War, Rowse argues that the prime use of history

> is that it enables you to understand better than any other discipline, the public events, affairs and trends of your time . . . If you do not understand the world you live in, you are merely its sport, and apt to becomes its victim . . . In understanding is our only emancipation.[11]

Although his talk of 'emancipation' sounds liberal, Rowse's argument is rooted in a phallocentric conception of history. The 'Teach Yourself History' series was constructed according to Rowse's conviction that 'the most congenial . . . concrete and practical approach to history is the biographical, through the lives of great men'.[12] Each volume looks at a pivotal period in history through the prism provided by a particular 'great man': *Luther and the Reformation, Raleigh and the British Empire* and so on. There are two problems here for women. First, the lack of women who figure as 'great': out of the 46 'Teach Yourself History' volumes only three feature women.[13] Secondly, as Lerner argues, 'the customary periodisation of traditional history' is not appropriate to women's history:

> Since for so long in their history women were not active or visible in the public arena of warfare and politics most of them were affected differently than were men by the historical changes set up as signposts in the traditional historical narrative.[14]

The kind of history promulgated by Rowse would seem to be of limited use to anyone interested in how women have been affected by historical change, or in how women can avoid being the victims of history. To find out about women's lives in history we have to look elsewhere, and we need a different conception of history.

This was precisely the point made over two decades earlier by Eileen Power, one of the pioneers of social and economic history in the early twentieth century. As she wrote,

> For a long time historians foolishly imagined that kings and wars and parliaments and the jury system alone were history: they liked chronicles and Acts of Parliament, and it did not strike them to go and look in dusty cathedral archives for the big books in which medieval bishops entered up the letters they wrote and all the complicated business of running their dioceses.[15]

What Power found in those dusty cathedral archives were the records which allowed her to produce her monumental study of convent life, *Medieval English Nunneries* (1922),[16] a text which re-visioned what constituted 'history' in ways that enabled the development of women's history.

Given the overall paucity of evidence about medieval women's lives, Power's work was especially valuable, providing a rich mine of information about nuns' daily lives – their finances, education, food, clothes, sexuality – as well as glimpses of individual women's stories, often tantalizingly incomplete but of the kind which have obvious attractions for a novelist. Women, she found, entered convents for a variety of reasons: 'A career, a vocation, a prison, a refuge; to its different inmates the medieval nunnery was all these things'.[17] In particular, she argued that the practice of using convents as a place to 'dump' unmarried or otherwise unwanted women (including political prisoners) helped to erode the spiritual *raison d'être* of the convent system. More positively, convents offered one of the few places where women were educated (to what degree Power admitted was unclear), and where they could wield power and influence.

For historical novelists, the question 'What is the use of history?' has a further set of meanings in that they use 'history', in the form of recorded information about historical events and personages, as a source of the 'facts' which they transmute into 'fiction'. The historical material provided by Power has obvious appeal for a female historical novelist, particularly given Power's own conviction that literature was an important source for the historian (*Medieval English Nunneries* discusses nuns in medieval literature). The availability of such material provides one reason why women writers might turn to the convent as a setting for historical novels. Another reason is the part played by convents in the development of historiography. Some of the earliest historical writings by women were the chronicles of individual orders and the biographies of abbesses and mystics written by nuns.[18] As well as information, such texts have the potential to provide alternative narrative models for women's history and for women's fiction.

The narrative form given to raw historical material in shaping it into a novel will depend on a novelist's conception of 'History' in an abstract sense – metahistory as a narrative of progress or decline, for instance. Here I want to introduce briefly the theories of two critics of the historical novel whose work, in part through their omission of women's texts, helps to clarify the ways in which women writers use both 'history' (the raw information) and 'History' (metahistorical narratives). In his seminal work, *The Historical Novel*, the Marxist critic Georg Lukács valourized the historical novel for the accuracy of its representation of the reality of the past as the 'prehistory of the present'.[19] Lukács takes as his exemplary historical novel Scott's *Waverley* and from this he argues that what he calls the 'classical historical novel' has a dialectical view of history which he finds reflected in its plot structure. That is, such novels depict the conflict of two opposing forces out of which comes a synthesis which represents the middle way of progress. For Lukács, even the anti-Fascist 'historical novel of democratic humanism', however laudable its politics, is still inferior to the 'classical historical novel' because it reduces history to a 'parable of the present'.[20]

In contrast, the novelist Umberto Eco (most famous for *The Name of the Rose* [1980],[21] a postmodern historical detective novel set in a medieval Benedictine monastery) argues that there are three ways of narrating the past in fiction. The first is romance, where the past is used 'as scenery, pretext, fairytale construction, to allow imagination to rove freely', while the second is the swashbuckler.[22] Although Eco does not mention this, this distinction has a gendered element: 'romance' has come to mean a love story written for and about women, while the swashbuckler (an adventure story) has come to be seen as a male form. The third method of narrating the past Eco calls rather imprecisely the 'historical novel' which may use invented characters but in which 'what the characters do serves to make history, what happened, more comprehensible'.[23]

The earliest convent novel I want to discuss here, Florence Barclay's *The White Ladies of Worcester: A Romance of the Twelfth Century* (1917), written before Power's work, uses its historical setting precisely as 'scenery, pretext, fairytale construction' for a love story. The protagonist Mora de Norelle enters a convent when the man she loves, Hugh d'Argent, goes off to the crusades and both are told (untruthfully) that the other has married someone else. When Hugh returns and discovers the deception, he disguises himself as a nun to gain access to the convent and reclaim her. Eventually, after much heart-searching, Mora is convinced that it is her duty to marry him and become 'the Madonna in the Home'[24] rather than remain as Prioress of the White Ladies.

This use of a historical background as a 'pretext' for the fantasy of romance has been an important one for twentieth-century popular women writers, from Barclay through Georgette Heyer to Rosemary Rogers's erotic bodice-rippers. Barclay's 'historical' setting (which owes more to Victorian fiction than to archival research) works to legitimize not only the romance, but also an overheated sentimental religiosity, which is late Victorian rather than twelfth century. The heightened emotion in this text is spiritual rather than sexual (although a Freudian critic might argue that the vocabulary of spiritual passion stands in for sexual passion) but earthly love is only acceptable when it receives spiritual sanction.

However, Barclay also uses the historical setting as a way of coding a polemical allegory or parable about women's 'duty'. Mora's story and the conflict between her vows as Prioress (a kind of career) and her promise to Hugh can be read as a parable with particular relevance for women in 1917. The message of Barclay's book (dedicated 'To faithful hearts all the world over') is that women's 'duty' is to wait faithfully for their soldier men to come back from the war and then to vacate their war-time jobs, returning (in Deirdre Beddoe's phrase) 'back to home and duty'.[25] 'History' is used to naturalize this reactionary vision of women's place.

These uses of history – as a fantasy space for desire or as a way of coding and/or naturalizing a political message – are common in women's historical novels. But they can be seen as ways of denying history: by constructing 'the past' as a fantasy space outside history or by using it as a veneer to disguise what Lukács called a 'parable of the present'.[26]

With the exception of Barclay's novel, the other novels I want to discuss are historical novels in the sense of Eco's third definition. That is, they recreate history in order to make it more 'comprehensible' rather than using it as a fantasy or allegorical space (although they may still have political motives). However, their view of history and their use of narrative differ radically from that in the 'classical historical novel' idealized by Lukács.

In contrast to Barclay's vaguely romantic picture of *The White Ladies of Worcester*, the kind of historical material made available by Power is used to create a detailed, naturalistic and often ironic picture of convent life in Sylvia Townsend Warner's socialist-realist *The Corner That Held Them* (1948). Warner, a writer whose work consistently modifies Marxist ideas by subjecting them to her thinking on gender, evokes the life of Oby, a convent in Norfolk, concentrating the main action between 1345 and 1381. These dates, Arnold Rattenbury points out, place the book between Chaucer's birth and the failure of the Peasant's Revolt.[27] Rattenbury maintains that the novel is a political allegory about fascism (the Black Death) and the failure of popular political risings (the Peasant's Revolt). Warner was, he argues, 'deeply engaged with her own times, . . . only and always political' and, whatever period she is writing about, 'the actuality is *now*'.[28]

To read the novel only as a 'parable of the present', however, is reductive. Its strength is that it works on several levels, as an evocation of a past way of life for its own sake and as an exploration of women's ostensible exclusion from the worldly events which constitute 'History'. The convent paradoxically both removes women from history, since they have renounced the 'world', and yet makes them visible as a female community. Warner is acutely aware of the ambiguities of this position, especially given that the majority of nuns have not chosen a sequestered life. 'A good convent should have no history,' she writes, 'Its life is hid with Christ who is above. History is of the world, costly and deathly, and the events it records are usually deplorable.'[29] This echoes but ironically rewrites Power's comment: 'Happy the nunnery that has no history.'[30] 'Yet', as Warner goes on to add, 'the events of history carry a certain exhilaration with them' (*CHT*, p. 7). To be sequestered from them does not automatically bring either spiritual serenity or, indeed, security as the convent is vulnerable to the Black Death as well as the machinations of men.

Warner's concern was to write an explicitly Marxist novel which would '[get] its teeth into the religious life – a sitting target for it'.[31] Her historical materialist account focuses, like Power's study, on the economics, rather than the spirituality, of convent life. After the Black Death, the Prioress reckons up the convent's dead in terms of profit and loss, itemizing retained or lost dowries for the dead nuns and labour lost among the peasants who worked on the manor. Later, the nuns are condemned by the Bishop not for spiritual shortcomings but for what he alleges to be scandalously sloppy book-keeping. Warner further underlines the spiritual bankruptcy of the convent system by providing her convent, ironically founded in memory of an adulterous wife, with a fraudulent priest.

In reconstructing women's history, Warner's novel rejects the dialectical plot and central protagonist typical of the realist historical novel idealized by Lukacs – 'It is not in any way a historical novel', she wrote, 'it hasn't any thesis, and so far I am contentedly vague about the plot'[32] – and deploys instead the chronicle form, itself one of the earliest forms of historiography. This is also the form used by H. F. M. Prescott in *The Man on a Donkey: A Chronicle* (1952), who develops further the use of multiple points of view.

Like Warner, H. F. M. Prescott explores the economic and social aspects of convent life but, unlike Warner, she validates the religious beliefs which the nuns have neglected. *The Man on a Donkey* deals with the ill-fated pilgrimage of Grace led by Robert Aske to save the northern monasteries from dissolution and is partly set in Marrick, a Yorkshire convent. Prescott's Prioress Christabel, like Warner's Prioress Alicia and Chaucer's Madame Eglentyne, is a worldly rather than spiritual woman. Personally ambitious, Prioress Christabel attempts to bribe Cromwell to save the convent and maintain her own power. But, as in Warner's novel, the convent is at the mercy of the men who control both church and state and thus the events of public history. In contrast to the corruption of those who are supposed to uphold the tenets of Christianity, Prescott shifts the spiritual centre of the novel out of the convent and situates it instead in the mad serving-woman Malle, whose mystical visions recall those of Julian of Norwich.

As a female community, the convent appears to offer the potential for female solidarity. However, both Warner and Prescott confirm Nina Auerbach's contention that a female community, in contrast to a male one, tends to be a 'furtive, unofficial, even underground entity' suggesting 'an antisociety, an austere banishment from both social power and biological rewards'.[33] Both Warner and Prescott suggest that for women without a religious vocation, the monotony, privation and lack of privacy of the cloistered life led to petty squabbling and jostling for power.

It is precisely women's frustrated desire for power which destroys the convent in Julia O'Faolain's *Women in the Wall* (1975). Drawing on chronicles, letters and biographies by Bishop Venantius Fortunatus and the nun Baudovinia, O'Faolain's novel retells the sixth-century story of Saint Radegunda. Forced to marry Clotair, the King of Gaul, after he massacred her family, Radegunda endured several years of marriage but eventually founded a convent. For O'Faolain's Radegunda, the convent is a refuge from the violence of the world, as well as from her own fleshly urges, which she sublimates through pain and self-denial into mysticism. Offered the chance of worldly power, she jumps at the chance to engage in political plotting: 'What she really wants is power, power in the world, in this country now,' reflects her biographer Fortunatus.[34]

Writing in the 1970s, O'Faolain is more concerned than Warner or Prescott to explore the buried sexuality which she detects between the lines of historical documents. 'It has usually been held that [Fortunatus's] playful and passionate letters to [Radegunda's protégée Agnes] expressed a purely chaste feeling,' she comments, 'Perhaps. Perhaps not' (*WIW*, p. 11). Similarly, O'Faolain lays bare the sublimated erotic elements in Radegunda's mysticism, which involves submission to a 'Mystic Bridegroom' who tells her that 'Human Love is only an image of this. Give yourself totally, Radegunda' (*WIW*, p. 177).

More importantly, O'Faolain shows Radegunda's lack of control over both historical events and their representation within historical narratives. Radegunda's 'most scorching memory', the massacre of her family, has become a public story: 'Half Gaul shared it with her for it was in every harpist's repertory... Once she fainted at a banquet during a particularly graphic retelling of it' (*WIW*, p. 15). Even she can no longer 'unravel the bloody tapestry of her history and disentangle what she had seen from what she hadn't' (*WIW*, p. 16). Radegunda's life is further appropriated and misrepresented when Bishop Fortunatus writes his *Life of Radegunda*. In a continuation of this, Gerda Lerner notes that Baudovinia's version of Radegunda's *Life*, written in an attempt to supplant Fortunatus' biography and construct Radegunda as a role model for other nuns, has been disparaged by scholars in comparison with his text.[35]

In figuring women's relationship to history, both *Women in the Wall* and Moy McCrory's *The Fading Shrine* (1990) use the image of a damaged or partial artefact to symbolize the fragmentary and partial nature of the history they reconstruct. O'Faolain writes of attempting to put together the 'odd slivered images' or 'few surving sherds' to 'try for the shape of a lost and curious pot' (*WIW*, p. 11). In *The Fading Shrine*, McCrory uses a palimpsestic painting of Saint Polycarp, which when restored reveals another picture, of a tower and an odd group (possibly a man, a nun and a child). This painting links together the parallel narratives in the novel: the present-day narrative of Sister Cecile, a twentieth-century nun and history teacher who loses her faith, and the story of a tenth-century convent destroyed at the turn of the first millennium. Despite Cecile's attempts to interpret it, the painting will not give up the mystery of its meaning and, like so much of women's history, remains enigmatically obscure. The parallel narratives McCrory uses in *The Fading Shrine* are typical of the historiographic metafictions of the 1990s, but she also invokes the chronicle form in which the tenth-century nuns endeavour to record their own history and knowledge. Set against the apocalyptic happenings and unnatural sightings recorded in tenth-century chronicles, *The Fading Shrine* explores the millennial anxieties and fear of an ending evoked by metahistorical narratives such as Christianity and uncannily replayed in the secular 1990s.

In contrast, Philippa Gregory's *The Wise Woman* (1992) initially looks like a popular historical romance or bodice-ripper. However, Gregory has a doctorate in eighteenth-century literature and her best-selling novels have consistently subverted popular forms to explore feminist-Marxist ideas about women's history. *The Wise Woman* places its protagonist, Alys, in a situation which parallels the triangle of Henry VIII, Catherine of Aragon and Anne Boleyn. Alys has two 'mothers', the Abbess Hildebrande and the witch Morach, representing two forms of women's knowledge at the time of the Reformation.[36] Burned down in the opening pages, the convent represents a self-sufficient female world lost when the monasteries were dissolved for, Gregory suggests, blatantly economic reasons: King Henry's visitors, Alys recalls, had 'found us wealthy and pretended we were corrupt'.[37] Believing (like Anne Boleyn) that the most effective route to power is through bearing a son to a powerful man, Alys denies and betrays both her 'mothers'.

Through the expectations of the blockbuster format, Gregory teases the reader with the possibility of a romance ending (like that of *The White Ladies of Worcester*) where Alys will marry Lord Hugo but then, in an extraordinarily subversive ending for a popular novel, she has Alys choose instead to be burnt at the stake with her 'mother', the Abbess Hildebrande. Through this Gregory exposes the ideological meanings of the romance plot which has imposed 'happy endings' not only on the woman's realist novel but also on historical novels by women.[38]

In different ways, these novelists all emphasize the fragmentary and discontinuous nature of women's history and their exclusion from the 'big events' which act as 'signposts' in the grand narrative of 'History'. By using the chronicle form in particular these novelists reject the coherence implied in Lukács' 'classical historical novel' and, indeed, any metahistorical narrative of progress. As Lerner argues,

Not for [women historians] the systematic story of progress, the methodical building of thesis, antithesis and synthesis, by which succeeding generations of male thinkers grew taller by 'standing on the shoulders of giants'....[39]

Warner takes an ironic snipe at the tyranny of the dialectical model with its neat (and gendered) binary oppositions in *The Corner That Held Them*. The Abbess Alicia reflects that the advantage of the Trinity (as a motif for embroidery) is that it gets away from the antithesis which is 'monotonous in art' (*CHT*, p. 131). The same is true of the chronicle form – it gets women writers away from the monotonous and ideologically laden structures of the realist novel and the romance novel.

In these novels the convent itself, as I have suggested, acts as a figure for women's exclusion from and yet vulnerability to history. Warner's titular image of the 'corner that held them' suggests retreat and refuge but the full quotation used as an epigraph – 'For neither might the corner that held them keep them from fear'[40] – makes it clear that a retreat from history cannot necessarily keep history at bay. The nuns may be sequestered but the world comes into these convents through the ravages of famine and the Black Death, political machinations, rioters from the Peasant's Revolt or marauding soldiers. With the exception of *The Corner That Held Them* which ends with an apostate nun leaving on a pilgrimage, these other novels end with the convent destroyed: through famine and storms in *The Fading Shrine*, invasion by soldiers in *Women in the Wall*, dissolution ordered by Henry VIII in *The Man on a Donkey* and *The Wise Woman*.

In each case, a female community is destroyed. This destruction of the convent, perceived in these novels as one of the few spaces for women's learning, culture and history in each period depicted, figures the way in which women have been repeatedly cut off from their history. Such discontinuities, according to Gerda Lerner, have been one of the most insuperable barriers to the creation of a feminist consciousness:

> Marginalised from the male tradition and largely deprived of know-
> ledge of a female tradition, individual women have had to think
> their way out of patriarchal gender definitions and their constraining
> impact as though each of them were a lonely Robinson Crusoe on a
> desert island, reinventing civilisation.[41]

When McCrory's Scolastica becomes an anchoress, for instance, her knowledge of medicine and midwifery is lost to both her convent and following generations. Prescott's novel ends with the image of a copy of Julian of Norwich's *Revelations of Divine Love* among the other books in the convent torn up by the suppressors and the pages scattered around the cloister. These novels suggest that the Reformation, which destroyed the convents (however imperfect) and relocated the centres of learning to the male-only universities and grammar schools, was yet another disastrous setback for women.

If history is dangerous for women, to have no history is a kind of death. This is symbolized at its most extreme in the figure of the anchoress who haunts these texts, literally walled up in a cell too tiny for her to lie down in *Women in the Wall* and *The Fading Shrine*. This is an extreme retreat from the world – in O'Faolain's words, a 'form of death willingly embraced' (*WIW*, p. 252). In both novels, the anchoress immures herself as a penance for perceived sin: O'Faolain's Ingunda to atone for her own illegitimate birth, McCrory's Scolastica because she has aborted a foetus which she subsequently believes to have been developed enough to have a soul. Another version of this in *The Fading Shrine* is the sunken abbey inhabited by the Sisters of Compassionate Darkness. This abbey, reached by long tunnels, is literally underground and the Sisters live in total darkness except for their shrine. This neatly illustrates Auerbach's contention that a female community tends to be an 'underground entity'.[42] The image of the anchoress is evoked in *The Man on a Donkey* through the writings of Julian of Norwich which provide its spiritual subtext. And it is ironically alluded to in *The Corner That Held Them* through Dame Lilias' desire (inspired by a false vision of St Leonard, patron saint of prisoners) to become an anchoress.

If we introduce gender to the question of the uses of history and ask 'What is the use of history *for women*?', these novels suggest that without an understanding of their own past, specifically of the shifting developments of 'long history', women will continue to be the victims of history, walled up like the anchoress in her cell. They suggest that women's relationship to history has been radically different from men's and that therefore different narrative forms, both literary and historical, are needed to explore this. Perhaps most importantly they confirm Joan Scott's contention that we need a critique of history that characterizes it 'not simply as an incomplete record of the past but as a *participant in the production of knowledge that legitimized the exclusion or subordination of women*'.[43] For women writers, then, one of the uses of history is to undo 'History'.

Notes

1. See, for instance, Joanne Shattock, *The Oxford Guide to British Women Writers* (Oxford: Oxford University Press, 1994), p. 238.
2. Julian of Norwich, *Revelations of Divine Love*, trans. James Walsh (London: Burns and Oates, 1961).
3. Simone de Beauvoir, *The Second Sex*, trans. H. M. Parshley (1949; Harmondsworth: Penguin, 1983), p. 19, p. 18.
4. Mary R. Beard, *Woman as Force in History* (New York: Macmillan, 1946), p. 270; Gerda Lerner, *The Creation of Feminist Consciousness: From the Middle Ages to 1870* (1993; New York and Oxford: Oxford University Press, 1994), p. 15.
5. Mary R. Beard, *Making Women's History: The Essential Mary Ritter Beard*, Ann J. Lane (ed.) (New York: The Feminist Press at the City University of New York, 2000), p. 167.
6. Indeed, this is a tradition which dates back to the eighteenth century and Sophia Lee's *The Recess* (1785). Christine A. Colón, in Chapter 6 of this book, makes a similar point regarding the need to consider a long tradition of historicizing women's experience in her reading of the remarkable similarities between Churchill's *Vinegar Tom* and Baillie's *Witchcraft*.

7. Florence Barclay, *The White Ladies of Worcester: A Romance of the Twelfth Century* (London and New York: G. P. Putnam, 1917); Sylvia Townsend Warner, *The Corner That Held Them* (1948; London: Virago, 1988); H. F. M. Prescott, *The Man on a Donkey* (1952; London: Phoenix, 2002); Julia O'Faolain, *Women in the Wall* (1975; London: Virago, 1985); Moy McCrory, *The Fading Shrine* (1990; London: Flamingo, 1991); Philippa Gregory, *The Wise Woman* (1992; Harmondsworth: Penguin, 1993).
8. Another genre of convent novels, such as those by Antonia White and Kate O'Brien, deals with girls attending convent schools. There is also a tradition in male writing, as in Diderot's *The Nun* (1760), of associating convents with perverse female sexuality.
9. Bonnie G. Smith, 'The Contribution of Women to Modern Historiography in Great Britain, France, and the United States 1750–1940,' *American Historical Review*, 89 (1984), 721.
10. See, for instance, Marc Bloch's *The Historian's Craft* (Manchester: Manchester University Press, 1954) and A. L. Rowse's *The Use of History* (1946; London: English Universities Press, 1963) discussed below. John Tosh in *The Pursuit of History* (London: Longman, revd 3rd edn, 2002) includes a useful summary of the issues.
11. Rowse, *The Use of History*, p. 13.
12. Ibid., p. vi.
13. Alice Buchan, *Joan of Arc and the Recovery of France*; J. Hurstfield, *Elizabeth and the Unity of England*; Gladys Scott Thomas, *Catherine the Great and the Expansion of Russia* (listed in Rowse, *The Use of History*).
14. Lerner, *Feminist Consciousness*, p. 13.
15. Eileen Power, *Medieval People* (London: Methuen, 1924), p. 61.
16. Eileen Power, *Medieval English Nunneries* (Cambridge: Cambridge University Press, 1922).
17. Ibid., p. 25.
18. Lerner, *Feminist Consciousness*, pp. vii–viii.
19. Georg Lukács, *The Historical Novel*, trans. Hannah and Stanley Mitchell (1962; Lincoln and London: University of Nebraska Press, 1983), p. 53.
20. Ibid., Chapter Four, p. 388.
21. Umberto Eco, *The Name of the Rose*, trans. William Weaver (1980; London: Minerva, 1983).
22. Umberto Eco, *Postscript to The Name of the Rose*, trans. William Weaver (San Diego, New York and London: Harcourt Brace Jovanovich, 1984), p. 74.
23. Ibid., p. 75.
24. Barclay, *The White Ladies of Worcester*, p. 421.
25. Deirdre Beddoe, *Back to Home and Duty: Women Between the Wars 1918–1939* (London: Pandora, 1989).
26. In her essay on contemporary historical novels and seventeenth-century history, Katharine Hodgkin, in Chapter 1, offers a particularly sensitive exploration of the ways in which treating history as a 'lens' through which to explore the fantasies and preoccupations of the present denies the difference and complexity of the past.
27. Arnold Rattenbury, 'Literature, Lying and Sober Truth: Attitudes to the work of Patrick Hamilton and Sylvia Townsend Warner', in John Lucas (ed.) *Writing and Radicalism* (London and New York: Longman, 1996), p. 231.

28. Ibid., p. 23.
29. Townsend Warner, *The Corner That Held Them*, p. 7. Further references will be given in the body of the text using the abbreviation *CHT*.
30. Power, *English Nunneries*, p. 473.
31. Martin Seymour-Smith, 'Notes on Sylvia Townsend Warner's Poetry', *PN Review*, 23, 8:3 (1981), 57.
32. Letter to Paul Nordoff (9 April 1942), in Sylvia Townsend Warner, *Letters*, William Maxwell (ed.) (London: Chatto & Windus, 1982), p. 79.
33. Nina Auerbach, *Communities of Women: An Idea in Fiction* (Cambridge, MA and London: Harvard University Press, 1978), p. 11, p. 3.
34. O'Faolain, *Women in the Wall*, p. 267. Further references will be given in the body of the text using the abbreviation *WIW*.
35. See Lerner, *Feminist Consciousness*, p. 249.
36. See Chapter 1 for a discussion of the implications of the portrayal of the figure of the witch as wise woman in contemporary historical fiction.
37. Gregory, *The Wise Woman*, p. 1.
38. See, for instance, Rachel Blau DuPlessis, *Writing Beyond the Ending: Narrative Strategies of Twentieth-Century Women Writers* (Bloomington, IN: Indiana University Press, 1985), on the ideologies of endings.
39. Lerner, *Feminist Consciousness*, p. 220.
40. *Bible*, Wisdom of Solomon, 17.4.
41. Lerner, *Feminist Consciousness*, p. 220.
42. Auerbach, *Communities of Women*, p. 11.
43. Joan Wallach Scott, *Gender and the Politics of History* (New York: Columbia University Press, 1988), p. 26 (emphasis mine).

12
The Revenge of the Stereotype: Rewriting the History of the Gothic Heroine in Alice Thompson's *Justine*

Maria Vara

Since the 1790s the Gothic genre has teamed with women characters that have been solidified into tropes or key motifs which have generated an enormous breed of contemporary avatars. Although the persecuted heroine – the maiden in flight – is the emblem of classical Gothic, it is the 'madwoman in the attic', this prominent literary figure exemplified by Bertha Mason in Charlotte Bronte's *Jane Eyre* (1847), who has been intertextualized in Gothic fiction and who forms a vital Gothic trace in the topography of women's writing.[1] Susanne Becker informs us that the 'resonant "madwoman in the attic" is a clue to the attractions of gothic form for feminine fictions',[2] with her transgressive potential stimulating many critical debates. Conversely, Justine, an equally subversive heroine, first introduced by the Marquis de Sade, and the recent rewritings of her story have been cursorily dealt with by commentators[3] on the 'heroine-centred' Gothic and on the Gothic in general because her discussion entails an encounter with the disturbing narrative dynamics of passivity, where the structures of narrative power are considerably more obscure.

This chapter will focus on reading Alice Thompson's *Justine* (1996) as a palimpsest that encapsulates Justine's history within the genre and unravels the complex implications of her appearance in Gothic fiction. Thompson's *Justine*, read in the light of Angela Carter's *The Sadeian Woman*,[4] can be seen to unpick the intertextual thread of the stereotype of the passive heroine and to unpack a narrative tradition that spans more than two centuries. I will attempt to show that this much-abused iterative trope is a 'textual negotiation with history'[5] in which the Gothic circulates. *Justine* registers that part of history that takes account of the changing notions of subjectivity and agency, and it also follows closely the permutations of the genre's history over the centuries, exemplifying, in Victor Sage's and Allan Lloyd Smith's words, the 'peculiar unwilling-ness of the past to go away'.[6] It also foregrounds a turn of contemporary women's writing in exploring how recent novels by women attempt, in bad faith and in accord with an aesthetics of postmodernism, to rescript the history of the Gothic canon.[7] In other words, I want to venture the claim that Justine, the malleable heroine, stands for the Gothic genre itself.

Set in contemporary London, *Justine* comprises seventy-six small sections, with a mischievously teleological first-person narration, which ends by deflating the readers' expectations of a satisfying solution by turning full circle back to the beginning. This is one of the novel's opening paragraphs and also its finale:

> The library is from where I am writing to you, writing out the story of Justine... The shadows on the shelves around me are only books. When I hold up their pages to the light, the paper of many of them is so thin that the words on the other side shine backwards, through.[8]

The unnamed male narrator and art-collector is here writing out what at first seems to be the story of his obsession with the 'Perfect Woman': 'Justine, I imagined, could be my Sleeping Beauty. All I had to do was to bend over her and wake her up with a kiss' (p. 57), he proclaims, echoing Noah, a medical expert in 'the reconstruction of human bodies' in Thompson's other novel, *Pandora's Box*, whose 'dream come[s] true' when he turns a heavily burned face into one resembling 'a textbook photograph of an idealized woman's face'.[9]

Justine reads like a *fin-de-siècle* narrative of Wilde or Huysmans – of extravagant aestheticism and sensuousness – until, that is, the narrator's account of a recurrent dream of a Gothic house, the first self-conscious Gothic digression, slyly invokes the genre. Justine's presence crystallizes the Gothic element in the text, first as a portrait haunting the narrator's mind and later in the flesh when the narrator spots her in a library:

> Standing next to her, I took out a book at random and opened it up.... It was only then that I realized that I had picked out the novel *Justine* by the Marquis de Sade. The pages of the book were so thin they were almost transparent and the print from the other side shown backwards, through. (p. 54)

The last two lines of this extract are, obviously, repeated once again, with the text returning on itself, an intertextual gesture to the Sadeian repetitive excess. The Marquis de Sade's *Justine* is the story beneath the story, 'the moment beneath the moment'[10] of palimpsest Gothic writing, whereby the traces of the old textual layer (relics from a distant past) become visible so as to upset the chronotope of the narrative together with the reader's complacency. Such an overt engagement with an earlier literary text is also apparent in the work of several of the writers explored in this book, namely Angela Carter, Michèle Roberts, Jeanette Winterson, Sena Jeter Naslund, Susan Kenney and Sarah Waters. Just as Waters' novels, for example, as Mark Llewellyn argues in Chapter 14, 'are acts of writing but are also responses to and results of acts of reading' (p. 196), so is Thompson's *Justine* an act of writing that entails an act of reading/interpreting the power structures of the Gothic tropes in the Sadeian text.

Justine and her sister Juliette (whom the narrator tries to seduce in order to approach Justine), moving portraits, the Gothic house, a strange maze, all these mingle together in an implausible, highly artificial plot that is constantly alluding shorthand style to the classical Gothic of the 1790s. The text's visible Gothic elements are surviving accounts from other narratives. Thus, it is impossible to come to the novel as an innocent reader, without prior readings or without knowledge of Justine's traits of character: Justine enters the plot from another story, representing the 'ideal feminine' stereotype, particularly in her capacity for 'virtuous passivity'. The text holds her presence not as a fixed point of origin but as a signifier of the continuous interweaving of texts, as an agent of an ongoing process of layering. There is no such thing as a new story (or a new history), the novel seems to argue. Thus, de Sade's text is a significant strand but not the Ur-story beneath Thompson's text; Justine has already been there, in other texts, in the narrative mystique of fairy tales and mythology.[11]

Justine's story was rewritten three times by de Sade and subsequently published in three different versions,[12] but Thompson's narrator does not specify which version of *Justine* he has selected. Nevertheless, we can assume it is the second one, *Justine ou les Malheurs de la Vertu* (*Justine, or Good Conduct Well Chastised*) first published in 1791,[13] which is the best known. In this novel by de Sade, the Gothic genre (its iconography, thematic intensity and preoccupation with power and its ramifications) is given an equal share with pornography, so the portrayal of Justine can actually be read as a radical rewrite of the classical 1790s Radcliffean heroines. Emily in *The Mysteries of Udolpho* (1794), for example, is initially portrayed as a vulnerable maiden, a potential victim fleeing her persecutor, just like Justine. But unlike de Sade's text, the enigma to be deciphered by Emily leads to a form of narrative resolution, which grants the text a 'primitive' teleology and the reader pleasure and satisfaction.

Classical Gothic novels employ the so-called 'explained supernatural'[14] where all plot lines are drawn finally into the marriage or death of the heroine. By contrast, readers of de Sade's *Justine* will find no trace of narrative linearity, no mystery to be solved, no increasing awareness on Justine's part and thus gain no insight into the nature and meaning of her misfortunes. The more Justine turns to social and legal institutions for aid, the more she is persecuted, until she is struck by lightning, indicating that in the end chance and contingency prevail at the expense of the formation of any rational narrative pattern. This haphazard ending on a surface level turns Justine into a parody of her synchronic avatars. But the text is not simply parodic: the readers of *Justine* find themselves complicit with her innocence and bad luck when they feel entrapped in the narrative effect of circularity, in endlessly repeated events. Justine never learns her lesson, in parallel with the reader, who desperately but unsuccessfully awaits a solution, a climactic point that will render the heroine's stubborn adherence to virtue meaningful or rewarding. Since hers are not misfortunes of an Aristotelian, cathartic nature, the reading practice cannot become an exercise of 'pity' and 'fear' that would endow Justine's virtue and passivity with moral value. There is no transcendence, no room for hope. Passivity is not glorified; on the contrary it is rendered contingent and redundant by Justine, whose stubborn devotion to virtue results in the production of narrative excess that threatens the ideology of the Enlightenment in its entirety.

In other words, the eighteenth-century passion for dictionaries and encyclopedias, 'the search for totalizing categories and a universal order' is pushed to its limits in *Justine*. De Sade's manic attempt to expose his heroine to all the possible dangers that Radcliffe's texts only imply but never actualize[15] is a plot structure that can be seen to parody the principles of the Enlightenment. As Dalia Judovitz observes, the 'ostensible encyclopedic ambition' of the Sadeian text to 'say everything' and 'to show everything' results in both the 'saturation of the classical order of representation and its actual violation'.[16]

From the moment of its appearance the Gothic was a flexible register for historical changes. It was born from 'the inevitable result of the revolutionary shocks which all of Europe . . . suffered',[17] according to the Marquis de Sade who, recently acknowledged as a Gothic writer himself, in his 'Reflections on the Novel' in 1800 was the first to link the rise of the Gothic with the historical circumstances that made the French Revolution possible. Faithful to the permutability of the Gothic, Angela Carter has a plot line going straight from de Sade to another important moment of history, the politicized 1970s. In direct contravention of the feminist imperative of the 1970s to feature strong and active women characters so as to restore a lost sense of agency as a necessary foundation of women's empowerment, Carter, in *The Sadeian Woman*, focused on the plot and narrative structure in de Sade's *Justine* and *Juliette* – a gesture which, at the time, provoked a vehement reaction amongst feminist critics because of its pornographic implications, pornography being an issue that was already causing strong internal disagreement. Carter called the notorious Marquis a 'moral pornographer' and invited us to look back from the viewpoint of 1970s poststructuralist thinking to the 1790s story of Justine in order to notice beneath the simplistic pornographic tale a writing of excess that slyly destroys the fairy tale of the blameless, passive woman. For Carter, Justine's innocence, virtue and excessive passivity are not 'the continuous exercise of a moral faculty', but 'a sentimental response to a world in which she hopes her good behaviour will produce her some reward'.[18] This makes her 'self-conscious in her innocence', someone who 'knows how to make a touching picture out of her misfortunes . . . She presents herself emblematically in the passive mood as an object of pity.'[19]

In consciously attempting to present a specific ideology through her virtue, Justine is as egocentric as Juliette, and that is how, Carter believes, the myth of the Virtuous Woman is debunked by de Sade. In Carter's eyes, to be blameless is to be outside history, to have no place in the world, to become a myth and thus a 'consolatory nonsense'.[20] The central point of her argument, in Lorna Sage's words, is that 'sexuality must be understood as historical, not timeless or fixed'.[21]

This is what Thompson's *Justine* contrives to make more visible. On a first reading, the text forces us to see double: there are Justine, whom the narrator is pursuing, and Juliette, her sister. The beauty of the art objects he collects is set against his aesthetic fear of decay. His angel face is in contradiction to his deformed foot.[22] We are thus entangled in his first-person narrative of binaries from where he attempts to hold on to a location and an identity, making us *see* how the myths of timelessness are made and disseminated. But the story gradually pulls out of the narrator's hands in spite of him. While he is supposedly following his own carefully crafted plan to seduce Justine with Juliette as his accomplice (he views Justine as an art object or 'ventriloquist's doll', who 'sanctified' his plan [p. 104, p. 30]), Justine, with grim irony, mercilessly teases the narrator's expectations. Justine *is* Juliette; they are the same woman. Thus, she proves to be an impostor, a larger, more vicious plotter, who wishes to avenge herself on all who are suspected of complicity in the making of the myth of the 'Perfect Woman':

> Did...you really think you could divide me up that easily? Like a child sorting out two colours of brick...While the real me was climbing between the two phantoms of Justine and Juliette, living somewhere in the space between the two...The characterizations are so basic. Omnipotent Justine and needy Juliette, virgin and whore. Just enough to titillate the preconceptions....So now you know...*My* story was the real one...I am talking about the story I have really written, the story of Justine. The story I have got you, my ghost writer to write for me...But you chose to ignore *my* story. As have all the men in my life. You were too busy making up your own. If I was to be the heroine of your book, you could at least have given me the speaking part. But now that you have acted out my story, I think it's time that you put it down in writing, too. (pp. 123–4, emphasis in original)

Justine highlights the instabilities and dangers of power structures that usually lie beneath the essentialist discourses of myth making, the 'bankrupt enchantments' and 'fraudulent magic' of the 'ideal feminine', as Carter puts it in *The Sadeian Woman*, that leave women in 'voluntary exile from the historic world, in its historic time that is counted out minute by minute'.[23] (See Chapters 2 and 7 for a more detailed discussion of Carter's definition of myths.) In line with Carter's point of view, Justine here resents the reductive reading of women as helpless victims and wishes to do away with the dualities of myth not by merely reversing the roles (the passive turned active), but by levelling things out. The narrator finally comes to a full understanding:

> She had certainly acted at all times as if she had been in absolute control. She even had her sense of control under control. For had she not acted out the implacable image of Justine just as she had acted out the passionate incoherence of Juliette, with equanimity? She was not mad at all. She was simply a woman possessed by a lucid sense of revenge. Hell hath no fury. (p. 124)

The narrative has escaped the narrator's control, with his line of authority and dualistic philosophy abruptly broken. The story of the *revenge* of a much-abused stereotype which he is forced to write has come full circle. The text that has mocked him, making him the author of a subplot, performs a self-reflexive gesture with Justine as the agent of dissemination of narrative power. Justine does not have an important role in the story but, with hindsight, she is the narrative agent of the text, the one pulling its strings. This turn of the plot provides us with reading tools to approach a number of controversial novels that were published in the 1970s and turned the portrayal of heretical heroines into a radical challenge to the feminist 1970s' demand for realism. It was at this same moment that the Gothic that had been marginalized during the 1950s and the 1960s reappeared as a strong narrative element in women's writing, particularly as a means of addressing issues of gender politics. Lise in Muriel Spark's *The Driver's Seat* (1970), Elena in Joyce Carol Oates' *Do With me What you Will* (1973), N. in Diane Johnson's *The Shadow Knows* (1975), Ghislaine and Annabel in Angela Carter's *Shadow Dance* (1966) and *Love* (1971) respectively, form an array of Gothic avatars of Justine that generated vitriolic responses from feminist critics, as they were seen to desecrate the then literary sanctuary of *agency* as activity.

Take Ghislaine, for example, in Carter's *Shadow Dance*.[24] 'There is no mysterious virtue in her suffering', Carter says about Justine, which also applies here. Ghislaine only makes three brief appearances in the novel. Otherwise, she is constantly dreamt of and talked about by the two male characters, Honeybuzzard and Morris. She is in the background, forming the backbone of the narrative, and the actual narrative power proves to be with her, when she provokes her own ending, *making them* kill her in a way similar to Lise in Spark's *The Driver's Seat*. Lise, who was propelled relentlessly along the tracks of her fate, has a need to enact control over her life, even if this means enacting agency against herself by demanding death. She can be read as deliberately, consciously a victim, rehearsing with precision the overt provocation of her murderer so as to mock normative femininity.

Since they know that the role of the victim is the only place allotted to them, these heroines see things from the end, are already enlightened. Unlike de Sade's Justine, they have learned their lesson. They are not in the process of finding out the limits of their powers. Neither they nor we are in the dark, so that the tragic dignity and the glory of the traditional persecuted heroine is denied to them. There is a pervasive feeling of unfreedom as well as a sense of euphoria emanating from these texts because we are in a way 'enlightened', we now see it all. We can now revisit the controversial passive heroines of the 1970s, having become adept readers, knowing the story in advance, which grants us the interpretative tools for detecting there an ingenious narrative structure that refracts de Sade's *Justine* and anticipates Thompson's.

Justine's avatars in the 1970s rescript the story of the passive heroine anticipating, in line with Foucault, the recent feminist tendency towards reading the body both as, in Butler's words, 'a field of interpretive possibilities'[25] and as historical and material, with a nomadic subjectivity in constant process.[26] These passive heroines of the 1970s, by rejecting blamelessness in a crafty way, have illustrated the mechanics of the intricate agency formations distilled in Carter's argument that 'Flesh comes to us out of history'.[27]

By being a cunning palimpsest, *a story beneath a story*, Thompson's *Justine* manages to reanimate her precursors. The old textual layers are now retraceable, which enables a better understanding, and highlights the Gothic as a genre that traverses many texts and accommodates a fluid subject position. Justine, through the centuries, has offered not a fixed history of subjectivity, but its deconstruction, by divesting the persistent myth of the 'Perfect Woman' of its allure and by exposing any strategy by which women are compensated for their powerlessness by being turned into goddesses as suspect. At this moment in history, when Sleeping Beauty's brood of avatars continues to thrive in popular culture,[28] 'illusory metaphysics' remains with us because, as Carter grimly put it, 'if the goddess is dead, there is nowhere for eternity to hide', which frightens us because the result would be the 'final secularization of mankind'.[29] To recast the history of the passive heroine through the Gothic, then, as women writers have ventured to do in recent decades, is to reconfigure, to *remake* the stories and histories we are told. In other words, to mistrust myths and bankrupt ideologies, to do away with the lure of suffering by holding Justine's prolific image as the narrative agent of the text, is a way of postulating that fiction can become a means for women to step into the demythologizing business, a way for them to enter history.

Notes

1. Charlotte Perkins Gilman's *The Yellow Wallpaper* (1892), Daphne Du Maurier's *Rebecca* (1938) and Jean Rhys's *Wide Sargasso Sea* (1966) are some famous examples. The 'madwoman in the attic' paradigm was first theorized by Sandra M. Gilbert and Susan Gubar in *The Madwoman in the Attic: The Woman Writer and the Nineteenth-Century Literary Imagination* (New Haven, CT: Yale University Press, 1979).
2. Susanne Becker, *Gothic Forms of Feminine Fictions* (Manchester: Manchester University Press, 1999), p. 10.

3. Notable exceptions are two articles by E. J. Clery and Angela Wright that address the issue extensively. See E. J. Clery, 'Ann Radcliffe and D. A. F. de Sade: Thoughts on Heroinism', *Women's Writing*, 1, 2 (1994), 203–14; Angela Wright, 'European Disruptions of the Idealized Woman: Matthew Lewis's *The Monk* and the Marquis de Sade's *La Nouvelle Justine*', in Avril Horner (ed.) *European Gothic: A Spirited Exchange 1760–1960* (Manchester: Manchester University Press, 2002), pp. 39–54.
4. Angela Carter, *The Sadeian Woman: An Exercise in Cultural History* (London: Virago, 1979).
5. Victor Sage and Allan Lloyd Smith (eds), 'Introduction' in *Modern Gothic; A Reader* (Manchester: Manchester University Press, 1996), p. 10.
6. Ibid., p. 4.
7. Emma Tennant's *Two Women of London* (1989), Valerie Martin's *Mary Reilly* (1990) – both rewrites of Stevenson's *The Strange Case of Dr Jekyll and Mr Hyde* – and Elspeth Barker's *O Caledonia* (1991), based on Sir Walter Scott's *The Lay of the Last Minstrel* (1805), are only a few examples of novels that set out to rewrite earlier narratives. For an extended discussion of Tennant's and Barker's novels, see Carol Anderson, 'Emma Tennant, Elspeth Barker, Alice Thompson: Gothic Revisited', in Aileen Christianson and Alison Lumsden (eds) *Contemporary Scottish Women Writers* (Edinburgh: Edinburgh University Press, 2000), pp. 117–30.
8. Alice Thompson, *Justine* (London: Virago, 1996), p. 137. Further references appear in the text.
9. Alice Thompson, *Pandora's Box* (London: Virago, 1999), p. 7, p. 14.
10. David Punter, 'Postmodern Gothic: The Moment beneath the Moment', *Etudes Britanniques Contemporaines*, 23 (December 2002), 1–17.
11. Mario Praz in his seminal study *The Romantic Agony* as early as 1933 traced the emergence of the *persecuted maiden* in medieval romances (Oxford University Press edition of 1970, p. 166). More recently, Angela Carter spotted Justine's mutability as a trope, when she maintained in *The Sadeian Woman* that she is 'the heroine of a black, inverted fairy tale and its subject is the misfortunes of unfreedom' (p. 39).
12. First composed in 1787 as *Les Infortunes de la Vertu* (*Justine or the Misfortunes of Virtue*) it appeared in 1791, after considerable re-vision, as *Justine, ou les Malheurs de la Vertu* (*Justine, or Good Conduct Well Chastised*) and finally became a much larger work, *La Nouvelle Justine* (*The New Justine*), in 1797. See Jean-Marc Kehr, 'Libertine Anatomies: Figures of Monstrosity in Sade's *Justine, ou les Malheurs de la Vertu*', *Eighteenth-Century Life*, 21, 2 (1997), 100.
13. I have consulted a recent anthology: The Marquis de Sade, *Three Complete Novels: Justine, Philosophy in the Bedroom and Other Writings* (London: Arrow Books, 1991). This book contains the second version of Justine: *Justine, or Good Conduct Well Chastised*.
14. The 'explained supernatural' is a narrative device whereby, as E. J. Clery puts it, 'apparently supernatural occurrences are spine-chillingly evoked only to be explained away in the end as the product of natural causes'; see *The Rise of Supernatural Fiction, 1762–1800* (Cambridge: Cambridge University Press, 1995), p. 106, p. 108.
15. In Ann Radcliffe's *The Mysteries of Udolpho* (London: Penguin, 2001), Emily is always on the verge of being abused. She is either about to be married

against her will (to Count Morano) or even raped (by Montoni), but nothing is ever actualized. Conversely, Justine's fears are actualized to the utmost degree. She undergoes numerous hardships at the hands of powerful men, is unjustly accused of crimes and repeatedly raped and tortured.

16. Dalia Judovitz, 'Sex, or the Misfortunes of Literature', in David B. Allison, Mark S. Roberts and Allen S. Weiss (eds) *Sade and the Narrative of Transgression* (Cambridge: Cambridge University Press, 1995), p. 172.
17. D. A. F. de Sade, 'Reflections on the Novel', *The 120 Days of Sodom and Other Writings* (London: Arrow Books, 1991), p. 109.
18. Carter, *The Sadeian Woman*, p. 54.
19. Ibid., p. 47.
20. Ibid., p. 5.
21. Lorna Sage, *Angela Carter* (Plymouth: Northcote House Publishers, 1994), p. 39.
22. Carol Anderson makes a similar point when she refers to Thompson's male narrator: 'Byronically club-footed yet "angel-faced" he embodies the novel's many Gothic dualities and doublings' ('Emma Tennant, Elspeth Barker, Alice Thompson: Gothic Revisited'), p. 122.
23. Carter, *The Sadeian Woman*, p. 109, p. 106.
24. Angela Carter, *Shadow Dance* (London: Virago, 1995; first published in 1966). For a more extended reference to the relation between de Sade's Justine and Carter's Ghislaine (and a brief, earlier version of the discussion of Thompson's novel *Justine* which mostly focuses on its metafictional, 'Borgesian-like' nature), see my article 'Justine Revisiting', *Etudes Britanniques Contemporaines*, 23 (December 2002), 19–30.
25. See Michel Foucault, *The History of Sexuality: Volume One. An Introduction*, trans. Robert Hurvey (London: Penguin, 1990). Judith Butler, 'Sex and Gender in Simone de Beauvoir's *Second Sex*', *Yale French Studies*, 72 (1986), 45.
26. See Rosi Braidotti, *Nomadic Subjects* (New York: Columbia University Press, 1994).
27. Carter, *The Sadeian Woman*, p. 11.
28. In Anne Rice's novels for example, written under the pseudonym A. N. Roquelaure: *The Claiming of the Sleeping Beauty* (1983), *Beauty's Punishment* (1984) and *Beauty's Release* (1985).
29. Carter, *The Sadeian Woman*, p. 141, p. 110.

13
The Resisting Writer: Revisiting the Canon, Rewriting History in Sena Jeter Naslund's *Ahab's Wife, or The Star-Gazer*

Jeannette King

'American literature is male'. So Judith Fetterley insisted in *The Resisting Reader*, one of the most influential examples of second-wave feminist criticism. She argued that 'to read the canon of what is currently considered classic American literature is perforce to identify as male',[1] specifically to identify with a male protagonist on the run from civilization, domestication and marital responsibility. The woman reader is, therefore, interpellated into a position from which she must identify against herself – unless she becomes the resisting reader of Fetterley's title. While writers like Toni Morrison and Alice Walker have transformed the canon which Fetterley so deplored, others have responded to her challenge by becoming 'resisting writers'. Although Fetterley argues that 'women obviously cannot rewrite literary works so that they become ours by virtue of reflecting our reality',[2] this is in a sense what some contemporary women novelists have done. The American bestseller *Ahab's Wife, or The Star-Gazer* (1999) by Sena Jeter Naslund[3] constructs a richly imagined life for the woman briefly referred to in Herman Melville's epic *Moby Dick*, engaging intertextually not only with Melville's novel but with Owen Chase's *Narrative of the Shipwreck of the Whale Ship Essex of Nantucket* (1821),[4] the true story which inspired Melville. In the process, Naslund illuminates areas of experience which 'resist' the male orientation of the classic American canon, and joins Angela Carter in the 'demythologizing business' which Michael Sinowitz explores in Chapter 7 of this book (p. 102).

Fetterley was not, however, the first critic to identify this orientation. As early as 1959, Leslie Fiedler argued in his influential study of American fiction that it consisted largely of boys' adventure stories, quoting Melville's statement that he wrote *Moby Dick* for 'the discriminating male reader'.[5] Describing her daughter's enthusiasm for Melville's novel, Naslund nevertheless records her own disappointment that 'there was no wonderful woman character... with whom she might identify'.[6] By placing a woman at the centre of *Ahab's Wife*, which builds on Melville's original in so many ways, she as it were fills the gap left by this absence. The extent of her engagement with that giant of the American canon is evident from the moment that the reader opens *Ahab's Wife* and finds what appears to be a facsimile of a nineteenth-century novel, complete with etched illustrations and with echoes of its predecessor in the layout of its contents page and the series of 'Extracts' which preface both novels. The style similarly echoes Melville's syntax, imagery and cadences, and in the chapters set in New Bedford, allusions to the opening of *Moby Dick* come thick and fast: to the pulpit in the Whaleman's Chapel which the minister enters via a rope ladder, pulling it up behind him; to Mrs Hussey's chowder and the Try Tops Tavern and to the brindled cow who feeds on fish remains and wears a cod's head on each foot. Naslund's heroine is, moreover, conceived not just as Ahab's wife but as his mirror image. When Una Spenser first sights Ahab, she experiences a flash of recognition, seeing his scarred cheek as a sign that he too *'has stood next to lightning'* (p. 178), as she did on the balcony of her uncle's lighthouse. She calls him 'a male version' (p. 291) of herself, since he too has achieved insight only through experiencing horrors. More surprisingly, perhaps, Ahab also recognizes his likeness in Una, a woman less than half his age: she is 'a girl-child... with his spirit' (p. 18). He tells her, 'Thou art as I am, though we be female and male' (p. 358). By establishing this equivalence between male and female, Naslund foregrounds the way that, in contrast, the reader of *Moby Dick* is encouraged to identify with experiences constructed as exclusively male.

Naslund recasts the classic adventure narrative in female terms, simultaneously jettisoning the conventional narrative of nineteenth-century womanhood. Cutting off her hair to disguise herself as a cabin boy represents Una's deliberate rejection of the constraints of femininity, and that domesticity which she wishes to escape just as much as any nineteenth-century American hero. As Melville's Ishmael puts it, 'every robust healthy boy with a robust healthy soul in him'[7] wants to go to sea, a rite of passage towards male adulthood in the nineteenth-century whaling communities in which *Ahab's Wife* is set.[8] Una's success at carrying out such a deceit challenges the rigid sexual distinctions inscribed in nineteenth-century gender ideology. Able to climb the mast like a man and as sharp-sighted as any of the men sent aloft to sight whales, Una's achievements close the gap between male and female aspiration and experience. Her decision to go to sea marks her break with her destiny as a young woman, which she accurately identifies as marriage and motherhood, associated with the pain and loss of child-birth and miscarriage. Una is conscious of rewriting history, determined not only to live a life different from that of other women, but to be able to tell a different tale. She wants no more 'uniquely female' stories (p. 142). Once she has 'begun to see [her] own life as a story and [herself] as the author of it' (p. 158), she claims a degree of autonomy and self-determination not usually associated with women of the time. Even marriage, when it comes, is not for her the end of the story, as it is for so many nineteenth-century heroines.

Naslund's challenge to the male adventure narrative is not, however, confined to her representation of Una's dramatic life at sea, for she suggests that there is also adventure to be found in the more traditional patterns of a woman's life. Although the difficulties may be mental rather than physical, Naslund finds equivalents for male experience in female lives. Una speculates on her mother's sewing: 'Had her needle trudged, as a man's foot might trudge, over a journey of a thousand miles? . . . And when one stitches, the mind travels, not the way men do, with ax and oxen through the wilderness, but surely our traveling counted too, as motion' (p. 70). Una does not need therefore to cross-dress to prove herself the possessor of 'masculine' courage. After she returns to Nantucket, and her ill-fated shipboard marriage to Kit comes to an end, she experiences a kind of rebirth into identification with the female at the hands of Mrs Macy, who bathes her with glycerine and rosewater, so that Una emerges feeling both 'new and clean' and yet 'her own old self again' (p. 349). Una is in effect being prepared for her marriage to Captain Ahab, which results in pregnancy and appears to reinsert Una into the traditional woman's narrative. But these experiences result in further trials of her courage, awakening her to an under-standing of the heroism inherent in those 'uniquely female' stories. Naslund's language draws attention to the analogies between male and female experience of being tested. When Una returns home to Kentucky to have her child, she and her mother seem 'a little ship of sorts' (p. 403). In labour she 'circled without progress on a sea of pain' (p. 405), but does not reach 'the port of motherhood' safely (p. 4). Una has to endure not only the agonies of birth in a snowbound log cabin, helped only by a young escaped slave, but also the death of her child and her mother, who heroically attempts to seek help. Although this event occurs relatively late in Una's life, Naslund opens her novel with it, in order to establish the nature of female heroism and tragedy firmly in the reader's mind before introducing the more familiar world of masculine adventuring.

Naslund emphasizes, moreover, that Una is to be regarded as a representative rather than a unique figure. Responding to a reader's suggestion that Una is a twentieth-century woman placed in the nineteenth century, Naslund explains that she 'flanked' Una with the historical figures Maria Mitchell and Margaret Fuller specifically 'to suggest that there were women of tremendous intellect and courage and curiosity at that time', and to counter any suggestion that women like Una did not exist.[9] Mitchell, a pioneering astronomer and abolitionist, tells Una that Nantucket is 'famous for [its] independent women as well as for [its] intrepid whalers' (p. 600).[10] Since whalers' wives were alone for up to five years at a time, they took sole responsibility for the family, often protected their husbands' financial and business interests and sometimes took paid work themselves.[11] Some historians have argued that the domination of colonial Nantucket by Quakers, who insisted on spiritual equality for all, further enabled women like the pioneering feminist Lucretia Mott to develop an assertiveness unusual for the period. Una's adventures therefore have their roots in a local tradition of female independence which undermined traditional notions of sexual difference. When Una meets Fuller, this influential nineteenth-century American feminist, author of *Woman in the Nineteenth Century* (1845), sums up her book's argument for women's emancipation with the words, 'Let them be sea captains – if they will!' (p. 381).[12] Although Una's time at sea anticipates Fuller's dream, it is historically authentic, according to Norland's research into the diaries and journals of nineteenth-century women who went to sea in whaling ships.[13] Nor is her disguise as a boy unique. As David Cordingly writes, in relation to female sailors and pirates,

We will never know how many women went to sea as men because the only cases we have any evidence of are those in which the woman's sex was revealed and publicized in some way, or those cases where a woman left the sea and had her story published. . . . What is striking about the genuine cases of female sailors is how they were able to fool the men on board for weeks, months, and in some cases, several years.[14]

When therefore Fuller says to Una, 'You are the American woman' (p. 591), she is asserting that women, too, are part of the American tradition so firmly identified as male in nineteenth-century fiction.

Presenting Una as the female counterpart to the freedom-seeking hero of classic American fiction, Naslund engages with the defining features of that fiction as identified by Fiedler, for whom it is essentially about heroic quests undertaken in a natural setting from which women are excluded. In such fiction, beasts are 'monstrous embodiments of the natural world in all its ambiguous and indestructible essence',[15] which the hero must overcome. Like Angela Carter, in Sinowitz's reading of *Nights at the Circus*, Naslund responds to masculine myth-making by suggesting the material practices reflected by those myths. While demolishing the polarity which excludes women from the natural world, *Ahab's Wife* suggests that men and women have a different relationship with nature. Una's father defends killing her dog with the words, 'The Lord has given man dominion over the creatures of the earth' (p. 22). Ahab's injury by the white whale, however, appears to prove God's promise of dominion false, so that he must pursue and destroy the whale to prove he is still 'sovereignty in [himself]' (p. 510). His role in *Ahab's Wife* can also be interpreted in the light of another canonical narrative alluded to by Naslund – Edmund Spenser's *The Faerie Queen.* Giles Bonebright, Una's first love, is the first to link Una Spenser with her namesake, the lady of the Red Cross knight – 'pure of heart, steadfast, and clear of mind' (p. 110). He offers to slay dragons for her and does indeed save her life when they are both shipwrecked, but it is Ahab who most obviously embodies the dragon slayer, the great white whale being 'the King of Dragons' (p. 512), who has devoured too many young Nantucketeers. But while the harpooners remind Una of stories of knights and dragons, she does not confuse the whaler's role with that of the quest hero, finding nothing but 'sad blood' on the whaling ship, since the dragons in those stories had never been female, leaving behind a frightened 'chick' (p. 183). And where Spenser's Una represents truth, Naslund's actively pursues it. The novel's subtitle, 'the Stargazer', draws attention to her search for solace in the night sky and the knowledge that she is made of the same atoms as the stars: '*We are kin to stars*' (p. 502).[16] Where Ahab is driven by the desire to dominate Nature, Una hopes only to achieve a sense of oneness with it.

According to Fiedler, dominion over nature is, moreover, linked with a denial of the female which is also characteristic of nineteenth-century American fiction. As Naslund's Ishmael puts it, 'When we kill [the sea's] mightiest creature, . . . surely we show that we hate the oceanic mother' (pp. 644–5). Where Una experiences the breaching of gender boundaries as liberation, most of the men in the novel perceive it as a threat. When Kit tells Una, 'They've made a man of you, and they've tried to make a woman of me' (p. 187), he implies such feminization is a source of shame, even a signifier of his madness when he becomes 'unsexed' (p. 273). The threat to masculinity is felt even more strongly by Ahab. Losing his leg to the white whale inevitably makes him feel himself 'unmanned' (p. 513) by this threat to a way of life which epitomizes the manly virtues of courage and adventure and by a symbolic castration rendering him unable to give Una another child. To retrieve his manhood he vows to beget a new 'Justice' (the name of his only son), 'not with any woman. With the sea. She shall open her thighs and yield up the whale to me' (p. 513). But the concept of fatherhood – another defining element in traditional constructions of masculinity – is also feminized by the novel. Ahab ultimately fails in the role of father because, Naslund suggests, the 'good' father, as opposed to such bad fathers as Una's, combines traditionally 'masculine' and 'feminine' qualities. Captain Fry of the *Sussex*, for instance, has in Una's view 'the eyes of a true father' 'as though he were [her] mother but invested with power' (p. 151, p. 153). When his ship is destroyed by the white whale and the survivors take to the boats, Fry sacrifices his own life to save his son's, unaware that the blow intended to render the child unconscious, sparing him the sight of his father's suicide, has killed him. Giles describes this act as an 'answer to Christianity', since it replaces the father's sacrifice of his son, central to the Christian tradition, with an act which instead belongs in the tradition of self-sacrificial love more often associated with motherhood. In contrast, in an incident borrowed from *Moby Dick*, when the Captain of *The Rachel* asks Ahab, as another father, to join his search for his son, adrift in a whaling boat dragged away by the white whale, Ahab refuses to interrupt his hunt for the whale. His rejection of this appeal to his paternal feelings is also a rejection of the 'feminine' qualities of compassion and self-sacrifice which signifies the loss of his humanity.

In the classic American tradition, this denial of the female is also articulated in the substitution of what Fiedler calls 'the Holy Marriage of Males'[17] for the heterosexual marriage central to the nineteenth-century European novel. He cites the relationship between Melville's Ishmael and Queequeg as a love 'which develops on the pattern of a marriage: achieving in the course of a single voyage the shape of a whole lifetime shared, and symbolizing a spiritual education' in contrast to the 'spiritual death implicit in fleshly marriage with women'.[18] This 'innocent homosexuality'[19] is evident when Ishmael describes the crew working on the whale's spermaceti, where the ambiguity of the word 'sperm' and the 'loving feeling' generated when the men squeeze each other's hands by mistake all conduce to the homoerotic feeling of the scene. Naslund similarly describes Kit's hands becoming soft because 'spermaceti is like a ladies' emollient' (p. 186). She, however, makes the fear of the feminine more overt, and the homoerotic becomes explicitly sexual and violent, when Giles forces anal intercourse on Kit, an act Kit in turn forces on Una, venting on her his sense of degradation at being made a substitute for a woman.

The exclusion of the feminine from classic American fiction is, moreover, justified by what Fiedler cites as the corollary of that exclusion: the assumption that women are the guardians of a constricting domestic order, which is always a hindrance to male freedom. Naslund contests this demarcation between private domestic space and the wider, unexplored world which represents freedom by showing that Una first experiences freedom in her uncle's lighthouse, the most confined of spaces. Here she learns to reject the 'tyranny of religion and paternity' (p. 53) because here no one wishes 'to constrain or define' her (p. 37). In *Ahab's Wife*, woman no longer represents constraint but is herself actively involved in the struggle for freedom. From the maternal side, Una inherits a tradition of free thinking and living deeply connected, as already noted, to its historical and cultural context. She remembers her mother tearing down a poster offering a reward for the return of an escaped slave while reciting the opening of the Declaration of Independence. Una's initial desire for freedom of thought becomes absorbed into the struggle for female emancipation, as she resorts to living as a man in order to achieve the kind of freedom so readily available to Kit and Giles.

Ahab's Wife further suggests that freedom is too complex a concept to be identified simply with running away from constraint. The story of Una's son, who travels to Europe in a ship called the Liberty, enacts the classic American view that freedom is only to be found away from home. Not long before, however, the drowning of Liberty, the child of Una's cousin Frannie, like the stillbirth of Una's first child, also called Liberty, warns that true freedom is not so easily achieved; it has to be pursued with steady persistence, particularly by women. Nowhere is this more apparent than in the story of Susan, the escaped slave who helps Una through that first birth. Susan voluntarily returns to slavery out of love for her mother, having decided that freedom 'was Nothing' (p. 535), if nothing in the free world meant anything to her. She too names her child Liberty, out of her sustained conviction: 'We will have freedom, and we will have it right this time' (p. 661). In her penultimate letter to Una, she describes herself as Una's 'shadow self' (p. 538), and signs herself Susan

Spenser, adopting Una's maiden name. Her readiness to identify with
another woman's quest for freedom, across the racial divide, suggests a
close identification between female and racial emancipation.

Even in the classic American novel, Fiedler acknowledges that the
rejection of female ties seems a rejection of life itself, a kind of suicide,[20] a
suggestion for which there is some historical underpinning. Here again,
Naslund's approach can usefully be compared with Carter's, as discussed
by Sinowitz in this book, since Naslund engages with Melville's myth-
making by recuperating the material, historical conditions underlying
his creation of the symbolic quest for the white whale, particularly in
relation to the role of women in that history. In her study of women of
the whaling community, Lisa Norling argues that, while seafaring was
traditionally a highly gendered world, 'an aggressively masculine world
of "iron men in wooden ships" that marginalized and objectified real
women while feminizing the sea, ships, and shoreside society',[21] in the
period in which *Ahab's Wife* is set these divisions were reinforced by new
ideas of sexual difference imported from Europe, which defined men
and women as fundamentally different beings belonging to two separate
spheres. Central to this ideology was the ideal of domesticity, of the
home as a private and spiritualized haven where men could be renewed
after their brutalizing voyages. Women therefore assumed an enormous
symbolic importance, in addition to their practical responsibilities. For
Una, this importance is embodied in the red square, representing the
hearth, at the centre of the log-cabin pattern on her mother's quilt.
Giles also stresses the happiness to be found 'in the hearth and in the
heart' (p. 123), while insisting on his need to travel, and this 'push-
pull rhythm of movement between land and sea, home and work'[22] is
even more evident in Una's relationship with Ahab. Where Melville's
Ahab admits he would rather look into Starbuck's eyes where he can see
the 'bright hearthstone',[23] than at the sea or sky, Naslund constructs
the life this 'hearthstone' represents, the female ties which could have
been his salvation. She turns Ahab into a hero in the Romantic tradition which celebrated emotional intensity in love for another, another
tradition which Norling argues had a radical impact on perceptions of
sexual relations in America in this period. At sea, Ahab writes that Una
'completes' him for the first time: he feels 'full of life, not madness'
(p. 453). Returning home, he says farewell to his ship as to a 'seducer',
who has kept him from his true wife. The 'soft glow reflecting the hearth'
on his face is contrasted to 'the demonic burning from the try-pots'
(p. 473), likened to the fires of hell. The ambiguity of this central metaphor of fire is, however, addressed by Ahab himself when fire breaks

out in Nantucket: 'The fires of hell, the fires of creation – they are all one' (p. 358). He feels, moreover, that he needs to be purified by fire till 'fit for hearth and home' (p. 358). Ahab here asserts the indivisibility of the passions which drive him – the intensity of his love for Una and the 'rapture' he experiences in his hunt for the whale, also 'a kind of marriage' (p. 453) – at the same time as their essential incompatibility. This conflict is the source of both Ahab's tragic nature and the inevitably tragic outcome of his story.

The significance of Naslund's decision to oppose Una's story of survival to Ahab's tragic obsession with the white whale becomes clearer if we compare her engagement with her historical source with Melville's. Both *Ahab's Wife* and *Moby Dick* are partly inspired by the true story of the whaling ship, the *Essex*, as written by Owen Chase, the first mate, in 1821. Chase describes how the whale, a creature 'never before suspected of premeditated violence', 'appeared with tenfold fury and vengeance in his aspect' and deliberately rammed the ship twice, destroying it and forcing the survivors to take to the whaling boats, and ultimately to resort to cannibalism.[24] Melville ignores this final dramatic episode in the *Essex's* story to maintain his focus on Ahab's quest, but his novel nevertheless abounds in references to cannibalism – literal and meta-phorical. Literal cannibalism is embodied only in the non-Europeans of the whaling community, the 'savages' and 'cannibals' who haunt New Bedford, some of them joining the crew of the Pequod. Such savagery is projected onto the 'Other' races, obscuring the possibility that white Americans might resort to eating each other, in spite of the evidence in Melville's source. Metaphorical use of the term is more pervasive. The Pequod is described as 'a cannibal of a craft' (p. 82), because she uses the bones of her enemy, the whale, in place of wood. And in both *Ahab's Wife* and its precursor Ahab refers to himself as '*cannibal old me*' (p. 433).[25] Routinely described by Melville as black, Ahab is associated both with the 'savages', the dark races, and with the night which represents the darkness within. Ishmael, *Moby Dick's* narrator, equates the eating of any creature's flesh with the eating of human flesh, asking 'who is not a cannibal?'[26] when he compares Fijian islanders eating a missionary to survive famine with those who torture a goose before eating its liver as a luxury. Is Ishmael's analogy an admission that the hunting of the whale is an act of brutality equal to human cannibalism? Could it also be a tacit acknowledgement by Melville that his projection of this 'savagery' onto the black races is a falsification of maritime history? If Melville chose not to incorporate the story of the *Essex's* survivors into his narrative, this is perhaps because that story of man's ultimate helplessness in the face of nature, and their readiness to kill each other to survive, runs contrary to the story of heroic action and male bonding that Fiedler identifies as defining elements in the American tradition.

In contrast, Naslund bases a significant part of Una's story on that of the *Essex*'s survivors. Like the men of the *Essex*, the men of the *Sussex* refuse their Captain's advice to head for the nearest land, because they fear meeting cannibals there, heading instead for South America, two thousand miles away. They too are in consequence reduced to cannibalism themselves: as Giles points out, 'They should have feared the cannibal within' (p. 214). But cannibalism is the only means of survival, a reality confirmed when the remaining boat is found full of 'bones and human rot' (p. 309). Chase's narrative endorses their behaviour as acceptable in survival situations,[27] and explains that the generally agreed procedure was to cast lots, in keeping with 'biblical sortilege – the dependence on what looks like chance to know the will of God'.[28] Even the youngest of his crew, Owen Coffin, whose name was first to be drawn, faced his 'lot' with stoic acceptance, as does Naslund's first victim, Chester Fry, echoing Coffin's words with his own: 'It is as good a fate as any' (p. 225). But Giles breaks with this tradition, abrogating to himself the divine authority to choose who is to die. He is, in a sense, given this power when the dying Captain Fry passes his sword to him, in the hope that Giles will then protect his son. The sword clearly suggests the phallus, itself a signifier of the power that accrues to masculinity in a patriarchal society. While I have suggested that this act belongs to the tradition of self-sacrificial maternal love, it is also possible, therefore, to see it as a patriarchal act, since Fry acts 'in the name of the father', both in protecting his son and in passing on his phallic power, embodied in an instrument of force, to Giles. It enacts the principle of 'women and children first', which is one of the more benign consequences of patriarchal ideology. Una is further protected from the full horror of cannibalism because Giles feeds her, allowing her to keep her own eyes closed. But although Kit and Giles justify the deaths of the others in the boat as an act of love, the only means of preserving the 'knot of love' (p. 232) between the three friends, Giles takes the Captain's place not in any spirit of self-sacrifice, but driven by a belief in his own superiority which entitles him to assume the godlike power of life and death. Ultimately, Giles pays the price for his arrogance, meeting Icarus's fate by falling – or more likely jumping – from the masthead of the ship that rescues them. After such knowledge, for him there can be no forgiveness. For Kit, madness is the escape route from guilt. Both men prove their

masculinity in the terms in which patriarchal ideology defines it, by acts
of violence in the name of love which ultimately prove self-destructive.

Una can, however, be seen to be complicit in patriarchal ideology
in so far as she is saved from both death and madness by her friends'
murderous acts. She does not avoid the guilt of the survivor, although
she is able to live with it. For Naslund's narrative is essentially about
survival and the powers of endurance and belief which make survival
possible against terrible odds. In *Ahab's Wife*, moreover, survival is
gendered as 'feminine', if not 'female'. The power to endure passively
has traditionally been associated with woman, rather than man, who
has the prerogative of heroic action, and Una's survival at sea is secured
by the men who love her. But she is not the novel's only image of
survival. The other, inherited from Melville, is male – Ishmael. Ishmael
is also saved symbolically by love – floating to safety on Queequeg's
raftlike coffin. And as Fiedler notes, Ishmael has been feminized by his
relationship with Queequeg, which functions as a kind of marriage.
After Ahab's death, Una's free union with Ishmael satisfies her desire for
freedom while enabling the two to become truly 'one' (p. 651), because
in each the traditional gender boundaries have been broken down. The
fruit of their union is appropriately named Felicity. Ishmael, quoting
Melville's original (p. 271), tells Una that 'in the soul of man there lies
his one insular Tahiti, full of peace and joy, but encompassed by all
the horrors of the half-known life' (p. 643), and that if men turn away
from their Tahiti, they risk becoming savages. This is the fate of both
the crew of the Sussex and Ahab. In contrast, Ishmael and Una 'rejoice
in the hearth' (p. 663), and are saved by it.

Both Una and Ishmael are survivors of extreme situations, who live to
tell the tale and see their writing as a continuance of that tale, a means of
continuing the search for truth and of dealing with their demons. As Una
asks, 'Could the narration of pain, and of what had been of sustaining
value in difficult times, be in itself redeeming?' (p. 418). She and Ishmael
are in a sense writing 'the same book' (p. 663). Ishmael's book about
his experiences, about ships and whales, will become *Moby Dick*, which
Una invokes in her final paragraph, echoing Melville's riveting opening,
'Call me Ishmael', with the words, 'I shall call Ishmael' (p. 666). But Una
is also conscious of writing a story which provides a female alternative
to the traditional American male-centred narrative:

And if one wrote for American men a modern epic, a quest, and
it ended in death and destruction, should such a tale not have its
redemptive features? Was it not possible instead for a human life to

end in a sense of wholeness, of harmony with the universe? And how might a woman live such a life? (p. 417)

Through her re-visioning of Ahab's story, Naslund achieves Fetterley's aim of exposing the male bias in American literature which 'neither leaves women alone nor allows them to participate. It insists on its universality at the same time that it defines that universality in specifically male terms.'[29] Together, the two narratives of Melville and Naslund constitute a more complete, more 'universal', story of Ahab and his wife, the Romance as well as the epic adventure. When Tim Cahill, in his 1999 introduction to Chase's narrative, comments that it 'inspired one of the great masterpieces of American literature, and even today, one can hardly read it without imagining that there is at least one more great novel buried, gemlike, somewhere in its wonderfully stiff and stoic prose',[30] he has clearly not had the chance to read *Ahab's Wife*.

Notes

1. Judith Fetterley, *The Resisting Reader: A Feminist Approach to American Fiction* (Bloomington, IN: Indiana University Press, 1978), p. xii.
2. Ibid., p. xxiii.
3. Sena Jeter Naslund, *Ahab's Wife, or The Star-Gazer* was first published by William Morrow in 1999. All further references to the novel will be to the paperback edition (New York: HarperCollins, 2000) and will follow the relevant quotation in the text.
4. See Owen Chase, *Narrative of the Most Extraordinary and Distressing Shipwreck of the Whaleship Essex*, Tim Cahill (ed.) (New York: Lyons Press, 1999). Nathaniel Philbrick has added to Chase's account that of Thomas Nickerson, the *Essex*'s cabin boy, found in 1960; see *In the Heart of the Sea: The Epic True Story that Inspired 'Moby Dick'* (New York: HarperCollins, 2000).
5. Leslie A. Fiedler, *Love and Death in the American Novel* (London: Paladin, 1970), p. 225.
6. See interview on Kentucky Educational Television's Bookclub (http://www.ket.org/bookclub/books/2000_jul/), downloaded January 2005.
7. Herbert Melville, *Moby Dick or The White Whale* (New York: New American Library, 1961), p. 23.
8. See Lisa Norling, *Captain Ahab had a Wife: New England Women and the Whalefishery, 1720–1870* (Chapel Hill, NC: University of North Carolina Press, 2000), p. 140.
9. See Kentucky Educational Television's Bookclub online interview.
10. Maria Mitchell (1818–1889) discovered a comet with her telescope at the age of twenty-eight, and became the first woman to be admitted to the American Academy of Arts and Sciences and the first Professor of Astronomy at Vasser College. See Susan Raven and Alison Weir, *Women in History: Thirty-five*

Centuries of Feminine Achievement (London: Weidenfeld & Nicolson, 1981), pp. 236–8.

11. See Norling, *Captain Ahab had a Wife*, pp. 148–54.
12. Margaret Fuller's exact words were: 'let them be sea-captains, if you will'. See her *Woman in the Nineteenth Century*, Larry J. Reynolds (ed.) (New York: Norton, 1998), p. 102.
13. Further corroborative evidence is provided by David Cordingly, *Women Sailors and Sailors' Women: An Untold Maritime History* (New York: Random House, 2001).
14. Ibid., pp. 60–1. Cordingly confirms that a number of young women were, like Una, capable of working aloft and succeeded in their disguise because they were able, given the dress of the time, to look like adolescent boys.
15. Fiedler, *Love and Death in the American Novel*, p. 334.
16. In contrast, Melville's other sailor hero, Bulkington, cannot stay away from the sea because 'in landlessness alone resides the highest truth' (*Moby Dick*, p. 116).
17. Fiedler, *Love and Death in the American Novel*, p. 355.
18. Ibid., p. 346, p. 355.
19. Ibid., p. 355.
20. Ibid., p. 325.
21. Norling, *Captain Ahab had a Wife*, p. 2.
22. Ibid., p. 140.
23. Melville, *Moby Dick*, p. 507.
24. Chase, *Narrative of the Most Extraordinary and Distressing Shipwreck*, p. 27, p. 21.
25. Melville, *Moby Dick*, p. 508.
26. Ibid., p. 293.
27. By the early nineteenth century, in Philbrick's words, 'cannibalism at sea was so widespread that survivors often felt compelled to inform their rescuers if they had *not* resorted to it' (*In the Heart of the Sea*, p. 164), since the assumption would otherwise be that they had.
28. Chase, *Narrative of the Most Extraordinary and Distressing Shipwreck*, p. xxv.
29. Fetterley, *The Resisting Reader*, p xii.
30. Cahill, Introduction to Chase, *Narrative of the Most Extraordinary and Distressing Shipwreck*, p. ix.

14
Breaking the Mould? Sarah Waters and the Politics of Genre
Mark Llewellyn

Imagine Jeanette Winterson on a good day, collaborating with Judith Butler to pen a sapphic Moll Flanders. Could this be a new genre? Whatever it is, take it with you. It's gorgeous.[1]

As many of the chapters in this book demonstrate, historical fiction has become increasingly prominent during the last twenty years. In this final chapter, I want to explore 'historical fiction in action' by providing an overview of one of its current, most visible and popular practitioners: Sarah Waters. My interest in this piece is to bring together some of the issues that have been raised throughout this volume in relation to the present condition of 'women's' historical fiction and suggest ways in which we might read the self-reflective strain in contemporary works in this genre.

Defining what historical fiction now does in terms of contemporary fiction is not easy. *The Independent* reviewer's suggestion (above) that Waters' debut, *Tipping the Velvet* (1998), might constitute a new, hyper-fictionalized-historicized-theorized textual style which cannot yet be categorized points to a conscious desire to situate Waters' work beyond what might be defined as historical fiction. This is strange given her work has obvious connections with many of the writers already explored in this book: like Byatt, Carter, Roberts and Winterson, Waters is interested in challenging a patriarchal view of history and women's bodies, desires and emotions within it and, as in the work of the writers discussed in this section in particular, Waters seeks to make that challenge through rewriting or at least engaging textually with the written histories of previous generations.

As Anne Cranny-Francis indicated in the early 1990s, genre fiction plays an important role in the cultural and financial marketplace:

'People enjoy genre fiction; it sells by the truckload. As a conscious feminist propagandist it makes sense to use a fictional format which already has a huge market.'[2] A genre that was once overlooked, historical fiction has a clear potential to reclaim a sexually pluralistic past which also has the ability to reflect upon our own postmodern sexually politic landscape. Waters, during her time as an academic, wrote that '[t]hough frequently dismissed as romantic, escapist or historiographically naïve, women's historical fiction often constitutes a radical rewriting of traditional, male-centred historical narrative'.[3] She went on to suggest that she had 'always suspected that one of the reasons why the historical novel has received such poor and patchy critical attention is that... it has been a genre dominated by women'.[4] In her critical essays, Waters argues that historical fiction has always been a genre that has attracted lesbian and gay authors; she categorized her first three novels as 'lesbo Victorian romps', a phrase which 'has come back to haunt' her, but signals 'the way the books bring two traditions together; the thoughtful historical novel and lesbian fiction'.[5] The bringing together of literary traditions is important, because Waters' novels are at every level engagements with other literary works. Repeatedly, Waters signals that her novels are not only acts of writing but also the responses to and results of acts of reading; as Byatt has commented, this is one of the 'less solid reasons' to write historical fiction, 'to keep past literatures alive and singing, connecting the pleasure of writing to the pleasure of reading'.[6] It is these acts of reading and their importance in the construction of both historical narrative and individual identity which I want to follow in Waters' novels from *Tipping the Velvet* (1998) through to *The Night Watch* (2006).

When writing about the historical fiction of the last twenty years, it has become useful to think in terms of 'historiographic metafiction', a phrase that denotes 'those well-known and popular novels which are both intensely self-reflexive and yet paradoxically also lay claim to historical events and personages'.[7] It would, however, be an over-reading to identify Waters' work with such a label. It is rather telling in the context of the issues I wish to explore here that when even well-known (literary) figures are named in Waters' texts it is in order for the narrative to make the distinction that the protagonists are not like them: see, for example, Mrs Prior's declaration to her daughter in *Affinity*, 'You are not Mrs Browning, Margaret – as much as you would like to be',[8] a fact Margaret spends much of the narrative trying to disprove. Where Waters' texts do share a thematic with 'historiographic metafiction' is in their desire to reveal 'history as a shaping force (in the narrative and in human destiny)'.[9]

The fact that her narratives have become more complex affairs appears to signal a consciousness about the ways in which the plurality of historical voices might be constructed through the fictional text: *Tipping the Velvet* is a kind of lesbian *bildungsroman* with a coherent single narrative voice (Nancy Astley) and an auto(erotic)biographical style; *Affinity* is a dual narrative which switches between the years 1873 and 1875 in its diary accounts of the relationship between Margaret Prior and Selina Dawes; *Fingersmith* likewise has two narrators, but rather than have them chronologically separated, both tell the same narrative events from their respective positions, a signal perhaps of the need to re-read and rewrite the story at every turn; finally, and most recently, *The Night Watch*, a novel set in the 1940s and thus a historical leap forward for Waters' project of looking back, carries the accounts of four lives, three women and one man, and the narrative unfolds from end to beginning, a device which seems to play consciously with acts of reading backwards and the retracing of human stories within a larger series of historical events.

Tipping the Velvet: towards a democratic voice

My interest in Waters' first novel relates not so much to how the narrative deals with history but how it negotiates a particular element in the individual's relation to an unfolding narrative beyond their control. *Tipping the Velvet* functions as a coming-to-lesbianism novel about the various pitiful pitfalls and eventual redemption of the good girl turned bad girl who develops a social conscience. It is this social, even socialist, element of the text which proves most illuminating in the context of Waters' subsequent fiction, particularly the way in which the character's gradual emergence as a subject with a political knowledge is centred round literary works.

The scene in which Nan comes to engage with a literary-political understanding of the world is one where knowledge, conviction and self-recognition come about through the diversity of written, and thereby read, textuality. Asking Ralph and Florence, her socialist companions, who Eleanor Marx is, Nan tells us of her embarrassment and the immediate clash between the different literary milieux in which she and her friends have been educated:

I blushed: this was worse than asking what *cooperative* meant. But when Ralph saw my cheeks, he looked kind: "You mustn't mind it.

Why should you know? I'm sure, you might mention a dozen writers
you have read, and Flo and I would not know one of them."

"That's true," I said, very grateful to him; but although I *had* read
proper books at Diana's, I could think, at that moment, only of the
*im*proper ones – and they all had the same author: *Anonymous*.[10]

The difference here is between knowing the author of the text and not
knowing; between the acknowledgement of one's voice and responsibilities and the desire to hide behind the catch-all '*Anonymous*'.
This concern with authorial identification reflects a self-awareness
concerning the re-visionist's need to question the authenticity of
accounts, narratives, histories, as they are received by her. If one knows
one's author and one's own authority then one can begin to place the
events that have happened into a logical literary context; thus Nan
berates herself: 'What a fool I'd been! . . . I had believed myself playing
in one kind of story, when all the time, the plot had been a different
one' (*T*, p. 398).

But authorship and reading also play out on another historical level
in this novel, and with a far greater emphasis on the political. This
happens when Nan and Florence begin to come to an understanding
that their lesbian relationship is not about the individual but rather
serves a political purpose; identity becomes ideology and is informed
by it. It is not surprising that this realization occurs in regard to a
book nor that a physical eroticism is subsumed into a literary erotic
space:

We said nothing more, then; only kissed and murmured. But the
next night she produced a book, and had me read it. It was *Towards
Democracy*, the poem by Edward Carpenter; and as I turned the
pages, with Florence warm beside me, I found myself growing damp.
(*T*, p. 437)

The fact that the ensuing passages are about how the women caress
one another as they read the poem together, with Florence remarking
that 'I think Mr Carpenter would approve', highlights the way in which
so much of Waters' period detail concerning the emergence of Nan's
awareness of the world outside the sordidness of sex at Diana's or the
double-standard of Kitty's performances both on and off the stage is
located in the textual sphere. By keeping '*Towards Democracy* beside the
bed permanently, after that [night]' (*T*, p. 438), Florence and Nan are

actively engaging in a social revolution; embracing the possibilities of literature, thought and sexual desire in one and the same moment. It is all the more telling, then, that although Waters' first novel ends with the hopes of the physical and intellectual urge 'towards democracy', her second, moving backwards in time, has at its mysterious heart the very 'class division' and sexual divide that Carpenter and his followers sought to overcome.

Affinity: setting the past alight

The point about *Affinity* is that the one voice we never hear, that of the maidservant Ruth Vigers, is the key. The text enacts its own historical silencing upon us and in the very act of revealing the voices of the past draws attention to our failure to recognize the other class-marginalized individuals in the story; the narrative, in a sense, only draws back the medium's curtain so far and in looking for a world beyond, we fail, like Margaret, to recognize the realities of the world around us. It is not until the end of the novel that we realize that we have been duped not by the narrative but by our romanticization of the characters and the situations described to us. In presenting us with diary accounts in which we act as privileged readers of Margaret's inner thoughts, Waters allows us to collude in our own deception. The voice of the educated Margaret is tentative from the outset, and her first diary entry opens with a declaration of her own inadequacy as a story teller or creator of narrative in deference to the authority with which her father could construct 'a tale': 'Pa used to say that any piece of history might be made into a tale: it was only a question of deciding where the tale began, and where it ended' (*A*, p. 7). Unfortunately, for the readers, Waters' text hinges on the way in which Margaret seeks to emulate her father's style of accounting, recording and placing facts; Margaret becomes an imitator of male-authored history until it is too late. Although she recognizes that 'the great lives, the great works' her father worked on could be easily 'classif[ied]', she herself spends most of the narrative divided between the competing impulses of charting her passion and producing a more sedate record of the prison she visits, the inmates she meets, the research she carries out. Indeed, Margaret draws a conscious distinction between the narrative drive which has emboldened her to undertake her diary and her need to find solace and peace from the tempers of her heart in logic, reasoning and a masculine view of the role of the chronicler of history. This occurs when Margaret compares her previous attempt at authorship, the diary of her love for her now sister-in-law Helen, with the account of her visits to Millbank Prison:

> I have been thinking of my last journal, which had so much of my own heart's blood in it; and which certainly took as long to burn as human hearts, they say, do take. I mean this book to be different to that one. I mean this writing not to turn me back upon my own thoughts, but to serve, like the choral, to keep the thoughts from coming at all. (*A*, p. 70)

It is possible that Waters is providing a kind of ironic comment on the escapist impulse to both write and read historical fiction. Margaret cannot allow herself to return to her past, she cannot 'turn . . . back', yet the nature of the narrative she authors does exactly this: each diary entry is inescapably a 'turn . . . back', be it on the events of the day or the implied return to the individual past.

For Margaret the only escape from her betrayal is to be found in self-destruction rather than self-authorship. Even before the revelation of her ultimate abandonment Margaret toys with the idea of destroying her work: 'I almost burned this book to-night, as I burned the last one. I could not do it' (*A*, p. 241). Yet by the end of the novel this irresolution – which revolves, it seems, around the fact that the narrative is Margaret's only means of self-authority – has been overcome with the acknowledgment that writing one's history is not the end of the matter, that one must act upon it. In burning her diary, as she did the previous one, Margaret challenges our received interpretation of history even as she purports to destroy the evidence that would counter it:

> This is the last page I shall write. All my book is burned now, I have built a fire in the grate and set the pages on it, and when this sheet is filled with staggering lines it shall be added to the others. How queer, to write for chimney smoke! But I must write, while I still breathe. I only cannot bear to read again what I set down *before*. (*A*, p. 348)

The emphasis is interesting because it shows Margaret cannot bear past words, she cannot face the history of her relationship with Selina any more than she could endure the continued existence of that other diary of her love for Helen. The past hurts here, and lesbian desire is not portrayed as any more rewarding than its heterosexual counterpart; even the fleeing 'criminal' and her maid are trapped in a seemingly passive/dominant relationship with the novel's ominous final words,

'Remember . . . whose girl you are' (*A*, p. 352). Without a voice, without the words, for one's 'queer' emotions, the past's system of historical documentation is both a recording and a silencing depending upon who wields the power of the pen. While Selina and Ruth have the possibility of a subversive narrative beyond a materialist and textual explanation, Margaret, because of her class, education and parental relationship, does not.

Diana Wallace, amongst others, has commented on the prominence of spiritualist characters in more recent historical fiction, remarking that 'the female medium becomes a suggestive figure for the historical novelist herself, ventriloquising the voices of the past'.[11] This play with the idea of voicing the past is apparent in works like Byatt's 'The Conjugial Angel' where the metaphor can draw comfort from the fact that not all mediums are portrayed as 'dishonest', but Waters' medium is a fake. As in some ways a coauthorial representative with Margaret, Selina's duplicity must do something to call into question the role of such 'ventriloquising' itself. It is for this reason that Waters' second novel is her most disquieting. There is no resolution to the narrative for Margaret other than death by her own hand, an act prefigured by the destruction of her diary, and by implication her voice and identity, in the fire.

Fingersmith: crossing the finger

> I looked at Maud, who stood, still fumbling with the fastening of her glove; and I took a step, meaning to help her. But when he saw me do that, the old man jerked like Mr Punch in the puppet-show, and out came his black tongue. 'The finger, girl!' he cried. 'The finger! The finger!'[12]

Chastized by a man whose tongue is stained by black ink in the way his mind is stained by the imprint of his encyclopaedia of pornography, Sue Trinder is left in no doubt of the temper awaiting those who cross the demarcation line on her mistress's uncle's study floor. 'Set into the dark floorboards', Sue tells us, 'in the space between the doorway and the edge of the carpet, [was] a flat brass handle with a pointing finger' (*F*, p. 76). In this scene, Sue learns of the boundaries of knowledge – classed, gendered and sexed. The finger points to the inclusive/exclusive divide between those who have access to material print culture and those who are merely its subjects; narratives themselves, pornographic or otherwise, become histories in which people like Sue might be written about, but upon which she herself is supposed never to blacken her tongue.

The study of Maud's uncle illustrates the importance of textual and sexual understanding in the novel. As Sue takes an encompassing look around her, she sees Maud entrapped in the centre of a seemingly endless labyrinth of print: 'All about her, over all the walls of the room, were shelves; and the shelves had books on – you never saw so many. A stunning amount. How many stories did one man need?' (*F*, p. 75). The fact that Sue recognizes that it is men who need the stories and have possession of them is intuitive; to her, reading and learning, as she imagines to be the activities of Maud's uncle, are the realm of men. But Sue's naivety is more than matched by Maud's own education in a literature which has as its primary concern the relation of pleasure through story. The friction between the fictional world which Maud chronicles and also narrates on behalf of her uncle and his friends is dramatized in Maud's simultaneous ability to despise the textual framework of her existence even as she recognizes its gradual appropriation of her identity:

> My cunt grows dark as Barbara's, I understand my uncle's books to be filled with falsehoods, and I despise myself for having supposed them truths. My hot cheek cools, my colour dies, the heat quite fades from my limbs. The restlessness turns all to scorn. I become what I was bred to be. I become a librarian. (*F*, p. 201)

Both the naturalness and unnaturalness of Maud's condition are united in the final two sentences: as a woman she is 'bred to be' whatever her uncle, as male guardian, determines as her role; her education, which should be an advantage, has only made her 'a librarian', the guardian of texts which she can catalogue and index but never strictly speaking possess. Her train of thought continues as she describes the queerness of her existence, narrating multiple lives and yet remaining in a static no-place at the margins of her uncle's enterprise and on the fringes of the texts which she reads aloud:

> So my life passes. You might suppose I would not know enough of ordinary things, to know it queer. But I read other books besides my uncle's . . . I am worldly as the grossest rakes of fiction; but have never, since I first came to my uncle's house, been further than the walls of its park. I know everything. I know nothing. (*F*, p. 203)

Maud has already told us she has 'become a librarian' but we see how books and the fictions they contain are both an education and a betrayal. To 'know everything . . . know nothing' is a reflection on the emptiness and hollow centre of the pornographic text. Time plays its role in this vision and the inevitable passing of a chronological existence outside the patriarch's house may remain uncharted but it is not unremarked. Maud, in the time away from her uncle's study, questions what he thinks she does away from the books:

> Now and then I wonder how he supposes I spend my hours, when not engaged by him. I think he is too used to the particular world of his books, where time passes strangely, or not at all, and imagines me an ageless child . . . My uncle himself . . . I have always considered to have been perfectly and permanently aged; as flies remain aged, yet fixed and unchanging, in cloudy chips of amber. (*F*, p. 206)

One might consider this an indictment of the 'fixed and unchanging' nature of the patriarchal order, but Maud is casting her condemnation onto time itself, the way in which it is not a fixed, unified or chronologically egalitarian idea(l), but rather a commodity. Time, its movement, its progress, can be bought and sold like the pornography of Maud's uncle or, indeed, like the women who are traded within that same pornography; even Maud herself is a commodity, not bought but rather endured for the material benefit and assistance she can provide to her uncle, her working hours spent reading 'from an antique text' (*F*, p. 262).

For Maud, the fictions come to life at the same moment as her desires in a scene in which Waters seems to offer not only a sense of how Maud's own reading (supposedly innocent and unknowing) influences her understanding of her relationship with Sue, but also an indictment of the male-authored and male-centred world of such literary production. Maud writes:

> Even my uncle's books are changed to me; and this is worse, this is worst of all. I have supposed them dead. Now the words – like the figures in the walls – start up, are filled with meaning. I grow muddled, stammer. I lose my place. My uncle shrieks – seizes, from his desk, a paperweight of brass, and throws it at me. That steadies me, for a time. But then he has me read, one night, from a certain work . . . Richard watches, his hand across his mouth, a look of amusement dawning on his face. For the work tells of all the means a woman may employ to pleasure another, when in want of a man.

'And she pressed her lips and tongue to it, and into it –'

'You like this, Rivers?' asks my uncle.

'I confess, sir, I do.'

'Well, so do many men; though I fear it is hardly to my taste. Still, I am glad to note your interest. I address the subject fully, of course, in my Index. Read on, Maud. Read on.'

I do. And despite myself – and in spite of Richard's dark, tormenting gaze – I felt the stale words rouse me. I colour, and am ashamed. I am ashamed to think that what I have supposed the secret book of my heart may be stamped, after all, with no more miserable matter than this – have its place in my uncle's collection. (*F*, pp. 279–80)

The anger Maud feels towards the texts which have simultaneously opened up her understanding of her desires and have tainted her approach to other women is released when she slashes her uncle's priceless collection a few pages later (*F*, pp. 289–90). What is perhaps more important here is the way in which the triangular exchange of the female between two males is partially undercut.[13] Instead of the excitement of this scene deriving from the cross-talk between the two men about the relative merits of female–female sexual activity, Maud's reading aloud to them is portrayed as a moment of transgression in which, rather than being the passive narrator of amusements for the men's titillation and thus demeaning the nature of the tale she tells, she is herself '[a]rouse[d]' by them. It is debatable whether this reclaiming of a pornographic heritage is a liberation for the female characters, or readers. Although it points to a sense of the lesbian reader, identification with male-focussed pornography might not be considered such a positive move.

At the end of the novel, a similar scene occurs as Maud reads to Sue from her uncle's books and removes from her any illusions about the works that Maud and her uncle spent so much time cataloguing; Sue narrates:

She stopped. Her heart was beating harder, though she had kept her voice so flat. My own heart was also beating rather hard. I said – still not quite understanding:

'Your uncle's books?'

She nodded.

'All, like this?'

She nodded again.

'Every one of them, like this? Are you sure?'

'Quite sure.'

I took the book from her and looked at the print on the pages. It looked like any book would, to me. So I put it down, and went to the shelves and picked up another. That looked the same. Then I took up another; and that had pictures. You never saw any pictures like them. (*F*, p. 545)

'You never saw any pictures like them': the phrase holds an ambiguity about it because Sue's words appear to throw the pornographic back at us, the contemporary readers. Is Sue indicating her own naivety or is Waters turning to us through Sue and suggesting that we would be shocked by the surprisingly obscene nature of the 'art' before her? There certainly appears to be an authorial play in action here, with Waters mocking us for our popularly prudish understanding of the Victorian period's views on sex; her 'Notes' at the end of the novel lay the emphasis on the true story of Henry Spencer Ashbee and his various indexes of pornography from the 1870s and 1880s, even declaring 'All the texts cited by Maud are real.' Like most historical fiction writers, Waters underlines the accuracy of her detail and places the strength of her 'truthfulness' on the existence of these other texts.

The fact that Sue's narrative ends with her and Maud's assumption of the role of pornographer proves a possibly less than satisfactory resolution. Maud, envisioned as the light bringer in a house of moral and literal darkness, is, nevertheless, taking on the mantle of her uncle's occupation: 'She took up the lamp. The room had got darker, the rain still beat against the glass . . . She put the lamp upon the floor, spread the paper flat; and began to show me the words she had written, one by one' (*F*, p. 548). One could argue that there is a kind of poetical justice in the victims/passive figures in pornography adopting a more active stance (see Maria Vara's discussion of 'the revenge of the stereoype' in Alice Thompson's *Justine*), but the embracing of what Nan, while Florence reads *Towards Democracy* to her in *Tipping*, calls 'books written especially for this sort of thing' (*T*, p. 437) could be considered a backward step. On the other hand, because the events of *Fingersmith* occur in a period before the narrative of *Tipping*, it could also be that Waters' is making her own intertextual reference – that the secret women pornographers

of the 1860s and 1870s made it possible for women's lesbian relationships to be positive acts 'contributing to the social revolution' (*T*, p. 437)
several decades later.

The Night Watch: 'Oh, so what? It's not the nineteenth bloody century'[14]

In an interview about her new novel, Waters declared, not presumably
in all seriousness, that 'I'm going to write a farce next, or a screwball
comedy.'[15] While that would indeed signal a move to a wholly new genre
for Waters, *The Night Watch* (2006) itself cannot easily be considered as
part of the same group of texts as her first three novels. An author who
finds a niche and can sell well within it takes a brave step when deciding
to offer her readers something new. Waters' motivation in making the
leap from the mid-nineteenth to the mid-twentieth century appears to
arise from a fear of being periodized and genreized; as she puts it, 'I felt
I was becoming a bit stuck in the Victorian period. I was beginning to
feel I was writing a pastiche of myself.'[16]

The Night Watch brings together many elements of Waters' previous
novels: there is a small part for spiritualism and a prison features quite
prominently (both elements linked to *Affinity*), as do the fluidity of
gender boundaries – in wartime – and the possibilities of cross-dressing
(from *Tipping*). The role of the (lesbian) author of stories (as played out
in the conclusion to *Fingersmith*) is more consciously brought centre
stage in the figure of Julia, an author of detective novels. There might
even be considered to be a certain self-reflective intertextuality in the
plight of Helen (Julia's lover) in *The Night Watch*: unlike her namesake in
Affinity she does not desert her female lover and seek to align herself with
normative heterosexuality, indeed, in Helen here is rather the paranoid
Margaret-figure, insecure in her relationship though not with her sexuality. It is Helen who becomes the unwitting object in a female-to-female
exchange between Julia and Kay just as Maud was placed in relation to
Rivers and her uncle in *Fingersmith*. References to other texts again act as
a means to place the time of the novel and provide an ironic comment
on the narrative itself: *Blithe Spirit*, a play about the return of former
lovers, is mentioned, as is Daphne du Maurier's *Frenchman's Creek*, which
contains a cross-dressing subplot; perhaps ironically, regular references
are made to Dickens' work, especially *Oliver Twist*.

Ultimately, Waters' latest fiction does not sit comfortably with the
previous three because the wider themes of social change, class division
and the realization and assertion of lesbian identity are passed over for a

narrative concerned with the complexities of love in a more generalized sense: the story of Duncan is that of an adolescent first homosexual love, while the narrative of Duncan's sister Viv is firmly located in the sphere of heterosexual desire. In this tale, female lovers do not come together in the historical moment but rather drift or are torn apart, like their male counterparts and the pairings of opposite sexes. This, though, is part of Waters' point because history in this novel is far more about the personal than the political. As Helen says in 1947, about those who come to use the dating agency where she works, 'People came to look for new loves, but often – or so it seemed to her – only really wanted to talk about the loves that they had lost' (*NW*, p. 14). Despite its wartime setting, there is very little sense of momentous events taking place behind the narrative: the listless absence of purpose that Kay feels as the novel begins in 1947, and thus after a period in which women like her were needed and became seen, is present in the earlier/later parts of the novel too.

Individuals in the text look backwards in a way that the characters of *Tipping the Velvet, Affinity* and *Fingersmith* never do: even the youngest, like Duncan, try and recreate a past that they can never have known, sublimating and almost erasing their own identities into that of things, materials from an unknowable yet more comforting and earlier period. As Viv thinks of the house Duncan shares with Mr Mundy, she dwells on the fact that the surroundings are much older and, in fact, would be more in keeping with one of Waters' earlier novels:

There were yellow, exhausted photographs: of Mr Mundy as a slim young man; another of him as a boy, with his sister and mother, his mother in a stiff black dress, like Queen Victoria. It was all dead, dead, dead; and yet here was Duncan, with his quick dark eyes, his clear boy's laugh, quite at home amongst it all. (*NW*, p. 25)

Duncan collects china and bric-and-brac from the past (*NW*, p. 25), and even lives with a much older man. For Duncan, it is the present rather than the past that he sees as a nightmare from which he must awake, and this is the argument which his friend Alec uses against boys like them having to go and fight in the war that has been designed by their parents' generation: 'Old men! It's all right for them. It's all right for my father, and your father. They've had their lives; they want to take our lives from us . . . They want to make us old like them' (*NW*, p. 448). Alec escapes this fate by ending his own life rather than let these 'old men' risk ending it for him; Duncan fails in his part of their suicide pact, and yet because of his imprisonment for this crime he, too, manages to escape the war, although it is this guilt which leads him to move in with Mr Mundy, who has been one of his prison warders.

The text contains many references to ghosts and haunting: for Kay, the cross-dressing lesbian in a post-war world, 'it seemed. . . that she really might be a ghost' (*NW*, p. 4) as she slips through the streets in her own form of night watching, or when she takes a break during her work as an ambulance driver during the war and picks up a copy of *The Invisible Man* (*NW*, p. 96); and Julia and her father, an architect, spend their war assessing damaged buildings, or as Julia terms it 'recording ghosts' (*NW*, p. 251). The point Waters seeks to make here, it seems, is one she expresses through Kay and her regular trips to the cinema where she watches the end of the film first: 'people's pasts, you know, being so much more interesting than their futures. Or perhaps that's just me' (*NW*, p. 99). For none of these characters is there a future: the possibilities opened up for Kay and her friends during the war have ended, just as the war itself ended the future potential of Duncan and Alec's relationship. History in this novel is not something that can be rewritten, re-interpreted, re-examined or re-read (except by us as readers who are forced to read backwards), and it is therefore questionable whether Waters is able to add anything to our perception of the 1940s period; it is commonplace, for example, when writing about gender in relation to both the Second and First World Wars that boundaries became more fluid and even sexual desires or behaviour outside the 'norm' were, if not accepted, at least not as harshly persecuted as at other times. In this sense, it is rather the characters' personal attempts to escape from history which are put under the spotlight, and in most cases the attempts fail. Individuals connected to one another at the end of the novel (1941) remain tied if not constrained to each other at the novel's start (1947). Events move on, wars end, but the tragedy to be found in the ordinary, 'little' life remains unresolved.

Conclusion: the future of looking backwards

Putting lesbian characters into the sphere of Victorian fiction might explode a few clichés in the popular imagination, but it does not, ultimately, change history or the way in which the majority of us view the past. Historical fiction has, for most of the last century, been an adaptable and ever-moving form; it was certainly changing before Waters appeared on the literary scene and her work develops from the same impulses as that of many other contemporary women writers. Waters has added to the debate about what constitutes 'historical knowledge' by giving her narratives a distinctly political motivation, but it is narrative politics and the narratological impulse to create histories in pluralistically gendered and sexed terms which drives her historical fiction. As one reviewer wrote of Waters' first novel, 'If lesbian fiction is to reach a wider readership... Waters is just the person to carry the banner. Less ostentatious and self-referential than Jeanette Winterson... she has more flair for narrative and a stronger grasp of her characters.'[17] Waters is both political and postmodern with a small 'p'; she is not interested in the ambiguity and androgyny to be found in Winterson's work and its often ahistorical approach. Emphasizing difference in desire, Waters underlines the importance of choice in relation to the construction of the self; it might be no accident that one of her own favourite characters in literature is the identity-switcher Tom Ripley;[18] like him she has a talent for the (re)telling of (hi)stories, though thankfully she uses it for better ends.

Notes

1. Reviewer in *Independent on Sunday*: cited on back cover of paperback edition of *Tipping the Velvet* (London: Virago, 1999).
2. Anne Cranny-Francis, *Feminist Fiction: Feminist Uses of Generic Fiction* (Cambridge: Polity, 1990), p. 2.
3. Sarah Waters, 'Wolfskins and Togas: Maude Meagher's *The Green Scamander* and the Lesbian Historical Novel', *Women: A Cultural Review*, 7, 2 (1996), 176.
4. Ibid.
5. Carla Long, 'Romp and Circumstance: Sarah Waters', *The Times*, 26 March 2005; 'The Eye', p. 24.
6. A. S. Byatt, *On Histories and Stories: Selected Essays* (London: Chatto & Windus, 2000), p. 11.
7. Linda Hutcheon, *A Poetics of Postmodernism: History, Fiction, Theory* (London: Routledge, 1988; repr. 1996), p. 5.
8. Sarah Waters, *Affinity* (London: Virago, 1999), pp. 252–3. Hereafter *A* with page numbers in parentheses.
9. Hutcheon, *A Poetics of Postmodernism*, p. 113.
10. Sarah Waters, *Tipping the Velvet* (London: Virago, 1999), p. 386. Hereafter *T* with page numbers in parentheses.
11. Diana Wallace, *The Woman's Historical Novel: British Women Writers, 1900–2000* (Basingstoke: Palgrave Macmillan, 2005), p. 208.
12. Sarah Waters, *Fingersmith* (London: Virago, 2002), p. 76. Hereafter *F* with page numbers in parentheses.
13. For a discussion of women as bodies of exchange in the relationship and bonding of men, see Eve Kosofsky Sedgwick, *Between Men: English Literature and Male Homosocial Desire* (New York: Columbia University Press, 1985).

14. Waters, *The Night Watch* (London: Virago, 2006), p. 301. Hereafter *NW* with page numbers in parentheses.
15. Benedicte Page, 'Love Among the Ruins', *Bookseller*, 28 October 2005, pp. 20–1.
16. Mario Basini, 'In the Frame: Sarah Waters', *Western Mail*, 22 March 2003. This and the following two sources were accessed online via http://www.infoweb.newsbank.com where page numbers are not provided.
17. Miranda Seymour, 'Siren Song: *Tipping the Velvet*', *The New York Times*, 13 June 1999.
18. Julia Stuart, 'The 100 favourite fictional characters... as chosen by 100 literary luminaries', *The Independent*, 3 March 2005.

Index

academia, 9, 84, 116, 124, 129, 149,
150, 151, 152, 196
accuracy, 136, 137
Adler, Louise, 78, 85 n.23
aestheticism, 173, 176
agency, 53–4, 56, 57, 117, 173,
174, 178
ahistoric, ahistoricism, 48–9, 50, 209
Akalaitas, Joanne, 154
ALAS, 85 n.4
Albert, Prince, 129
Alexander, Meena, 146 n.5
allegory, 112, 130, 163
America, 1, 5, 30–44, 110, 182–94
anachronism, 15, 24, 91, 151
anarchy, 33
anchoress/anchorite, 168, 169
Anderson, Carol, 180 n.7, 181 n.22
Anderson, Linda, 27 n.4, 133, 140,
145 n.1, 146 n.9
androgyny, 123, 151, 209
'Angels of the House', 118
apocalyptic, 107
Aragon, Catherine of, 167
archives, archival, 47, 49, 162, 202
Armstrong, Judith, 86 n.27
art, 116, 167, 176, 205
artist, 84, 109, 113, 125–6, 138, 139
Ashbee, Henry Spencer, 205
Aske, Robert, 164
Atwood, Margaret, 1
audience, 31, 92, 93, 94, 95, 99, 112,
138, 144, 149
Auerbach, Nina, 165, 169, 171
n.33, n.42
Australia, 1, 5, 6, 7, 73–86
authenticity, 16, 23, 31, 49, 68, 75,
136, 185, 198
authorial identity, 76–86, 198, 206
authority, 77, 80, 133, 134, 137, 138,
140, 177, 198

authorship, 54, 76, 78–9, 80, 83–4,
102, 198, 199, 200, 205, 206
autobiography, 24, 25, 29 n.27, n.28,
31, 61, 74, 78, 112, 119, 197

Baillie, Joanna, 8, 20, 89–101, 169 n.6
Witchcraft, 90, 169 n.6
Bakhtin, Mikhail, 33, 44 n.7, 154
Barclay, Florence
The White Ladies of Worcester, 159,
162–3, 167, 170 n.7, n.24
Barker, Elspeth, 180 n.7
Barnes, Julian
Flaubert's Parrot, 140
Barnum, P. T., 108, 109
Barrett Browning, Elizabeth, 196
Barthes, Roland, 77, 79, 80, 82, 83,
126, 129, 131 n.20, 132 n.26
'The Death of the Author', 31, 77,
81–2, 85 n.16, n.17, n.19, 86
n.36, n.47
Barton, John, 150, 151
Basini, Mario, 210 n.15
Baudelaire, Charles, 103
Beard, Mary R., 158, 169 n.4, n.5
Beardsley, Monroe C., 81, 86 n.38
Beauvoir, Simone de, 158, 159,
169 n.3
Becker, Susanne, 172, 179 n.2
Beddoe, Deirdre, 163, 170 n.25
Behn, Aphra, 9, 90, 149–57
The Rover I, 9, 149–57
Beloff, John, 146 n.3
Bennett, Susan, 92, 100 n.14
Bentley, David, 73, 80, 84 n.2
bible, biblical, 32, 34, 37, 69, 120, 171
n.40, 191
bildungsroman, 197
Black Death, 163, 164
Bloch, Marc, 170 n.10
body, 46, 53, 54, 56–7, 59, 63, 117,
129, 179, 195

211

Drabble, Margaret, 5
drama, 8, 21, 35, 89–101, 156
dream, 33, 128
Drury Lane Theatre, 92
'dual temporalities', 6, 16, 22–3
DuPlessis, Rachel, 54, 58 n.17,
    171 n.38

Easton, Alison, 114 n.11, 115 n.35
Eco, Umberto, 162, 163, 170 n.21,
    n.22, n.23
economics, 96, 151, 160, 164, 167
education, 3, 49, 168, 199, 201
Egypt, 133, 134, 143
Eliot, George
    Middlemarch, 122
Ellmann, Richard, 105, 109, 114 n.17,
    115 n.30, n.33
emancipation, 59, 110–11, 112, 160,
    176, 185, 186, 188, 189, 192
emotion, 117, 126
England, Englishness, 28 n.8, 71 n.27
    early modern, 17, 91, 151
Enlightenment, 91, 175
episteme, epistemic, 50, 56
equality, 150, 185
eroticism, 19–20, 165, 198
Erskine, Barbara, 27 n.1, n.6, 28 n.17
escapism, 1, 196, 200
eschatology, 126
ethnicity, 3, 5
Europe, 30–44, 188
evangelism, 19
Eve, 69, 70, 141
Ezell, Margaret J. M., 101 n.20

fabrication, 80, 138
fairytale, 20, 35–6, 63–4, 122, 123,
    130, 138, 142, 162, 174, 180 n.11
    Little Red Riding Hood, 64, 66
    Sleeping Beauty, 56, 63–4, 179
Falcus, Sarah, 8–9, 27 n.5, 118, 133–46
fantasy, 26, 29 n.23, 31, 130, 163
fascism, 162, 163
fatherhood, 61, 187
femininity, 16, 42–3, 61, 90,
    99, 123, 178, 183, 187, 188,
    189, 192

feminism, 11, 20, 24, 45, 89, 99, 113,
    114, 152, 155, 166, 185, 196
    anti, 153, 154, 156
    ecological, 20, 22
    first wave, 61, 150
    lesbian, 29 n.23
    liberal-humanist, 149, 150
    post, 20
    proto, 20, 22, 150, 185
    second-wave, 10, 61, 150, 153,
        154, 178
    socialist, 90, 91
    third wave, 61
feminist theory, 7, 59, 196
femme fatale, 43
Fetterley, Judith, 10, 182, 193, 193
    n.1, n.2, 194 n.29
Fhlathuin, Marie Ni, 77, 85 n.18,
    86 n.43
fiction, historical, *see* novel
Fiedler, Leslie, 182–3, 186, 187, 188,
    191, 192, 193 n.5, 194 n.15, n.17
Figes, Eva, 1, 6, 7, 59–72
    Days, 7, 59, 61–5, 66, 69, 70,
        71 n.18
    Little Eden: A Child at War, 61, 71
        n.16, n.27
    Nelly's Version, 7, 59, 62, 65–7, 70,
        71 n.19, n.27
    Patriarchal Attitudes, 64, 71 n.26
    The Tree of Knowledge, 7, 59, 62,
        67–70, 71 n.17
film, 35, 36, 41, 42–3, 44
Finney, Brian, 105, 114 n.15
Flaubert, Gustave, 8, 133, 138
folklore, 20, 34, 39, 64, 102, 122
Ford, John (director), 35, 36
Ford, John (playwright), 35, 36
    'Tis Pity She's a Whore', 36–7
Forster, E. M., 131 n.13
Foucault, Michel, 20, 28 n.15, 54, 58
    n.18, 82, 85 n.21, 179, 181 n.25
fragmentation, 3, 16, 52, 94, 139,
    166, 167
France, 120, 129, 138
French Revolution, 129, 136–7, 176
Freud, Sigmund, 123, 127
Freudian, 20, 66, 163
Friedan, Betty, 51, 57 n.15

London, 134, 143, 173
Long, Carla, 209 n.5
Lukács, Georg, 117, 130 n.6, 162, 163,
    164, 167, 170 n.19, n.20
Lyotard, Jean-François, 32, 44 n.3, 59,
    70 n.2

McAuley, James, 86 n.33
McCann, Maria, 27 n.1
McCrory, Moy, 166
    The Fading Shrine, 159, 166, 168,
    169, 170 n.7
McDonald, Roger, 85 n.10
Mack, Phyllis, 28 n.11
madness, 10, 17, 49, 51, 143, 144,
    187, 191, 192
'madwoman in the attic', 10, 118,
    172, 179 n.1
Mallarmé, Stephane, 138
Malleus Maleficarum, 28 n.18, 98–9
Malley, Ern, 79, 84 n.2, 86 n.33
Man, Paul de, 77
Manne, Robert, 85 n.10,
    86 n.26, n.34
Mansfield, Katherine
    Daughters of the Late Colonel, 69,
    72 n.33
Manton, Jo, 146 n.5
marginality, 47, 59, 137, 144, 199
marketplace, 150, 195–6, 206
Marlatt, Daphne, 1, 6, 45–58, 62
    Ana Historic, 6–7, 45–58
Marr, David, 85 n.10
marriage, 68–9, 96, 97, 113, 138, 164,
    174, 184, 187
Mars-Jones, Adam, 114 n.7
Martin, Valerie, 180 n.7
Marx, Eleanor, 197
Marxism, 163, 164, 166
Mascuch, Michael, 29 n.28
masculinity, 8, 42–3, 61, 67, 90, 111,
    155, 184, 187, 191, 192
'cosmic', 8, 116–32
materiality, 16, 17, 102, 105, 106,
    109, 112, 113, 144, 179, 186, 189,
    201, 207
Maurier, Daphne du, 17, 28 n.7,
    179 n.1
    Frenchman's Creek, 206

Melville, Herman, 10, 182, 183, 189,
    190, 193
    Moby Dick, 10, 182, 183, 190,
    192, 193
memoir, 23, 139
memory, 4–5, 9, 33, 40, 50–2, 63, 65,
    78, 104, 125, 138, 139, 166
menopause, 91
menstruation, 91
metafiction, 1, 3, 11, 31, 35, 45, 119
    historiographic, 3, 7–9, 45, 119,
    158, 166, 196
metahistory, 1–2, 3, 129, 159,
    161, 166
metamorphosis, 122, 123
metaphor, 46, 70, 108, 116, 121, 125,
    129, 189, 190, 201
Michelet, Jules, 117, 129
Middleton, Peter, 3, 4–5, 11 n.8,
    12 n.14
midwives, 20–1, 28 n.18, n.19, 168
Miles Franklin Award, 85 n.4
millennium, 1, 166
Milton, John, 7, 68–70, 72 n.31, n.34,
    n.35, 154
'minority' cultures, 5
misogyny, 8, 20, 154
Mitchell, Maria, 185, 193 n.10
modernism, 8, 103, 107
Moggach, Deborah, 27 n.1
Moi, Toril, 90, 100 n.6, n.7, 123, 131
    n.19, n.23, n.24
monstrosity, 52–6
Monstrous Regiment, 89
Moorman, Mary, 146 n.5
Morley, Rachel, 7, 31, 56, 73–86
Morrison, Toni, 182
mother, 36, 48, 51, 52, 62, 69, 70,
    135, 138, 141, 188
    absent, 35, 47
    death of the, 36, 47
    single, 94
motherhood, 21–2, 36, 60, 67, 93,
    134, 135, 136, 141, 145, 184, 191
Mott, Lucretia, 185
multiculturalism, 75, 76, 78
Munns, Jessica, 150–1, 157 n.12, n.13
mysticism, 158, 165

poetry, 45, 103–15, 118–19, 139, 141, 198
politics, 6, 24, 31, 60, 61, 68, 80, 91, 151, 160, 163, 197, 209
polysemy, 83, 127, 128, 130
popular culture, 9, 149, 150, 179
  literature/fiction, 1, 5, 149, 166, 195
pornography, 10, 39, 174, 176, 201–6
possession, 8, 16, 116–32
postcolonialism, 38, 58 n.19, 77
postmodern/ism, 1, 3, 4, 11, 46, 73, 84, 85 n.3, 119, 162, 173, 196, 209
  (post), 84
poststructuralism, 77, 82, 176
poverty, 89, 94
Powell, Mary, 72 n.31
power, 17, 24, 90, 95, 97, 98, 99, 113, 118, 165, 174, 177, 191
Power, Eileen, 160–1, 164, 170 n.15, n.16, n.17, 171 n.30
Praz, Mario, 180 n.11
Prescott, H. F. M., 159, 165
  The Man on a Donkey, 159, 164–5, 168, 169, 170 n.7
progress, 59, 167
prophet, figure of, 6, 15–29
Proust, Marcel
  Remembrance of Things Past, 116
psychoanalysis, 65, 66, 134
Punter, David, 180 n.10
Puritan, Puritanism, 6, 15–29, 32–3, 34, 39, 43
Purkiss, Diane, 28 n.16, 29 n.21

Quakers, 17, 185
queer, queering, 54, 56, 202
quest narrative, 125, 186

race, 25
Radcliffe, Ann, 174, 175
  The Mysteries of Udolpho, 174–5, 180 n.15
Radegunda, Saint, 165, 166
radicalism, 96, 100
  religious, 17–19
rape, 103, 153, 154, 180 n.15
rationalism, 33, 103, 127
Rattenbury, Arnold, 163, 170 n.27, 171 n.28

re-vision, 9, 103, 116, 120, 150, 151, 161, 179, 184
  see also Rich, Adrienne
re-writing, 46, 145, 149–57, 172–81, 195, 197, 208
reader, 16, 23, 31, 50, 78, 80–1, 155, 174, 175, 183
  resisting, 182
reading, 2, 11, 76, 79, 80–1, 83, 105, 126, 174, 195–210
realism, 54, 91, 123, 167, 178
reality, 6, 32, 48, 80–1, 137, 162
Rees, Celia, 28 n.17
Reformation, 168
reincarnation, 107
Reinelt, Janelle, 100 n.15
Reisert, Margaret, 28 n.17
religion, 17, 25, 68, 127, 145, 158–71
  female-centred, 21, 158–71
repression, 38, 54
  sexual, 19–20
  of women, 111
research, 16, 21, 22, 47, 159, 199
Restoration, 9, 17–18, 67–70, 150, 151, 153, 154, 156
Restoration comedy, 9, 149, 153, 155
resurrection, 129
revolution, 17
Rhymer's Club, 108
Rhys, Jean, 5, 179 n.1
Rice, Anne (pseudonym 'A. N. Roquelaure'), 181 n.28
Rich, Adrienne, 7, 12 n.19
  're-vision', 7–9, 12 n.19
Riemer, Andrew, 79, 85 n.5, 86 n.31, n.32
Riffaterre, Michael, 47–8, 57 n.6, n.8
Roberts, Michèle, 1, 8–9, 117, 133–46, 174, 195
  Fair Exchange, 133, 136–8, 140, 142, 145
  In the Red Kitchen, 133–6, 138, 139, 142, 143
  The Looking Glass, 133, 138–42, 145
  The Mistressclass, 133
  The Wild Girl, 133
Rogers, Rosemary, 162
Roman Catholicism, 127